The Prophet

K.M.Bishop

—Shellville Press—

Shellville Press

Printed by Shellville Press in the United States of America

Cover illustration, map, and chapter illustrations by Dirk Macorol

ISBN: 978-1-7334487-4-1

Shellville Press
a division of Shellville Design LLC
www.shellvillepress.com

10 9 8 7 6 5 4 3 2 1

The Eternal Realm

PREFACE

It is said, in the beginning, there was nothing. There were no stars, nor land. Darkness consumed everything that ever there would be, and it is in this condition that our world began, as a vast nothingness. Yet, out of that nothingness came the gods. They were a beacon in the shadows of nonexistence and from them grew the essence of life.

The first to originate were the earth goddesses Behr and Gher, twins that sprouted from a speck of dust. Through them spread the land, vast and fertile, as lush grasses and trees sprung up from the once barren soil.

The second to come into existence was the wind god Mahk who formed within the pure air the trees had created. Seeds floated upon his breeze further growing the land the goddesses had begun.

The third to arise was the fire god Vremir who was sparked by a bolt of lightning as it struck a tree, igniting him into life. Through his flames, the sun burned, the stars shone, the land was shaped, and canyons and mountains were created. Through the ashes left in his wake, the land began to grow a sustainable source of food.

Then there was the last being, the water god Vron, who was formed when a single drop of rain hit the ground. From him gushed forth rivers and the seas that coursed through the land further creating a habitable place.

For several hundred years, the five gods and goddesses lived in harmony, content with the world they had created. But, after a time, the goddesses yearned for something more. They wished to fill the land with more than just plants and small creatures. They wanted to make new life, human life.

So it was agreed, and as the gods laid with the goddesses, man was created and the land was populated. This pleased all the gods and goddesses for a time as they looked lovingly upon their creations. All but Vron. Vron saw humans as weak and exploitable; he saw them as tools, instruments to be used.

Buried deep within the earth was a special mineral beraxium—a metal that, when harvested and harnessed, gave the gods great strength. Vron wanted this precious metal for himself, and casting a haze over the minds of men, he forced them to mine it for him.

Appalled by his actions, the other gods confronted Vron about his greed and cruelty. They encouraged him to stop his misdeeds and he agreed. Vron, however, had lied. He hid his misadventures from his siblings further enslaving the human race until one man stepped forth.

Strahm Mahrkai, a man of great will, prayed to the other gods for help, for deliverance—and for his faith the voice of the gods was planted within him. They foretold the destruction of Vron's enterprise, a liberation of those enraptured by his power. They told him that man should be prepared.

And, so, Mahrkai preached to the people, readying them for what was to come. However, there was a traitor among them and word got back to Vron who was more than ready for a fight.

It was not long before a great battle ensued. Volcanoes erupted, the earth split, the seas and rivers raged, the wind howled. But in the end, it was not enough. Vron, who had long been harnessing the power that beraxium gave him, could not be stopped, not without great sacrifice.

With great love for the world they had created, the gods and goddesses combined their strength, giving all they had to Vremir. In a tornado of earth and fire, Vremir captured Vron, taking his powers from him, but in doing so, he depleted himself of life. After it was over, a powerless Vron laid in a pile of ash, angry and embittered, but alive.

As punishment, he locked away what was left of Behr, Gher, and Mahk in an unbreakable prison. To those men that turned against him, he had banished to an island, their skin blackened like the charred earth. All, but the family of Mahrkai.

Hidden by a small piece of Vremir's power, the family of Mahrkai lived on, preaching that one day he would return. One day a new prophet would raise an army and save the realm once more.

But no one listened, no one could. Because as long as Vron walked the realm no one was free...

Part 1

SACRIFICE

CHAPTER 1

"What have you done?" a scratchy male voice asked angrily.

The girl shifted where she sat in the back of a covered wagon, trying to remain hidden. She wondered where her mother was. She had not seen her for a long time, perhaps even a couple of days. She whimpered as her stomach growled. When had she eaten last? She couldn't remember.

"This does not concern you," came a second male voice.

They were arguing. About her?

"Does not concern me?" came the first man. "You have lied to us! You have lied to the coven and broken your vows!"

The girl squirmed. She was dirty and tired from hiding in the trunk of that tree until those men found her.

"Oh, what do you know of vows?" the other man retorted. "Do not act as if you are so righteous."

The first man laughed. "I can't wait to hear what The Leaders will say about your discretion. What do you think your punishment would be? Perhaps they will kill her and not you."

"I will rip the heart from your chest before you speak another word!"

"Quiet, the both of you!" came a hushed, yet stern, female voice. "The child can hear you."

There was a pregnant pause.

"The child has already been through enough without you two tearing each other apart just a few yards away from her."

Again, neither of the men replied, the tension between them palpable.

"Is she truly your daughter, The—"

A large black hawk, perched in a nearby tree, squawked, a deafening noise. She blinked at it, realizing that it was staring back at her.

"Yes," came a reply. "She is my daughter. Though she doesn't recognize me. I have not been back for at least a year."

"And her mother?" the female voice asked.

There was a sharp intake of breath followed by a long pause. "She is dead," the man almost whispered, his voice riddled with pain and anguish. "I must bury her. Please allow me to bury her."

"This is unacceptable!" came the first male voice. "The Wind, you have to agree with me!"

Another pause.

"Do you know who this child is, The—"

Again, the hawk let out a shrill noise, obstructing her ability to hear what was said.

"Should that matter?" came the reply. "She is the product of his disloyalty."

"No," said The Wind calmly. "She is the future of this realm."

Dahlen opened her eyes and blinked at the roof of her tent. The Wind. The Wind had been there the day she was found all those years ago. But who were the other two? She knew The Master was there the day she was found. He must have been the second voice. Her father. The one who had vouched for her.

She sighed and rolled over to see Dohrrn already sitting up and smiling at her.

She smirked at him. "Have you been awake long?"

The boy shrugged. *A few minutes.*

She yawned as she nodded, the unspoken words of the young boy running through her head as her own thoughts. She slowly sat up.

The boy offered his hand to help her, but she politely refused. She was now more than six months along, and though unsettled by her growing bulk, she refused to be treated any differently due to her condition.

The two of them pushed their way out of their tent into the still darkness of the early morning, the top of the sun just starting to push its way up and through the trees.

Dohrrn made a gesture with his hands. *Let's go to the river and watch the sun rise.*

She nodded and smiled as he took her hand and led her through the woods to the river where they stood, their feet being tickled by the morning current. They listened in silence as the rest of the wildlife awoke; the birds chirping, the squirrels chittering, the wind making the leaves rustle against themselves.

Dohrrn seemed content, but she seemed distant. She stood staring off into the sky, clutching the necklace of her family seal in her hand. She stroked the small wing as she thought about her dream.

"The Wind was there when I was found," she thought. "The Wind knew who I was all those years ago, knows who my father is."

Were they talking to you again?

She looked over at the boy. "Who?"

Dohrrn lifted a brow.

"Right," she replied with a sigh. "Your sisters Behr and Gher." She didn't reply for a few moments. "I guess they were."

And?

She shrugged, placing her hand on her swelling stomach. "Just another small fragment to a more confusing puzzle," she told him. "Oh!" she exclaimed. She took his hand and placed it on her belly. "She is kicking."

Dohrrn's face lit up with delight.

"Do you feel her?"

He nodded excitedly. *What does it feel like?*

She shrugged. "I don't know," she replied. "Kind of like a weird bit of pressure or maybe something like this!" She bent over and began tickling the boy making him shriek in delight. It was the only sound he really made.

"Dahlen!"

They both looked back into the woods.

She patted the boy on the head. "I am being summoned," she said with a smirk. She motioned with her head. "Come on. Let's go before he disquiets himself again."

The boy made a funny face as he took her proffered hand and let her lead him back into the woods.

"Dahlen!"

"We are here, Mohrr!" she replied.

"You mustn't take off like that," he half scolded her. "Not in your condition."

A concerned father.

She shot the boy a wink before returning her gaze to Mohrr. "I am not a piece of glass," she told him. "I am fully capable of walking a few hundred yards to the river and back. Besides, we were still within the bounds of the settlement."

Mohrr gave a small huff. "Yes, but you could at least ask someone to go with you."

She held out a hand indicating the boy. "Who better to protect me than the god of fire himself?" she retorted.

Dohrrn shot her a look.

"I wish you would just let me take care of you for once," Mohrr told her.

Dahlen turned to him and pressed her hand lightly against his cheek. "I am honored that you want to take care of me, but it is not what I want. I have been taught to be self-sufficient and that is how I will always be."

He smiled and gave another small huff. "Yes, that and stubborn."

She shrugged. "Stubbornness should be a virtue," she responded taking his arm as they walked. "It is the most underrated quality."

He chuckled and kissed her forehead. "I will take your word for it."

"Has Marten returned from his journey yet?" she asked as they approached the camp.

"I think he is expected back soon."

"He has been gone almost three months," she added.

Mohrr nodded.

"And he has sent no word?"

Mohrr shook his head. "No, not yet."

She sighed. "Well, this place is driving me a little insane. I feel as if I need a change in scenery."

"Dahlen," Mohrr started, his voice a little stern. "You need to start thinking about the child inside of you. *Our* child."

"Start thinking?" she repeated. "She encompasses my every waking moment. I am not sure if *you* have noticed but the fact that I am with child is difficult for me to ignore." She placed her hand on her lightly protruding stomach again.

As the three of them reached the camp, they were greeted with deep bows and whispers of *Ver Jatahl* or 'My Lord' in ancient Vremerian.

Dahlen looked down at the boy. "I hope you don't expect me to bow down to you," she told him. "Especially not in my condition."

Dohrrn narrowed his eyes at her playfully.

"There you are, my child," came a booming voice. Vorce Brahn emerged from his tent, his massive arms wide to embrace her. He kissed her forehead as he assessed her. "You are glowing as your mother did when she was carrying you."

Vorce was not her actual father. In reality, she did not know who her father really was. And for some reason unknown to her, Vorce, who trained and fought alongside her father, refused to tell her, claiming that it was not the time for her to know. That too many lives were at stake.

"I think you like to remind me of my change in condition every day," Dahlen told him flatly.

He chuckled, a deep purring sound that shook his whole body. "Are you ready for your training after we break our fast?"

"No," Mohrr said, a little sternly. "Forgive me for being so unceremonious, but don't you think it is time to slow down with the training? You are now more than six months along."

"Yes, but just think of how good I will be with a sword once the child is born," she replied repressing a smile. "Once my movements and balance are no longer hampered by this." She circled her belly with her hand. "Perhaps I will even be better than you with a sword."

"You are teasing me," Mohrr remarked.

Dahlen exchanged a quick glance with Vorce. "I am not altogether being serious," she replied. "But," she continued holding a finger up, "as I said before, I am also not made of glass." She squeezed his arm. "Please trust that I know my body's limits."

Mohrr pressed a hand to her face. "This child is important," he reminded her gently. "Not just because she is *our* child, but because of her bloodline and what she means for the realm." He gestured with his hand, making a wide arch.

She shot a glance at Dohrrn who shrugged and walked away.

I'm hungry.

She narrowed her eyes at the boy for leaving her. "Traitor," she thought.

"Dahlen," Mohrr said, bringing her back from her thoughts, "why don't we go for a walk instead of training? I know you hate sitting still and doing nothing, but I am only thinking of the child."

A large, strong hand landed on Mohrr's shoulder. "Trust AnnJella," Vorce said, still using her original name given to her at birth. "She will tell you when she is ready to quit. But it is important to keep moving. Heavy with child or not."

"Watch it," Dahlen replied in a sing-song voice. "I am far from *heavy*."

"I feel as if my opinion is overruled more often than not here," Mohrr replied.

"Ah, that is because you are a prince!" Vorce exclaimed. "You are not used to being opposed!"

Dahlen hid a smirk. "Whether or not that is the case," Mohrr started, "I feel as if I have some say in your condition. That is also *my child* you are carrying. I feel as if I have a right to be concerned."

"And you do have a right," Dahlen reassured him, "but, as Marten always says, you should also have faith. This child is part of the gods' and goddesses' plans, so shouldn't we trust that they will keep her and myself safe?"

He frowned at her. "That is not how it works," he explained. "You still have to be conscious of your surroundings and what you're doing. There is no reason to tempt fate. And besides, you didn't even believe in the gods and goddesses until six months ago."

"Fine," Dahlen said taking his hand. "You are right."

"Thank you."

"Vorce and I will take it slowly today." She quickly gave him a peck on the cheek and moved in the same direction Dohrrn had gone.

Vorce let out a small chuckle.

"Wait, what?" Mohrr asked. He turned to follow her when Vorce's large hand took him by the shoulder again. He looked up at Vorce who shook his head.

"You will never be able to contain her," Vorce told him. "And the more you try, the more she will resist you. Like a tiger in a cage, she will always be planning her escape."

Mohrr didn't reply.

"You have done much for her, but sometimes it is enough to let her do something for herself," Vorce continued. "Take a step back and you will see."

CHAPTER 2

THE CLANGING OF SWORDS RANG OUT THROUGH THE FOREST, FOL-
lowed by grunts of exertion and the fluttering of wings as startled
birds flew from where they were perched. Dahlen parried an attack
before striking, letting out a yell as the sword came down on Vorce's.

Sweat streamed down both of their faces as they continued, Vorce
yelling encouragement over the sounds of their sparring.

In truth, Dahlen missed this. She missed the excitement of fighting, of fulfilling a contract. Before this, before she found out who
she was, she had been an assassin raised by the Brotherhood of The
Nameless, a secretive society that trains small children to be assassins, mercenaries, or spies. She had been found by a few members
of the coven, as it is known, after her mother was murdered, and,
for almost twenty years, she had no idea who she was. It was not
until recently, until fate had brought Vorce back into her life, that she
found out about her birth. About the prophecy surrounding her life.

Born AnnJella Mahrkai, she was the last remaining descendant of
the original prophet, Strahm Mahrkai, who had predicted the god
Vremir's first coming several hundred years ago. There had been a
second prophet, one who had predicted a second coming of Vremir,
one whose prediction contradicted the teachings of the temple,

and because of the prophet's heresy, the temple wanted the entire Mahrkai bloodline eradicated.

The temple first sought the help of the coven, but was refused. The coven did not believe in the destruction of families, and the slaughtering of innocent women and children, so instead, they chose to save them. By the time Vorce had arrived with Dahlen's father, only her mother was still alive, the temple having found assistance from the Order of Zeln.

The Order was an even more secretive society than the coven. The only knowledge Dahlen had of them was from a book given to her by one of The Leaders of the coven from the forbidden section of their library. It was not a very thick book, but it provided her with more information on them than she had before.

The Order was a group of men and women dedicated to the god Vron, the god of water, the one responsible for the chaos and ignorance that plagued this realm and the next. They were trained, much like she was, to take out all of those that depose Vron and the origin story, the one falsified and spread by Vron himself.

In Vron's version, Vremir was the aggressor, a rogue god whose jealously drove him to commit heinous acts upon mankind. It was Vremir who sought to take over the realms and it was Vron who stopped him. As with all histories, the victor's versions of events are passed down through the generations, making Vron the hero and Vremir the villain.

For centuries after, however, Vron roamed the realms, lost. His powers had been greatly diminished by his fight with his brother, and, so, he spent his days watching, embittered by his derailment, as the humans around him lived on. But he was still there, slowly regaining his power and spreading his deceit and will over the minds of man.

And that is where Dahlen came in. It took her months to come to terms with it, to truly believe it, but she was revealed to be the next prophet—the key to what the gods have in store. She laughed at the idea when Marten and Mohrr explained it to her, but when she watched Dohrrn, a mere child, set a man on fire with nothing more than a thought, her attitude toward it all began to change.

Dohrrn is the second coming; he is the god of fire, knowledge and free will; he is Vremir.

DAHLEN WIPED THE SWEAT FROM HER BROW AND GAVE A SMALL EXCLA-mation of surprise as she pressed her hand to her stomach.

Vorce dropped his sword and held her by the arms. "What is wrong?" he asked in alarm.

She huffed laughingly. "Not you too!" she replied playfully. "I am fine. She is just kicking is all. It startles me sometimes."

Her adopted father nodded, giving a sigh of relief. "Perhaps, that is enough for today."

"Am I wearing you out?" she asked with an arched brow.

Vorce laughed. "Yes, and no," he told her, gently patting her back. "But there are a few things I must attend to today."

She nodded. "I think I would like to take a ride," she told him. "I need to clear my head."

"Take the prince," Vorce told her. "He is feeling neglected by you."

"Must I always venture with someone?" she replied, playfully groaning.

He kissed her forehead. "He cares deeply for you, AnnJella," he explained. "And though you do not express how you feel, I know you care for him as well."

She shrugged. "It's complicated."

Vorce shook his head. "No, it is not. You will not get anywhere by pushing him away." He gently slapped his hand on her cheek. "He is the father of your child, so let him be that." He picked up his sword and sheathed it before walking back to the settlement.

She watched him go for a few moments before she took his advice and sought out Mohrr. She found him rereading the book about beraxium, for what had to be the third time.

"I am glad someone found that book interesting," she said with a smile. "I don't think I got further than the second chapter."

He closed it and smiled up at her. "It can be a little dry, but it will be useful," he told her. "We need to know how to find it and where my father intends to start mining for it."

"Are there not old mines off the coast of Skahrr?"

He nodded. "Marten is supposed to inquire about them while he is gone." He shook his head. "But chances are, they are depleted. And hopefully so. It will make it more difficult for my father to find."

"And if he were to find any?"

Mohrr shook his head again, solemnly. "He will seek out Vron and give it to him, strengthening him. Then who knows what he will do once he regains his power? Whatever it is, I am sure it will only end in destruction."

She took his face in her hands. "I am sorry your father appears to be on the wrong side of things," she told him, knowing Mohrr would be willing to kill his father to prevent that from happening.

He placed one of his hands over hers. "He was never much of a father to begin with, but I appreciate the sentiment."

She dropped her hands from his face and took one of his hands in hers. "Come," she goaded him, motioning with her head, "take me riding."

Mohrr needed no further encouragement as he quickly stood and walked with her to the stables.

"Where do you want to go?" he asked her. "Just around the settlement?"

She shook her head. "I am tired of these walls," she told him. "I need to get out."

Mohrr hesitated. "Dahlen, this is where it is safe," he reminded her. "These trees are protected. While you are in here, the Bornnenian's soothsayer cannot see you. This is where Vremir hid your family centuries ago during his battle with Vron. This place is what kept your family from his notice and why your family was not ostracized to Meht."

She took a deep breath and tried to keep herself from rolling her eyes. "Yes, I know the story," she told him. "I was there when Marten told me."

"So why leave?"

"Because sometimes I feel trapped and the need to escape is sometimes," she paused and let out a breath, "overwhelming."

Mohrr looked at her.

"And if you don't come with me, then I will just go by myself," she told him defiantly. She stopped in front of the stables, her hand on the door. "So?"

Mohrr sighed, but relented.

A tiger in a cage as Vorce had told him.

"I have been giving some thoughts on names," she told him as they rode along a forgotten path in the woods not far from the settlement border.

"What are they?" Mohrr asked a little excited.

"I like Vera," she told him. "And Tessa is a strong possibility."

"Are those all?" he asked after a moment.

"I thought about the name Lahpren, but only for a second. It seemed silly."

"Ancient Skahrrian for peace?"

She nodded. "It was just a thought."

"I like it," he said, "but I also like Mirabelle."

She looked over at him. "After my mother?"

He shrugged. "Why not?" he asked back. "You were named after your grandmother, were you not? It only seems fitting."

She smiled. "Mirabelle it is," she replied.

They fell into a pleasant silence, both of their minds filled with the possibilities of what their future could hold. Not too long ago, starting a family would have been impossible for Dahlen. Before she was released from the vows she took while still belonging to the coven, all of this would have been forbidden. Those of the coven are not allowed to marry or procreate. It was the same vow her father had broken. It was the reason she was even here. Some days, it still felt impossible. Some days, she still couldn't believe that she was here, that she was about to be a mother.

She often wondered what The Master, one of The Leaders from the coven that essentially helped raised her, would think. Would he be pleased or disappointed? They had not left on the best of terms. She was rather angry with him, believing The Master not to have had her back when she needed his support, but she had since forgiven him. She even missed him and wished she could reach out.

"What are you thinking of?" Mohrr asked her, breaking her away from her reflections.

She shrugged. "Of how different my life was only a few months ago from what it is now."

He nodded. "A lot has changed in such a short time," he agreed.

There was another silence between them.

"There is something else I would like to discuss," Mohrr started slowly.

Dahlen looked over at him. "What's that?" she asked, noticing the hesitancy in his voice.

He shifted in his saddle and cleared his throat. "I have for a while now wanted to bring the subject up again, but I know you have your reservations about it. I, on the other hand, have remained unshaken."

"You want to discuss the subject of marriage again," she stated calmly.

He nodded.

"Mohrr, I told you, I do not want you to feel obligated to bind yourself to me just because it is your child I am carrying," she explained to him. "You are free to come and go as you please."

He frowned and looked at her. "Is that what you truly think of me?" he asked, offended. "If that were the case, if I truly wanted to come and go as I pleased, I would have already done so." He shook his head. "But I have not. I have been here, with you, offering my assistance, though you take it but little. I feel no other sense of obligation than a man who is in love and wants to be with the woman he is in love with."

Dahlen averted her eyes, her face flushed. She still wasn't used to Mohrr's openness, how he readily and willingly shared his feelings. It was not her way. She spent a lifetime repressing her feelings, pushing them aside.

"Is it because you do not love me back?"

"I did not say that," she quickly replied.

"Sometimes, it is not what you say, but what you do not say that matters."

They came to the river bank and Dahlen stopped to get off. Despite being angry, Mohrr helped her down. Their closeness made her heart skip a beat. She embraced him, placing her head on his chest.

"I don't know how to love as you do, Mohrr," she told him as he wrapped his arms around her. "Please, have patience with me. My life changed overnight and I am still coming to terms with a lot of it." She took a step back and looked up at him. "You have always known who you are. The crown prince of Skahrr. But, me? I am still discovering who I am and where I came from." She gave him a small smile. "I love you in my own way; it just happens to be different from yours."

Mohrr smiled down at her, brushing back one of her black curls before gently kissing her.

Somewhere nearby, the sound of a bird cawing caught Dahlen's attention. Her skin prickled as she pulled away from Mohrr and looked around them in the trees.

"What's wrong?" Mohrr asked.

The bird cawed again, a piercing sound that echoed off of the water. Dahlen looked up into the trees and saw it, perched not ten yards from them. A black hawk clutching a snake in its talons. Her blood ran cold and her heartbeat quickened.

Run, she heard Dohrrn's voice warning her.

"We need to leave," she said, trying to remain calm.

Not far away, the sound of a twig snapping made her panic increase.

"What's happening?" Mohrr asked, searching the woods around them.

The hawk cawed again as an arrow pierced through the air, skimming Mohrr's arm and landing in his horse's neck. Mohrr clutched his arm and gritted his teeth as his horse let out a horrendous squeal and fell to the ground.

"Get on your horse now!" he yelled.

"I will not leave you!" Dahlen yelled back.

"For once, just do as I tell you!"

Another arrow landed in a tree trunk by her head.

"Go now!" Mohrr commanded as he helped her onto the horse.

"We can ride together!"

He shook his head. "It will only slow the horse down!" He gave the horse a slap on the rear causing it to lurch forward.

Dahlen glanced behind her, watching as Mohrr retrieved his sword from his now dead horse. Her chest ached as she continued on, cursing her condition for making her so vulnerable. She should have stayed and fought. There was no telling how many were out there and he was injured.

She was so distracted with leaving Mohrr behind that she had not been focusing on where she was going. As she came to a bend in the road a man with a bow and arrow stepped out and took aim at her. She reared her horse just in time, causing the poor creature to sacrifice itself for her. She screamed as she fell backward, grabbing a nearby branch just in time before she fell to the ground. She let go of the branch, landing a little heavily on her feet as she rolled into a ditch, holding her belly to help protect it. She staggered up and hobbled a few yards before hiding behind a tree.

She pressed a hand against her mouth to quiet her breathing and exhalations of pain. She gingerly put her left foot down and winced, hoping it was only sprained. After a few seconds, she took in a calming breath and listened for the slightest movement behind her. She waited, quietly retrieving the throwing knives she never went anywhere without from a concealed belt.

She waited, calmly, unmoving until the sounds of crunching leaves were not far off. She closed her eyes for a moment, envisioning her surroundings, before she moved from behind the tree and threw two knives into the chest of the man who was pursuing her.

He fell with nothing more than a grunt escaping his lips.

Dahlen limped over to him, slitting his throat for good measure before prying the bow from his hands and relieving him of what arrows he had left. It was clear to her that he was not the only one pursuing her. The first arrows had come from the direction she ran from and this man had been waiting for her down the road.

He knew where she was going.

She walked slowly back to her horse who was also limping, the arrow miraculously missed, having only grazed its back leg. The would-be assassin must have shifted his aim at the last minute. Her horse brayed as she patted its nose. The animal was in no condition to ride, just as much as she was in no condition to walk.

She quickly glanced around her, knowing she should not be out in the open for too long. She kissed her horse on the nose. "Go home," she pleaded with it. She then did as Mohrr had and slapped it on the butt sending it on its way.

She moved back into the woods, using the trees for cover, stopping to rest every few yards and listen. The pain in her ankle was starting to get worse, throbbing with every little movement. She was trying to focus on where she was going and for anything she might recognize, but the pain was distracting.

Behind you!

Dahlen spun on her one good foot and took aim with the bow as a hooded man jumped from a tree, sword raised. The first arrow caught him in the left side, but the second landed in his chest when he tried to rise from the ground.

She moved toward the man, his mouth foaming with blood as she took his sword and put him out of his misery.

"They weren't lying when they told us you would be difficult to kill," came a voice behind her.

She quickly turned, gritting her teeth to keep from wincing.

"Are you any good with that thing?" a man said motioning to the sword in her hand, his bearded chin the only thing visible under his hood.

A wave of fury rushed through her, but she shook it off. "I guess we are about to find out," she replied, holding the sword out in front of her.

The man rolled his shoulders. "I've never killed a woman before," he told her as he pulled out a sword of his own. "But I guess there is a first time for everything." He charged Dahlen while she remained still, waiting.

She took in a deep breath through her nose and let it out calmly as she parried at the last second, using the man's weight and strength against him as she kicked him, causing him to stumble sideways. She winced as she re-shifted her weight back to her good foot.

The man laughed. "That was a good move," he told her, sounding a little impressed. "Tell me, where did you learn to fight?"

"Forgive my rudeness," Dahlen replied as she studied the man's movements, "but I am not one for talking to those I am about to kill."

The man laughed again. "Cold and calculated," he replied wagging a finger at her. "My kind of woman." He moved toward her once more bringing his sword down on hers, swinging with great force, as she blocked. "It is a shame I have to kill you though," he said as he swung again.

Dahlen blocked it, her arms shaking as the man pushed against her. The sword inched down, coming closer to her face when a surge of strength rushed through her. She let out a scream as she kicked the man in the groin causing him to topple over before she punched him in the face.

The man gasped for air, his face red as Dahlen stepped towards him, raising the sword.

"You fight dirty," the man croaked, still holding his crotch. His mouth twitched into a smile regardless of the pain.

"It is not just myself I am protecting," she replied.

Before she could bring the sword down, however, a sharp pain coursed through her abdomen. She let out a scream as she placed her hand on her belly, the sword falling to her side. The pain flared again as she fell to her knees.

"No!" she thought as she saw the man rising from the ground.

"T!" she heard someone yell in the distance.

"Marten," she gasped as another pain hit her.

"Are you with child?" the man asked confused, finally noticing her swelling belly. His face twisted into a look of horrified surprise. "Well, this is awkward." He let out a breath and brushed back his hood, revealing his bald head and almond-shaped eyes. "I was not told you were going to be with child. I was skeptical when I was asked to kill a woman, but a pregnant woman is a whole other issue." He scratched at his beard.

She glared up at him with confusion. "Who are you?"

"Well, I'm not a monster," he told her. "At least not a big enough one to kill a pregnant woman." He held out his hand for her to take.

She grimaced again.

"T!"

"Dahlen!"

Her eyes lit up. "Mohrr!" she tried yelling back.

"Come on," the man told her, still holding his hand out for her to take. "I promise, I am not going to hurt you."

She furrowed her brows at him.

He bobbed his head from side to side. "Yes, strange coming from the man who literally just tried to kill you, but on my honor as an assassin of the brotherhood of the Nameless, I am voiding my contract."

"The Nameless," she repeated breathlessly. She took his hand and allowed him to help her up. When she was finally standing, she took him by his left wrist and pushed back his sleeve to reveal the 'X' tattoo. "You're of the coven."

He didn't have time to reply before Mohrr tackled him to the ground and began pummeling him with his fists, the two of them rolling on the ground in a tumult of dead leaves and twigs.

Dahlen moved to stop them, but the pain in her ankle and abdomen were too great.

"T!" came Marten's voice, his face riddled with fear and relief as he ran through the woods to get to her. He embraced her, holding her close. "I am so sorry I could not get here sooner," he told her.

"Stop them," Dahlen ordered in a whisper, unable to talk through her pain. "Before they kill each other."

She slid back to the ground as Marten complied, dragging Mohrr off of the other man just enough so he could roll away.

"Let me go!" Mohrr yelled as he pulled against Marten, kicking in the man's direction.

Just then a rush of hot wind flew past them followed by a scream. All of them looked to see a man holding a bow and arrow being consumed by flames. His screams soon faded as the flames devoured him and he was nothing but ash.

"Ah," said the last of the assassins, spitting out blood and pointing to his dead comrade. "You missed one."

Dahlen turned to see Dohrrn running through the woods to her, Vorce and some his men not far behind. The young boy, the god of fire, embraced her, his dark skin warm against hers. He then pressed a hand to her stomach.

You are in pain.

She nodded, not having the energy to fight. "The baby," she replied, blinking back her tears.

First, we must get you out of here.

Vorce, as if he too had heard Dohrrn, swiftly picked her up from the ground. "Bring that man," he ordered in a booming voice. "Alive!" He then turned and carried Dahlen out of the woods.

CHAPTER 3

"You're fine," Marten told her once they returned to camp. "You just badly sprained your ankle."

"And the baby," she inquired with anxiety.

He gave her a soft smile. "The child is fine. You merely pulled a muscle in your abdomen."

She let out a sigh of relief.

"Maybe it is time you toned down your training sessions," he scolded her gently.

She returned a weak smile. "You should know me better than that by now," she shot back.

He shook his head. "What were you doing out there?" he asked her.

She shrugged. "Nothing," she replied. "The same thing I have always done, just existing."

"Things have changed, T, you know that," he told her.

"I know," she replied as she sat up, wincing as the pain seared through her.

"You don't have to prove anything to anyone," he told her. "You are allowed rest."

"I need to speak to that brother," she told him sternly. "I saw his tattoo, Marten. He is of the coven. Someone hired the coven to kill me."

Marten's face paled.

"He only spared me when he saw I was with child."

Marten nodded. "The coven has always been against the killing of the innocent," he responded. "We have always had a strange way of looking at things."

"I want to talk to him."

"Fine," he relented. "But I will have him brought to the main house where Vorce, Mohrr, and Dohrrn will also be in attendance."

She narrowed her eyes for a moment before lowering herself back onto her pillows. "Fine."

Mohrr burst into the tent a few minutes later having spoken with Marten. "Absolutely not!" he exclaimed furiously. "There is no need for you to meet with him."

"Mohrr, I understand you're angry, but we must find out who sent those men," she told him. "We have to know who and what we are up against."

He shook his head. "I think we should just kill him and be done with it," he replied. "We know who sent him. The Order sent him, or even Bornnen! What does it matter?" Mohrr winced and pressed a hand to the back of his head.

"You're hurt," she said with concern.

"That bastard knocked me in the back of head when I wasn't looking, like a coward," he told her. "It's nothing."

"And your arm?"

He walked over to her bed and sat next to her. "It's just a scratch." He put his hand on top of hers and gave it a squeeze. "I don't remember ever being more terrified of anything else in my life than I was today. The possibility of you dying today was unbearable," he told her softly. "Promise me, no more. No more going out of the boundaries of the settlement. Please. I don't want to go through what happened today ever again."

She silently nodded. "I promise," she whispered. "But I am still going to talk to the assassin, or at least see what Marten can read from him. No harm can come from him while he is bound and guarded."

Mohrr looked agitated but nodded. He moved to leave when Dahlen took hold of his arm.

"Please, stay," she said softly.

He looked at her for a moment.

"I was scared today, too," she confessed, shaking her head. "I thought you were dead as soon as I rode away. I don't know how I would have survived it." She pressed her lips together and took a deep breath through her nose. "I am sorry," she told him. "I promise I will no longer leave the boundaries of the camp until after the baby is born."

Mohrr smiled softly as he sat back on the bed and embraced her.

CHaPteR 4

THE ASSASSIN, BOUND BY HIS HANDS AND FEET, WAS DRAGGED IN AND made to kneel before Dahlen, Mohrr, Dohrrn and Vorce while Marten stood silently off to the side. One of the assassin's eyes was swollen and his lip was busted, but he forced a smile regardless of the pain it caused him.

"Evening," he said cheerfully looking up.

Mohrr grunted.

"Do you know who I am?" Dahlen asked from her seated position, a stern look on her face.

The man shrugged. "An unfulfilled contract," he replied.

Mohrr took an angry step forward but his advancement was cut off by Vorce who pressed a large hand against the prince's chest.

Dahlen pulled up her sleeve to reveal an identical 'X' tattoo on her wrist.

The assassin on the ground shifted uncomfortably. "You're a vow breaker, then," he said giving another shrug.

"I have broken no vows," she explained. "I was released from my vows by The Leaders themselves. While I was of the coven I was known as The Tigress, an assassin much like yourself."

His eyes grew wide with recognition. "The Tigress," he repeated.

"I have heard of you. The knowledge of your release had," he paused looking for the right words, "mixed views amongst the rest of us."

"Who hired you to kill me?" she asked, disregarding his comment.

"Tsk, tsk, tsk," he replied, shaking his head. "You know I can't tell you that. I am bound by the confidentiality clause of my contract to not divulge that kind of information."

"What is your title?" Marten asked, remaining in the shadows of the tent.

The assassin grinned. "I am known as The Viper."

"A snake is a befitting title for someone like you," Mohrr responded bitterly. "Only a snake would be so callous as to attack a woman heavy with child."

Dahlen shot him a warning side glance.

"Hey, to be fair, you can't tell she is with child under that baggy tunic she's wearing and I had no knowledge of it until she was about to cut my head off," he said with a nod in her direction. "Most impressive, by the way. The Tigress, indeed. I am a little ashamed that I let a woman with child get the better of me. I was offended when they sent those other men with me, as if they didn't trust me alone to do the job, but they were right to have been so cautious."

"Who sent you?" Dahlen asked again.

The Viper shook his head. "You of all people should know I cannot tell you," he reaffirmed.

Marten stepped forward out of the shadows. "I have heard your name mentioned among the coven," he told him. "You are about as honorable as your name implies."

The Viper turned his head to look at Marten, a movement so quick it was almost unnoticeable. "Do I know you from somewhere?" he asked, narrowing his eyes. "You look familiar."

Marten showed him his tattoo as well.

"Ah, another defector."

Marten shook his head. "I am still of the coven."

"Hmm, now I remember," The Viper mused. "You're one of our

spies. I've seen you around before. I think I received my title the year after you did. You're The Monk."

Marten nodded. "I am."

"Word is, you're The Leaders' little pet," he continued. "Running around and doing their bidding."

Marten frowned, but ignored The Viper's comment. Instead, he placed both of his hands on The Viper's face and closed his eyes.

The Viper gave a small jerk. "What is he doing?" he asked, more in confusion than in alarm. "Why is he touching me?"

No one answered as they watched, a strange tension filling the room as Marten twitched and spasmed, still holding the captive assassin's face in his hands. After what seemed like several minutes, Marten took a large gulp of air as if he had been holding his breath the entire time. He took a few steps back from The Viper, panting slightly.

"Marten?" Dahlen asked, a little concerned.

"What just happened?" The Viper asked, looking confused. "What did you just do to me?"

Marten shook his head. "It is the same man who hired Tristan Stahrs to hand you over to the Bornnenians."

Tristan Stahrs was a man Dahlen had been traveling with on a mission to Bornnen who had ultimately betrayed her. It was a name she wished she could forget.

"But Tristan was never able to tell me who that was," she replied. *Vron is behind this.*

As if he had heard Dohrrn as well, Marten added, "There were several instances where I saw a black hawk, Vron's familiar." He shook his head again. "The man I saw, I can't decipher his face. Every image I have of him is distorted. But I can feel that it's the same man who hired Tristan."

Mohrr frowned slightly. "You can feel?"

Marten wrinkled his nose in thought. "It's difficult to explain," he started, "but when you *read* someone or have a vision of them, you get a sense of their aura."

The Viper snickered. "What in the greater realms are you talking about?"

"We should torture him," Mohrr growled. "Get the answers out of him that way."

Vorce rubbed his hand over his mouth pensively, scratching his beard. He shook his head after a moment. "As much as I might wish to tear this man limb from limb—"

"Pleasant seeming fellow," The Viper muttered.

"—something does not feel right," Vorce said.

This is what they want. They want us to kill him. We cannot play into their game.

Dahlen cursed. "You're right," she said shaking her head. "We can't kill him. He plays some role in their scheme."

"Yes!" The Viper said in agreement, motioning his tied hands in Dahlen's direction. "What she said about not killing me. I vehemently agree with her on that point. The second half of what she said, however," he shook his head, "I'm a little confused about. I have no knowledge of a scheme."

"We will keep him here," Vorce said. "He will be our prisoner until he can be disposed of or found useful to our cause." He gave a wave of his hand and two of his men dragged The Viper back out.

Mohrr shook his head in defeat and stormed out, angry the man who attacked Dahlen wasn't going to get punished.

"He seems a little hotheaded today," Marten commented.

"I believe he is angrier with himself than anything," Dahlen explained. "He felt helpless today."

Marten nodded.

"Did you see this attack happening?" she asked him.

He looked over at her and sighed. "Are you all right to take a walk?" he asked motioning her to follow him.

She glanced over at Dohrrn who had sat down and appeared to be meditating. She nodded and, taking his arm for support, allowed

Marten to lead her out into the camp, limping slightly.

"I saw this happening about two weeks ago," he told her as they walked past the other tents. "I was in Harpren visiting Mohrr's sister Princess Rain. She is with child as well and is due about the same time as you are."

Subconsciously, Dahlen rubbed a hand over her belly. "I am happy for them."

Marten gave a quick smile. "It was in the middle of the night while there that I saw the attack. I wasted no time in coming back."

"You made great time," she told him. "Harpren is at least two and a half weeks away."

He nodded. "I changed horses a few times and rode through the night most days. I still barely made it back in time."

They stopped walking just past the construction site, where permanent houses were being built. Dahlen sat down on a stump and grimaced.

"Are you alright?" Marten asked.

She nodded. "My abdomen," she replied pressing her hand where it hurt.

He gently took her hand. "Do you mind if I look?" he asked.

She hesitated. It always made her uncomfortable when he read her, but after a moment she nodded.

He took her hand in his and she watched as, after a moment, a haziness fell over his eyes. She watched as his eyes darted back and forth, his body twitching slightly. Then it was over. His eyes returned to their normal hue and focused on her face.

Marten immediately dropped her hand and looked away.

Dahlen frowned. "What did you see?"

He gave a heavy sigh. "Then it has not changed," he said just above a whisper.

"What did you see?" Dahlen repeated herself.

"I have to pray on this first, T," he replied still not looking at her.

"Tell me, Marten!" she commanded.

"I will!" he replied with equal force, finally meeting her eye.

Dahlen jumped, startled by the anger staring back at her.

He rubbed his face with his hands and then put a gentle hand on her shoulder, giving it a light squeeze. "I will," he repeated in a softer tone. "I promise, but there are things I need help interpreting and for that, I need to pray and meditate on what I have been seeing the past few weeks."

Dahlen shook her head. "If you need to talk to Dohrrn, I can help."

"No," he replied, forcing a small smile. "I need time to reflect." He bent over and kissed her forehead. "I promise I will talk to you when I am ready." He held his hand out for her. "Let me escort you back to Vorce."

She let him help her up. "Actually, if you could take me back to my tent, I would appreciate it," she told him, looping her arm through his. "I'm exhausted."

He nodded and patted her hand. "Thank you for trusting me, T," he said after a short silence.

She rubbed his arm. "You are the closest thing to family I have ever known for years, Marten. And no one has ever trusted or believed in me as much as you have."

A shiver ran down his spine as he squeezed her hand and he forced a smile. "I will always believe in you, T."

CHAPTER 5

"We must take her with us," said The Wind. "We can take her to The Rest and—"

"No!" came a male voice.

The young child jumped, the sound of yelling waking her from a restless sleep.

"I will not have her becoming one of us. I will not put her through that."

"What other choice do we have?" The Wind offered gently. "We cannot leave her here or at some orphanage. The Order will find out she is still alive and come after her."

There was a pause.

"Do you understand what I am telling you?" The Wind asked. "That little girl, your daughter, is in danger. We are the only ones who can offer her protection, offer her the means to protect herself. With us, she will be nameless, untraceable. Out there, she will be easy prey."

The child heard the man sigh. "I know you are right," he finally replied, sounding defeated.

"There is one more thing," The Wind told him. "She must never know who you are."

Weeks had passed since Marten returned to the settlement and he still had not explained to Dahlen what he had seen. Her confinement grew closer every day and her belly was becoming cumbersome. Her training sessions with Vorce had stopped but it did not deter her from swinging a sword by herself, or shooting a bow, or throwing her knives. With child or not, she was becoming more restless.

Spring was fast approaching, bringing with it new beginnings. Dohrrn could feel the excitement of the change of seasons as he, like the trees, began new growth. He often would take Dahlen's wing necklace, wearing it as he meditated or tested his growing powers.

Mohrr made plans to return to Skahrr after the child was born. He wanted to go back to check on what his father was doing and see if there was any way to stop him from helping Vron in what was bound to be a cataclysmic war.

Marten was often vacant. He would rise early before the others, going out of the boundary of the settlement to pray and would, more often than not, not return until dusk. He apologized for his absence, but gave no explanation. Dahlen's curiosity burned and her patience waned. On a couple of occasions, she went to Dohrrn for answers, but he would only shake his head.

I am not the only god who is at work here, he would tell her.

She was frustrated, but had come to understand this was how the gods worked. Nothing seemed to be straightforward. Everything was a long, drawn-out procedure, an enigma they expected you to solve.

So, it did not surprise her that it took Marten almost two months to come to her with his answer about what the gods had revealed to him. She was inspecting the little house being built for her, smiling to herself, imagining what it would be like when her daughter was born. Then she heard shouting.

She stepped out of the partially finished house to see Mohrr storming angrily out of Marten's tent. They made eye contact for a brief moment before he hurried off in the opposite direction. A few seconds later Marten emerged, his head bowed for a moment in solemn repose. When he looked up and saw her, a small, sad smile flashed across his lips.

"I will reveal everything to you tonight," he told her before he too walked away.

Dahlen laid her hand on her belly, feeling the child inside her stir, and for a moment she was filled with uncertainty. She roamed the camp looking for Dohrrn so he could give her some sense of comfort, but he was nowhere to be found. Even as the sun began to sink behind the trees and dinner was being prepared over the evening fires, Dohrrn had yet to return.

It wasn't until Marten approached her that she asked if he knew where Dohrrn was.

Marten shook his head. "I believe he went this morning to meditate in the woods, but I have not seen him since."

She nodded. "It's not like him to miss dinner."

Marten took her by the hand. "T," he said softly, "Mohrr and I need to discuss something with you."

She nodded and allowed him to lead her to his tent where Mohrr was leaning against a table, looking distant. He did not meet her gaze when she entered.

"I apologize for taking as long as I have to come to you with my visions," Marten started. "A lot of what I see is not always clear and takes time to decipher, or has holes in it, meaning I have to wait to receive more visions to fill them in." He pressed his lips together and averted his gaze to the floor.

Dahlen looked from Marten to Mohrr, who kept staring at nothing, an indecipherable look on his face.

"And have you?" she asked looking back at Marten.

"Received more visions?"

"Filled in the holes?"

Marten cleared his throat and nodded while Mohrr shifted slightly where he stood, crossing his arms over his chest.

"I have."

"From the look both of your demeanors, can I assume that the outcome is not favorable?" she asked slowly seating herself.

"It might not be what you had hoped for," Marten replied matter-of-factly.

"Gods be blessed! Stop being so cryptic, dammit, and tell her," Mohrr growled in a low voice.

Dahlen could feel her heart sink in her chest. "Will my child not survive?" she asked, putting a protective hand on her stomach.

Marten shook his head. "Your child will live, and she will thrive."

She let out a sigh of relief. "Then what is wrong?"

Mohrr pushed off the table he was leaning against and walked to the other side of the tent, agitated. Marten rubbed his mouth with his hand, his eyes searching for the words he seemed hesitant to say.

"Mohrr's sister, Rain, will lose her child," Marten started slowly. "And as far as I can see, will not be blessed with another opportunity."

Dahlen frowned and shook her head. "That is awful and will be very hard on her. Someone as kind as her does not deserve such a fate. I am so sorry, Mohrr."

Mohrr did not reply.

"How will this happen?" Dahlen asked.

Marten swallowed and rubbed his lips together. "There is going to be an attempt on her life," he responded. "The Bornnenians are going to raid the capitol Harpren. Rain will be evacuated from the city, but during her escape she will go into labor." He took a deep breath and let it out slowly. "It is during this time she will be found by Bornnenian soldiers. Her entourage will be slaughtered and she—"

"She will be killed?" Dahlen said softly.

Marten shook his head. "She will be hurt, but she will survive, while her child will not."

"They will stab my sister in her womb," Mohrr added lamentably. "Killing her child and taking away her ability to carry another."

Dahlen gaped at Marten. "Is this true?"

He nodded.

"Can we not prevent this?" she asked incredulously.

He shook his head. "The gods have willed this," he replied mournfully. "Any scenario I can image brings the same outcome. It does not matter. We will only arrive just in time to save her."

Dahlen shook her head. "I don't understand the gods. Why would they let something so awful happen to such a good person? It doesn't make sense to deny Rain the chance to be a mother when she is so deserving of a child's love and affection."

Marten opened his mouth for a moment to continue speaking but shook his head to reconsider what he was going to say. "But she *will* be a mother," he finally replied after a moment.

Dahlen blinked at him. "I don't understand. If her child dies and she can no longer bear them, how will she be a mother?"

"Because she will be the mother to yours," Marten replied softly.

Dahlen didn't move or speak for several seconds as Marten's words sank in. "You expect me to give up my child?" she asked shakily, her face starting to flush with anger.

Marten took in a deep breath, closing his eyes as he let it out slowly. "Yes," he almost whispered.

She shook her head vigorously. "No!" she yelled, struggling slightly to stand. "No! I refuse! You cannot make me!"

"T, you have to understand," Marten started gently, "the both of you run a greater risk of being found and killed if you are together. Think of what happened just a few weeks ago. This is the only way."

She shot an angry glance at Mohrr who would not, or could not, meet her eye.

"If we keep her hidden," Marten continued, "then she will be safe."

She shook her head again. "Keep her safe?! You want me to hand my child over to a city that, by the time she is born, has been attacked by the Bornnenians! How is that keeping her safe?"

"Bornnen is no match for Thren, you know that," Marten replied calmly. "After this failed attack, Thren will tighten its borders and increase its guards. It will be the safest place for anyone, especially a princess. She will be safe."

Dahlen pressed her hand to her chest and let out a ragged breath. "I can keep her safe! I can protect her!"

"T, please, try to understand your child's importance, her role, in securing the future of this realm," Marten tried to explain.

"Dahlen," Mohrr finally said quietly, "there is no other way."

"What?" she said, hurt, shaking her head and frowning. "You agree with this?"

Mohrr took in a sharp breath, shaking his head. "I don't like it, in fact, I hate it, but for selfish reasons. It hurts to think that our child will grow up not knowing we are her parents and how much we love her, but it will hurt more if something were to happen to her." He took a few steps toward her as if to take her in his arms. "She will be safer this way."

"No!" she yelled, recoiling from his touch. "Where is Dohrrn?" She moved out of the tent, the two men following her from a safe distance. "Dohrrn!" she screamed, tears starting to fall down her face. "Dohrrn! Where are you?"

The child emerged from the woods. *I am here.*

Dahlen's chest heaved angrily as she looked down at him. "Is this what I should do?" she asked bitterly. "Is this what you and the other gods are telling me needs to happen?"

Dohrrn did not reply.

"Tell me! Is this what you wish of me to do?"

Dohrrn, his eyes shimmering with his own tears, did not look away from her. *I wish it.*

"Damn you!" she yelled, putting a supportive hand on her belly as she fell to her knees. "Damn you!"

Mohrr and Marten moved to help her but she swatted them away.

"I never wanted any of this! I never wanted to be who I am! I only wanted a quiet life, a life of my own. But I have finally come to terms with my role in this prophecy. I have accepted who I am, even embraced it!" she cried. "And the one good thing to come out of this, the one gift you have given me, you are now telling me I have to give away!" She pressed a hand to her mouth to suppress a sob. "Why?"

Dohrrn approached her and gently took her face in his small hands. *Life cannot happen without sacrifice.*

CHAPTER 6

Princess Rain, future queen of Thren, was due to have her child at the end of spring. She was elated, overjoyed at the prospect of being a mother and bringing a new prince or princess to the realm. Her husband, Castuhl, who had as gentle of a demeanor as she did, believed the child could only add happiness to their marriage.

Castuhl told her he only wished for a healthy child, but she secretly prayed for a girl. She lit a candle for the goddesses Behr and Gher every morning, telling them of her hopes for her first born. She wanted a healthy child, of course, but beyond that she prayed for her child, her daughter, to be strong, independent, and fearless while still being gentle and understanding.

She walked the shoreline of the Dormant Sea daily, letting the salty water run over her feet as she dreamt of her child's future. This was everything she wanted. It was difficult to imagine how, just a little over a year ago, she opposed the match between her and Castuhl. A pang of guilt struck her every time she thought about how she begged the assassin, The Tigress, to kill him so she wouldn't have to marry him. She had wished to be free of a loveless marriage, but what she and Castuhl turned out to have was anything but loveless.

"I received a letter from my sister River this afternoon," Rain told

Castuhl as they walked the shoreline together one evening. "She wishes to visit soon. She says she will try to convince our father to leave now so she can be here before our child is born."

"Your sister River is the wild one, is she not?" Castuhl teased.

Rain's grip tightened slightly on his arm as she smiled. "She is the adventurous one out of all of us," she agreed. "Mohrr is the realistic one, level-headed and cautious, while I am reserved and shy, but River is exactly how her name implies. Unpredictable, bold and daring. I used to wish I was more like her."

Castuhl kissed her forehead. "I do not wish that," he told her. "I wish you to remain exactly as you are. Kind, understanding, and compassionate. That is all I have ever wished for in a wife."

Rain felt her cheeks blush as she smiled. "And what about beautiful?" she teased gently.

He gave a small laugh. "Your being beautiful is certainly wonderful, but I would never have wished it above everything else."

Rain smirked and raised a brow. "How sly you are," she said laughing. "I cannot believe that for a minute!"

She saw him smile in the fading light. "It is true. I am grateful for your beauty, but beauty will fade, your compassion and kindness will not," he explained. "That is what matters to me."

She rested her head on his shoulder. "How good you are to me, Castuhl," she told him. "I have truly been blessed."

"We have both been."

"Oh," she uttered in surprise. "Our child is kicking," she said taking his hand and pressing it to her stomach.

Castuhl smiled broadly as he felt his child moving inside his wife's womb. "I believe I am the more blessed one," he told her. "I could not be more overjoyed." He kissed her gently before resting his forehead on hers.

After a few moments, shouting could be heard from the direction of the castle. Both of them looked up to see a guard carrying a torch, yelling for them.

"Your royal highnesses," he said when he caught up to them, "there is a raid upon the city!"

"What?" Castuhl asked in concern.

"Bornnenian soldiers, they have entered the capitol! Your father requests your presence," the guard told him. "He says we must get the princess away."

"No!" Rain said grabbing Castuhl's arm. "I will not leave you!"

Castuhl turned to her. "You must," he told her. "For our child's sake."

She shook her head. "I will not leave without you then!"

"My love, I cannot leave my city while the Bornnenians attack it," he replied. "I must stay to protect my people, *our* people. It is what a king would do."

Tears began to run down Rain's cheeks. "Promise me you will be alright," she pleaded.

He took her in his arms and gently kissed her forehead. "I will meet you shortly. We will drive the Bornnenians from our borders in no time." He then turned to the guard who informed them of the attack. "I am entrusting my wife and child to you."

The guard nodded. "King Caston has ordered her a guarded entourage. I shall take her to them so that she might escape the city safely."

Castuhl gave Rain one last kiss before running back to help defend his city.

Rain stared after him, her lips quivering and eyes filling with tears.

"Come, princess," the guard said, holding out his hand. "There is no time to waste."

She nodded. This was not the time to be afraid, she told herself, rubbing a protective hand over her belly. This was the time to be courageous.

DAHLEN SAT UP STRAIGHTER ON HER HORSE AS A SHOT OF PAIN coursed through her back. She gave a small gasp but continued at her pace, trailing behind the others. They had left almost two weeks ago, making their way further south in Behr Wood to somehow find and rescue Princess Rain.

Marten explained to her that they would find her in enough time to save her life from her wounds, but her child would die as soon as the knife entered its mother's body.

"Just because her child dies, does not mean she would be convinced to look after one that is not her own," Dahlen bitterly explained to him as they made their way to their destination.

"The plan will fall together," Marten told her.

"I'm sure it will," she whispered back.

Dahlen fidgeted again in her saddle. After twelve days of traveling, her body was sore. She had been stagnant too long at their settlement, she thought. She was used to traveling, moving from one location to another. Even when she was growing up in the coven, there was always some excursion to go on with one of The Teachers.

She held back a groan. When they began their journey, she was offered a spot in the covered wagon, but she quickly refused. She was angry, and felt used, but she was not going to hide herself away. Now, however, a more stable place to sit and maybe even lie down was sounding more appealing. Her stubbornness prevailed, nonetheless, and she continued to shift uncomfortably on her horse.

You are in pain.

She looked over at Dohrrn who had a worried look on his face. "I am fine," she replied looking away a little haughtily. "Not that my pain actually matters."

Dohrrn didn't say anything in response. She had been bitter toward everyone for weeks now. She felt wronged by all of them.

"Does your back trouble you?"

Dahlen turned to see the midwife slowing her horse to match her speed. "I have been more comfortable while traveling, yes," she replied.

The middle-aged woman looked mildly concerned. "You will let me know if the pain persists or worsens," she said in a gentle command.

Dahlen opened her mouth to say something sarcastic, but thought better of it when she saw the woman was being genuine. She nodded. "I will. Thank you."

The midwife, Ehris, smiled gently. She was well respected among Vorce and his ruffians for being a wonderful healer and midwife. She had saved several of the men's lives back at the camp and even, several months before, helped tend to a cut in Dahlen's leg. A cut she sustained from fighting against the Order of Zeln. She liked Ehris. She was gentle and kind, yet forceful when she needed to be.

"I am glad it is you who came with us," Dahlen told her.

"I was asked by Vremir himself," she replied smiling modestly.

Dahlen looked over at Dohrrn.

"The god of fire looks after us all," Ehris told her as if reading her mind.

"I'm sure he does."

chapter 7

The wagon moved slowly through the woods, its wheels creaking. The young girl huddled in a corner. She had no idea where she was going. All she knew was that she wanted her mother.

She wiped away a tear as it fell not wanting the boy that slept nearby to hear her crying. She wanted to know where she was going and why Vorce had not found her yet. She knew something was wrong, but she just couldn't figure out what it was.

"You don't have to be afraid," came a soft voice.

She started.

It was just the boy. He had not been sleeping after all. He sat up and scooted closer to her.

"Are you scared?" he asked in a low voice.

She hesitated, but nodded after a moment.

"You don't have to be," he reassured her. He took out a piece of jerky from his pocket and offered it to her. "Are you hungry?"

Tears flooded down her face as she nodded, gratefully taking what was offered to her. She ate it as she cried, wiping away giant tears as she chewed.

"Momma," was all she was able to utter as she finished.

The boy bowed his head. "I'm sorry, but your mother is," he paused for a moment, "she is with the gods."

She cried harder, not understanding what he was saying.

The boy gently shushed her, taking her into his arms. "You're going to be okay," he whispered soothingly. "The gods have big plans for you."

She sniffed as she looked up at him.

"It's going to be alright, AnnJella," he told her.

"What's your name?" she asked still wiping away her tears.

He smiled at her. "My name is Marten," he told her. "And I am going to help look after you."

Dahlen shot up from bed as a hot blaze of pain rang through her. She brought her hand to her mouth to stifle her agony as she struggled to get up from the ground. The others in her group were still sleeping, the fading embers of the fire barely giving off any light. She got to her hands and knees and crawled to a tree stump. Confusion overcame her as a wetness trickled down her legs.

The child was coming.

She dug her teeth into her fist as another wave of pain hit her. She leaned against the trunk of the tree for support, wanting so much to stand but lacking the strength. Despite the crisp, night air, sweat began to gather at her brow. She panted heavily as she pushed herself off of the ground, using the stump for support.

Pain ripped through her as she gritted her teeth. Tears streamed down her face as she pushed herself up from the ground only to fall back to her knees. She held a supportive hand on her stomach as another wall of pain hit her.

She let out a cry without even knowing it.

"Dahlen!" Mohrr had said from somewhere.

"She is in labor," she heard Ehris say next to her as if she suddenly appeared from nowhere. Her gentle hand rubbed her back. "Keep breathing, my child," she told her. "Deep breaths. We must breathe through the pain." She gently, yet firmly, took Dahlen by the arm and guided her back toward camp.

Mohrr and Marten were compiling blankets on the ground for a makeshift bed while Vorce awakened his men.

"We must have boiling water," Ehris commanded with a nod to one of Vorce's men.

He took a pot and ran to the nearby river as another man built the fire back up. The whole camp was now awake. The five men Vorce chose to bring along were scurrying about the trees collecting wood for the fire or tearing strips of cloth for Ehris.

"What can I do?" Mohrr asked in a panic as Dahlen let out another cry of pain.

Ehris waved him away. "Give us room," she told him. "A woman's body can handle more pain than a man. She is strong and will be fine."

Mohrr looked torn between listening to Ehris and staying.

"You go!" Ehris said shooting him a look. "You are a distraction. Not what she needs. She needs focus."

"Dahlen," Mohrr said taking her hand for a moment. "I will be close by if you need me." He kissed her forehead and walked to where Marten and Dohrrn were standing, looking just as helpless.

Dohrrn then approached her and knelt by her side, taking her hand.

Dahlen shook her head and gritted her teeth through the pain. "Go away!" she told him. "I don't need you here!"

And, yet, I am still here. I will always be here.

Tears streamed down her face as Ehris called for her to push.

Whether or not you hate me for what is to come, I will always be here.

"Push, child!" Ehris goaded. "You must push!"

After what felt like hours, Dahlen gave a final push, falling back exhausted on her makeshift bed. And, for a moment, it was silent. The air was calm and peaceful as Dahlen's cries were replaced by that of her child's.

THE WAGON SWAYED GENTLY AS IT MOVED ALONG, LULLING THE BABY to sleep. Dahlen stared down at her, unable to remove her eyes from the miracle that had grown inside her. She watched as her daughter's tiny hand gently clenched and unclenched, grasping at nothing.

Dahlen placed one of her own fingers in her daughter's palm and felt her surprisingly strong grip as she clasped onto it. She bent down and kissed her wrinkled forehead which caused a slight twitch of the child's mouth that could have been a smile.

Dahlen's eyes filled with tears and her chest tightened. Two days is what Marten had said. Two days was all she would have to hold the child she created, the child she had carried inside of her for months. Two days was all she would have to comfort and nurse her.

She tried not to think of all of the other days she would miss. She tried to focus on what was in front of her at that moment, her sleeping child that inspired more love and hope inside of her than anything or anyone else could ever have done. She tried not to let her feelings of bitterness toward the situation haunt her, but she could not.

It tore her to pieces to think of everything that would not be between her and the child she bore and she cried silent, bitter tears as she looked down at her. She knew giving her child away was for the best, in her mind she understood that. But in her heart, she could not. As the prospect of handing her baby off to another woman grew closer, a different kind of emptiness grew within her, a sense of loneliness she had never known before.

The wagon stopped moving for a moment and Mohrr came in. He crouched to avoid hitting the canvas covering as he made his way to her.

"How are you feeling?" he asked as he sat next to her. "Are you in any pain?"

She shot him a side glare. "Physically, I am fine," she told him. "Whatever Ehris has given me has helped greatly with the pain."

"She is beautiful," he whispered as he looked over at his daughter, his eyes shimmering with pride. "Can you believe we have made something this perfect?"

Dahlen couldn't respond. Her overwhelming feelings of anger and emptiness would not allow her to.

"Might I hold her?" he asked not looking up from the child.

She wanted to say no; she wanted to scream and yell at him and deny him the chance to hold his daughter, but then she understood. Mohrr was losing all of the same opportunities as she was. He would not be able to witness his daughter grow either.

For a moment, her bitterness melted away and she nodded as she gently handed him his daughter. "Ehris said you must always support her head," she told him protectively.

He nodded as he took his daughter in his arms and held her close to him. She stirred slightly at the disturbance but quickly settled into her father's arms. He smiled down at her and stroked her tiny face. He shot the same smile up at Dahlen, but she turned away.

His hand found hers and he squeezed it gently. "I know this is not going to be easy," he said gently, quietly. "Looking at this miracle we created, I have never felt more love for anyone or anything than I do her."

"Don't," Dahlen replied in almost a whisper.

"The mere thought of giving her away rips a hole in my heart I know will never be filled."

"Don't," she repeated a little more firmly.

"And I know you must feel the same," Mohrr continued despite her pleas for him to stop. "No, I know you feel it more having carried her inside of you."

"I said don't!" she said in a harsh whisper, flashing him a glare. "I don't want to talk about how I feel or how you feel. Because it does not matter. It will not make a difference in what has already been decided for us." She looked away. "I will give my child up because that is what I was told to do. That is what the god of fire has wished of me," she told him bitterly.

They were silent for a moment. An almost palpable tension between them.

"I don't speak as eloquently as Marten in situations such as this," Mohrr started, "nor am I able to say anything wise, but I believe this is the right thing to do and I know Rain with her gentle loving nature will take great care of her. She will make a wonderful mother."

Dahlen's muscles tensed at the word, *mother*. The role she was being denied. "I am sorry, truly sorry, for what is going to happen to your sister," she started unsuccessfully holding back her bitterness, "but it does not make me feel any better for doing what I am about to do."

"We can have another," Mohrr told her with sincerity.

"What?" she replied with astonishment, appalled he could even suggest such a thing.

"We can have more children," he repeated, reaching out to take her hand again.

She pulled away, horrified. "You mean try to replace her?"

Mohrr shook his head. "No, but this does not have to be the end. What if this is the beginning of what is to come?"

"You are right," she told him after a few moments. "You do not speak as eloquently as Marten or have anything wise to say." She held her arms back out to take her child.

Mohrr sighed dejectedly, but gently handed their daughter back to her. "I did not choose this, Dahlen," he reminded her softly. "What we are doing here does not make me feel less for you. In fact, being able to hold our child in my arms, even for a moment, has made my feelings for you stronger."

Dahlen closed her eyes for a moment, suppressing a surge of emotion.

"I have not given up on us," he continued. "And I hope you have not either." He gave her a kiss on her forehead before he exited the wagon.

Dahlen looked down at her child and held her close. Giving her up would change everything for her. She was sorry for it, but she would have no hope left.

CHAPTER 8

RAIN SLOWLY PACED THE ROOM, TAKING DEEP BREATHS THROUGH THE pain. She had been in labor for over two hours when they came across a small abandoned structure in the middle of the woods. Knowing she could not give birth on the run, she made her escort stop and take shelter. The building was in need of repair, but it provided a roof which was all she wanted.

It had been dusk when they arrived, but now the only light was the moon dimly shining through the windows. Her head guard insisted on no fire so their position would not be given away, so she had to make due as she slowly walked from one side of the small room to the next, her hand tracing the wall to help guide her in the dark.

She took a deep breath and let it out slowly as another contraction hit her. She leaned against the wall for support.

"Just keep breathing, your highness," her midwife cooed gently.

Sweat moistened Rain's brow as she gritted her teeth through the pain. She wished Castuhl was there. She wished he was the one gently rubbing her back and offering her words of comfort. She would be less frightened if he was.

"It's too early," Rain said when the midwife first told her the baby was coming.

"'Tis not abnormal for the first to come early," the older woman had replied. "The babe will be fine nonetheless. 'Tis not so early to be concerned."

Rain's eyes filled with tears as another contraction nearly brought her to her knees.

"Perhaps you should lie down, your highness," the midwife suggested.

Rain shook her head. "No," she replied sternly. "The pacing helps with the pain." She pushed off the wall and began walking again from one side of the small room to the other. She wiped her brow and took a sip of water offered to her from the midwife.

"How much longer?" she asked panting.

The midwife shook her head. "I cannot tell unless you lay down and I check." She pressed her hand on Rain's stomach. "The baby has at least turned. I feel its head. The birth should not be difficult."

Rain nodded wordlessly.

Just then shouting could be heard from outside. The midwife ran to the window and whispered something under her breath.

"What is happening?" Rain asked.

"They have found us, your highness," the midwife said with a sense of panic. She scrambled around the room looking for a place to hide. "We must get you out of here. There must be someplace to hide."

The shouting continued. Rain, finally having made it to a window, saw the glowing of torches as the Bornnenian soldiers grew closer and her heart sank.

"There is nowhere to go, Sera," she told her almost calmly. "I cannot run in my condition."

"No, your highness," the midwife replied. "We must get you out!"

Rain let out a small scream as another contraction coursed through her. She braced herself on the wall again, breathing deeply.

It was then that the half-rotted door was kicked from its rusted hinges and a large mass of a man stepped in, the glow of his torch bouncing ominously about the room.

Sera stepped protectively in front of Rain, her arms spread out. "Leave us," she pleaded. "We are helpless women; we could do you no harm."

The soldier, without a word, grabbed Sera by the throat.

"No!" Rain yelled. "Leave her alone!"

The man tossed her to the ground, kicking her until she no longer fought back.

Rain stood with her back against the wall, her body shaking from pain and fear.

The soldier sneered at the princess, stepping over the dead body of her midwife as he advanced toward her.

Her breath caught in her throat for a moment as another contraction enveloped her, but she soon recomposed herself.

"I do not fear you," she started, trying to remain brave, "as much as what will happen to you in the afterlife. The goddesses do not look kindly on those who would kill a woman in the midst of birth."

The soldier came closer to her, pulling out a knife, its blade reflecting the flames of the torch.

A tear rolled down Rain's cheek as all of her hopes for her child vanished in midair, but still she refused to beg, knowing it would have no effect. "You are not a man," she whispered, looking him in the eyes defiantly. "You are not even human."

No response came as a different pain coursed through her. If she screamed, she did not notice; all she saw, in the dim light of the torch, was the dark pooling of blood that surrounded her as she fell to the ground.

CHAPTER 9

THE CARNAGE WAS JUST VISIBLE IN THE PALE LIGHT OF THE FULL moon. Mohrr had rushed ahead of the others, jumping off of his horse and bringing his sword down upon the first Bornnenian soldier he found.

Anger and fear fueled him as he swung, and thrust his sword. He bellowed a furious battle cry as he cut his way through the Bornnenians with Vorce and the others not far behind.

When he came across the small, stone structure, he entered, ready to further his fight, but what he found floored him. Three soldiers sat at a small table, drinking, gambling, and laughing while his sister lay on the floor in a pool of her own blood.

The soldiers, stunned for a moment by his entrance, stood and reached for their weapons, but Mohrr was too quick for them. He kicked one of the soldiers in the face as he bent over for his sword, and ran through another as he lunged at him. Mohrr yelled furiously as he brought his sword down on the soldier he had kicked, thrusting his sword into his chest where he laid on the ground.

The last soldier swung at Mohrr, landing a sloppy punch on the left side of his face. Mohrr stumbled and wiped the blood from his lip as he sneered at the soldier.

"You're going to wish you picked up your sword," he told him as he let his drop to the ground. He cracked his knuckles before charging the soldier, releasing upon him all of the anger and frustration that had piled up within him in the past several weeks. Mohrr could feel a sharp pain shoot through one of his hands, but he didn't care. He didn't stop, couldn't stop, until the man before him was lying lifeless on the ground.

He fell to his knees exhausted, panting heavily, his bloodied hands shaking. He thought for a moment that he was the only one left alive in the room when a small sound alerted him to his sister.

"Rain?" he said in the near darkness.

There was a soft groan in response.

Mohrr stood and ran to his sister. He fell by her side and rolled her over, horrified to see a knife still sticking out of her body. Tears misted his vision as he held his sister close to him.

"Rain," he said again, "I'm here."

His sister's eyes fluttered in response and her lips parted.

He brushed back her matted hair. "Do not be afraid."

She made a small gasping sound as if she were in pain. Mohrr moved to remove the knife, hoping to ease her pain when a stern voice stopped him.

"Do not touch the knife!" Ehris commanded, rushing over to him.

"She is dying," he told her.

"Yes, but that knife, though it caused her wound, is slowing her blood loss," she informed him. "If you remove it, she will die."

"Then what can we do?"

"I need light," she told him. "Bring me light. Build me a fire and boil water. I will stay with her and do what needs to be done." She knelt beside the princess and opened her bag of herbs, pulling several out.

One of Vorce's men stepped into the room.

"Boh," Ehris said without looking up, "have the dead bodies removed and have someone make a bed for this girl."

Boh bowed and moved back out of the room to tell the others

their orders.

Ehris then looked back up at Mohrr. "You must leave."

Mohrr looked down at his sister who looked ghastly pale. Once again, he felt helpless. "I am trusting you, Ehris," he replied. "Please save my sister."

She waved an indifferent hand at him. "Do as I say and she will live. Now, go!"

D**AHLEN DID NOT, AND COULD NOT LEAVE THE WAGON AS THE OTHERS** rushed to save Rain. Only Vorce, Dohrrn and Marten stayed behind to help her. Her daughter, who had been fussy earlier was now sleeping again in a basket next to her.

She rocked it gently, watching as she slept.

"This is it," she thought. "These are my last few moments with my child." She was gently counting her daughter's little fingers for the hundredth time when Marten poked his head in.

"T," he said softly.

"Do you think the reason men wish to take life so often, is because they will never truly understand the miracle of creating life?" she asked not wishing to start whatever conversation he wished to start.

He hesitated for a moment. "I don't know. I never really thought about it."

"Do you think they envy the ability?"

Again, Marten was slow in his response.

"Taking a life is easy. Humans are so frail. Killing someone can take only a moment. But creating life, giving life, takes time. It is a long, drawn out process. It is something that is as rewarding as it is painful. It's a humbling yet empowering experience." She looked at him. "I have given this realm a life. Created it inside of me and for the past two days kept that life alive by feeding it from my own breast." She looked back down at her daughter. "I now fully understand just how frail a man's body is compared to mine, to any woman's. Men often take us for granted, but what miracle can any of you perform?"

Marten remained silent, but nodded.

"You were there that day, weren't you?" she asked him after a moment.

He looked at her quizzically.

"The day the coven found me and took me in."

He nodded. "I was. As I have told you before, I led them to you."

"Yes, but you have not told me you were there when they found me."

Marten looked over at the sleeping baby. "It is true I was with the group of brothers and sisters that found you, but I was not there until several hours after you were found."

"I have asked you this before, Marten, and I want you to tell me now, truthfully," she started. "Do you know who my father is?"

He held her gaze. "Truthfully, I do not."

She rubbed her mouth pensively with her knuckles. "But he was there that day."

He furrowed his brows. "You know this?"

She nodded. "The goddesses have been helping me piece together my past. I'm in the back of a wagon, much like this one, and I can hear two men arguing about me. One of them is being scolded for having fathered me when The Wind interrupts them for talking too loudly. I could not make out the voices but I know The Wind was there and by admission, I know The Master was there. Can you remember any-one else?"

Marten shook his head. "T, that was a long time ago," he told her.

"Do not play games with me, Marten," she replied sternly. "I know you remember despite that."

Marten nodded as he sighed. "The Boar was there. The Storm, too," he paused for a moment to think. "I believe The Horn was there as well."

"The Horn?" she repeated. "He never told me that."

Marten shrugged. "Our pasts are of no consequence at the Rest, remember?" he told her. "There would have been no reason to have told you."

She thought for a moment. "He would have been pretty young, wouldn't he?"

"I believe he had only received his title a few years before."

She nodded. "Who else was there?" she asked. "The others you named couldn't be my father. The Boar died five years ago, and The Storm is a woman. And I know from Vorce that my father is still alive."

Marten took a deep breath and let it out slowly. "The Terror, The Hunter, The Current, and The Gallant."

"The Gallant was there?" she asked him incredulously. "Are you sure?"

Marten nodded. "I am pretty sure, yes," he responded, frowning slightly. "At least he started the journey with us. I do not remember seeing him on our way back to the Rest, but, again, it was a long time ago."

Dahlen thought for a moment on the possibility that The Gallant was her father, but was not convinced. He had never shown any interest in her during her time at the Rest. She remembered seeing him on occasion, but he was never truly present in her life. It was not until her last visit, the visit where she was released from her vows, that he actually spoke to her.

No, it couldn't be him. If The Horn had been, perhaps, five years older, she would have guessed it was him over The Gallant.

"I," Marten started, interrupting her thoughts.

She shook her head as she tucked in a loose corner of her daughter's blanket. "There is no need, Marten," she replied. "You have come to apologize for something you claim the gods wish of us, but I have no desire to hear it." She glanced over at him, noticing his solemn face. "Your apology will not make what I am about to do any easier. It will not soften the blow of the pain I am likely to feel for the rest of my life."

"I cannot bear the thought of you being in pain," he told her. "And that it is of my own doing," he shook his head. "I couldn't—"

"Then don't," she said interrupting what he was trying to say. "You are sorry, you are in pain, you regret the burden your gift makes you carry. Please, leave it at that." She took a ragged breath. "I am tired of talking about it."

Marten nodded. "Do you mind if I sit with you, then?"

She slowly shook her head. "Would you like to hold her?"

Marten's eyes lit up in the dark wagon. "May I?"

Dahlen gently picked up her sleeping child and handed her to Marten who, at first, took her awkwardly in his arms. But after a moment, he settled more comfortably.

He smiled broadly. "She is so small," he said.

Dahlen nodded. "She did not feel that small while I was giving birth to her," she replied half smiling.

Marten laughed through his nose. "I am proud of you, T," he told her. "I have always been proud of you." He reached out and squeezed her hand.

Dahlen gently squeezed his back unsure of what to say.

Marten held the baby for a few more minutes until she grew fussy and Dahlen took her back to nurse her. It was then, as her child was falling back to sleep that Dohrrn came to her.

It is time.

Dahlen's heart caught in her throat as she stared down at her daughter. "Must I do this?" she whispered, almost begging, hoping at any moment she would be told this was just a bad dream, a joke.

Dohrrn, however, did not reply, he merely waited.

Shakily, Dahlen stood, half crouching as she walked to the wagon's opening. The sun was just beginning to rise and she paused a moment to look at it. Mohrr then helped her down and followed her as she slowly made her way to the stone structure where she would leave her child with another woman.

She walked proudly, as tears streamed down her face. The others in the group bowing their heads respectively as she passed. She hesitated when she reached the broken door of the stone building, her knees almost failing her.

You cannot have life without sacrifice. That is what Dohrrn had said. But why must her sacrifice be so great?

She stepped forward into the darkened room just making out the shape of Ehris hovering over Rain lying on a pile of blankets. Ehris turned upon hearing her enter.

"She is just resting," she said answering a question no one asked. "She will perhaps sleep for another day, but she will live."

"How will she eat?" Dahlen asked referring to the child, her voice shaking.

"I will get her to feed on the princess," Ehris explained.

A gentle hand landed on her shoulder. "Ehris will take good care of the both of them," came the deep voice of Vorce. "My men will stay behind to guard them. And we have already sent another to find Castuhl."

Dahlen didn't respond.

It is time.

She closed her eyes as a stream of tears fell down her cheeks. She gently kissed her daughter's forehead and held her close for the last time before she handed her to Ehris and walked out of the room without looking back.

CHAPTER 10

DAHLEN WAITED A FEW HOURS AFTER THE SUN HAD GONE DOWN BEFORE she left her house. She paused a moment to place her hand on the door frame of the entrance. It had just been completed two months before. Only a week before she left to give up her child.

She took a deep breath and let it out slowly as she picked up her belongings and carried them to the stables where she fastened them to her horse. She paused a moment as a strong sense she was forgetting something came over her. She stood in the darkness, her eyes searching for the answer until a thought hit her. She gave a small laugh and shook her head as the placed thought developed.

This is Mahk's idea, she thought. *I would never think of something so ridiculous.*

She sighed and scratched the nose of her horse, saying she would be back in a few minutes before she slipped back out into the dark.

She crept slowly between half-built houses and tents until she got to the one she was looking for. She cursed herself seeing two guards standing in front of the entrance, but she had to get in there.

She walked up to them and they bowed. "Good evening," she said. "Vorce would like a word with the both of you. I will look after the prisoner while you are gone."

The two men looked a little confused for a moment, but complied; they would never dare question her. She quietly slipped in as she watched them disappear into the night.

"I'm going to make this quick," she said causing the man inside to jump. "We only have a few minutes."

"Only a few minutes?" he repeated. "It could be a lot better for the both of us if we had more time."

Dahlen scowled. "We only have a few minutes before the guards I sent away realize I lied to them," she explained stepping closer.

The Viper sat up in bed, the chains on his arms and legs rattling as he moved. "Now why would you do that?"

She took a deep breath and let it out slowly. "Because I am going to set you free."

The Viper arched a brow. "Same question."

"Because I want to take you with me."

"With you?" he asked. "Where are you going?"

Dahlen thought for a moment. "I haven't gotten that far yet," she replied. "I just know I can no longer stay here."

The Viper nodded. "And you want the man who was hired to kill you to come with you?"

She smirked. "That contract was voided as soon as you learned I was with child."

The Viper sucked his teeth. "True."

"And I could use someone with your specific set of skills to come with me on my," she paused trying to think of what she was trying to say, "expedition."

The Viper rubbed his chin, intrigued. "What kind of expedition?"

"A dangerous one," she replied.

He grinned. "Now you have my attention."

"I cannot pay you now," she explained. "But if you agree to join me, I will give you your freedom."

The Viper moved his tongue across his teeth as he thought. "I hate verbal contracts," he told her, "but I am rather tired of being chained to this bed. You have yourself a minion."

They shook hands and Dahlen smirked as she pulled out the keys she had swiped from one of the guards. She quickly undid his chains and led him silently back to the stables where they saddled their horses.

They quietly led the horses out of the stables and moved silently to the southern gates where Dohrrn and Marten were already waiting for them.

"Well, this attempt failed," The Viper said with a huff.

"Quiet," she replied shooting him a glance. "They aren't here to stop us. Just open up the gates."

The Viper shook his head. "I witnessed that kid throw a ball of fire at a man and incinerate him where he stood," he told her. "That is not how I want to die."

"Trust me," she said sternly.

The Viper looked from her to them and then back at her before he slowly, without turning his back on Dohrrn, made his way to the gate.

"We have ordered the guards to retire for the night," Marten said as he stepped forward and handed her a bag of coins.

"How long have you known?" she asked him.

"Since the day you gave up your child," he told her softly. His eyes glistened in the pale moon light. "I *am* sorry, T," he whispered.

She nodded. "I know, Marten," she replied. "But this has nothing to do with you."

He nodded too. "I know." He took a step closer and took her face gently in his hands, placing a soft kiss on her lips. "Please, don't let your anger get the best of you," he told her as he pulled away.

She gave another nod, half dazed.

He pulled her in for a hug and gave her another kiss on her forehead as he walked away without another word.

Dohrrn stepped forward and she made eye contact with him for a moment before looking away.

You feel as though I have failed you, he said.

She shook her head. "No, I feel as though I have no control over what I do with my life."

The Viper, who had returned from opening the gates, looked around confused. "Who are you talking to?"

I only want what is best for the realm. For my people.

She nodded. "I understand that," she replied. "But what was best for the realm was at my own expense and I am not ready to understand that."

"Are you talking to the kid?" The Viper asked still confused.

There is still more you do not understand. He walked closer to her. *I do not wish you to go.*

Dahlen shook her head. "But I wish to go," she replied. She then took off her necklace, her family seal, and gave it to Dohrrn. "I know how much you like this," she said placing it over his head. "I want you to hold on to it for me."

He shook his head but accepted the gift. *You cannot run from who you are or your role in what is to come.*

"I am not running," she explained. "I am seeking."

Dohrrn was silent for several moments before he bent over and plucked a stone from the ground. He closed his fingers around it, holding it tightly as his hand began to emit an orange glow.

The Viper looked from the boy to Dahlen and then back. "What is he doing?" he asked in a small panic. "What is happening right now?"

No one answered him.

After half a minute, Dohrrn opened his hand to reveal a polished red opal that gently glowed in the night.

Carry this with you. This will offer you strength and protection when you need it most. As long as you have it, their soothsayer will not be able to see you.

Dahlen nodded.

The small boy then wrapped his arms around her waist.

Her eyes filled with tears as she gently placed her hand on his head.

Dohrrn released her after a moment and stepped back.

"Don't tell Mohrr until he returns from Skahrr," she said as she mounted her horse. "I don't want him coming after me. And tell Vorce I'm sorry. He deserves more than me vanishing in the night, but I know he will understand."

Dohrrn nodded.

"Are you ready?" she asked The Viper.

"Ready?" he repeated. "I am unnerved, and unsettled by this bizarre episode, but yes, I am ready to get the hell out of here."

Dahlen shot one last glance at Dohrrn. "Don't reach out to me," she told him firmly.

Dohrrn only stood there.

"And take care of Marten." She turned her horse toward the gates and rode off into the night.

Though your faith in me has waned, my faith in you will never waiver.

———

Part 2

HALANA NEYA
(THE SCATTERED FOREST)

CHAPTER 11

THE WIND PICKED UP, PUSHING THE SMALL VESSEL MORE SWIFTLY across the sea. It had been over a week since a bird could be seen in the sky, but now, after almost three weeks out to sea, the crew and passengers silently rejoiced as the first gull landed on deck.

The Viper took a deep breath in and let in out noisily. "Aaaah!" he exclaimed joyously. "Ganavan is not far off now."

Dahlen readjusted her veil to keep the burning sun off of her face.

"You will never find honey sweeter anywhere else than in Ganavan," The Viper said with a smirk.

"Something tells me you aren't talking about actual honey," she replied.

"Women," he told her. "Ganavan has the sweetest selection of them."

Dahlen huffed. "Great. Of all the people I could have chosen to travel with, I chose a libertine."

The Viper chuckled. "I am a man of honor, Dahlen," he told her, "but I am a man with a weakness."

"Well, I don't care what you do while we are here as long as we get what needs to get done first," she told him.

"Tsk, tsk, tsk," he replied clicking his teeth. "Trust me, what we are looking for is buried deep in the brothels of this place."

Dahlen made a face. "I would hope the priest I am looking for has a stronger moral backbone than that."

The Viper laughed. "Priest, priestess, man or woman, we are all sinners," he said. "Your religious inclination cannot save you from temptation. But that is not what I was referring to."

Dahlen looked at him quizzically.

"Come now, Dahlen," he playfully goaded. "Do you really think that you, a priest, and myself are any match for the journey you have set before us?"

She looked out to the horizon, glimpsing a small strip of land in the distance.

"No," The Viper continued. "We need backup."

It was her turn to smirk. "And you believe we will find backup in the prostitutes of Ganavan?"

The Viper coughed to stop him from laughing. "Perhaps, not the prostitutes themselves, no, but amongst their clients we are sure to find more hands to share in the joy of our task."

"We are setting out to find a secret organization and eliminate them," Dahlen said. "Do you find joy in that?"

The Viper smirked and shrugged. "Joy is something different to everyone."

"We need to find you a hobby."

"Death *is* my hobby."

"Then we need to find you a new one," she said leaning on the railing of the ship.

The Viper imitated her. "Tell me more about this priest you are looking for."

She shrugged. "I don't know who he is yet," she replied.

The Viper nodded. "Yes, you mentioned that, but you also mentioned you know you have to find him. How do you know?"

She took a deep breath and let it out slowly. "It's difficult to explain. But it's almost like an urge or a feeling. It's something I know

I have to do."

"And you believe the gods have given you this *urge*?" he asked without skepticism.

She nodded slightly. "Yes, like the night I freed you," she explained. "I felt a small push to do it, a random thought I knew was not my own."

"Ah, the gods have been good to me!" The Viper exclaimed with a small laugh. "So, how will you know the priest is the one you are looking for when you find him?"

She shook her head. "I just will," she told him. "I think," she said to herself. She stroked the red opal Dohrrn had given her. Since then, she had wrapped it with leather string and strung it around her neck, a replacement for the necklace of her family seal. It was always warm and often glowed. Holding it comforted her as it did just then as she thought of where her journey might take her.

"So, you are a prophet?"

She shot The Viper a glance. She had explained this to him more than once during their several months of traveling together. "Yes, the gods speak to me."

"And that small boy who can throw fire? Who is he?"

Dahlen shot The Viper a look. This was not the first time he had asked her and it was not the first time she had avoided the question. "He is just an orphan from Meht. I took him with me when I left the coven. He had been a trainee that I had become attached to on my last visit. After noticing he was not fitting in, I asked for his release with mine."

"Right," The Viper replied a little skeptically. "And how exactly did he learn to throw fire?"

"Vorce's men taught him a few tricks. Most of Vorce's men are from the Lost Tribes and, therefore, know their way around simple magic tricks.," she half lied. Vorce's men were from the Lost Tribes and were known for their magic, but she couldn't tell The Viper who Dohrrn really was. Not yet, at least.

He lifted a quizzical brow.

"I have explained this to you several times by now," she replied.

He put his hands up defensively. "I just want to get it all straight. From a normal person's point of view, it sounds a little crazy."

"You think I don't know that?" she asked. "How do you think I felt when this all started? Do you think I just believed it without question?"

The Viper shrugged. "Must have been difficult not to." He stood up straight and stretched. "Well, we have certainly come to the right place to have questions answered. For as religious as Ganavan is, it sure has a lot of brothels."

"You seem very fixated on these brothels," she said with an arched brow.

He flashed her a grin. "Sweetheart, don't you know the best places to find out anything are brothels?"

"Don't call me that."

He nodded. "That's fair."

"But, yes," she replied. "I do understand that men like to talk or brag to the women whose company they are buying. I have used brothels as a source of information before."

"Then, that is where I shall start," The Viper told her. "You can find your priest while I do some," he shrugged, "digging."

She huffed. "Fine," she replied. "Just remember what we are looking for."

"We are looking for any information on The Order of Zeln," he told her. "A secret order with men and women who wear yellow silken pajamas." He shook his head. "I'm telling you, if anyone on this Island knows, it will be the sordid women."

The boat docked late in the afternoon the same day. Dahlen quickly paid the captain and pushed her way onto the pier.

"Over there," she indicated with her head. "The Green Panther Pub. We meet back here in four hours."

The Viper whistled. "I can get a lot done in four hours."

"Good," she replied. "Then I won't be disappointed."

She turned and headed down the familiar streets of the port city Anat and breathed in the intoxicating smell of roasted almonds and spices. She was almost excited when Mahk, for it had to be him, had urged her to go here.

She turned down a lane of mud houses and made her way to the end of the street that opened into a stone path lined with palm trees. People happily bowed at her as she walked by, smiling as they offered a blessing. Betal aht lahm, or God is good, passed through the lips of one person to the other.

Ganavan, she almost forgot, was monotheistic. They believed in one god that ruled over everything. Perhaps looking for a priest preaching about the Eternal Four here was not the best idea. But she knew she was right. This was where she had been summoned.

She had not gotten more than two miles when she heard a Ganavanese man and woman talking heatedly.

"Ehl aht metar eh fen pondta la ekla ehl burm la."

He's crazy and needs to return from where he came from, the man said, irritated.

"Ehlma hetra whet aht dar eek betal."

Everyone knows there is only one god, the woman replied shaking her head.

Dahlen approached them and gave a small bow. "Alet eer," she said. *Forgive me.* "Fa aht dartalem gatan dehere?" *Whom are you noble people speaking about?*

The man and woman seemed pleased to see a foreigner speaking their language and smiled politely at her.

"Your accent is quite good," the man told her in Ganavanese.

The woman agreed. "Your inflection is almost perfect."

Dahlen smiled at the unnecessary niceties. "Thank you," she replied keeping her patience. "Whom were you speaking of just now?"

"Oh, yes," the man said nodding. "There is a priest from Skahrr."

"Ridiculous man, talks too much," the woman added.

"He speaks of this god Vremir who has returned to save us from ourselves and once the other three gods are released, they will all save us from another god Vron."

"Silly man. Why would there be a god out to harm his creations?"

"Could you please point me in his direction?" she asked them ignoring their lead into a conversation.

They looked at her skeptically but pointed down a different avenue where the cobble stones were not as smooth.

"He is in a small, red building," the man told her.

"He calls it the house of flames," the woman added with a smirk. "And you will know it is him because his accent is so terrible."

Dahlen bowed and thanked them gratefully. "Betal aht lahm," she said as she set off in the direction they indicated.

"Betal aht lahm," they both replied as they continued the way they were going.

Dahlen picked up her pace, confused as to how she found the priest she was looking for so easily. She almost doubted her good fortune as she came upon the small red building. She paused for a moment as she approached, noticing a crowd had gathered out front. Several men and woman were shuffling, encircling someone.

Dahlen started to get a bad feeling as shouting rose up among the people gathered and that feeling increased as the crowd began to cheer. She ran, forcing and pushing herself through the people. When she finally got to the opening in the crowd she stopped.

"You have got to be kidding me," she said with a sigh.

There in the middle of the ring were three men. One was restraining another man, presumably the priest clad in long red and white robes, while a third hit and threw insults at him. To make matters worse, Dahlen could not have been any more surprised as to whom the priest was.

She sighed, stepping into the makeshift ring as the third man raised his fist again to strike the priest and held her hands up. "Evalat!" *Enough*, she screamed causing the assailants to look at her.

The priest blinked through the blood trickling from a cut on his forehead.

"What crime has this man committed?" she asked the crowd in Ganavanese. "Do you punish him based merely on his different religious views? I thought the people of Ganavan more civilized than that."

The man who had been hitting the priest straightened his back. "We do not punish him because of his teachings," he replied. "We punish him because he deflowered my sister."

Dahlen pressed a hand to her mouth and nodded. "This *is* your doing, Mahk," she thought, suppressing a groan.

"She was set to be married tomorrow, but now, her fiancé will not have her because of this man."

Dahlen cleared her throat and wiped her mouth with her hand. "Was it consensual?"

The man looked confused.

"Did this *priest* force himself upon your sister or was it a mutual," she paused to think of the right word, "encounter."

The man shifted uncomfortably where he stood. "She says she is in love with him."

"So, mutual," she said. "There is no law in Ganavan against mutual encounters, but, though I am foreign myself, I understand there is one against willfully harming anyone."

The man gave her a challenging look.

"I am sure the barrister I just met earlier today would love to hear about this, especially after he told me of how safe his country was." She met his stare. "Strict punishment, I believe, is what he said made his country so safe. I saw him not half an hour ago; I am sure he is still where I left him." She turned slightly to indicate she could easily return from where she came to report the incident.

The man sucked his teeth and made a gesture to his friend with his head causing him to drop the priest on the ground.

"Ik aht obtah," the man told the crowd. *It is over.* "Ehlma, pondta ilhat." *Everyone, return home.*

A disappointed murmur rang out through the crowd as they slowly dispersed, almost everyone shooting her an annoyed look.

"Either I was hit in the head harder than I thought," the priest started as he slowly pushed himself off of the ground and brushing off his robes, "or you are actually here and you actually saved me."

Dahlen turned and gave him a disapproving look. "Tristan," she said with disdain. "I see you haven't changed."

"Dahlen," he smiled as he wiped the blood from his face. "It's good to see you. I knew I would meet you again eventually. And to my good fortune, I am glad it was today."

"What are you doing here?" she asked him.

"I am spreading the word of Vremir," he told her opening his arms out wide. "I have even opened my own place of worship." He shrugged. "Sort of."

"In Ganavan? Why?" She shook her head and put her hands up. "It doesn't matter. I don't actually care."

He huffed. "I see *you* haven't changed."

"Me?" she asked. "I am not going around deflowering people's sisters and getting into fights."

He gave a small laugh. "Trust me, that girl was deflowered well before I came around."

Dahlen twitched, trying to suppress her anger. She took a calming breath before forcing a smile and looking at him. "Look," she started, "I am here because I was guided by Mahk, the god of wind, and, apparently, ill-timed humor, to find," she put her hand out and gestured to him, "you," she finished, releasing a sigh.

Tristan blinked at her. "You came here to find me?" he asked pointing to himself. "You believe that the god of wind sent you here to find me?"

Dahlen squinched up her face, smiling forcefully and nodded. "Yeah, I do," she replied almost painfully.

Tristan smiled broadly. "I thought you didn't believe in the gods."

"Circumstances and feelings can change," she replied blandly.

Tristan nodded. "Why me, do you think?"

Dahlen shrugged. "You specifically?" She shook her head. "Mahk has been known to play a joke or two on people."

He frowned.

"But, I might have prayed for more help and guidance on a self-given mission. So," she put her arms out, palms up, "here I am."

Tristan opened his mouth for a moment to speak, but closed it again. He then smiled and wagged his finger at her. "You came here to seek me out in order to ask me for help on your mission?"

"Ugh, here we go," she whispered to herself. "Yes," she said slowly. "It appears I have."

Tristan laughed joyously. "This is the best news I have heard in a long time."

She pursed her lips a little annoyed. "This mission will be dangerous," she told him. "It will involve a lot of unsavory actions and situations."

He grinned at her. "Are you trying to convince me or dissuade me?"

"You might have to kill some people. And sleep outside in the wilderness. There won't be a lot of inns where we're going."

"I'm in," he said without hesitation.

"I haven't even told you what the mission is."

"You came from the docks, right?" he said, pointing. He started in that direction without waiting for an answer.

"You are seriously considering going then?" she asked catching up with him.

He nodded. "If it is a mission for the gods, then, yes. And if it is a mission where you have to seek out my help, then absolutely."

"'Have to' is a relative term," she muttered.

"Nevertheless, I am at your service."

"And if this mission is a self-serving mission?"

"If you truly believe Mahk brought you to me, and he did, then it is not such a self-serving mission after all," he told her matter-of-factly.

"He obviously wishes me to help, so, I am."

She pushed a curl back inside her veil. "This ought to be interesting," she mumbled to herself. "It's only been about eighteen months, Tristan, since we last met," she told him. "What has made you change so much?"

He smiled pensively. "There was a man I met while we were among Vorce's people," he started. "Hamon is his name."

She nodded. "Yes, I know him."

"He taught me about Vremir, the true Vremir, while I was there," he continued. "It was different from the version you told me, but it resonated with me, stayed with me. After you and I parted ways, I had a lot of time to think about what I had done with my life and where I wanted to go. First, I went home to the Hills. I resumed my old life for a time, but something was missing. And then I remembered what that one monk had said to us while on his pilgrimage in Bornnen. Do you remember?"

She shook her head. "No."

"When we told him I was taking my vow of silence, he told us that his eyes had never seen nor his ears had never heard before than when he was taking his vows."

She gave a nod. "Now I remember, yes."

"So, I did it. I left home, I went out to the woods, traveled down to the sea, climbed up the mountains, and I just looked, and listened, and felt."

Dahlen turned and looked at him with a subtle awe.

"I have never felt more at peace with myself than I did during that time."

"And you made it the whole year?" she asked not holding back her skepticism.

"Well," he said, bobbing his head from side to side, "mostly. I did have a few slip ups. But for the most part, yes, I was silent for an entire year or two and a half months."

"Well, I am rather impressed," she replied. "You took a single experience and turned it into qualifications for you becoming a priest." She shot him a glance.

He nodded. "Okay, so I am a little self-proclaimed, but this has been the best experience of my life." He paused for a moment. "Well, other than my stepmother's conviction."

"Conviction?"

He gave a sad smile. "Turns out she murdered my father because he was trying to get me legitimatized," he explained. "They found incriminating letters and the poison she used among her things."

"I am sorry she did that," Dahlen said.

He shrugged, and gave a small laugh through his nose. "Turns out killing him didn't matter. The paperwork still went through."

She lifted her brows. "So, you are no longer a bastard?"

He smiled. "Legally speaking, no."

She smiled back. "So, what does that mean for your father's silk trade? Does it fall to you now?"

He nodded. "Yes, I inherited it, all of it, but to be fair to my brothers and sister I had the assets split four ways."

She regarded him for a moment. "That was very noble of you," she told him. "Were they not always cruel to you?"

He gave another shrug. "My brothers were only cruel because their mother told them to be. My sister Esther was always nice to me at least."

"Truly, Tristan, I am impressed," Dahlen said. "You have done a lot of growing since we last met. So, now instead of being just a self-proclaimed priest, you are a rich and generous self-proclaimed priest."

He gave her another sad smile. "I have you to thank, you know," he told her.

"Me?"

He nodded. "There are not a lot of things I regret doing in my life," he started, "but I do regret what I did to you. Most of my mistakes or bad decisions have shaped me, but that time I— It often keeps me awake at night."

Dahlen didn't reply. The topic of his betrayal was still a sore subject with her.

"I often pray for your forgiveness," he said softly.

She shot him a glance. "Perhaps this is why Mahk chose you," she replied. "By helping me, you might just earn it." She thought for a moment. "By the way, are you just going to leave your temple?" she asked motioning with her thumb behind her.

"What?" Tristan asked. "Oh, right, yeah, that building wasn't exactly mine," he explained. "I was trying to get the people of Ganavan to want to help me purchase it as a temple for Vremir."

Dahlen pressed a hand to her forehead. "I take back some of what I said about you changing."

Tristan put his arms behind his head as he walked. "It's going to be like old times, Dahlen," he said a little triumphantly.

"You're still an idiot."

CHAPTER 12

THE VIPER WAS WAITING FOR THEM AT THE GREEN PANTHER WHEN they walked back through the market. He gave a look of surprise at Tristan's appearance.

"Did you have to force him to come along?" The Viper asked pointing to the cut on his brow.

Dahlen tilted her head to one side. "I had to save him from a little scrape he got himself into."

"You saved him?" The Viper asked. "Isn't he supposed to help save us or something?"

Dahlen ignored his question. "Tristan, this is The Viper. The Viper, Tristan."

The Viper gave Tristan a two-fingered salute who nodded his head in acknowledgment.

"So, did you find anything out, or were you just taste testing the honey?" Dahlen asked The Viper, smirking at her own joke.

He chuckled. "Cute," he replied. "You would be proud to know that not only have I received some good tips, but I might have found us another recruit."

"We are not taking a prostitute with us," she told him.

The Viper tilted his head and shrugged. "However regrettable that might be, I was not talking about a prostitute." He smiled. "That being said, the person we are looking for is in one of the brothels."

She blinked at him. "And this person couldn't or wouldn't come out to meet with us?"

He shrugged. "She, uh," he smiled, "she said she wanted you to come in and convince her."

Tristan coughed to suppress a laugh.

Dahlen arched an eyebrow. "She?" she repeated. "And she is not a prostitute?"

The Viper nodded.

Dahlen held her hand out. "Lead the way."

The Viper led them through the market and up a hill where a large white building stood out against the setting sun. Dahlen remembered having seen the place on another occasion that brought her to Anat. It was hard to forget. Had The Viper not told her it was a brothel beforehand, she would have thought it was the house of some nobleperson with its lush landscaping and bulbous towers with golden roofs.

As they entered what could have been a small palace, they were greeted by half naked women who caressed and complimented them. Dahlen politely rebuffed one woman's advances.

"Back so soon, I see," playfully said one of the women who had her hands all over The Viper. "And I see you have brought friends."

The Viper chuckled as he placed his hands on the woman's waist. "I enjoyed my time so much I just—"

Dahlen cleared her throat.

The Viper paused and smiled. "Though I enjoyed our time immensely," he started over, "we are actually here on a small business matter."

The woman pouted. "How boring," she replied. She gave a small shrug. "Oh, well. Let me know if you change your mind." She winked and sashayed away.

Dahlen backhanded The Viper on the chest who gave a small

jump. "Shall we continue?"

"Yes, right," he replied, tearing his eyes away from the woman still strutting along.

"I think I will stay here for a few minutes," Tristan told them as they turned to move down the hall.

Dahlen grabbed him by the neck of his garb and pulled him along, ripping him from the woman who had been rubbing her hands all over him. "She's not actually interested in you," she told him. "She just wants your money."

"I am well aware of what she wants," he replied, reluctantly following them.

The Viper led them through a long hallway where the smell of steam drifted, making the air humid and a little thick. Laughter and splashing could be heard the closer they came to the end of the corridor. They paused at a doorway and moved aside the beaded curtain before entering.

The room was filled with naked women laughing and splashing around in a large bath. Sitting in the bath against the wall, with her arms resting on the shoulders of two prostitutes was someone Dahlen had not seen in years.

The woman leaned forward and smiled as they entered. "The Viper wasn't kidding," she said with a grin. "The Tigress, as I live and breathe. If that is what you still go by. I heard the coven released you."

Tristan, who had been studying the room of naked bodies glanced over at Dahlen. "Released you?" he repeated, confused.

Dahlen nodded. "The Defiant," she said addressing the other woman, "it is good to see you again."

The Defiant winked at her. "So, how is life on the outside?" she asked her, playfully kissing the shoulder of one the girls beside her. "Does it bore you?"

"Not necessarily."

"It must, or you wouldn't be here," The Defiant replied. She whispered into the ears of the girls on her arm and they giggled as they stood, water rolling off of their skin as they exited the bath.

Tristan watched as they both adorned loose robes that clung to their still wet bodies and left the room.

"It has its moments," Dahlen replied.

The Defiant shot a glance at The Viper as if to confirm.

He shrugged. "I was hired to kill her."

"Wait! What?" Tristan said snapping to attention.

"Really?" she replied lifting a quizzical brow. "Interesting." She clapped her hands. "Pardon us, ladies," she said to the other naked women in the room, "I was wondering if you could give us the room for a few minutes."

"You are not going so soon?" one of the girls with a slight accent asked. "You promised some time with me."

The Defiant smiled and nodded at her. "I won't leave without paying you a visit, Zo, I promise."

The girl smiled. "Good," she replied happily. "You will know where to find me." She gave a small wave before following the other women out of the room, her still wet feet leaving prints on the ground.

"Nice," The Viper said watching the women leave. "Were they all for you?"

The Defiant's smile broadened. "Well, when you take care of your lover, word gets around."

"Lover?" Tristan asked confused. "As an assassin, aren't you not supposed to engage in sexual activities?"

The Defiant lifted a brow and sucked her teeth as she looked at Tristan. "That vow doesn't apply to me," she told him.

He looked confused. "How so?"

The Defiant stood, revealing a muscular, yet, slightly feminine body riddled with tattoos. She brushed back her dark hair with her hand. The sides of her head were shaved and she tied what was left in a bun. She walked shamelessly out of the bath, letting the water drip off of her. "Because those vows pertain to men and women sharing a bed. It is the act of procreation that is prohibited." She shot Dahlen another wink. "And, the last I checked, two women were incapable of procreating."

Tristan's cheeks flushed red and he let out a small breath.

The Defiant smirked at him. "Making my sexual dalliances," she paused a moment and gave a small shrug, "sanctified."

Tristan put a hand over his mouth and swallowed hard.

The Defiant gave a small laugh at his reaction. "So, what does The Tigress have in mind?" she asked turning her attention back to Dahlen. "The Viper mentioned you might be interested in my help. I want to know what an ex-assassin could possibly need help with."

The Viper nodded his head in Dahlen's direction. "She gave herself a new name," he told The Defiant. "She goes by Dahlen now."

Tristan turned his head slowly and looked at her. "You chose to go by the name I created for you?" he asked her.

She looked at Tristan briefly and held a hand up as if to say 'not now.' "The Viper is right. He *was* hired to kill me," she said turning to address The Defiant. "Not because I left the coven, but because of who my family was before the coven."

The Defiant narrowed her eyes and rubbed her mouth pensively.

"I am the seven times great-granddaughter of Strahm Markai, the first prophet," Dahlen continued.

The Defiant grinned. "No shit."

"And, now, I am the next prophet of our realm."

The Defiant arched a brow at The Viper who shrugged.

"I believe her," he said. "I have seen a few strange things happen since I've started tagging along. Things I am not really sure how to explain."

The Defiant gave a nod. "Neat," she replied as she took a flask out from her belongings and took a swig. "And this little mission you want me to follow you on, it involves The Order of Zeln?"

Dahlen looked from The Viper and back to The Defiant. "You have heard of them?"

She shrugged as she took another swig from her flask. "I have been active a little longer than you," she explained. "I am on my seventh year and I have learned that there isn't a secret a man won't sell at the right price, or if it's whispered into the ear of a pretty woman."

The Viper pointed to himself. "That is basically what I said."

The Defiant wrapped her chest in cloth before slipping on a robe and tightening it around her waist. When she was done, she looked more like a beautiful man than a woman. "They are an elite group," she continued. "I have seen them fight. Their men are cruel and hold nothing back. If I am being completely honest, I think their skill set can only be matched by the best the coven has to offer."

"You are one of those," Dahlen said. "Your skills as an archer and with the short sword were always spoken of at Dead Man's Rest."

The Defiant gave a small bow.

"Other than that, do you know where they reside? What their plans are?" Dahlen pressed.

The Defiant shook her head. "I have heard they are moving a lot of men to Meht for something. I am not sure what though," she replied. "As far as their home base," she shrugged, "I couldn't tell you. To be honest, I think they might be nomadic in nature."

Dahlen thought for a moment. "So, you don't think they have a set base, just set times when they meet?"

The Defiant nodded. "That is the impression I have from received information."

Dahlen thought for a moment. "Received information," she repeated. "Were you seeking this information or was it given freely?"

"I have had some run-ins with them," she explained.

Dahlen raised a brow, waiting for her to explain.

The Defiant shrugged. "They can get a little rough with the women they hire," she continued. "I encountered a couple a few months ago in a brothel in Meht. I heard screaming coming from a room so I rushed in to see two men beating one of the women, raping her. So, I interceded."

"You killed them," Dahlen clarified.

The Defiant smiled. "More or less." She took another swig from her flask. "It got me curious, so I asked the woman about them. She told me they had been coming in and out of the area for a month or so and every time they came, those two would select a woman and take turns beating and raping her." She frowned. "That rubbed me the wrong way, so I decided to talk to the other prostitutes about them. I found out they have been planning something in Meht, some expedition."

Dahlen scowled. *They must have found something,* she thought.

"Anyway," The Defiant went on, "I thought of pursuing them as my curiosity was getting the better of me, but I thought better of it at the time. Going alone to attack a group of highly trained ruffians sounded a little risky, even for my standards." She jutted her chin in Dahlen's direction. "But I have a feeling that is what you are going to ask me to do."

"I don't have a lot to offer as payment," Dahlen told her, "but I would be honored and grateful if you would be willing to join us."

The Defiant thought for a moment and shook her head. "I don't need payment," she replied. "Money is trivial to me, but I do need a favor."

Dahlen exchanged a small glance with The Viper who nodded.

"Name it," she said turning back to The Defiant. "If it guarantees your loyalty and skills, then we will do it."

"Perfect," she replied. "But first," she moved her brows up and down and smiled, "meet me outside in thirty minutes," she told them. "I have a promise to keep."

CHAPTER 13

"Is that them?" Dahlen asked, watching a group of men come out of the Green Panther later that evening. She adjusted her position, leaning against the corner of the building so her back was to them.

The Defiant bobbed her head lightly as she put her arm up on the wall and moved closer to Dahlen. "They are supposed to make another run to the Lost Tribes tonight," she said leaning in as if to whisper into her ear.

The men passed them on their way to the docks. Dahlen put her hands on The Defiant's waist, putting on the illusion they were lovers stealing an intimate moment in the dark. When the men were a safe distance away, they followed, staying far enough away so as not to be suspicious but close enough not to lose them.

There were five of them, and very likely more on their vessel.

"They're sex traders," The Defiant had told her earlier that day when she was explaining what she needed done. "They have been kidnapping young children and women and selling them as sex slaves to the highest bidder. I have been watching them for a few months now. I know this is their main port, but I haven't figured out who their boss is. I know his name, but not what he looks like, only a description of a scar he has running from his ear to the base of his neck. Turns out, he sometimes likes to make these runs with his men. And tonight is one of those nights."

Dahlen and The Defiant continued to follow the men until they reached the docks. They hid behind large barrels as they watched the men board a lavish ship with four guards patrolling the deck.

That made at least nine men total.

"I hope your skills have not gotten rusty," The Defiant told her.

Dahlen huffed. "I survived The Viper's attack," she responded.

The Defiant gave a small laugh. "Good." She whistled and The Viper peered over the roof of the building he was hiding on.

He whistled back and descended. He crouched as he ran to them, using the darkness as cover. He handed them both their weapons when he reached them. "I am glad I can be your mule," he told them satirically.

"Four men on deck, five went inside," The Defiant told him, ignoring his comment.

He nodded. "Plan of action?"

"The Defiant is the best archer," Dahlen said. "I say you and I take the two on the starboard side and she take out the two standing guard on the portside. The Viper, you and I can climb up from the water, take out our men, and then The Defiant can take out hers."

The Defiant moved her tongue along her gums and nodded. "I like it."

"Wait, what can I do?" Tristan, who had followed The Viper down from the roof, asked.

The three of them turned to look at him.

"I am capable of handling a bow and arrow," he told them matter-of-factly.

"Have you used a bow and arrow to kill a man before?" The Defiant asked him.

Tristan thought for a moment. "Well, no."

"Have you used it to hunt or kill anything?" The Viper asked.

Tristan opened his mouth to speak, but shut it. "No," he replied after a moment or two. "But I was always good at hitting the target."

"How far away was this target?" The Defiant asked.

"Was it a stationary target or a moving target?" The Viper added.

Tristan looked put off by their interrogation. "What does all that matter?"

"Everything," the other three said in unison.

He narrowed his eyes lightly. "But I have killed before. While in battle!" He put extra emphasis on the word 'while.' "Tell them, Dahlen. Tell them how I saved your li—"

"Listen, Tristan," Dahlen started, interrupting him, "this might not be a task for you. This takes a little more finesse than just running in there and swinging a sword."

"It takes experience," The Defiant said.

"Stealth," The Viper added.

"Precision," The Defiant continued.

"I got it," Tristan said holding up a hand to stop them, dejected. "I will just stay here and watch our stuff."

"There is one other thing you could do," The Defiant said as she strapped her quiver of arrows to her back.

"Yeah?" Tristan replied brightening up.

"You could pray." The Defiant grinned and slipped out from behind the barrels and into the dark.

"We will be back," Dahlen told him, checking that her knives were secure.

The Viper gestured with his head to get going and they both moved swiftly to the other side of the docks. They ran, staying in the shadows as they continued up a pier parallel to the one the ship was docked at. They silently slipped into the water, ignoring the chilliness of it as they swam up to the ship.

They climbed up the anchor chain and scaled the edge of the ship, pausing when they heard voices.

"We shippin' out soon?" came a gruff voice.

"Cap'n says we 'eaded for the west islands. Those women be in 'igh demand in Ganavan," came another voice.

"In my opinion, I think we should go to Meht," said the first voice. "There be pretty women there as well."

"Well, luckily your opinion don't matter," answered the second voice. "Ain't no one here want a girl from Meht."

Dahlen and The Viper exchanged a glance realizing the men were right above them. They shifted slightly, one moving a little more left while the other went a little more to the right.

"You don't know that," the gruff voice said, sounding a little annoyed. "Mehtian girls be just as exotic as those ones from the Lost Tribes. And that's what they want. Exotic women."

Dahlen held up three fingers, counting down until they took the men out. When Dahlen got to zero, the two of them climbed over the railing and, grabbing the men from behind, slit their throats. When they were finished, small thuds could be heard as the two men on the portside fell dead, each of them with an arrow sticking out of their necks.

The Defiant then calmly walked up the plank and stepped on the deck. She tapped her ear to tell them to listen as the sound of foot-steps could be heard coming up from below. The three of them hid behind large boxes, Dahlen with The Viper, and The Defiant still on the other side.

The Defiant took out a little mirror and slowly moved it to the corner of the box, using it to view around the corner. She held up two fingers.

Dahlen nodded and took out one of her throwing knives. She gestured to The Defiant who nodded and quietly readied her bow. Again, Dahlen counted down from three with her fingers. When she was ready, she and The Defiant stood and took aim only long enough for the men to register movement, but not long enough for them to react. They were both dead before they could utter a word.

The Defiant gave Dahlen a nod of approval.

The Viper got up and ran swiftly to the door of the hull, pressing his back against the wall. He held up two more fingers as he heard more men climbing the stairs. He waited for the men to reach the top before he wrapped his arm around the throat of one man to silence him while simultaneously stabbing the second through his ribcage piercing his lungs. When he lay dead on the floor, he broke the neck of the struggling man still in his grip.

The Defiant gave him a silent clap and he bowed.

They dragged the bodies out of the way, hiding them from plain sight as they contemplated how many men were left.

Dahlen held up one finger and furrowed her brows as if to say, "One more?"

The Defiant totaled up the body count. In response she held up one finger and shrugged. "One or more?"

The three of them moved to go down the stairs when a shouting could be heard from the pier.

"Behold the power of Vremir, god of fire, wisdom, and free will!"

It was Tristan and he was yielding a bow with a flaming arrow.

"What the hell is he doing?" The Defiant whispered harshly.

"He will come again to save us all from Vron, the god of water, jealousy, and destruction!"

Tristan let the flaming arrow fly.

The three of them watched in horror as it whizzed through the air and landed with a 'thunk' into a pile of wooden boxes covered by a canvas sheet. They watched, helpless, as the canvas quickly caught fire.

"That man is an idiot!" The Defiant proclaimed.

"You are sure this is the man Mahk led you to?" The Viper asked.

"Led me to kill him," Dahlen said gritting her teeth.

"Fire!" Tristan yelled from the docks. "Fire! Fire on deck!"

The Viper, The Defiant, and Dahlen hid behind a stack of barrels next to the stairs to the hull, watching as not one, but seven men emerged from the downstairs to the deck. They rushed, grabbing buckets to put out the growing flames.

Dahlen sighed. "He's an idiot, but he's a useful idiot," she said. "Those men are not armed and they certainly are not worried about intruders."

"We need to take them now," The Defiant replied as she pulled out her two short swords.

"Works for me," The Viper said pulling out his own sword.

Dahlen nodded as she charged, coming up from behind the first man and ramming one of her knives into the base of neck.

The boat erupted into chaos as the quickly moving flames were forgotten, and the crew tried to defend themselves from an attack they didn't know was coming; most of them were dead before they could even reach for a weapon.

Screams and curses filled the night air as the flames crackled about them. But it did not last long.

When The Defiant was pulling her sword from the last of the men, the three of them exchanged glances.

The Viper shrugged. "That worked out pretty well," he said.

"Yes, but is the boss among these men?" Dahlen asked as she looked over the bodies littering the deck.

"He is not," came a voice from behind them.

They whirled around to see a man holding a crossbow aimed toward them. Dahlen moved to grab one of her knives, but it only made him shift his aim to her.

"You can't take down all three of us with that," Dahlen told him, challenging him.

He gave a small nod. "No, I cannot," he replied with a small smile. "But I can at least kill one of you before you reach me. So? Which one of you is willing to sacrifice yourself for the safety of the others?"

Before either of them could answer, an arrow fell from the sky and landed in the man's thigh. At first, he stared at it, the realization of what had happened not yet sinking in. Finally, after a few moments, his eyes grew wide and he let out a shrill scream as he fell to his knees, screaming in pain.

The Defiant went over to him, a slight grin on her face. The man tried to lift the crossbow in defense, but she kicked it out of his hands.

"Please, don't kill me," he begged.

The Defiant grabbed the man by the hair and pulled his head to the side seeing a long, curved scar trailing from the back of his ear to the base of his neck. "Hello, Amrin Tenga," she said triumphantly as she raised her arm.

"No, whatever you are being paid, I will tri—"

The Defiant did not give him time to finish before she cut him down. She turned and rolled her eyes. "I hate when they try to bargain with you. It's so pathetic."

"Right?" The Viper agreed. "Die with some dignity."

Dahlen turned to see the flames starting to make their way toward them. "We should probably leave," she told them.

The others nodded.

"Huh," The Defiant said looking around at the other ships around them. "I'm not sure your priest thought this plan through. The entire dock is likely to catch fire."

"I have an idea," The Viper told them.

They exited the boat, but not before they disconnected the anchor from the ship and released its sails. The three of them watched as the flaming ship glided through the water, making it several yards before it collapsed into itself and sank to the bottom of the Dormant Sea.

"That was amazing," came a voice from behind them,

The Defiant turned and landed her fist square in the middle of Tristan's face who fell flat on his back.

"One," she started, holding up a finger, "never sneak up on me. Two," she held up another finger, "your little act could have gotten us killed."

"Uuugh," Tristan groaned, holding his hand up to his bleeding nose. "I was trying to save you. You went in there thinking there were only nine men when there were sixteen. I saved you."

"How did you even know there were more men on board?" The Defiant asked skeptically.

Tristan shrugged from the ground. "I looked at the log book. Ganavan is very particular about keeping tabs on people coming and going. So, I thought I would check."

The Viper held out his hand for Tristan who took it a little begrudgingly. "He is kind of right," The Viper said with a shrug. "His plan did end up helping us."

"Fine," The Defiant told him. "But don't sneak up on me. You're lucky I didn't put a sword through you."

"That's enough," Dahlen said sternly. "We should leave before a crowd is drawn."

The other three nodded as they turned and vanished into the night.

CHAPTER 14

"So, you go by Dahlen permanently now?" Tristan asked once they were safely aboard another ship the next day.

Dahlen sighed as she watched Ganavan's shoreline vanish in the distance. "I do," she told him. "After I was released from my vows, I thought it ridiculous to continue to go by The Tigress and AnnJella just didn't sit right with who I was."

Tristan smirked. "But the name I chose for you did?"

"Don't get overly excited about it," she replied.

He shrugged. "How is an assassin released from their vows in the first place?" he asked after a moment.

"Your cousin paid for my release," she said annoyed after mentioning Mohrr when she had successfully avoided doing so for the past few months.

"My cousin?" Tristan asked, almost horrified. "My cousin the prince?"

Dahlen gave a small nod.

"Mohrr paid the coven to release you from your vows?"

"Yes," she replied trying to remain calm.

"What? Did he just waltz right into Dead Man's Rest and drop a bag of money on the ground and demand you to come with him?" he asked bitterly.

"Why is there such animosity between the two of you?" she replied curiously. "Why do you always seem to be at odds with each other?"

Tristan shrugged. "We used to be close, I guess, when we were younger," he replied. "Being close in age, we were playmates growing up."

"What changed?" Dahlen asked him.

He shook his head. "That might be a story for another time," he told her.

She let out a sigh. "Of course, it is."

There was a brief silence between them.

"So, what did his buying your freedom entail?" Tristan asked after a minute or two.

Dahlen shot him a glance. "He gave the coven a bunch of money and livestock for my release and for the guarantee that they will side with Skahrr in the next war. Though with the way King Breht is behaving, I doubt that will happen."

Tristan shook his head. "I meant for you," he told her.

She glared at him. "It entailed nothing for me," she replied harshly. She shifted uncomfortably against the railing of the ship. "I was free to do as I pleased," she said after recollecting herself.

"And he did not expect anything in return?"

Dahlen stared out into the horizon. "No," she replied with a sigh. "He truly expected nothing more in return. I could not tell you what he had hoped, but he did not put any pressure on me to do anything I did not want to do." Regret panged her as she thought of Mohrr and the child she was forced to give up. She wondered, as she often did when she could think of nothing else, how her daughter was. How was Princess Rain as a mother? It hurt her to think of it, more than anything she could remember, but it was something she had yet to hide herself from.

What could she have truly hoped for with either of them? Would she really have been content with a stagnant life? These were questions she asked to save herself from regret.

She repeatedly told herself no, an act of self-preservation, perhaps. But it rarely worked.

"Well, I am glad he did not force himself on you," Tristan told her.

Dahlen creased her brows. "You think so little of your cousin, then?"

Tristan shook his head after a moment. "No, I do not believe him capable of that kind of cruelty," he replied.

"Do you think he would have succeeded if he were?"

Tristan smiled and laughed through his nose. "Certainly not. You would have slit him from nose to navel."

Dahlen nodded.

"Do you love him?" he asked after another pause.

Dahlen did not shift her gaze from the horizon. "I am not with him, am I?" she replied softly.

Tristan shrugged. "He's an ass anyway."

Dahlen twitched. "If I am being completely honest," she began, her voice a little tense, "Mohrr gave me more than any other man or woman has and I owe him a debt of gratitude. If he is an ass, I was never witness to it."

Tristan opened his mouth to say something else, but decided it was better not to push the issue. Instead, he changed the subject. "So, now you are a prophet?" he asked.

Dahlen nodded. "Yes, I suppose I am. But not a self-proclaimed one," she replied shooting him a smirk.

Tristan shrugged. "Well, we all can't have your good fortune, can we?" he replied sardonically. "Tell me about it. What is it like to speak to the gods?"

Dahlen took a deep breath and let it out slowly. "Oddly enough, I believe they do most of the talking," she told him. "I hardly ever ask them of anything, except when I asked for more help."

"And you were led to me," Tristan added a little too triumphantly.

"Yes," she replied blandly. "Other than that, I believe they are the ones who reach out to me." She thought for a moment. "Well, perhaps that is how it is with Mahk, Behr, and Gher. I suppose I did speak a lot more with Vremir than the others."

Tristan looked at her in wonder. "And does he talk back?"

Dahlen thought of Dohrrn and another pang of regret and anger hit her. Sometimes, it was difficult to believe that the small child she had spent so many months with was actually Vremir, the god of fire. Even though she had witnessed his power firsthand, he was still just a boy to her.

She cleared her throat. "Yes," she finally replied. "He tends to have a lot to say."

"So, does that mean he has returned?" Tristan asked excitedly, turning to look at her.

She nodded. "Yes, he has returned."

"Has he appeared to you?" he asked. "What does he look like?"

Dahlen shifted, ready to be done with the conversation. "I do not believe he is in true form yet," she replied.

The Viper then joined them. He took in a deep breath of sea air and let it out in a noisy exclamation.

"Don't you just love the freedom the sea gives you?" he asked, wedging himself between the two, leaning against the ship's railing. "The smell of salty water has always been a welcome scent to me."

"It has always reminded me of The Rest," Dahlen replied. "Where is The Defiant?"

"Swindling the men on the ship out of their money," he replied with a grin.

"So soon into our voyage?" she asked. "She is going to get herself into trouble before we are even halfway to Meht."

The Viper shrugged. "It will be an interesting journey to say the least."

"So, we are headed for Meht then," Tristan said, breaking in. "Why again?"

"That is where a large number of the Order are headed, remember?"

she replied. "According to a prostitute or two who told The Defiant."

"And why do you think they are headed there?" Tristan asked.

"Beraxium," Dahlen replied.

"Good, good," Tristan said nodding his head. "What is that?"

"Beraxium is a precious metal coveted by the gods," Dahlen explained. "They draw strength from it. My bet is, if the Order is heading to Meht, there must be a supply of it there. And, if I am correct, there should be an old mine or hoard of it in one of their forests. My bet is the Scattered Forest, or Halana Neya. Its remoteness and location make it the most likely location. All of the other forests are inhabited, so a mine, even an ancient one, might have been noticed by now."

"Vremir told you this?" Tristan asked curiously.

She shook her head. "No, I read it in this very old book." She pulled out the book on the element she took from Mohrr's things before she left. "It's a dry read, but it's good if you are having trouble sleeping. Knocks you right out."

Tristan gave a nod. "So, we are going there to—what? To mine it?"

"To find the Order," The Viper said, piping in. "They are looking for the metal as well in the hopes of giving it to Vron so that he might regain his power and take over the realm again." He looked proud at having retained the information Dahlen had told him earlier in their journey together.

"Should we not take some to help the eternal four regain their strength?" Tristan asked.

"My plan is," Dahlen started, "to kill those of the Order there and take whatever processed beraxium they might have."

"But nothing else?"

"Do you know how to mine?" she responded lifting a brow. "If you do, I would be very impressed. It is a skill I lack."

"I suppose you are right," Tristan said. "But what if they have none?"

The Viper gave him a strong pat on the back. "Then we will come up with a new plan," he replied. "Not all plans come into fruition and they are never perfect. We just have to adapt to them."

"That is less than comforting," Tristan mumbled.

A strong, yet gentle, wind swept across the boat and filled the sails, pushing them onward.

"It seems Mahk agrees with us," Dahlen said as she watched the billowing sails push them along.

CHAPTER 15

"WELCOME TO YOUR NEW HOME," SAID THE MAN KNOWN AS THE Master.

The little girl stirred from his lap and looked in the direction he was pointing, just making out rows of houses past several rows of trees. She had been traveling for almost two months and was exhausted always being on the move.

"Is momma here, too?" she asked in a small voice.

"No, child," The Master told her. "Your mother is dead. She is no longer among the living."

The boy, Marten, had explained it to her before, but she still did not understand how she would never be able to see her mother again. It pained her to think it.

"I am proud of how brave you were on this journey," The Master told her. "I believe you will do well here among the Nameless. Perhaps, you will even become an assassin." He chuckled.

"Yes, she rarely cried the entire time," The Wind agreed as she rode up beside them. "And I don't remember her complaining. She will do well. More importantly, she will be safe here."

"What say you, The Gallant?" The Master asked with a sneer.

The Gallant shot The Master a glare. The girl often saw him looking *at The Master that way though she didn't understand why.*

"I believe I have no say in the matter," The Gallant replied a little bitterly.

In the distance a black hawk cawed after them. The sounds of its shrill voice faded away as they moved further toward her new life.

"Wow," Tristan whispered as they got off the boat in the port city of Hese in Meht. "I never expected Meht to be so—" he shook his head as he thought of what he wanted to say.

"Hot?" The Defiant suggested as she patted at the sweat forming on her neck with a handkerchief.

"Humid," The Viper added taking a swig from his canteen.

"Lavish," Tristan finally said as he stood in awe at the many green, lush trees and perfectly manicured buildings that lined the streets. "It seems so clean here."

Dahlen nodded. "Meht is never what outsiders expect it to be," she told him. "Most people expect to find a wasteland when in reality, it is anything but."

"We just had to come during the summer months, didn't we?" The Viper said tugging on his loose garbs to create a breeze.

"When else would we come?" Dahlen asked. "We could not risk giving the Order more time to compile beraxium. We had to act as quickly as possible."

The Defiant pulled out a hand fan and began fanning herself. "Understandable, but this is almost unbearable."

Dahlen shot the two of them a look. "Really? I would expect this from Tristan, but not from you two."

"Don't get me wrong," The Defiant started, "I will still do whatever it is you need me to do. I will probably just hate it."

"Agreed," The Viper added.

Dahlen sighed. "Why don't you two go find yourselves a brothel and start making inquiries?" she asked. "Would that not make you at least feel a little bit better?"

The two of them smirked.

"I suppose it couldn't hurt," The Viper replied.

"Definitely worth a shot," The Defiant chimed in.

"Good," Dahlen said. "I will secure us lodgings for the night at the Blue Inn. We can reconvene there later this evening. Until then, I am going to figure out the best way to reach the Scattered Forest."

She turned to move up the street when she noticed that Tristan hadn't moved.

"Are you not going with them?" she asked.

He shook his head. "No, I think I am going to go with you and explore the city a little bit more."

She shrugged. "Suit yourself," she told him as she made her way through the bustling streets of the port city.

"I am truly surprised by the beauty of this city," Tristan said after walking past the market. "All of the buildings are intricately adorned and ornamented. Even the road we are walking on seems to be a swirling mosaic of stones. Not even Ganavan could boast such beautiful pathways."

Dahlen gave a nod. "They pay their laborers next to nothing here," she explained. "When you are paying your workers very little, you are able to afford more expensive material."

"Has Meht always been this prosperous?" he asked as he looked around at the expensive houses and the women strolling the streets with silken robes and diamond crested jewelry.

"For the most part, yes," she told him.

"Then why all of the pirating?" he asked, confused.

"Because this is just how the rich live," she explained. "Most of Mehtians are poor and unable to provide for their families. So, they turn to what might seem like an easy way to bring in money."

Tristan nodded.

"The rich are very rich in this country, while the poor are very poor." She handed a small bag of dates she bought at the market to a desperately skinny child sitting under a tree. The young girl smiled gratefully and hurriedly ran through an alley, her ragged clothes barely clinging to her. "To be honest, Meht is not much different than the rest of the realm in that aspect," she added. "The rich of the realm are all about how they can become richer without a second thought about how to help their fellow man. There is a small difference though."

"Which is?"

"Meht is more about appearances. They want to appear rich and lavish. While other countries of the realm are about power."

"Why are they so focused on appearance?" Tristan asked.

"Because the rest of the realm has bastardized them," she explained. "Remember in the original story of the gods? Meht was said to be born of the women whom Vremir had raped and were banished from the mainland. And even in the true version, the people of Meht were those that had sided with Vremir and who Vron had their skin blackened and banished here. They are the unwanted and disregarded, so they are trying to make up for it by putting on a show of grandeur."

Tristan shook his head. "It might be a show but I am convinced," he told her. "We walked through the entire market and three blocks past and, besides that little girl you gave the dates to, I have not seen one beggar." He shrugged. "They seem to be better off than any of the other countries of the realm, including Ganavan."

Dahlen smirked. "That is because begging is illegal in Meht," she replied.

Tristan blinked at her. "What?"

She nodded. "Had there been an enforcer around, that little girl would have been either shooed away or dragged to the stock for public humiliation. Children, of course, get off lighter, but I have seen a man whipped for asking for a loaf of bread for his starving family."

"That seems a little harsh," Tristan muttered.

"There," Dahlen said, pointing to a small, whitewashed building with a wooden hanging sign that read 'Batan.' "That is the place we are looking for."

"What is it?"

"It's like an outpost," she replied. "We can buy supplies there and, more importantly, a map."

Tristan nodded.

"I just hope the shop owner speaks the shared language," Dahlen said just above a whisper as they moved to the door of the shop.

"I thought you spoke Mehtian?" Tristan whispered as they walked through the door.

"My Mehtian skills are well enough to help me get by, but I struggle with pronunciation. My inflection is not the best."

"Inflection?"

"Different inflections on words give them different meaning. It has gotten me in trouble in the past."

"Then, you ah fortunate I speak your language," came a deep accented voice from behind a shelf. "Theahfoh, you do not have to butcha mine." A tall, dark-skinned man emerged from around the shelf where he had been stocking supplies. He shot them a toothy grin. "Please, come in."

Dahlen gave a small bow. "I am very grateful for your language skills," she told him stepping forward.

"It is impohtant to be familiah with sev-ral languages in my line of wohk," he replied giving her a small bow back. "What can I help you with?"

"We are looking for some supplies for a small expedition," she replied. "We are looking to rent a few horses and buy a map of the surrounding jungles."

The man glanced from her to Tristan, a stoic look on his face. "What jungles?" he replied. "We have sev-ral on Meht. There ah even two on eitha side of Hese."

"We will be travelling from here to Stem," Dahlen replied.

The man nodded. "Then you would pass through the Fian jungle."

He moved to the back of the store and rifled through some papers before pulling one out. "Fian is an easy jungle to navigate," he told them. "The paths ah well used and mostly cleah, but in case you need it, heah is a map."

Dahlen took the proffered paper and thanked him. "Would you possibly have a map of the entire island?" she asked.

The man gave a slow nod. "Of couhse," he replied. "I can get that foh you." He moved to look for the other map when Tristan leaned in and whispered to her.

"Why don't you just ask for a map of the Scattered Forest?"

The man froze and Dahlen closed her eyes in annoyance.

"What business do you have in Halana Neya?" the man asked suspiciously.

Dahlen narrowed her eyes at Tristan for a moment before turning her attention to the shop attendant. "Religious," she replied not entirely lying. "We understand that the Scattered Forest, or Halana Neya, has significant meaning to the eternal gods."

"Ah theah not enough places on thee main land with reelijus meaning?" he asked skeptically.

"Yes, there are plenty, to be sure," Dahlen started, "but what you learn from one religious journey is never the same as what you learn from another."

The man regarded her for a moment without blinking before he moved to the back, returning with the map of Meht a tense minute later. "Halana Neya is not a sacu-red place," he warned them. "It is a place of ghosts and death. You would do well to avoid it."

CHAPTER 16

"WHAT WAS HIS DEAL?" TRISTAN MUTTERED AS THEY LEFT THE SHOP leading their rented horses.

"His deal," Dahlen started, "was trying to prevent two foreigners from getting lost in a very sacred, yet, very hostile area."

He narrowed his eyes at her. "I thought it was nothing more than a jungle?" he said.

"Morons with views like that are more than likely the ones that never return from the Scattered Forest."

He blinked at her. "Why wouldn't we return?"

"I am not saying that we won't," she replied.

"But you are saying there is a chance?"

Dahlen hesitated in her response. "The Scattered Forest has lot of legend behind it. A lot of silly stories to explain why so many people go into the forest but do not return from it."

Tristan gulped. "What kind of legends?" he asked.

Dahlen shrugged. "The usual. Angry ghosts or spirits of those that died horrible deaths, or were unsatisfied in life, tearing unsuspecting travelers limb from limb."

He stared at her wide-eyed. "And that's where we're going?"

She smirked. "We survived the man-like bears of Behr wood,

didn't we?"

"Yes, but those were just men in bear skins," he replied.

"And who is to say whether or not the ghosts or spirits are just men in 'skins' as well?" She arched her brow at him.

Tristan didn't reply.

"Listen," she started, "I do not believe for one second that there is something supernatural in that jungle. I would believe, however, that the legends are built upon the actions of actual men. Just like the tales of the man-like bears were of Vorce and his men."

He gave a small nod.

She squeezed his arm. "We will get through this just like we did with them."

He shot her a small smile. "Honestly, I feel safer traveling with you more than I do with anyone else. Especially with the other two as companions."

"We will be just fine," she reassured him. "Now, let's go set up our accommodation."

"Did we find more than pleasure at the brothels?" Dahlen asked as The Viper and The Defiant met up with them later that night.

The two of them exchanged glances.

"It appears that the Order of Zeln has beat us here by only a week or so," The Defiant replied.

The Viper nodded. "Several of the prostitutes have had clients wearing bright yellow garbs. Some of those men bore a tattoo of a black hawk on their chests."

"They had been around, scouting previously, but never in the large numbers they came in and left just a week ago," The Defiant added.

"Did any of the men tell them where they were headed?" Dahlen asked as she scanned the pub they were supping at for eavesdroppers.

The Defiant nodded. "At least one of them let it slip that they were headed to the Scattered Forest to mine for an ancient precious metal."

"Then I was right," Dahlen all but whispered to herself.

Tristan returned from the front with plates of food.

"There is another thing I was told," The Viper started. "Soldiers from Skahrr are here too. Until a few days ago, they had been frequenting the respected brothels of Meht."

Dahlen rubbed her mouth pensively with her knuckles and sighed. "Then King Breht knows as well," she surmised as she shook her head.

"King Breht?" Tristan replied. "What does he have to do with anything?"

Dahlen looked from The Viper, to The Defiant, and to Tristan. "King Breht is also looking to mine beraxium in order to give it to Vron. He thinks that by doing so he will gain enough power to take over the entire realm. What he doesn't realize is that that power will never belong to him. Vron will only take advantage of his efforts and use the beraxium to regain his strength and retake the realm and the will of man for himself."

Tristan blinked at her. "This is what you meant about the way my uncle was behaving?"

The Viper put his growler down. "Uncle?" he repeated. "You're King Breht's nephew?"

"His father's sister was King Breht's late wife," Dahlen quickly explained.

"The gods rest her sweet soul," Tristan said with a nod.

"Does his involvement in this affair change your fealty?" The Defiant asked with a raised brow.

Tristan raised his hands. "Absolutely not. There is very little love lost between us. Especially on his side. He would be ashamed to call me nephew in front of anyone."

The Viper and The Defiant stifled sniggers.

He thought for a moment. "Wait," he started, "does this mean my cousin Mohrr is in on it as well? Does he know about my uncle?"

Dahlen nodded. "He does know, but he does not agree. In fact, he is working against his father."

"If he is working against his father, then why isn't he here with us?" Tristan asked a little begrudgingly.

She shifted in her seat and sighed. "Because this is my mission," she replied defiantly. "He has his own to tend to."

The Defiant waved her hand as if to dismiss the argument. "So, this expedition to find beraxium," she began clearing her throat, "you expect us to— what— stop the Skahrrian soldiers and those of the Order from mining it?"

Dahlen looked at The Defiant. "We are going to try."

"Seems pretty risky," The Defiant replied with a shrug. "What's the plan?"

CHAPTER 17

The four of them woke before dawn the next morning and snuck out of the town of Hese and into the Fian jungle. The air in the jungle, though cooler without the sun, was still thick with moisture.

Tristan let out a sigh and pulled on the neck of his tunic to create his own personal breeze. "I have never been in a forest where the air was not fresher than the air beyond its borders." He dabbed at the sweat forming on his brow. "Meht is a strange place."

The Viper slapped a bug on his neck. "I have only had to come here a handful of times," he said, wiping his hand on his pants. "And I have never been impressed."

The Defiant shrugged. "I could do without the bugs swarming me every three feet, but other than that, the jungle seems quite peaceful."

Dahlen studied the map as her horse gently moved about the trail. "I have some charl root serum in my bag," she said, not looking up.

"Perfect," The Viper replied, moving his horse towards her.

Tristan made a face. "What is that?"

"Keeps bugs away," Dahlen asked as she handed the bottle to The Viper.

"Please leave some for all of us," The Defiant replied watching The Viper slather a thick layer of the earthy smelling mixture onto his face.

"If we make good time today," Dahlen said ignoring the little tiff going on behind her, "we should make it to Stem in about two days. We can then replenish our supplies and from there, the Scattered Forest might take us another three days to get to."

"We aren't likely to run into any pirates, are we?" Tristan asked, tentatively smelling the bottle of charl root serum.

"In Meht?" The Defiant replied. "No, not likely."

"The pirates are only known to raid the shorelines of the main land and large cargo ships on the Dormant Sea," The Viper continued.

"But they don't raid the people of their own country?" Tristan asked.

"Mehtian laws are a little harsher than they are on the main land," Dahlen explained. "If a pirate is caught on the main land, only the pirate will lose his life. If someone is found pirating on Meht, their family, up to four members, lose their lives as well."

Tristan looked bewildered. "Even if the other members of the family are innocent?"

The Viper nodded. "Even if one of those family members is nothing more than a child."

"How can they justify something like that?" Tristan asked.

"It's a way to get rid of a 'bad seed,'" The Defiant replied. "Kill them all before it can spread further."

"A wicked father does not necessarily mean a wicked son," Tristan commented.

"Just as a good father does not necessarily mean a good son," Dahlen replied. "Regardless, that is their law. They are part of our realm, but it is by far a very different culture."

The Viper shrugged. "At any rate, the law has done its job."

"How so?" Tristan scowled.

The Viper smiled. "There isn't a whole lot of raiding going on, is there?"

LATE THE THIRD MORNING, THE FOUR OF THEM EMERGED FROM FIAN Jungle into the less-than-impressive streets of Stem. Stem was certainly a busy village, but being a fishing village in a hot and humid climate did not always mix well. The streets reeked of dead fish and the air buzzed with insects waiting for their turn to land on an unsupervised parcel of meat.

Tristan choked down bile as a sea breeze wafted the unsavory scent of the market over him.

"They must have had a bad haul," The Defiant said clearing her throat.

The Viper gave a shrug. "I've smelled worse," he stated as the four of them dismounted their horses.

"How come Hese doesn't smell this bad?" Tristan asked as they traversed the vendors trying to force them to buy their pungent-smelling goods.

"Probably because Hese's market isn't in direct sunlight," The Defiant replied holding a scented kerchief to her nose.

"There is the trading post," Dahlen said, nodding with her head. "Let's exchange our horses and buy our supplies so we can leave the stench of this place behind."

"I am guessing the owners of the fishing vessels are further up on those hills," The Viper pointed out, motioning to the luxurious villas in the distance, a stark contrast to the small shacks the actual fishermen lived in by the market.

"Shall we split up here like we did in Hese?" The Defiant asked just wanting to get out of the streets.

Dahlen nodded. "Yes," she replied. "I think it would be helpful to see how far behind we are."

The Viper and The Defiant didn't argue.

"Did you not want to go with them?" she asked Tristan skeptically.

He shrugged. "I don't have an appetite for anything in this smell," he told her. "I'll just tag along with you again."

The two of them quickly made it to the trading post on the edge of the village, grateful that the owner had the sense to keep the windows closed.

"How can I help you today?" asked a young woman behind the counter in a slight accent, a beaming smile on her face.

Dahlen smiled back. "We need four fresh horses, dried meats, nuts, dates, and a bag of apples and oranges," she replied, though the smell of the market made it difficult to think about food.

The woman gave a small frown. "I apologize," she started. "But we ah out of on-ges and only have a few apples left. We also only have two bags of roasted almonds left from Ganavan."

Dahlen nodded. "That is fine," she said. "I will take what is left of the almonds and apples."

"We also have smoked fish, cooked here in Stem," the woman offered.

Dahlen's stomach churned. "How about two dozen eggs instead?"

The woman nodded. "Yes, it is hahd to imagine fish with the awful smell."

Tristan put a jug of wine on the counter. "We will take this too."

The woman nodded and smiled as she piled what was asked for on the counter for them. "Wheah ah you headed?" she asked as she tallied up the cost.

"We are going across the river and up to Diak," Dahlen replied.

"Ah, you ah visiting the gahdens theah?"

Dahlen nodded. "I have heard they are beautiful and we want to pay our respects to the Goddesses in which the gardens are dedicated."

The woman's eye twitched slightly. "You have come a long way to pay your respects," she stated.

Dahlen gave a small nod.

"It is never too far to pay your respects to the eternal four," Tristan commented, taking the bagged goods from the counter. "What would a pilgrimage be if you only had to go a few yards to complete it?"

The woman smiled. "That is a good way of seeing it," she replied.

"I did not mean to question you."

"There is a bridge we can use to cross the river, is there not?" Dahlen asked averting the woman's attention back to her.

"Theah ah sev-ral," she responded. "Do you have a map?"

Dahlen put hers on the counter.

"Heah," the woman said pointing. "Heah, and heah."

Dahlen marked them on her map.

"I reco-mend taking the middle bu-ridge," the woman told her. "Theah is anotha post fo you to buy moh supplies."

"Is there not a post before or after the first bridge?" Dahlen asked. "The one closest to Stem?"

The woman's skepticism returned. "Theah used to be a post," she replied in an even tone. "But it has been sev-ral yeahs since it was open. People do not often travel to Goun. So, it was not deemed necessary."

"Do people not travel out of Goun? Would they not need a place to stock up supplies?" Dahlen asked.

"Goun is no longa inhabited," she replied matter-of-factly. "Theahfoh, you have no cause to take the south bu-ridge."

Dahlen nodded. "Understood," she responded, catching the woman's intentions to cut the subject short. "Thank you for your help. I am grateful for the information you provided. The second bridge is a lot more convenient."

The woman gave a small bow. "I am happy to help."

Dahlen gathered the rest of the things Tristan could not and took a deep breath before exiting the building.

"The smell is so much worse," Tristan complained. "It's as if I forgot how bad it was when I was inside the trading post and then got hit twice as hard on my way out."

"Have you secured the horses?" Dahlen asked.

He nodded. "There is a man around back bringing them to us."

"Good," Dahlen replied shifting where she stood.

"You alright?" Tristan asked her.

She furrowed her brows. "Yes," she replied. "I just have a strange feeling that the smooth part of the journey we have experienced thus far is about to end." She looked at him. "I hope you are prepared for it."

CHAPTER 18

A strange, cold wind drifted off of the sea, making the four of them shiver slightly. Dahlen pulled on her sleeves to make them longer and lifted her veil over her head.

Tristan pulled his arms into his wide sleeves. "At least we have left the smell of rotting fish behind," he said, shivering again as he remembered.

The others nodded in agreement, but a gloom lingered over them.

The Viper and The Defiant did not bring back good news from the brothels. By the prostitutes' accounts, they were almost two weeks behind the Order and a week behind the Skahrrian soldiers.

"If this forest is truly uninhabited or not used by the locals, as you say," The Viper started, "then there won't be a path for any of them to travel on. So, they will have to make their own." He shrugged. "That should slow them down several days and saves us a lot of work."

The Defiant nodded. "That's true," she agreed. "The locals believe the forest is haunted and refuse to talk about it, much less venture near it. According to some of those locals," she cleared her throat and smirked, "a Mehtian has not set foot in Halana Neya in over two hundred years. So, the paths to gain access to anywhere in the forest should be completely overgrown."

Dahlen pressed her lips together as she thought. "The shopkeeper at the trading post also said that the village that borders the forest is now abandoned. No one dares to even live near it."

Tristan looked from Dahlen to The Viper to The Defiant, then back to Dahlen. "Has anyone said why?" he asked, a slight panic in his voice. "Have either of you thought to ask why they believe it is haunted and why no one who lives near the forest has ever dared to go into it? Or why an *entire* town that borders the forest is no longer inhabited?" He searched their faces again. "Anyone?"

The other three looked at him quizzically.

"No?" Tristan replied. He nodded. "That's fine. I am sure there is no reason whatsoever why people who have lived here all their lives won't go into a deep, dark, creepy forest. Perfectly fine."

The Defiant smirked. "You aren't getting scared, are you, priest?" she asked playfully.

Tristan cleared his throat and shook his head. "No, just concerned," he replied. "Concerned as to why I am the only one bothered by all of this."

"If you don't think we are taking the threats or dangers of the Scattered Forest into account, you are wrong," The Viper told him. "We take rumors and local legends like this very seriously."

"Well, the lot of you appear a little too calm," Tristan said.

"The appearance of calm doesn't mean the absence of fear," Dahlen told him.

The day passed almost silently as they moved through the rural borders of Stem and onto the Zan River. The heat from the past few days having broken and the cool breeze from the Southern Dormant Sea made traveling a lot more pleasant. They were all surprised when they reached the southern bridge just as the sun was beginning to set.

They paused for a minute as they decided whether or not to cross the bridge and stay the night in Goun or to stay on the side they were already on and cross in the morning.

"We have made decent time today," Dahlen said. "It would not hurt if we didn't cross today, but I don't see why we shouldn't."

Tristan fidgeted on his horse and sniffed, rubbing his hand across his mouth.

The Viper shrugged. "The village of Goun looks only to be a few miles off from the bridge," he commented. "I think we will be able to make it there with enough light left to set up camp."

Tristan rolled his shoulders.

"I agree with The Viper," The Defiant said. "We should make up as much ground as we can."

Dahlen nodded. "Then we shall continue to Goun."

Tristan shook his head. "I don't know," he finally chimed in. "I am getting a strange feeling about this. I think we should wait until tomorrow."

The other three regarded him for a moment.

"I don't care how the three of you look at me, I know how I feel and I will not waiver," Tristan said defiantly. "I don't know what it is, but something is telling me we should wait until tomorrow to cross."

The Defiant lifted a brow and smirked.

"Dahlen," Tristan pleaded, turning his full gaze on her, "I know this is a lot to ask of you, but if there was ever a moment for you to trust me, please let that moment be now."

A strong breeze encircled them, making their garments flap about before it ceased, creating a strange, silent calm.

Dahlen sighed and looked at The Viper and The Defiant. "We will camp here for the night," she said dismounting her horse.

Tristan let out the breath he didn't realize he had been holding. "Thank you," he replied getting off of his own horse.

The other two shrugged, but followed suit, getting ready to set up camp.

"If the concern for our safety is so high," The Defiant started as she built the fire back up after dinner, "we should set up a watch through the night."

The Viper nodded. "Agreed," he said as he straightened his bedding.

Tristan nodded as well. "I think that is a good idea," he added.

"Good," The Defiant said. "You can take the first shift."

Dahlen bowed her head to hide her smile.

Tristan did not seem dejected by the suggestion. "Alright."

The Defiant stood, giving a curt nod. "Then I will leave you to it," she said moving to her horse to grab her bedding.

"I am not sure The Defiant likes me too much," Tristan said later that evening, poking at the fire with a stick.

Dahlen shrugged as she glanced over at the other two, resting peacefully a short distance from the fire. "The Defiant just doesn't fully see you as an asset yet," she told him.

"Is that what she said?" Tristan asked sounding a little offended.

Dahlen suppressed a small laugh. "No, she has not relayed anything to me," she replied. "It is just— I understand her." She sighed. "Does she not remind you of me?"

He moved his head from side to side. "I guess in a way she does."

"You are an outsider to her," Dahlen continued. "She is not going to trust your ability to have her back right away. You have to prove to her that you are useful."

Tristan blinked at her a moment before giving a slow nod. "Is that still how you feel about me?" he asked. "Do I still have to prove myself useful to you?"

Dahlen took in a deep breath and let it out slowly. "I believe that Mahk led me to you for a reason," she said. "I do not know what that reason is yet, but that is what I believe."

He nodded. "I am glad," he replied after a few moments.

She gave a small smile in reply absentmindedly rubbing her necklace between her fingers, comforted by its warmth.

"Are you not going to sleep like the others?" he asked after a minute.

She shook her head, not ready for the dreams the goddesses had in store for her for the night. "No, not yet," she told him. "I have too much on my mind."

"Like what?"

She shifted uncomfortably where she sat. "Everything," she responded distantly. Everything being her daughter. She often wondered how she was doing and what Princess Rain had named her. She would often lie awake at night wondering if her daughter was fast asleep or fussing to be held. She often tried to imagine what she looked like. Was she taking on more of hers or Mohrr's traits? Was she a calm baby, or was she restless? Was she happy?

It hurt her to not know, but she couldn't change it now. What was done, was done. In time, she knew she would learn to move on, but she also knew she would never cease to wonder about her.

"Why did you choose to name yourself Dahlen?" Tristan asked, breaking her from her thoughts.

She looked at him, the light from the fire danced about them as a symphony of crickets played in the background. She chuckled lightly. "I don't know," she told him. "I guess I felt it suited me better than my given name. AnnJella just seemed so foreign to me."

His lips curled into a subtle smile. "I am glad I could give you a name," he told her.

She laughed through her nose. "I guess I do have you to thank for it," she replied.

Tristan moved closer to her. "Might I ask what has happened between now and the last we met?"

She made eye contact with him briefly before looking away. "Nothing substantial."

"Are you sure?" he pressed gently. "You seem so changed."

"Other than me being released from my vows, there is nothing to report," she told him.

He shook his head. "I don't believe you."

She regarded him for a moment. "I have changed that much?"

He gave a nod. "Before you seemed stoic, maybe a little distant at times," he explained. "But, now, now you seem," he paused for a moment, "sad."

Dahlen averted her gaze back to the fire. "Perhaps, I have always been sad and you are just now noticing," she replied.

Tristan shook his head. "No," he said a little sternly. "You might have had a brooding moment or two before, but this is different. You aren't just brooding; you are regretting something."

She cleared her throat and rubbed her mouth with her hand. "If I were sad, as you say, I have not changed enough to want to talk about it."

Tristan nodded, pressing his lips together. "Understood," he told her. "Just know that, if the time comes that you do want to talk about it, you can always talk to me."

She gave him a weak smile. "Thank you," she responded. "I appreciate it." She took a deep breath and let it out in a huff. "But today is not that day."

"I understand," he replied.

There was a brief pause between them as they both stared into the fire.

"Does it have anything to do with your necklace?" Tristan asked, once again breaking her from her thoughts.

"What?" she replied, a little confused.

He shrugged. "You used to always play with your other necklace. The little, silver wing," he explained. "Now you have a different necklace." He reached out to take it in his hand when she pushed it away gently.

"Are you asking whether my new necklace has any connection to the sadness you think I am feeling?" she asked with a raised brow.

He gave a small nod. "Yes."

She thought for a moment as she held the warm red opal in her hand. "I believe we both agreed that if or when I was ready to talk," she started, "I would."

"Fair enough."

Somewhere in the distance, their conversation was interrupted by the sounds of a barking or howling. The both of them looked over their shoulders in the direction of Goun, the symphony of crickets now silent.

"Wolves?" Tristan said, unsure.

Dahlen listened for a moment before shaking her head. "None that I have ever heard before," she replied. "No," she continued as another howl sounded in the distance, "that is something else."

Tristan shifted in his seat. "Do you think whatever they are will come this way?" he asked.

"I think you better keep the fires burning."

CHAPTER 19

"Steady your aim," the teacher titled as The Calm told the girl as she struggled to hold up her bow.

The girl let the tension out on the bowstring and took a deep breath before she pulled back on it again, taking aim.

"Release!" The Calm said.

The arrow whizzed through the air and landed in the target twenty-five feet in front of her with a 'thunk.' The girl smiled in triumph though she missed the bullseye by nearly a foot.

The Calm gave her a soft pat on the head. "You are getting better, child," she told her. "Keep practicing."

The girl nodded and picked up another arrow, taking a deep breath as she aimed. She let go and watched as the arrow hit the target again, this time much closer to the bullseye.

"Very impressive," came a familiar voice.

The girl turned and beamed. It was The Master.

"You have come a long way these past two years," he told her. "I am very proud of you."

A few of the other children in the class looked over at them, their jealousy of her being noticed by a distinguished member apparent on their faces.

"But you still have much to learn," he continued. "You should not breathe as you aim, but you should breathe as you pull back on your string. Hold your breath as you take aim and then exhale with the release of the arrow. This will help steady you."

The girl nodded.

"Come," he beckoned her. "Let us take a walk."

The girl looked at The Calm who nodded. "We are done for the day," she told her, allowing her to leave with The Master.

"I have not seen you in over a month," she said as they walked along the Rest's market place. "Have you been out on a mission?"

The Master gave a small smile. "A personal errand really," he replied pulling two apples from a stand and handing her one.

The girl took it joyfully.

"But I wanted to give you something," The Master said pulling something from his pocket.

It was a silver necklace with a small birdwing for a charm.

A strange sense of familiarity flashed through her as she looked at it. She had seen it before. But where?

"That is for me?" she asked gently taking it in her small hands.

The Master nodded.

"It is so pretty," she said smiling up at him. "Thank you."

There was a flash of movement in the alley next to them. The girl turned her head and saw a man shrouded in the shadows. He paused for a moment, perhaps, looking at her before he rounded the corner and hurried off in the other direction.

The girl blinked as she watched him go, a sense of sadness surrounding him. After a moment, the incident was forgotten and she turned her attention back to her necklace.

"Am I allowed to wear it?" she asked innocently.

The Master nodded. "Of course," he told her, helping her put it on.

"Where did you get it?"

"One day, I will tell you about this necklace, and the importance of it." He turned her so she was facing him. "But for right now, just know *that you were meant to wear this."*

The girl smiled down at the small wing dangling from her neck. "Thank you."

The wind gently blew about her and followed the path of the shrouded man.

DAHLEN WOKE, CONFUSED BY HER DREAM. SHE VAGUELY REMEMBERED the day when The Master had given her mother's necklace to her, but she did not remember the presence of the other man. She blinked into the dusky morning light and contemplated what she had seen.

It would be so much easier if you just told me what you were trying to tell me, she thought, directing it to the goddesses. *What am I supposed to learn or understand by all of this?*

She stretched before she emerged from her bedding and began to roll everything up. The Viper and The Defiant were still sleeping soundly as she packed up her horse. She walked over to the now dead fire and smirked as she saw Tristan passed out in a seated position, a sword dangling from one hand and a charred fire poker in the other. She nudged him with her foot causing him to jump and fall from the log he had been perched on.

He jumped to his feet, half asleep, trying to hold up his sword.

His screams woke up the other two who, after realizing there wasn't a threat, began laughing at the scene before them.

"You alright?" Dahlen asked, trying not to add to his embarrassment by laughing.

Tristan cleared his throat. "Yes," he replied, sheathing his sword and straightening his clothes. "I was just stretching."

"As long as you weren't sleeping on the job," The Defiant said smirking as she packed her horse.

"I thought we were supposed to take shifts," Tristan grumbled.

The Viper yawned. "Whose turn is it to cook breakfast?" he asked.

"Yours," the other three answered without hesitation.

After a quick breakfast, the four of them were on their way to Goun, the last village, now ghost town, before the Scattered Forest. The Defiant and The Viper started the journey by cracking jokes, mostly at Tristan's expense, but he never let what they had to say get to him.

Dahlen, though generally ignoring them, played mediator from time to time when she had had enough of their antics. Everything stopped, however, when they reached the town. There was a strange hush that came over them as they moved along the abandoned buildings.

It was an eerie sight to see. Several of the houses and small buildings had collapsed into themselves, while the others had vines and other brush growing around and through them. Shattered windows and hole-filled roofs plagued almost every house and left behind furniture and children's toys littered the floors. It was a fleeting reminder of life's uncertainty. A once thriving village now dilapidated, a corpse waiting for nature to slowly reclaim what once belonged to it.

"We should search some of the buildings," Dahlen suggested once they reached the epicenter.

"Why is that?" Tristan asked. "There can't be anything in these buildings we could possibly use."

The Defiant gave a small huff. "We aren't looking for supplies," she explained. "We are looking for signs of life. For any indication that someone has been here recently."

"Whether or not anyone other than us has passed through," The Viper added.

"I got it," Tristan mumbled as he dismounted his horse.

The four of them moved through several of the buildings, searching for any indication of recent activity. Some of the houses, which were covered with dirt and dust from ceiling to floor, had the intimation of a disturbance. Footsteps, a week or so old, littered some of the floors and several fireplaces had remnants of recently-burned wood in them.

Tristan, on further inspection, however, found something a little more recent. Drag marks on the dusty floor of one house sent an ominous feeling through him. He called the other three over to him to see.

"Whatever was dragged, though I assume it was human because of the heel marks, was probably already dead, or at least unconscious," The Viper said, kneeling down to observe the marks.

"Why do you say that?" Tristan asked.

"There's no sign of a struggle," The Viper explained. "If someone or something was dragging you, would you not struggle against them?"

Tristan nodded.

"It is obvious another human dragged them out," The Defiant added, pointing at the floor. "The dead, or unconscious person, was grabbed from under the arms, half carried, half dragged."

"Is there any blood?" Dahlen asked as she moved around the small, one-room house.

Tristan shook his head. "None that I found, but I didn't venture further in once I saw the drag marks."

Dahlen nodded and followed the marks to where they started, by a window looking out the back. She narrowed her eyes at the view. It was of the forest. She turned her head slightly, eyeing a small shelf that had fallen from the wall, its contents broken and scattered on the floor. She moved over to them, kneeling on the ground so she could see them better.

She moved the pieces of broken vases and bottles with one of her knives. The outside pieces of the glass had dust caked on them, but the inside pieces had almost none. Whoever was dragged from this house was standing in front of the window when they were struck from the left, causing them to fall to their right, bringing down the shelf with them as they fell.

"Where are the other footprints?" The Defiant asked as she continued investigating the scene.

"Huh?" Tristan squeaked.

"This one set from the front door to the window belongs, most likely, to the person that was dragged," The Defiant explained. "But there aren't any left by the one that did the dragging."

"She's right," Dahlen agreed. "There aren't any prints of whoever dragged this person out of here."

Tristan gulped. "What are you saying?"

The Viper shrugged. "Maybe it's one of the ghosts of the forest that killed him," he suggested.

"You believe that then?" Tristan inquired. "You believe what the locals have said about the forest?"

"I believe I have seen a lot in my life to not discount something just because it might not seem logical," The Viper responded.

The Defiant gave a small huff. "You're both losing it," she snickered.

"I am not saying it was a ghost," The Viper defended himself. "I am just saying we cannot rule out the possibility. Especially given some of the things I have recently witnessed."

Something under a table in the corner by the window caught Dahlen's eye and she moved over to examine it.

"And what are some of these things you claim to have witnessed?" The Defiant goaded. "You have alluded to them before but are too vague on the details."

Dahlen lifted up the dingy cloth that hung from the table and narrowed her eyes at the small object under it. She reached out and took it in her hand, gently turning it over to examine it.

"You have no reason not to trust me," The Viper argued. "But, for contractual reasons, I cannot divulge this information."

The Defiant raised a skeptical brow. "You are so full of it," she told him.

"What is that?" Tristan asked moving over to Dahlen.

Dahlen stood and brought what she was holding to the window letting the light from the sun fall on it. At first glance, it looked like nothing more than a small, dirty rock, but as the sunlight hit it, a shine peeked through the dirt. She took out her canteen of water and washed the rock off, her heart beating faster as the silvery material underneath was revealed.

"Did you find something?" The Defiant asked curiously, stopping her bickering with The Viper.

The Viper looked over at Dahlen as well and frowned. "It's just a rock," he claimed.

Dahlen shook her head. "No," she corrected breathlessly, "this is beraxium."

CHAPTER 20

DAHLEN AND THE OTHERS RESUMED THEIR JOURNEY WITH A RENEWED energy. There was indeed beraxium in the Scattered Forest. And, if there was beraxium, the Order of Zeln would definitely be there.

Dahlen led the other three forward as she and her horse cantered their way through the town of Goun and, finally, to the edge of the Scattered Forest. She couldn't believe that she was almost there. Thousands of thoughts ran through her mind as she pushed her horse faster, taking it from its canter to a full gallop. The Order of Zeln was nearly in reach. Soon, she would avenge her mother and herself. Soon, she would fulfill her promise to Vorce.

She stopped her horse as she came to the edge of the forest, mixed emotions of exhilaration and anticipation coursing through her as she waited for the other three to catch up. She gazed upon the thickly wooded area, taking her horse up and down the edge to look for a path. She hesitated when she came across a narrow trail that seemed to be recently disturbed. She studied it for a few minutes, pacing back and forth as she took in its surroundings before she dashed back to the rest of her group who had yet to catch up.

"It seems almost too thick to take the horses in," The Defiant observed when she met up with them.

Dahlen nodded. "There is a narrow path just over there," she replied, pointing, "but it only allows enough room for one horse at a time."

The Viper shook his head. "I don't like it," he said with uncertainty.

"Nor do I," Dahlen admitted, "but we don't have many other choices. I ran up and down the edge of the forest and could find nothing else. Besides, it is obviously the trail the Skahrrians and possibly the Order took."

"You can see tracks?" The Defiant asked.

"Better," Dahlen replied. "I found their abandoned wagons."

Tristan frowned at this. "I don't like the sound of *that*," he stated.

The Viper shrugged. "If the trail only admits one horse at a time, then it certainly would not be large enough to admit a wagon," he informed him.

"Though the narrowness of the trail does pose an issue," Dahlen added.

"Makes us very easy targets for an ambush," The Defiant affirmed.

The Viper and Dahlen nodded.

"So, what should we do?" Tristan asked. "We aren't going to leave our horses, are we?"

Dahlen considered the question for a moment before taking a deep breath and letting out slowly. "No," she finally replied. "But I do think we should walk them."

The Viper agreed. "It will make maneuvering a lot easier."

The Defiant sucked her teeth as she thought. "First, let's see if there is anything valuable or useful we can take from whatever the Skahrrians left behind," she added. "Then we can decide just how narrow this path is."

A few minutes later, Tristan was shaking his head as he stared into the darkness of the forest, the other three being occupied with grabbing whatever they could use from the abandoned wagons.

"The path barely lets a horse in," he said loudly, so the others could hear them.

"We are going to be fine," Dahlen shouted in response as she found a decent piece of leather armor left behind in one of the wagons.

"Is that what the gods told you?" Tristan yelled back.

Dahlen came up next to him holding up the armor. "Would it make you feel better if I said, 'yes'?"

"It wouldn't hurt."

"Then, yes, they said we would be fine."

He eyed her skeptically, but took the piece of chest armor she proffered him. "Someone left this?" he mumbled to himself. "This is nice."

Dahlen looked at the late afternoon sun. "Alright," she said loud enough for everyone to hear. "We are losing daylight. We should get going."

THERE WAS NO DOUBTING THE FOREST WAS THICK. THE DENSE BRUSH barely let in enough light for them to see the path before them, but they pressed on regardless. Dahlen was in the front, leading her horse along the rough, leaf and debris littered path, while The Viper voluntarily brought up the back.

Birds flitted and cawed in the branches above them as they trekked through the moist air and spiderwebs. After the second one wrapped itself around her face, Dahlen picked up a long tree branch and waved it in front of her as she walked.

The four of them began their venture silently; all of them were on high alert for the slightest noise. But after about an hour of listening to nothing but the birds and the twigs snapping under their own feet, the silence was broken by an erratic whistling, the whistler missing half of the notes and horribly off key.

Dahlen stopped and glared back at Tristan who shrugged sheepishly.

"It's much too quiet," he reasoned. "I needed something to take my mind off the impending doom and gloom of the forest."

"This is not the time, Tristan," Dahlen told him. "We are listening for anything else that might be inhabiting the forest, while at the same time, not trying to attract any attention."

"What, like bears?" Tristan asked.

"Nah," The Defiant joined in, shaking her head. "In a jungle like this, I would bet there are more big cats than anything."

"Jaguars," The Viper added. "Definitely jaguars."

"Or, other people," Dahlen said starting to pull her horse along again. "The jaguars we can keep at bay with fire, but if there are other people, malignant to our cause, we need to be ready for them."

There was a rustling in the bushes next to the path and Tristan froze. "What was that?" he whispered, his voice uneasy.

The rustling started up again causing the bush to shake and move.

"Poke it with your sword," The Defiant told him.

Tristan looked at her like she was crazy, but after a moment pulled his sword from its scabbard and shakily reached out to the bush. He jabbed at it once causing the rustling to cease, but as he was drawing his sword back, a shrill screech rang out from it. Tristan recoiled backwards and fell as a small monkey leapt from the bush on top of him, screaming his dissatisfaction with being disturbed before scampering away to the other side of the path.

The other three chuckled at him as he clambered up from the ground, brushing off the leaves and dirt from him.

"Stupid monkey," he mumbled to himself.

"Terrifying creatures, really," The Viper said, poking fun at him. "Don't let their small stature fool you."

"Enough," Dahlen interjected before an argument could ensue. "We need to be more careful. There's more in this forest than just monkeys."

Tristan looked back at The Defiant who smiled and quietly mimicked the noise the monkey made. He scowled at her but grabbed his reins and continued following Dahlen.

Night fell quicker in the forest as what little light they had soon disappeared beyond the trees. Dahlen was disappointed, hoping to get further along the trail than where they had stopped. If she was correct, they had traveled only six or seven miles into the Scattered Forest and there had been no other signs of anyone else who may have ventured in. Other than the brush being beaten back, they appeared to be the only ones to have recently entered.

"The Skahrrian soldiers probably made camp further in," The Viper suggested.

Dahlen sighed. "Which just means we are falling further and further behind," she pointed out. "If we keep under pacing them, we will possibly reach them too late."

"How do you even know where we are going?" Tristan asked. "No one would give you a map of this place because no one ever dares to come here."

A soft breeze came upon them and wrapped itself around Dahlen before it continued on down the path. She nodded.

"Because I just know," she replied confidently.

CHAPTER 21

"MARTEN," THE GIRL EXCLAIMED HAPPILY AS THE OLDER BOY CAME *walking up to her.*

He smiled in response, but shushed her. "You are not allowed to use my old name," he reminded her for the hundredth time.

She shrugged. "Have you just returned from training?" she asked him as she held her hand out for him to take.

He hesitated but slowly took it. He took a deep breath and let it out in a huff. "Yes," he finally replied. "We spent a week working on survival skills in Behr Wood."

"Did you see any wolves?" she inquired curiously, gently pulling him along the street.

He gave a small laugh. "No," he told her. "There aren't any wolves in Behr Wood. There are some in the Stronghold Mountains and Vron Wood, but not that far east."

"What did you do while you were out there?" The girl continued to lead him down the road, weaving in and out of other children, teachers, and coven constituents.

"We learned how to survive on the land," he replied. "We hunted, learned what plants we could eat, cooked what we could catch. Things like that."

"Sounds easy," she boldly stated.

He laughed harder. "Says a young girl of no more than eight years of age," he retorted. "Where are you taking me by the way?"

"To the docks!" she proclaimed as she pressed her way through.

"What is so special about the docks?" Marten asked her, a brow raised.

"I want to watch the sunset," she told him matter-of-factly.

He laughed at the small girl's excitement. "But our docks face south," he told her.

"So?"

"The sun sets in the west," he explained. "The sunset won't be over the water."

The girl shrugged. "The water is still pretty to look at."

Marten nodded. "You're very right," he replied.

The girl led them to the edge of one of the piers and sat with her legs dangling over the edge. She patted the spot next to her for Marten to join her and he complied.

"This is my favorite place here," she claimed as she gazed out over the water. "It's so pretty and peaceful."

Marten sighed and nodded. "Do you," he hesitated, "do you remember what it was like before you came here?"

The girl furrowed her brows slightly in thought. "No," she told him unbothered. She rubbed the charm of her necklace between her fingers as she often did. "Do you?"

Marten gave a small nod. "Yes, but I was a lot older than you when I first came here," he replied.

The girl didn't reply. Instead, she pointed out a ship on the horizon.

"Ann–" Marten coughed and shook his head. "Do you wish that you did remember?" he asked her, steering her back to their conversation.

She looked up at him innocently. "I don't know," she peeped, afraid to give the wrong answer. "Am I supposed to?"

Marten smiled reassuringly and patted her arm, opening his mouth to speak when his eyes fogged over. His mouth hung open almost in *horror as he gripped the girl's arm who shouted in pain.*

She struggled against him. "Marten, you're hurting me," she pleaded. "Marten, let go!"

Sweat formed on Marten's brow as his chest rose and fell with shallow breaths; his eyes, however, continued to stare into nothing.

"Marten, you're scaring me!" the girl cried.

After several seconds of struggling, the girl was able to wriggle her arm out of his grip and she watched as his expression changed. The dullness of his eyes vanished and he gasped, gulping in air as if he had been holding his breath the entire time.

"You hurt me!" the girl pouted, holding back her tears of fear.

"I'm sorry," Marten replied almost breathlessly. "I am so sorry." He buried his face in his hands, his shoulders slumped as he mumbled apologies over and over.

The girl reached out and gently placed her hand on his shoulder, causing him to jump. She recoiled in response.

When he looked at her, she could tell he had been crying.

"You scared me," she told him almost in a whisper.

Marten gathered the girl in his arms and hugged her. "I am sorry," he said again. "I am sorry for everything. I would give my life for you before I let any harm come to you." He held her at arms' length and looked her in the eyes. "I will do anything to protect you."

Somewhere, either in her dream or the forest, a hawk called out.

DAHLEN WAS SO WRAPPED UP IN HER DREAM THE NEXT DAY THAT SHE barely heard anything that was said to her. Marten had had a vision about her that day at the docks. She vaguely remembered it. That might have been the first time she had dragged Marten to that spot, but it wasn't the last.

She tried to think. In her dream, he had hesitated taking her hand as if he didn't want to touch her. As if he didn't want to have a vision about her. Then, at the docks, when he touched her arm, that was when he had one.

It was after that that Marten no longer took her by the hand. He told her she was too old to be doing such things. It was also around that time he started wearing baggier sleeves. Was it to make sure his skin never came in contact with hers or others'?

His vision had obviously scared him. Or he would not have had such a horrible reaction. Then what was it about? Was that vision relevant to what she was going through now? Did it have a connection to her journey? Is that why the goddesses wanted her to see it?

"I think this might be one of their campsites," The Viper said, breaking her from her thoughts.

Dahlen turned in a daze.

"The brush and leaves are trampled in this area," he continued, taking a small step off of the path to look further into the woods.

Dahlen let the reins of her horse go and moved back along the path to where The Viper indicated.

"Perhaps this was the Skahrrian camp. Though it's difficult to tell." He prodded the area with his foot. He frowned at something on the ground, bending over to pick it up. He smiled as he held out a coin. "Definitely Skahrrian."

Dahlen took the coin and nodded at the brushed-up image of King Breht.

"We have only been traveling an hour," The Defiant stated. "We were not too far behind them when we camped."

She nodded. "We are making good time," she said, emerging back onto the path, "but there are only four of us. We should be making better time."

"Would we not make better time if we rode our horses?" Tristan asked, bringing up an old arguing point.

Dahlen shook her head. "We have been over this," she told him. "Walking our horses on a path this narrow makes for less surprises. Plus, our horses provide us with some cover."

Tristan shrugged. "Fine."

"At any rate, we aren't going to get anywhere faster if all we do is complain about it," she said. "The Viper, good eye on the campsite."

He bowed, still bringing up the rear.

"Let's keep pushing forward," Dahlen commanded.

Rain made for a particularly miserable day as the warm weather gave way for cooler winds and wet skin. The four of them shook the excess water off, continuing on with minimal complaints from Tristan who was often ignored.

On the next day, the weather cleared though warmed immensely around midday. The layers they had put on the keep out the chill of the rain, were promptly peeled off and packed away.

"Ugh," Tristan exclaimed for the fiftieth time. "At least the rain kept the bugs at bay." He slapped the back of his neck. "This is almost worse."

"Here," Dahlen said, handing him the charl root serum.

"Thank you," he graciously said taking the bottle. The wind changed as he opened the cork and he let out a 'whew' as a strong odor hit his nostrils. "Did this stuff go bad?" he asked.

The horses neighed, becoming uneasy, pulling slightly on their reins in agitation. The Viper, The Defiant and Dahlen all shook their heads. They knew that smell. Death.

The three of them silently took out their weapons, pausing slightly as they came to a bend in the path.

"Tristan," Dahlen whispered, "pull out your sword and be ready."

Tristan took his hand from his nose and obeyed.

Dahlen and the other two exchanged silent glances before they continued to move along the path. The Defiant, with her bow ready, brought up the back, slowly walking backward and scanning the trees for any life; The Viper slipped into the woods without a sound; Dahlen and Tristan remained in front, the awful smell of decay only worsening. As they reached the bend, they could hear an intense buzzing that only increased as they continued.

"What is that noise?" Tristan choked through the smog of

the smell.

"Flies," Dahlen whispered in return.

"Flies?"

She nodded. "A lot of them."

Sure enough, swarms of flies greeted them as they passed the turn, dark moving clouds hovering thickly in the air. The sound was almost deafening. Dahlen tied her veil around her nose and mouth as she pushed through them, half blind as she swatted at the flies with her hands.

"Light a torch!" she yelled.

Her command was obeyed and soon, the glowing light of a torch waved the mass hordes of flies away revealing the horror they had concealed.

"Oh, my gods," Tristan breathed in terrified surprise.

There before them, scattered about the jungle floor, were the rotting remains of no less than fifteen men.

"That explains the smell and mass of flies," The Defiant commented as she stole a glance away from her outlook.

"But it doesn't explain how this happened," Dahlen replied.

"Any thoughts, priest?" The Defiant asked.

She was answered by a retching sound.

Dahlen moved closer to one of the bodies and nudged it with her foot. "What do you think?" she asked to no one in particular. "Dead at least four or five days?"

The Defiant shrugged. "Hard to tell with all of the humidity and heat," she replied.

"Found a few more remains in the woods," The Viper interjected, emerging from the trees. "Dragged in there by a jaguar or other scavengers no doubt."

Tristan was heard retching again.

"These men are from Skahrr," Dahlen noted, seeing a tattered banner on the ground.

"Do you think the Order did this?" The Defiant asked. "It's obvious they were attacked by something."

Dahlen scanned the bodies and shook her head. All of them had the same green and brown uniforms. None of them wore the yellow and black attire of the Order.

"No," she finally replied. "This had to have been someone else. There aren't any other bodies."

"Maybe the Order killed them all without losing any of their own," Tristan said in a weak voice.

She shook her head. "Look at the sword in this one's hand," she explained. "There is dried blood almost up to the hilt on it. That is a fatal wound inflicted by this man and, yet, where's the body?"

The Viper nodded. "They all have their weapons out," he agreed. "There had to have been a fight."

"There are fifteen men here and more in the woods," Dahlen continued. "You're going to tell me none of these men were successful in killing even one of whoever attacked them?" She shook her head again. "I find that very hard to believe. Skahrrian soldiers certainly are not the best, but I cannot doubt their skill in combat so much to think they were incapable of killing even one man."

The Defiant nodded. "There appears to be blood on several of these men's swords," she added.

Tristan shrugged. "Maybe the winning side took their dead," he suggested matter-of-factly.

"Exactly," Dahlen said.

Tristan furrowed his brow. "And you don't think the Order would do that?"

"This path allows only one horse at a time," she pointed out. "No wagons, no carts. How would they transport them?"

"On the back of their horses?" Tristan suggested.

"No, a group in a hurry would not waste their time taking their dead," The Viper said. "That kind of sentimentality is frowned upon anyway."

"So, they buried them?" Tristan asked.

"For what purpose?" The Defiant replied. "Why waste the energy? And again, time?"

Tristan looked from one trained assassin to the other. "Then what are you supposing?"

"There's someone else in these woods," Dahlen said.

Tristan swallowed. "Ghosts and spirits," he whispered.

Dahlen smirked and shook her head. "As far as I know," she indicated to the bloody sword, "ghosts don't bleed."

CHAPTER 22

It was a restless night for all of them as the slightest noise indicated the possible approach of an ambush. Even with taking shifts to watch, none of them could get out the image, or smell, of what they saw earlier that day long enough to sleep. So, every sound in the jungle was a warning, preventing them from suffering a similar fate.

"So, you think that whoever, or whatever, killed those men is human?" Tristan asked as they continued to trudge along the path the next day.

Dahlen nodded as she took a swig from her canteen. "Yes," she replied. "I do."

Tristan nodded pensively. "Why?"

Dahlen took in a small exasperated breath and let it out slowly. "Do you remember when we were first attacked by Vorce's men in the Vron Wood?"

"I think about it often," he replied.

"Remember when I shot one of the men with my bow?"

He nodded slowly.

"Do you remember what the other man did?"

"He helped the other man get away," Tristan answered. "It saved his life."

"Yes," she said. "If he had left him, that man might have died and with it, the legend of the man-like bears."

Tristan thought about it for a moment. "Because if people stumbled on his body, they would learn that it was just a man disguised by heavy furs."

"Exactly," she smirked. "And it is the same with these 'ghosts' of the forest. They take their men so that they can vanish back into the jungle. If people learned that it was just ordinary bandits in the woods, there wouldn't be too much to be afraid of."

Tristan shook his head at this. "But why scare away your supposed victims?" he asked. "Why continue with the haunted forest façade?"

"Because they aren't putting on this façade to lure people into the forest to rob them," The Viper chimed in.

"They're doing it because they're protecting something," The Defiant added.

Tristan blinked. "The beraxium."

Dahlen nodded. "They are trying to prevent people from taking the beraxium."

"For what purpose?" Tristan asked. "It has no monetary value. Most people don't even know what beraxium is. I didn't until you told me."

"They know what beraxium is used for," Dahlen theorized. "Perhaps, they know it can be used to strengthen Vron and in order to prevent that from happening, they act as the mine's guardians."

"Which makes them extremely dangerous," The Defiant added. "They will have no fear of death and will, more than likely, fight until their last man is dead."

"They will not surrender, and they will not give up," The Viper concluded.

Tristan cleared his throat. "Maybe we should have brought more people with us," he muttered.

"Maybe you should start praying, priest," The Defiant replied with a smirk. "We might actually need it."

A light rain fell on them as they trudged along, dampening the midmorning heat into a thick humidity. In the afternoon, they came to a fork in the road where the sound of rushing water could be heard. The group stopped as they studied their choice of paths. One path led slightly north from where they were, while the other path continued straight on.

"Which way?" The Viper asked.

"My instincts tell me we need to take the northern path," Dahlen replied. "But I am not completely positive."

"Always a reassuring thing to hear," The Defiant said satirically.

"The path seems a little more used to the north than if we just continued straight," Tristan chimed in.

The others nodded.

"I agree," The Defiant said, sounding surprised.

"Well, before we go on too much further," Dahlen started, "I am going to fill up my water. I think we should all do the same."

Everyone agreed as they pulled out their canteens.

"The Viper and Tristan will stay with the horses while The Defiant and I go to the river and fill up," Dahlen told them as she took the containers. "The Defiant, bring your bow. I will fill everything up while you watch my back."

"Right," The Defiant replied, pulling out her bow.

"Stay vigilant," Dahlen reminded the other two as she and The Defiant slipped into the woods.

The two of them pushed against the branches and twigs of the dense forest, shielding their faces from the spiderwebs and falling debris as they made their way toward the sound of rushing water.

It was not long before they could smell the mist of the river and it was not long after that they could see it as it rolled from a cliff to a gurgling pool below. Dahlen and The Defiant took a moment to appreciate the sheer power of the water as it tumbled down the precipice, creating a tumultuous display of mist and bubbles. And all of this was surrounded by the lush green of the forest undisturbed by man.

They both took a deep breath, letting it out slowly. The scene was almost peaceful enough to make them forget the awful scene from the day before. After a moment, however, it passed.

"We should hurry," Dahlen almost yelled over the sound of the waterfall. "It's difficult to hear anything over the sound of the water."

The Defiant nodded as she scanned the trees with her bow at the ready.

Dahlen wasted no time as she opened the canteens and quickly filled them, only taking a brief moment to splash some cool water in her face. She relished the moment, taking another to wash some of the dirt from travel off of her hands.

It was then, as she was bending over to scoop more water in her hands, that she saw something strange move in the water's reflection. She blinked, thinking she had imagined it, but upon noticing it again she realized what she was looking at. It was a man in the tree above her. She hesitated, but not long enough, she hoped, that the man noticed. She slowly stood, wiping her hands on her tunic before she turned and took a few steps away from the water.

She made eye contact with The Defiant briefly before she spun around and threw a knife at the man in the tree, who screamed as he fell into the water below.

"Run!" Dahlen yelled as she began pushing her way back through the way they came.

They burst through the brush startling the other two who had been busy relieving themselves on a nearby tree.

"They're in the trees," Dahlen said, grabbing her horse's reins. "We need to go now!"

But before she could mount her horse, three men covered in leaves and brown clothing to camouflage themselves dropped down from the branches above just a few yards from them. Everyone froze as they considered their next actions carefully.

"Halana Neya he palende hayo sou ya!" one of the three proclaimed.

Halana Neya is a forbidden place.

"Chinda he dungo ya!"

You are trespassing!

Dahlen slowly removed her foot from the stirrup and inched her way behind her horse.

"Ome, Chinda he menno le ban ki itela!"

Now, by our hands, you will die!

The man lifted a spear in his hand to throw as Dahlen yelled and gave her horse a hard slap on the behind. Her horse reared in surprise and charged at the men causing enough confusion for Dahlen and the others to gain the upper hand.

The Defiant, without losing a beat, put two arrows in one man while Tristan sunk another in the other one. Dahlen had charged the man with the spear, breaking the wood in half with her sword before punching him in face. The man staggered back and Dahlen finished him with a thrust into his stomach.

No sooner, however, had she killed him was she grabbed from behind, her sword dropping to the ground. Large muscular arms wrapped around her and squeezed, her breath leaving her lungs in a 'woosh.' She struggled for several seconds, unable to catch her breath when he fell to his knees, releasing her and falling on his face. Six arrows were sticking from his back.

She didn't have time to voice her gratitude to The Defiant and Tristan as more men fell from the trees. Dahlen picked her sword back up, deflecting an attack just in time as one of the men came at her. She parried and thrusted and dodged a few more attacks before she was able to cut him down.

Panting from the exercise, she turned to see how her companions were faring. The Defiant now had her own swords out, yelling as she brought them down on one of the men. Tristan was wielding a sword in one hand and a shield in the other, using it to push back an advance. The Viper was seeming to have a wonderful time as he struck the men down before him, weaving and dodging blows and spinning to strike in return.

Dahlen moved in to help when she was again accosted from above. The man took her so much by surprise that she stumbled backwards trying to avoid his blow. His sword sliced at her, barely missing her flesh as it ripped the front of her tunic, exposing her chest. Caught off balance, Dahlen tripped over a branch and fell.

The man reached out to grab her, but instead caught her necklace in his hand, the leather band snapping as she continued to fall. The man gave a small laugh as he approached her but suddenly stopped.

He looked down at his hand and watched as it burst into flames. The man screamed as the fire burned through his flesh and ignited the leaves he used as camouflage. His screams of anguish filled the air as he smoldered and fell to the ground as ash.

Dahlen blinked. "Dohrrn?" she whispered. She looked around her, searching for him amongst trees.

"Heyatan!" came a booming voice.

Enough!

The fighting ceased as one of the men threw back his leaf covered hood and approached Dahlen who was pulling herself back off of the ground. She narrowed her eyes when she saw his face.

"You!" she said in disbelief.

The man nodded. It was the shopkeeper from Hese.

"What did you do to my man?" he asked nodding his head to the pile of ashen remains.

Dahlen shook her head. "I didn't do anything," she answered. "He just grabbed my necklace and then..." She let her statement hang in the air. The necklace.

The shopkeeper nudged the ashes of the man gently with his foot, finding the glowing, red opal still steaming.

Dahlen stared down at it for a moment before slowly retrieving it from the dust pile. It was no warmer than it usually was.

"What is that?" the man asked.

Dahlen looked at him defiantly. "It is a red opal," she replied matter-of-factly.

"Those ah quite uncommon."

"Would you like to see it?" she asked, holding out the rock for him to take.

The man recoiled. "Wheah did you get such a thing?"

"The god of fire gifted it to me," she told him. "Vremir himself made this for me."

There was a stirring among the other men as they whispered amongst themselves. The shopkeeper stared at her wide eyed.

"It is you, then?" he said, his eyes a little softer. "Maleya!" he called out, not taking his eyes off of her.

A few seconds later, a young woman emerged from the woods and Dahlen was even more surprised to see the shopkeeper from Stem approach her.

"Maleya, she has come," the man told her.

Maleya smiled at her. "I knew you werr diff-rent," she said. "I knew you would come."

"What's, uh, what's going on over there?" The Viper asked still holding his sword at the ready.

"I must apologize," the man explained, turning to Dahlen's companions. "Had we known who you werr, we would neva have attacked you. Please, put your weapons away."

They hesitated.

"Dahlen?" Tristan asked in confirmation.

Dahlen looked at Maleya, the shopkeeper from Stem.

"You are the chosen one, the pu-rophet," Maleya said. "We have been waiting a long time foh you."

Dahlen nodded. "Put your weapons down," she finally said. "They aren't going to hurt us."

Maleya bowed graciously. "We ah so happy you ah finally heah."

Dahlen smiled nervously in response.

"Manye, kochila!" Maleya ordered the men.

Everyone, clean up!

"Come," she said turning her attention back to Dahlen, her hand outstretched, beckoning her.

Dahlen gave her a weary look, but nodded.

Maleya gave a soft smile. "This way." She turned and led Dahlen into the forest as she motioned for the others to follow as they entered.

"Where are you taking us?" Dahlen asked.

"To our camp," Maleya answered. "We have one not fah from the path."

"What about our horses?" Dahlen asked as they pushed through brush.

"They will be looked aftah," Maleya replied. "You will get them back when you continue your journey."

"What is going on?" The Defiant whispered as they caught up with her.

"I am not sure yet, but I think we are going to be fine," Dahlen reassured her. "They aren't going to try to hurt us anymore."

"You're positive?" The Viper inquired skeptically. "We just killed several of their men."

"It is unfohtunate that we lost our people and they will be mourned," Maleya said in response. "But we ah not without unda-standing. You werr attacked and you defended yourselves. We cannot hold angah against you foh it."

"Who are you?" Dahlen asked.

"My name is Maleya," she replied. "I am the daughter of the chief of my people."

"Not that knowing your name isn't helpful," Dahlen replied, "but I meant who are you and those men?"

"You mean as a whole?" Maleya clarified. "We call ourselves Bame le gochen, the Ghosts of Vwemir. We have been chahged with gua-ding this fohest and the ba-xium that it holds."

Dahlen gave a small laugh through her nose.

"Our society has been pwefohming this task since Bame's last coming," Maleya explained.

"Bame meaning Vremir?" Dahlen asked.

Maleya gave a nod. "We have been told ovah the yeahs you would come. It had been fohtold by the first pu-rophet when he came to visit our people many yeahs ago."

Dahlen frowned. "Strahm Mahrkai came here?"

Maleya nodded. "It was he who found the mine. Meht was not yet inhabited back then. It was befoh Sha banished our people heah."

"Vron?"

Maleya gave another nod.

A brief silence came over them as they continued to walk.

"The opal you have," Maleya started, "I heard you tell Paya it was a gift from Bame?"

"Paya is the shopkeeper from Hese?" Dahlen verified.

"Yes."

Dahlen nodded. "Yes, it was a gift from Vremir," she told her. "He gave it to me before I left on my journey here."

Maleya let out a sigh of relief, a broad smile encompassing her face. "Then it has happened," she said softly. "He has come back. Bame has come back."

Dahlen gave a small nod. "Yes," she responded quietly. "Vremir has returned as promised."

"And you know him? You have met with him?" Maleya asked, the excitement apparent in her voice.

Dahlen cleared her throat. "I traveled with him for several months."

"I envy you the honah of being in his pu-resence foh so long," Maleya stated. "And it was Bame who sent you on this mission?"

Dahlen rubbed her lips together. "Yes," she lied. "And he gave me this red opal for protection. Though I had no idea what it was capable of."

"He gave a piece of himself to you," Maleya said. "His powahs flow thu-rough that opal."

Dahlen looked down at the opal still clutched in her hand now in need of another leather strap as the old one was incinerated with the man. It glowed gently as she held it, a small little beacon in the dark forest and she sighed. Dohrrn had saved her again and he wasn't even with her.

His power flows through that opal. Maleya was right. Dohrrn *had* given her a piece of himself and she had turned her back on him.

A feeling close to shame flushed her cheeks.

"We are heah," Maleya proclaimed as they came to a clearing several yards upstream from the waterfall.

Dahlen and the others looked around them, confusion riddling their faces. There was nothing there. There weren't any traces of fires, or discarded food, or any disturbance of any kind.

"I think your camp left you," The Viper said.

Maleya gave a small laugh. "You ah not looking hahd enough," she told him. She crouched down and reached into a pile of leaves, opening a hatch as she stood. "If we ah to be ghosts," she explained, "we must stay hidden."

Dahlen exchanged glances with her traveling companions before she entered the underground bunker. The smell of damp earth surrounded her as she descended, and the air cooled dramatically. Oil lamps lit a long hallway as she reached the bottom, and she paused to take it all in. She looked up at the tall ceiling, seeing the dangling roots of trees and plants and what looked to be small patches of sunlight.

"Those ah othah hatches for ventilation," Maleya pointed out, noticing her quizzical look. "It helps keep fu-resh air coming in."

Dahlen nodded.

"This is pretty remarkable," The Viper commented as he looked around.

"Come," Maleya said with a smile, "I will show you wheah you can rrest."

"Rest?" Dahlen repeated. "I think we still have a lot more questions."

Maleya nodded. "Yes, of couhse you do," she replied. "But first, you should rrest and eat."

Maleya continued to lead them down the hallway of her underground hideout which eventually branched off into several different sections. She made a second right down another hallway with doors on either side of the walls. She took them to the last four doors at the end of the hall.

"I hope you will find these chambahs to your liking," she told them as she opened the first door, and, borrowing one of the lamps from the hall, lit several in the room, illuminating it.

The four of them stared at the well-furnished room complete with bed, desk and water basin. Tapestries adorned the walls and furs the floor. It was a lot cozier than they were expecting an underground room to have been.

"This is nicer than the inns we have been staying in," Tristan muttered.

The others nodded.

Maleya lit the lamps in the three rooms. "I will have watah bu-rought to you all so you can fu-reshen up. Dinnah should be rready in a few hours." She turned to leave.

"Maleya," Dahlen said, stopping her. "I truly appreciate the hospitality, but we don't have time to stay here. We have to get to the mine."

Maleya smiled. "And you will," she told her. "We know your mission is impohtant, but so is what we have to tell you."

Dahlen creased her brow.

"Rrest," Maleya softly commanded. "I will be back soon."

Despite Maleya having given them four separate rooms, they gathered in one to reassess where they were. The Defiant immediately kicked off her shoes and jumped on the bed, while The Viper took the chair in front of the desk and Tristan leaned against the earthen wall. Dahlen paced for a few minutes before sitting on the foot of the bed next to The Defiant.

"I think there have been a few holes in what you have told us," The Defiant said, breaking the silence first. She propped herself up against the headrest. "Or what you have chosen to tell us."

"What did you mean when you told her you traveled with Vremir for several months?" Tristan asked.

Dahlen rubbed her mouth with her fingertips as she thought. "I meant just that," she replied. "Vremir has returned. He is living and breathing and walking around and," she took a deep breath, letting it out in a huff, "and I have spent about a year with him traveling and hiding from the Order of Zeln."

"Why didn't you tell us this before?" Tristan asked sounding perturbed.

"I told you he returned," Dahlen defended herself. "I didn't withhold that."

"Yes, but you failed to mention the close proximity in which you have lived with him," The Defiant clarified.

"What difference would that have made?" Dahlen retorted.

"It shows the lack of trust you have in us, for one," Tristan stated.

The Defiant shrugged. "What is the issue with telling us in the first place?"

Dahlen shook her head slightly. "Because Vremir is still vulnerable," she replied. "He is not what you would expect the god of fire to look like. He's—"

"He's a child," The Viper interjected. "The god of fire is a child."

"What?" The Defiant said.

Dahlen looked over at The Viper.

He smirked at her. "You didn't think I would figure it out, did you?" he asked, winking.

Dahlen cleared her throat. "Tristan, you would not have heard about this, but The Viper and The Defiant might," she began. "Eight years ago, a Mehtian pirate ship wrecked off of the coast of Dead Man's Rest. The only survivor was a pregnant woman that swam to shore. Not long after she was rescued, she gave birth to a baby boy, but having been so weak from the wreck, the mother died."

The Defiant nodded. "I do remember that," she said. "That was the year I was titled. I had been out on a training expedition, but I remember hearing about it when I returned."

Dahlen nodded. "That child was raised by The Wind, one of The Leaders, and was going to enter into the coven as another brother, but upon my release, I asked to take him with me."

"So, what are you saying?" Tristan asked. "You're saying that that child is Vremir?"

Dahlen nodded. "Yes," she responded. "I did not know it at the time. I thought he was just another kid, but fate, destiny, or coincidence brought us together."

Tristan shook his head. "So, Vremir is an eight-year old boy?"

"Yes, born of a Mehtian pirate woman."

"And you didn't want to tell us because you are protecting him?" The Defiant added.

"The Order has ears everywhere," Dahlen explained. "It's true even for his age, Doh- Vremir is capable of awesome power, but the use of that power weakens him and he needs time to recover. He is the god of fire, but, in many ways, he is still a child."

"I saw him turn a grown man into a pile of ashes in seconds," The Viper added, making an exploding gesture with his hands.

"What else have you not told us?" Tristan asked.

"Nothing that would make a difference to our current circumstance," she replied.

The Defiant narrowed her eyes at Dahlen and then The Viper. "Back in Ganavan, when we all first met up, The Viper said he was hired to kill you."

Dahlen looked over her shoulder at her. "That's true."

"Then why aren't you dead?"

Neither The Viper nor Dahlen replied.

"There are only a few reasons why you would not be," The Defiant continued. "Either you killed The Viper, which is obviously not the case, or," she paused and stood from the bed, "something rendered the contract void, something based on moral grounds." She looked from Dahlen to The Viper, studying their faces.

Dahlen looked back at her, her expression stoic, yet her body rigid with tension.

The Defiant opened her mouth to speak when there was a knock at the door.

"Come in," Dahlen said.

An older woman with a cart came in bowing and smiling. "Clean watah foh drink and wash," she explained in a broken version of the shared language. She moved to the water basin and filled it before carting her way to the next room.

"Thank you," Dahlen said to her as she stood from the bed.

The woman gave another bow.

"I am going to take Maleya's advice," Dahlen told the others. "I am going to wash up and rest before dinner." She paused at the door. "I apologize if my leaving out information seems distrusting. I only did it to protect those involved. I hope you can look past the disrespect you must feel and find understanding behind it."

Tristan followed her out of the room. "Dahlen," he said going into one of the rooms with her and closing the door behind him, "why bring me if you are only going to keep things from me?"

"Tristan," Dahlen replied a little exasperated, "I have already told you, I was trying to protect Vremir. Vron has been roaming the realm for centuries, slowly regaining his power, but Vremir has only just started to use his. The Bornnenians have a soothsayer. If she has a vision about one of our conversations referring to Vremir, then it could all be over. There will be no one to challenge Vron and the world will once again fall under his control and then he will enslave us all." She threw her hands up. "Is that what you want? Because that is what I was trying to prevent."

Tristan didn't respond right away. "But there is more, isn't there? Something that happened during your time with Vremir."

Dahlen blinked at him, her eyes riddled with defiance.

Tristan moved closer to her. "Why did you bring me?" he asked again, in almost a whisper.

"You know why," Dahlen replied. "Mahk led me to you."

Tristan shook his head. "But you could have walked away," he told her taking another step towards her. "When you saw it was me, you could have walked away. Why didn't you?"

She shrugged. "We have unfinished business," she said, her skin tingling as the tension between them rose. "I promised you I would kill you one day."

Tristan gave a small laugh. "No," he replied taking the last few steps between them. "It's because you wanted me here."

Dahlen narrowed her eyes at him. "You're wrong."

"I don't think I am," he replied reaching out to put his hand on her waist. He put his mouth up to her ear. "I think you feel something for me," he whispered.

She shivered. "Repulsion," she replied, in a shaky voice, her body quivering.

"Then why haven't you pushed me away yet?" Tristan asked not giving her enough time to answer as he pressed his lips against hers.

The kiss was hard and intense, and Dahlen could feel it through her whole body, but not because of passion or feelings for Tristan; it was a release from the tension and adrenaline, a release from the near death they all faced earlier that day, a release from the emptiness she felt inside.

Dahlen allowed him to pull her closer, one hand gently cupping the back of her neck, the other firmly on her lower back. She kissed him back, her body aching as she pulled on his tunic. Tristan moved them closer to the bed as his lips trailed down her neck.

Dahlen closed her eyes conceding to her deep need for human contact as he gently laid her on the bed. He hovered over her, loosening the belt that held her tunic in place, finding more skin to kiss.

Dahlen let out a small gasp, not knowing if she wanted or *needed* what was happening. Tristan's lips found hers again, and she pulled him to her, her hands trailing up his arms. She stopped when one of her hands ran over a warm, wet spot on his bicep.

She pulled away a second and looked at her hand now covered in blood.

"Tristan, you're bleeding," she said looking up at him wide eyed. She gently pushed him off of her, finally noticing the dark stain that ran down the sleeve of his tunic.

"It's just a scratch," he told her. "I'm fine."

Dahlen got up from the bed, retightening her belt. "Take your shirt off," she ordered.

He smiled subtly. "I was planning on doing that anyway," he replied, but as he stood from the bed to comply, the color rushed from his face and he fell to the floor.

CHAPTER 23

TRISTAN CAME TO A COUPLE OF HOURS LATER WITH DAHLEN GLARING angrily at him. He shot her a weak smile.

"How did I do?" he asked groggily.

"You are an idiot," she told him flatly.

"That bad, huh?"

"Why didn't you tell anyone that you had been hurt?" she scolded him.

He shrugged. "I didn't want to slow us down," he replied. "And I honestly didn't think it was that bad."

"That bad?" she repeated heatedly. "You had a six-inch gash on your bicep."

Tristan swallowed. "It didn't hurt, then."

Dahlen shook her head. "You are an idiot," she said again.

"Yes, so you have already told me." He groaned and pressed his hand to his forehead.

"Does your head hurt?" Dahlen asked indifferently.

"It could feel better," he replied.

She laughed through her nose. "That's what you get letting the blood rush from one head to the other."

"I didn't see you complaining," he shot back.

Dahlen cleared her throat and folded her hands in her lap. "Whatever happened or didn't happen earlier," she began, "will never be spoken of again. It was a mistake."

"You truly think that ill of me?" he asked softly.

She didn't reply right away. "That has nothing to do with it, Tristan," she finally told him. She took in a deep breath through her nose and let it out slowly. "I just don't think it is—" she struggled to find what she was trying to say. "I cannot be distracted from my mission," she finally decided on. "It has nothing to do with what I think or feel toward you."

"So, you're saying there's a chance?" he asked trying to lighten the mood.

She blinked at him, a stern look on her face.

Tristan let out a sigh. "Understood," he replied without a fight. He looked down at his arm, the wound cleaned and stitched closed. "Do I have you to thank for this?"

"No," Dahlen responded, standing. "Maleya is not only the daughter of the chief, she is also a talented healer." She shook her head. "It was very stupid of you not to say anything. You could have died."

"I swore the cut was not that bad," he replied stubbornly.

"No, but the infection would have been," she stated sternly. She sighed and moved to the door. "We are going to sit with the elders. They have invited us to dinner. You, however, are to remain here and rest. Food will be brought to you."

"That is not necessary, Dahlen," he argued struggling to sit up in the bed. "I am perfectly capable of— whoa." He took a deep breath and let it out slowly as he fell back onto his pillow. "Yeah, I think I am going to stay here."

"I will inform you of what goes on at dinner," she told him. "We can talk later." She walked out of the room and closed the door behind her.

Maleya and the other two had been waiting for her out in the hall.

"I hope you all have a good appetite," she smiled. "Come, the othahs ah waiting."

Maleya led them through the earthen labyrinth down several winding halls to a large round room with a massive, round table in the middle. Seven men, including Paya, and women stood expectantly behind their chairs shrouded in long brown robes. They smiled at their guests.

"Welcome," said one of the women.

The three of them bowed.

"Please, be seated," the woman gestured.

Dahlen, The Defiant, and The Viper did as they were told, their hosts sitting as well. Maleya took a seat next to The Viper who gave her a lingering side glance.

"I hope my daughtah has pwovided what you need to be comfohtable," the woman said.

Dahlen started for a moment. "Yes," she replied, regaining her composure. "Your daughter has shown us every kindness. Am I to presume you are the chief?"

The woman gave another small smile and nodded. "Yes," she replied in a soft voice. "My name is Fala and I am chief of Bame le gochen. And you," she started, "you ah the chosen one."

Dahlen gave a nod. "Yes."

"I apologize foh our attack on you," Fala said with sincerity. "Our mission is to gauhd the bahxium and we do so without bias. But we also have a mission to help you."

"There is no apology needed," she told her. "We only regret that it ended with the loss of some of your men."

Fala shook her head and waved her hand, gently dismissing Dahlen's concern. "They died foh theah mission," she explained. "It was a death they could hope foh."

Dahlen nodded out of respect.

Food was then served. Platters of green vegetables and mushrooms were placed on the table before them along with a variety of nuts, flowers and what appeared to be roasted beetles.

"I apologize if our food is not what you ah used to," Fala said. "We do not eat meat."

Dahlen shook her head. "What you have to offer is gratefully received."

The Viper shrugged, reaching for one of the beetles. "I assure you, we have been forced to survive on a lot worse than bugs," he added popping it in his mouth.

The Defiant eyed one of the young women who brought them the platters. "There is nothing wrong with beetles," she said returning her attention as the girl left the room. "Plenty of nutrition in them."

They fell into intervals of silence and polite conversation as they ate, their words forced and meaningless. Everything being said except what they were all there for.

"Forgive me, Chief Fala," Dahlen said after inquiries on where they were from were over, "not that I don't appreciate your hospitality, but I believe you have some information for me."

The chief nodded. "You are quite right." She looked at Paya and held out her hand.

Paya stood and cleared his throat. "Sev-rral days ago, we came upon an assembly of men. Theah weah about twenty-five of them. They weah wea-rring yellow and black clothing and mahched undah a yellow and black bannah with a—"

"Black hawk?" Dahlen interrupted.

Paya nodded. "You know of the Ohdah then?"

"They murdered my mother," Dahlen replied. "And not too long ago they chased me down and tried to kill me. If Vremir had not been there," she paused a second, "they would have succeeded."

"Then you have seen them fight?"

Dahlen nodded. "I know they are elite warriors."

"A group of our men, managed in killing only five of theahs while they killed all thehty of them," Paya told her.

The Viper gave a small cough. "They killed all thirty of your men?" he asked after he regained his voice.

Paya nodded. "Our watchman saw it all with hoh-rrah. Theah was nothing that could have been done. He said he watched as they toh-chad one of our men foh infohmation. Foh hours they hung him up in a churee just low enough so his toes could touch the gurround and beat him."

Anger flared through Dahlen as she remembered the torture Marten experienced not too long ago at the hands of the Order. They too strung him up in a tree and beat him mercilessly. It took months for him to fully recover.

"Thankfully, our man stayed honoh-rrable until the last," Paya concluded. "He was a good ghost."

"How long ago did this happen?" Dahlen inquired after a moment.

"Less than two weeks," he replied.

She nodded. "Do you know where they are now?"

"We have been watching them," Paya replied. "They made it to the mine ovah a week ago."

Dahlen's heart dropped. "We have to stop them," she said heatedly. "Why are you just watching them instead of attacking them?"

"Because moh have ah-rrived since our last encountah," Fala replied, stepping in. "Theah ah now fohty men in theah ga-rroup."

"Forty?" Dahlen repeated, bewildered. She exchanged glances with The Defiant and The Viper.

"Yes," Paya replied. "I have seen them myself."

Dahlen took a deep breath. "And how many warriors do you have?"

"We might have fifty oh moh." Paya told her. "Some, howevah, ah still young. They have no expear-ance in actual combat."

Dahlen gave a small nod. "And now you have us."

Paya smiled. "And now we have you."

"So what is the plan then?" The Defiant asked breaking in. "How far away is the mine and what course of action are we looking at?"

"The mine is anothah day and a half away," Paya answered. "As foh a plan, we have none yet."

Dahlen exchanged glances with The Viper and The Defiant. "You said you are watching them," she said turning back to Fala and Paya. "What is their layout? How is their camp set up?"

"Their tents are set up in a circulah position and set on the hill ovahlooking the mine," Paya replied. "They have high gurround on all sides."

"How many men do they have patrolling?" The Viper asked.

"Shifts of no moh than ten."

"And who is doing the mining?" The Defiant jumped in. "Is the Order doing it themselves?"

Paya's lips curled into a mischievous smile. "They have not found its opening yet."

Dahlen blinked at him for a moment. "What do you mean?"

"The coh-rect entu-rrance to the mine is hidden," Fala explained. "Bame le gochen ah the only ones who know wheah it is. Theah ah sev-rral false ones, but only one leads to the haht of the mine."

Dahlen nodded. "That's why you haven't attacked them," she said. "There is no need yet."

"Fohtunately, yes, theah has been no need," Fala replied. "Had they found the entu-rrance, we would have fought until our last man."

"We thank the goddesses foh theah pwotection," Maleya said with a slight bow of her head.

"Maheyo san Jiwane," the ghosts all murmured with a nod.

Thanks be to the Goddesses.

"But it is only a mattah of time until they find it," Fala stated. "We must act soon befoh it is too late."

Dahlen exchanged glances with the other two in her group and nodded. She then took a deep breath and let it out slowly. "So, we leave first thing in the morning then?"

CHAPTER 24

Tristan had not been happy to learn he was not going with them.

"What the hell did you bring me for then?" he asked after Dahlen finished explaining what had taken place at dinner and their plans to leave the next morning.

"What do you expect to do, Tristan?" she questioned back. "You're injured. You are much better off here recovering than getting yourself killed."

He scowled at her. "Don't you think that decision is mine to make?"

Dahlen shook her head at him. "No," she told him sternly. "You will stay here and recover and pray and learn from these people, but you will not be joining us tomorrow."

Tristan opened his mouth to talk when Dahlen cut him off.

"I am not going to risk the rest of our lives taking you with us. If you cannot defend yourself, then you cannot help defend us. My word is final." She stood from her chair and left without another word.

A few hours before the sun rose through the trees, Dahlen, The Viper, The Defiant, Maleya, Paya and an assembly of their best warriors left the comforts of their earthen sanctuary. All of them clad in the brown, leaf-covered garbs of the Bame le gochen.

The large group moved silently, yet, swiftly through the forest, paralleling the path as they used the forest as cover, their figures disappearing amongst the thick brush. Many of the ghosts swung from tree to tree.

For hours they moved through the forest, barely stopping to rest until the sun was high in the sky. Paya, who was leading them, put his hand up and made a fist, causing the whole group to stop. He then made a low whistling noise, waiting quietly for a response.

He was answered by the same call as several other ghosts emerged from their hiding places in front of them.

"Paheni!" Paya called.

Brothers!

The men and women bowed to each other.

"What news do you bring?" Paya asked them in Mehtian.

The watchmen exchanged glances with each other before a toughened woman stepped forward.

"When we left their campsite yesterday there had been new developments," she replied. "They still have not found the entrance, thank the eternal four. However," she said with a small smirk, "they have discovered a few of the traps."

The others in her group chuckled.

"At least ten of them have died, and another seven are injured," she continued. "But, two days ago, more of them arrived."

"How many more?" Paya asked.

She shook her head. "It was not a great amount. However, there was this man that arrived with them. He was not wearing the same garbs as the rest of the Order. He was wearing the colors of Bornnen."

Paya frowned. "What of this man?"

"He seemed to be giving the other men orders," the women told him. "We think he might be in charge."

Paya nodded.

"Do you understand what they are saying?" Dahlen whispered to The Viper.

He nodded. "They are talking about some guy from Bornnen that arrived the other day and began barking orders at the Order."

"Bornnen?" Dahlen repeated.

"Yeah," The Viper continued. "He's apparently very tall and rough looking."

"That's everyone from Bornnen," The Defiant muttered.

"Maleya," Dahlen said quietly, calling her over.

Maleya smiled at her and complied.

"How close are we to the mine?" she asked her.

"Soon, we will come to an incline," Maleya started. "Once we come to the peak, we will camp foh the night. Then it is anothah foh houahs befoh we ah at the mine."

"So, what are the sleeping arrangements?" The Viper asked her. "Are they co-ed? Do we have sleeping buddies or—"

Dahlen hit him over the head.

"Ow!" He rubbed his head, shooting Dahlen a small scowl.

Maleya gave a small laugh. "We mostly sleep in the churees so we ah not easy game foh the jaguahs."

"You know, a campfire would also keep them away," The Viper told her.

Maleya gave him a sly smile. "A fiah would defeat the pur-pos of staying concealed."

The Defiant snorted while Dahlen shot him a glare.

The Viper cleared his throat. "Yes, obviously," he replied.

"Manye, chicheya!" Paya called out.

"He wants us to continue," The Viper said regaining his composure.

Just as Maleya had said, they soon came to an incline and the trees began to thin out as the terrain became rockier, but this did not seem to slow down the Bame le gochen as they continued to swiftly climb to the top.

Tristan certainly would not have been able to keep up, was a thought that ran through Dahlen's head more than once.

Finally, after a few hours and a steady incline, they reached where they were going to camp. The mountain looked over a vast valley that came to another, smaller slope, with the sea glistening to the south.

"Theah," Paya pointed out. "The hill is wheah the camp is."

Dahlen nodded. "And the mine?"

Paya smirked. "They ah on top of it."

Dahlen blinked. "The mine is under their camp?"

He nodded. "They have no idea. They have been looking ah-rround it, but they have not discovahed it."

"How are we going to get down there unobserved?" Dahlen asked, noticing the thin line of trees that led to the sea on one side and the mountain that surrounded the valley in a 'U' shape on the other."

"We have a system of caves that rruns below the valley," Paya explained. "The entrrance to this is at the bottom of this mountain."

Dahlen nodded. "And does this system of caves also run underneath their camp?"

He shook his head. "No, they do not join."

Dahlen shrugged. "Of course, they don't," she mumbled. "That would have been too easy." She took a deep breath. "So, what is the plan?"

"I say we wait until dark tomorrow and slit their throats as they sleep," The Defiant voiced as she came up to them.

"Kill as many men as we can without raising an alarm," The Viper added. "Easiest course. Take out the guards so the rest of us can sneak in and—"

"To kill a man while he sleeps is to kill without honah," Paya replied sounding offended.

The Defiant made a sucking noise with her teeth. "Funny thing about assassins," she began, "we don't usually kill for honor."

Dahlen cleared her throat and shot The Defiant a stern look. "Though I understand your plight, Paya, or your hesitancy, The Defiant's plan is not a bad one. We stand better chances if we take them completely off guard than if we just ambush them. With them being on higher ground on all sides, we are at a great disadvantage."

Paya shook his head. "These men ah war-yahs and that kind of death is not suitable."

"Paya," Dahlen started, "we are past what is suitable. Do you think the Order would show you the same kindness?" She shook her head. "They kill unarmed women and children while they sleep, so what honor do they deserve?"

"Listen to her," Maleya said softly as she approached. "She speaks out of expear-ance."

Paya glared off to the side. "It goes against our teachings."

Maleya put a gentle hand on his shoulder, a gesture that was not lost on The Viper. "Sometimes we have to base our decisions on oth-ah's teachings, not our own."

Paya huffed.

"It is bettah this way," Maleya added.

"Bame le gochen ah not assassins," he replied gruffly, shaking off her hand. "We ah gauhdians."

"And as such, we must defend our mission at all costs," Maleya answered matter-of-factly. "A loss of honah is nothing compared to the loss of life we will suffah othahwise."

"And what will we tell Fala?" he argued. "What will she say when we tell her that we cut the thu-roats of these men while they slept? It will shame us."

"Fala will undahstand," Maleya told him, standing her ground. "These men ah not just some fohtune huntahs. They ah not here foh gold oh jewels. They ah heah to take bah-xium to Sha and we must stop that at all costs."

Paya glared at her. "You do as you like," he told her. "But I will not kill men as they sleep." He turned and stormed off.

"Your, uh, husband seems pretty angry," The Viper said, making The Defiant and Dahlen lift a brow in his direction.

"Husband?" Maleya repeated. "He is not my husband. He is my uncle."

"Oh, uncle," he said with a nod. "Nice, nice."

Dahlen sighed. "Is Paya not in charge?" she asked, a little concerned. "If he is, and he does not help us, will the others refuse to as well?"

Maleya gave a smile as she often did. "Paya is not in chahge," she told them. "I am." She took a step toward the edge of the cliff overlooking the valley. "Paya does lead his ghosts, but as long as I am heah, I have final say."

"So, what are you going to do now that he has defied you?" The Viper asked.

Maleya shook her head. "He has not defied me. He is just wanting to stick to our ways," she explained. "Bame le gochen ah men and women of honah. Paya is a ghost and he can be nothing else."

Dahlen nodded. "We understand," she replied. "We all have our own honor system. The Viper, do we not?" She turned and looked at him.

He nodded. "Yes. You cannot blame a man for sticking to his morals."

Maleya smiled again. "Paya is very stubbohn, but he will come to see things your way."

The Defiant shrugged. "He could at least lead the team to take out the guards," she suggested. "They shouldn't be sleeping."

"Yes, I will tell him this," Maleya replied. "Foh now, we should get some sleep. We have had a long day and we have anothah ahead of us." She gave a shallow bow and left.

The Viper moved to follow her when both Dahlen and The Defiant put a hand on his chest.

"Where do you think you are going?" Dahlen asked him.

The Viper shrugged. "I was going to, uh, see if she," he cleared his throat, "needed help with anything. Like bedding her—help with her bedding," he corrected. "I am going to see if she needs help setting up her bedding."

"If you're feeling so helpful," Dahlen started, handing him her pack, "you can help me set up mine."

The Defiant smirked at him.

"What?" he asked sulkily.

"You are way too obvious," she told him taking off her own pack and handing it to him as well. "I think that tree over there looks nice and sturdy for my bed."

"Hey," he said as the both of them started walking away. "Where are you going?"

"To eat," Dahlen replied over her shoulder. "You can join us when you are done setting up our beds and start thinking with the head on your shoulders."

The Viper huffed. "That will be never," he muttered to himself.

The group once again rose hours before the sun to start their journey, moving surefootedly along the line of trees down the slope of the mountain. At the mountain's edge, Paya lifted a hidden trap door, much like the one to their camp, and they slipped down into the darkness of the caves. Unlike the earthen walls of the camp, however, these walls were stone and wet with moisture.

"Come," Paya said a little bitterly. "We must move quickly."

The group pressed on, the light from the torches barely breaking through the darkness of the path.

"Stay close to the wall," Paya commanded, his voice echoing off of the stones. "Theah ah undahgurround cliffs at the next bend."

As if on cue, the ground beneath Maleya gave way and she let out a small scream as she began to fall. The Viper quickly grasped her by the arm and pulled her back up, his arms tightening around her waist.

"I got you," he told her.

Maleya smiled, though shaking slightly from the close call. "Thank you," she told him. "You saved my life."

The Viper smiled back at her. "It was my pleasure," he replied.

"Maleya, ah you well?" Paya asked, looking back from the front of the line.

"Yes," she answered a little breathlessly. She thanked The Viper again who carefully released her when she noticed a small light gleaming from Dahlen's pocket. She pointed it out. "Your pocket is glowing."

Dahlen looked down and, sure enough, the pocket where she had her opal was glowing dimly. When she pulled the stone out, it illuminated the surrounding area, forcing the darkness back and revealing the vastness of the cave.

"Well, shit," The Defiant mumbled now able to see the depths of the cliff barley three feet in front of them.

"The gift of light from Bame," Maleya praised.

"That would have been helpful a few minutes ago," The Viper whispered.

"I didn't know it glowed this brightly," Dahlen replied, shooting him a look. "It sometimes glowed softly at night, but nothing like this."

"It seems that stone does a lot moh than you thought it did," Maleya told her.

"Keep moving," Paya ordered.

The group trudged on, their hands trailing against the hard, wet wall of the cave as they avoided the edge of the cliff. Dahlen trailed behind Paya, the glowing red opal in the palm of her hand. For hours, they moved along the cave walls, avoiding cliff edges or gaps in the path until they finally came to a small incline.

"Ovah theah," Paya said pointing. "That is wheah we shall emahge from the cave. But we must be cautious. It is close to wheah they ah camped."

As they approached the entrance, Paya held up his hand.

"You wait," he commanded. "I will make sure it is safe."

Dahlen nodded. "Be careful."

Paya gave a curt nod before disappearing into the darkness.

"How long do you think he will have us wait?" The Defiant asked.

Dahlen shrugged. "He seems to be in a hurry."

"He seems to be a little bitter about our plan," The Viper commented before biting into an apple he pulled from his pack.

Dahlen brushed back one of her curls. "Yes, he did not agree with our plan whatsoever."

The Defiant shrugged. "He will thank us once he sees that it is much easier than letting the Order slaughter all of his men and women."

"Yes, and perhaps he is angry for no reason," Dahlen replied, shifting where she stood.

"What do you mean?" The Viper asked, creasing his brow and wiping the apple juice from his chin.

"When was the last time a plan of yours came into fruition?" Dahlen answered. "I am sure most of your ventures have been successful, but how often does a plan of yours come together without a hiccup?"

The Viper looked thoughtful for a moment, taking another bite of his apple. "So, you are saying our plan is going to fall apart?"

Dahlen shook her head. "I am saying that," she paused to sigh, "I don't know what I am saying. I just have a feeling that this isn't going to be easy."

The Defiant gave a small laugh through her nose. "Nothing worth doing is easy."

"Well said," The Viper commented, pointing at The Defiant with the hand holding the apple.

"Your apple has a worm," Dahlen pointed out.

The Viper inspected his apple and shrugged as he took another bite.

"Are you having doubts about our plan?" The Defiant asked bringing them back on topic.

Dahlen pressed her lips together for a moment. "No," she replied. "I think, for right now, especially not having seen their camp layout firsthand, it makes sense. It's difficult to gain the element of surprise running up hill."

"Then what are you so hesitant about?" The Defiant pressed.

Dahlen shook her head. "It's just a feeling that we don't have all of the information yet."

"You think Paya is holding out on us?" The Viper asked.

"No, I do not think Paya is doing anything of the kind," she told him. "There is just something we don't know yet. I can feel it."

The Viper nodded. "Like, one of the gods or goddesses is telling you something."

Dahlen took a deep breath and let it out slowly. "Actually, I think this might just be good old-fashioned intuition."

"Come now," Paya's voice whispered through the darkness. "The path is cleah."

Dahlen and the other two exchanged glances before nodding and following the voice of Paya with Maleya and the rest of the Bame le gochen in their wake.

"There were no scouts or guards?" Dahlen asked as she met up with Paya at the hatch.

"No," he told her. "I spoke with anothah ghost and they infohmed me the guads ah not back this fah."

She nodded as she pulled up the hood of her cloak. "Let us do this then."

DAHLEN COULD FEEL HER ENTIRE BODY TINGLE, HER SKIN PRICKLING with a flood of emotions; a mix of anticipation and anger made her shake as she looked down on the camp of the Order. She watched them from the high branches of a tree, disappearing into its foliage as she looked down on them. She could see them moving about, searching for the entrance to the mine, arguing amongst themselves, laughing or joking with one another.

"Heah," Maleya whispered beside her.

Dahlen looked over at her, a scowl on her face.

"Take this and look," Maleya told her.

Dahlen took the item proffered to her and gave Maleya a confused look. "What is this?"

"It is a looking glass," she replied with a smile. "You put the small end to your eye and whatevah is in the distance will look closah."

Dahlen pressed the object to her eye and looked through almost immediately pulling away from it. She looked at Maleya. "This is incredible."

Maleya nodded. "Yes, almost like magic."

Dahlen put the looking glass back up to her eye.

"Be cautious," Maleya warned. "Do not let the lens catch the light of the sun. It will give your position away."

Dahlen nodded as she scanned the Order's camp, amazed at how close they seemed through the looking glass. She looked from one man to the other, taking in the features of their faces until she hit on one she had seen before.

She pulled the looking glass from her eye and sat straight up in the tree, the color draining from her face.

"What is the mattah?" Maleya asked.

Dahlen swallowed hard and took another look to be sure she actually saw what she thought she did. But there was no mistaking it the second time she looked. The Bornnenian the ghost from yesterday had mentioned was General Ohtt. The man who took over Bornnen after she assassinated the late King Ahlenwei. The man who had once captured her and almost sold her to the Order.

What was he doing there?

CHAPTER 25

"General Ohtt?" The Viper said in surprise when Dahlen told them later.

Dahlen nodded as she paced the entrance to the cave they had emerged from earlier. "I saw him."

The Defiant shook her head. "What difference does that make?" she asked. "It should not change our plans to slit their throats while they sleep."

Dahlen sighed. "I know, but something about it makes me uneasy," she replied.

"Is he not supposed to be running Bornnen until King Ahlenwei's heir comes of age?" The Viper asked.

The Defiant laughed. "That boy will never come of age," she told them.

The other two looked at her.

"Seriously?" she said a little taken aback by their ignorance. "Prince Alihen is dead. You must know that."

"Why do you think so?" Dahlen asked.

The Defiant cleared her throat. "Do you know The Hawk?"

Dahlen and The Viper nodded.

"Several months ago, he was hired to find the prince and bring him safely to Thren," The Defiant explained.

"To Thren?" The Viper repeated.

"Apparently, his mother was a distant cousin of King Caston's. So, he hired The Hawk to take him from the clutches of Ohtt and his men and bring him to Thren where he would be safe."

"But?" Dahlen added when The Defiant hesitated.

"But," she continued, "there was no trace of the boy. No one had seen or heard from him almost since his father's death." She shook her head. "King Caston had even sent Ohtt a letter asking for his whereabouts."

"How long ago was this exactly?" Dahlen inquired, her brows furrowed.

The Defiant shrugged. "The Hawk told me this a few months before I left for Ganavan. Maybe eight months ago?"

"That must have been why Bornnen attacked Thren," Dahlen speculated.

"I suppose so," The Defiant agreed. "Ohtt couldn't let the fact he is a child murderer get out."

Dahlen shook her head. "No, it's different than that. Ohtt doesn't care about being titled a child murderer. It's because King Caston challenged him. He was trying to flex his power."

The Defiant nodded. "That attack was unsuccessful, was it not?"

"Fortunately, yes," Dahlen replied.

"Didn't Princess Rain give birth during this attack?" The Viper asked.

Dahlen felt her heart drop. "Yes, I believe she did."

"Though I heard the Bornnenians tried their best to kill her and the child," The Defiant added.

The Viper studied Dahlen for a moment. She had never told him what had become of her baby and he had known better than to ask. But he could tell the comment about Princess Rain's child made her uncomfortable.

"Well," Dahlen said with a forced smile, "since when have you ever known a Bornnenian to do anything right?"

"I STILL THINK WE CAN WIN IF WE ATTACK THEM WITH HONAH," PAYA said an hour before nightfall.

They had all met back in the cave to discuss the plan.

"And what?" The Viper said with a shrug. "We get slaughtered by them as we try to rush up the hill? They will pick us off with bows before we even reach the top."

Paya scowled at him.

"Paya," Dahlen said gently, "we cannot afford to lose this. Now, I understand if you do not want to fully participate, but we will need you and the rest of your ghosts close in case something goes awry."

"And you and the othah men ah needed to take out the guahds," Maleya added.

Dahlen nodded. "Now, do we have a sufficient number of ghosts in the surrounding trees with their bows?"

"The bow is a cowahd's weapon," Paya grumbled.

"Paya!" Maleya said sternly.

He gave a nod. "Yes, theah ah ten of our best ahchahs positioned wheah you suggested."

Dahlen nodded.

"So, we have ten men in the trees, ten men taking out guards, and ten including the three of us slipping into tents and slitting throats," The Viper calculated. "That leaves another fifteen or so more on standby."

"I say we are ready," The Defiant said with a twisted smile.

THEY WAITED A FEW HOURS AFTER NIGHTFALL, WHEN THE CAMP HAD been quiet and all of the candles had been snuffed out before they put their plan into action.

Clad in all black, Dahlen and her group waited for their signal to advance. The night was dark and humid and the sound of chirping crickets and buzzing cicadas only seemed to intensify it all. The night was still; the only movement was the intermittent swooping of bats as they caught a bug. It did not take long, however, for the signal, the low hooting of an owl, to break through the sound of the crickets and cicadas.

"Let's move," Dahlen whispered emerging from the woods and swiftly making her way up the hill, the others not far behind.

There were fifteen tents in total and, according to the watchmen, each tent held no more than three men with the exception of some of the men higher in rank, including Ohtt, who had tents of their own. At least ten men had died from the boobytraps set up around the mine, five more injured. Another twenty men had arrived with Ohtt a few days before.

Fifty men, minus the ten guards Paya and his men took out. Forty healthy men. If all went according to plan, Dahlen and her team only needed to take out four per person. Simple in theory. They split up into groups of two, each group moving noiselessly to a tent.

Dahlen waited until every group was at a tent before she gave the signal to enter. They were all going to strike as closely together as possible. She raised her hand in the air and as she brought her arm down to give the go ahead, a dark shadow flew over her.

She thought for a second it was just another bat, but it had been too big. She looked up at the top of the tent and could just make out the figure of a hawk in the moonlight looking at her, a snake clutched in its talons.

Fear stabbed at her heart, causing her to choke on her own breath. She tried to call out to the others, but it was too late. The hawk let out a shrill squawk of alarm causing mass confusion to come over the camp.

Regaining control of herself, Dahlen yelled for backup as men ran from their tents, their weapons raised. The once silent night erupted into a cacophony of cries, clashing metal, and the sounds of arrows breaking through the air.

Dahlen cut her way through, trying to reach Ohtt's tent when she was struck on the side of her face. For a moment she blacked out, the noise of the battle turning to a persistent ringing in her ears. When she came to, she was being dragged by her hair. She struggled against her captor, but his grip only tightened.

She reached for one of her knives but they were gone and the more she moved, the more the man shook her as he dragged her along. Pain seared through her head but holding onto his wrist she twisted in his grip helping her to regain some footing. She kicked out his legs and he let out a small yell of surprise as he fell to the ground, his grip loosening enough for her to wrench free. They both stood and faced each other.

"We have been searching for you," the man said pulling out a curved sword. "And luck has brought you to us."

Dahlen checked herself again for a weapon but felt only the warmth of the red opal in her pocket. She took it out and smiled. "You are wrong," she replied. "Death has brought me to you." She threw the opal at him, aiming at his heart, but its less than subtle glow gave it away and he caught it with a laugh.

"Is that all you have left? A pebble?" he asked with a sneer. "It is a shame killing you is going to be so easy."

"Perhaps not," Dahlen said in reply as the man's eyes grew wide.

She watched as the man's sneer turned to a look of horror as his hand burst into flames. The man screamed as the fire spread over him, illuminating the darkness and, as his smoldering ashes fell, they scattered in the wind and onto the surrounding tents igniting them.

The 'woosh' of the flames ate through the canvas tents scattering the men caught between them. Dahlen gathered her stone and ran to the red tent in the back, the one Ohtt occupied. She knew he would not be in there but still she rushed in, searching for something as the sounds of fighting continued outside.

Using her opal as a torch, she searched his room, looking but not knowing what for. She flipped through his table of documents and maps, skimming through their pages when a stack of letters caught her eye on a small writing desk.

Dahlen moved over to them gently fingering them and as she picked them up, she noticed an unfinished letter underneath, one written by Ohtt himself. She quickly looked around her, making sure she was in fact alone before she picked up the stack of letters and stuffed them in her pocket and exited the tent.

She paused to take in the scene before her. Bodies littered the ground as flames licked the night sky, the tents that fed the fires vanished into them. She searched the bodies, hoping to find Ohtt among them but he was not there.

"Dahlen!" she heard The Defiant cry out.

Dahlen turned to see The Defiant waving her over to safety. She moved toward her, putting her arm up to shield her face from the flames. She pushed through the heat, jumping over the remains of men from both the Order and the ghosts. As she ran between the burning tents, the squawk of the hawk caught her attention and she stopped. She turned to see Ohtt between two burning tents walking toward her. His massive figure an intimidating sight.

"Seems we meet again, prophet," Ohtt sneered over the roaring of the flames.

"And I will slip through your hands as I did the other two times," she replied.

Ohtt laughed. "I let ya go on our first meetin'," he told her in a gruff voice. "I knew you were not the Skahrrian princess and could only 'ave been there for one reason."

Dahlen tried to mask the surprise she felt. "You let me kill King Ahlenwei so you could take over without a fight," she concluded.

Ohtt smiled. "You're rather clever."

"And who told you who I was?" she asked. "Was it your soothsayer?"

Ohtt's lip twitched. "Ya know about her then?" He nodded. "She comes in pretty handy. She's been keepin' tabs on ya for quite some time. But a little over a year ago, ya seemed to disappear."

"How did you escape Vorce's men when they freed me?" she asked.

"You mean when I captured ya?" He huffed. "I had ridden ahead to meet with the Order. A mistake on my part."

"Did you hire The Viper to kill me?" she asked, ignoring him.

He sneered. "If I wanted ya dead, I'd have done it meself when I had ya in my grasp."

She believed him.

"Dahlen!" she heard The Defiant shout again. "We have to go!"

Dahlen hesitated, not wanting to leave until Ohtt was dead.

He smiled at her, seeing her reason for not leaving. "It will be the death of ya," he told her pulling out a sword that was almost as long as she was tall.

Dahlen held her ground. "That's your plan then?" she half growled. "To kill me while I am unarmed? I know you couldn't care less about honor but I can't imagine you would be satisfied to kill me so easily."

He laughed. "Ya know me so well, do ya?" he replied letting his sword fall to the ground. He cracked his knuckles and rolled his shoulders.

Dahlen turned sideways, creating a smaller target, as she waited for Ohtt to charge.

"Will be a shame to kill ya," Ohtt told her. "You're such a pretty li'l thing."

Dahlen gave a small laugh as she gripped the opal in her hand.

"I might even keep ya alive for a while. Until I'm done with ya."

"Are you always this talkative?" Dahlen goaded, ignoring the continued cries of her companions.

"In a hurry to die, are we?" Ohtt let out a guttural laugh before he charged letting out a roar.

Dahlen took a deep breath to calm herself, ready to evade his attack when without warning, a gust of wind rushed over them, toppling one of the flaming tents onto Ohtt entangling him. Dahlen watched helplessly as he screamed.

Suddenly, the ground began to shake and the earth opened up, swallowing Ohtt, his screams dying as he plummeted into the darkness. Dahlen jumped back in surprise just as Paya took her by the arm.

"We must go!" he yelled. "The bahxium beneath us is melting."

"What?" Dahlen asked.

"It is not stable in this heat," he explained. "The mine is collapsing."

Dahlen allowed Paya to pull her from the hill as the ground began to rumble again and the mine began to collapse into itself. They both turned and watched as the hill disappeared into a cloud of fiery dust, lighting up the night sky.

"The beraxium," Dahlen said breathlessly. "What are we going to do now?"

Paya shook his head. "Theah is not much we can do," he told her. "The bahxium will most likely continue to behn foh sev-rral gena-rrations to come. It is not minable."

Dahlen cursed under her breath.

"It is small mattah," Paya consoled her. "Theah may not be bahxium for Bame, but that means theah is none for Sha eithah."

She nodded. "This cannot have been the only beraxium mine left," she said. "There has to be another. How are we going to release Mahk, Behr and Gher and give them the strength they need in order to defeat Vron?"

"Theah will be anothah way," Paya told her, patting her gently on the shoulder.

"Dahlen," The Defiant said coming up to her, an angry look on her face. "I need to show you something."

Dahlen followed The Defiant to where The Viper was crouched over a body dressed in the Order's colors. He looked up at her with concern as she approached.

"What is it?" she asked.

The Viper pulled back the dead man's sleeve to reveal the 'X' tattoo on his wrist.

Dahlen's breath caught in her throat and her stomach dropped. "The Order has men inside the coven."

"How many men did we lose?" Maleya asked approaching Paya as they regrouped.

"Twenty," he replied with a solemn nod.

"But, we ah successful?"

He nodded. "Yes," he told her. "What was left of the Ordah was seen leaving on a boat."

"I am soh-rry your plan did not wohk," Maleya said turning to Dahlen and her companions.

Dahlen gave a small nod, her gaze distant. "Plans often fall through," she replied distantly.

"Did you know that man?" Maleya asked nodding her head at the man in question.

Dahlen shook her head. "No," she replied. "He does not look familiar to me."

"I believe I have seen him a few times at the Rest," The Defiant chimed in. "Though I cannot recall his title."

"The Thorn," The Viper said distantly. "His title was The Thorn."

"You knew him then?" Dahlen asked.

He nodded. "He took me and other trainees on training trips." He took in a deep breath and let it out slowly. "This brother taught me how to survive in the wild."

"We must get word back to the coven," Dahlen said. "We have to let The Leaders know that we have traitors in our midst."

"There is no 'we,' Dahlen. You are no longer of the coven," The Defiant reminded her. "You cannot just walk into the Rest and start demanding an audience with The Leaders."

Dahlen rubbed her tongue against her teeth and shifted where she stood. "You are right," she replied. "But the two of you could do it. Or you could at least get a message from me to The Master for him to meet me outside of the Rest."

The Viper and The Defiant exchanged glances.

"Dahlen," The Defiant started, "we are not even sure if The Thorn was an agent for the Order or for the coven."

"She has a point," The Viper agreed. "For all we know, the coven had him planted in the Order as a spy."

Dahlen looked from one to the other. "I see your point, but at any rate, the coven has to be told about his death or they will label him as rogue and send scouts out looking for him. That would be a waste of the coven's resources."

The two of them nodded.

"You're right," The Defiant replied. "The Viper and I will talk to The Leaders. We will inquire about this."

Dahlen nodded. "We can work out the details on our way back to the mainland."

"Paya!" came a distant voice, breaking the group from their thoughts.

They all turned to see a ghost carrying something large over his shoulders, a triumphant look on his face.

"Paya, watu he mado no tapale ya!"

Dahlen looked at The Viper who seemed to be smiling. "What is he saying?"

"He said he caught one," The Viper replied.

"Sha le chitake no tapale ya!"

"He has caught one of Vron's warriors," The Viper translated, grinning.

"He has someone from the Order?" Dahlen asked excitedly.

The Viper nodded. "And he's alive."

CHAPTER 26

"Wait, you guys had boats this entire time and you made us run the whole way?" The Viper asked a little bitterly as he watched Paya and a couple other ghosts uncover a few canoes they had hidden by the river.

"The boats ah foh a quickah way back," Maleya explained. "But they ah not as fast going upsu-trream."

"Besides, we did not have enough boats foh all of us," Paya added. "These two will hold six. You will go with Maleya and our captive along with Kaju. He is the one who caught him."

They nodded.

"Take him to Fala," Paya continued. "She will know what to do."

The Defiant lifted a brow. "If we're just getting information out of him, I know what to do already," she said pulling out a knife.

"No," Paya told her sternly. "He is not to be hahmed."

The Defiant shrugged, putting the blade away again. "Have it your way then."

"What will you do?" Dahlen asked.

"We ah going to stay and claim our dead if theah is any left to claim," Paya told her. "We nevah leave our men behind. And pahaps see how extensive the damage is to the mine. Maybe there is something salvageable."

Dahlen nodded. "Send me word if there is anything left."

Paya bowed. "Though I might not have agu-rreed with your ways of killing, it has been an honah fighting beside you."

Dahlen held out her hand for Paya to take. "You are an honorable man, Paya," she replied with a smile. "Thank you for all of your help."

Paya clasped his hand in hers. "May your voyage take you wheah you need to go," he replied.

They gave each other small bows before Dahlen moved to the boats.

"So, I am going to ride with Maleya and Achu," The Viper said pointing to the boat where Maleya was entering. "You and The Defiant have the prisoner, right? You're more than capable."

"His name is Kaju, not Achu," The Defiant replied as she pushed past The Viper to get to the boats.

The Viper shrugged. "Kaju, whatever."

Dahlen gave him a look. "Don't do or say anything stupid," she warned in a whisper. "Maleya has done a lot for us and I would hate for you to insult her by treating her like one of your beloved whores."

The Viper pressed a hand to his chest. "I am utterly offended that you think I would do such a thing," he replied. "She is pretty, to be sure, but I would never think of compromising our relationship with the Bame le gochen over wetting my—"

Dahlen cleared her throat, cutting him off.

"We ah all set to go," Maleya said coming up behind him and smiling as usual. "The sun is just stahting to come up, so our voyage back will be a pleasant, beautiful one."

The Viper smiled back. "It certainly shall," he exclaimed. "Let us go then." He extended his arm, gesturing for her to lead the way as he followed closely behind.

"So, Maleya," The Viper started as they paddled down the river, "what does the Bame le gochen like to do for fun?"

"Foh fun?" Maleya repeated, thinking. "Hmm, well, we sometimes hold competitions amongst ahselves. We like to see who is the fastest rrunah, oh boatsman. We even have climbing contests too."

The Viper nodded awkwardly. "Interesting." He nodded his head in Kaju's direction. "What about you, Kaju?" The Viper asked. "You look like a decent boatsman."

"Bacha?" Kaju replied, looking confused.

"Kaju does not speak the shared language," Maleya told him. She studied The Viper for a second. "You ah not impu-rresed with our way of life, are you?" she commented.

He shrugged lackadaisically. "I have no issue with it," he told her. "I am just wondering how you survive the isolation. Don't get me wrong, I have lived in and out of the forest, but I have always returned to civilization."

She smiled softly. "Yes, we do not have the city so close, but we pass the time in our own way." She took a deep breath. "The air heah is clearah than in Stem or Hese. Yes, they have othah things to entice one, and offah moh pleasahs, but theah is no beauty. This," she held out her hand to the scenery before them, the lush growth and the sun sparkling on the water, "this offahs moh to me than the city evah could."

The Viper smiled. "I see your point."

Maleya nodded. "The cities ah made by man, but what you see heah is made by the gods."

He nodded and cleared his throat. "So, what are the codes that Bame le gochen live by?" he asked after a brief pause.

"Codes?" Maleya shook her head. "They ah nothing special. We live and fight with honah and give wespect to those who desahve it."

"No, restrictive codes?" The Viper pressed.

She blinked at him.

"None that tell you that you cannot do a certain thing?"

Maleya shook her head slightly. "We do not kill unless we ah defending our mission. We also ah taught not to steal."

The Viper nodded again. "Those are good things not to do, but

I am talking about, uh, whether or not you are allowed to, uh, have relations with—"

Maleya chuckle lightly. "Ah you asking me if I am allowed to lie with a man or whethah I have?"

The Viper colored slightly. "Well, I think that—maybe not in so many words—I was just, you know—" He cleared his throat. "No," he said, deciding against it and shaking his head. "No," he coughed. "I meant something else."

Maleya raised a brow at him. "Like what?" she asked skeptically.

The Viper pressed his lips together and shook his head again. "Never mind. It's not important."

"Do you hear that idiot over there?" The Defiant asked Dahlen in the other boat. She gave a small laugh. "He sounds ridiculous."

Dahlen smiled. "I think he might actually like her."

The prisoner at the bottom of the boat stirred and The Defiant gave him a swift punch in the face, making him pass out again. "So, what else do you know about the Order?"

Dahlen looked up at her. "Nothing really," she told her. "I know only what I have told you. That they are a secret society that protect the old religion, as it should be called, by killing anyone who opposes Vron and his version of events." She took a deep breath. "I do not know where their base is located. The only thing I have read mentions the Island of Zeln."

"As in, where the gods originated from?" The Defiant clarified.

Dahlen nodded. "But only a god can find it, so I think Zeln is more of a metaphor for something else." She creased her brows. "When I was in Ohtt's tent, however, I found a stack of—" Her mouth dropped and she huffed laughingly.

"What?" The Defiant pressed.

"I found a stack of letters addressed to him and one he was in the middle of writing," she laughed. "I had completely forgotten. Finding The Thorn who was obviously involved with the Order completely distracted me."

"What do they say?"

Dahlen shook her head. "I have not had a chance to read them yet," she replied. "But once we get back to the camp I will. I am hoping there is some information about Bornnen's soothsayer."

"Soothsayer?"

"According to Ohtt, whom I had a heart-to-heart with just before I watched a burning tent fall on him, she has been tracking me for years," Dahlen explained. "I am hoping these letters give me her whereabouts."

"Hmm," The Defiant said with a grin. "I feel another mission coming out of this."

Dahlen nodded. "After we tell The Leaders about The Thorn, I think I would like to pay her a little visit."

The Defiant smirked. "These adventures of yours are starting to get more interesting."

Dahlen paced her room at the gochen fort as she skimmed through the letters she had taken from Ohtt's tent. Most of them were only updates on the Order's progress as they searched for the beraxium. But there were a couple in a delicate hand that caught her attention.

> My lord,
>
> I see her now as she returns to the Rest. She is hoping to find information on us. She will succeed in only learning our mission. But more importantly, once she leaves will be the time to strike. She is going before The Leaders to ask to be let go from her vows. In a few weeks' time, we should ready ourselves.
>
> X

Dahlen read it twice. This was a letter from the soothsayer. It had to be. She rummaged through the rest of the pile, looking for the same handwriting and pulled out four more in its likeness.

> *My lord,*
>
> *I have had a new vision and it tells of fire, death and new life. This letter might reach you too late, but I am now under the impression that Vremir might be with her. I cannot see his face, but I feel his presence. It obscures my visions of her, but what I cannot see, I can feel. The men we have sent after her, all will die. That I am sure of. Vremir will grow stronger by the day and she will soon fall heavy with child. If only we could prevent this.*
>
> *X*

Dahlen felt her knees buckle and the blood drain from her face. They knew. They knew about her child. They knew she was to have a child. She put her hand against the wall for support, but the feeling was overwhelming and she slowly slid to the ground. Rage and fear filled her as she read that sentence again. *She will soon fall heavy with child.*

How much did they know, she wondered? Did they know what happened to her daughter? Do they know where she is?

She flipped to the next letter and read anxiously.

> *My lord,*
>
> *I have seen a window of opportunity. We must act now. I am not sure of the exact day but it will be in early spring. I have seen her walking in the woods with the prince, her belly starting to swell. They have left the*

> protection of their camp and I can see them clearly. We must follow the Mahk River south on the western banks until we find a small clearing where a large oak has made a bridge over the water. That is where they will be. We must wait for them
>
> X

She nodded as the contents of the letter aligned with The Viper's account of events.

> My lord,
> She appears to have had the child. I can see the little whelp screaming, but fortunately for us, it does not appear to have lived. I have seen her crying and the child is nowhere to be found. We are safe.
>
> X

Dahlen pressed her hand to her mouth and let out a sob of relief. They believe her daughter to be dead. She is safe.

The last letter was of no importance. It only verified that the soothsayer was no longer able to see her. "She is shrouded by fire," it read.

Dahlen read through the letters more than once, hoping there was a clue to the soothsayer's whereabouts, but there was no mention of her location. She then picked up the letter Ohtt had been in the middle of writing.

> X,
> How do you expect me to stop the prophecy if I cannot stop the prophet? And how would I even begin to stop her if we do not know where she is? I do not keep you

Dahlen smiled softly. "I have you now."

She put the letters in her things and went to move toward the door when Tristan burst into her room, his injured arm in a sling. "You made it back!" he exclaimed upon seeing her. "I was beginning to worry." He wrapped his good arm around her and held her close to him.

Dahlen, tensing up at first, relaxed and allowed him to hold her a few seconds. "It's only been three days," Dahlen replied finally taking a step back.

He shrugged. "A lot can happen in three days. And when I didn't see you with the others, I wasn't sure what to think."

Dahlen laughed through her nose. "I'm fine."

"Well, were you successful?" he inquired after a brief pause.

Dahlen gave a half shrug. "We did not altogether lose," she sighed. "I did, however, run into an old friend of yours." She arched a brow at him.

Tristan gave her a confused look.

"Ohtt."

Tristan's face drained of all color before it flashed red. "He is not my friend, Dahlen."

"Calm yourself," Dahlen told him. "I was only joking. He is dead at any rate. I watched as a burning tent fell on him."

"Wait, was he with the Order?"

She nodded. "He appeared to be *giving* orders."

"As if he was in charge?" Tristan clarified.

Dahlen gave a half shrug. "It appears he could have been. I found a few letters to him and an unfinished one he was in the middle of writing."

"Anything useful?"

"There are a few things worth noting," she told him. "Including the name of a place where they likely gather."

Tristan's eyes grew wide. "Where is it?"

Dahlen shook her head. "It's called the summer castle."

Tristan frowned. "Never heard of it. Where is it?"

"I don't know," Dahlen replied. "But we are about to find out, hopefully. We brought back a prisoner."

Tristan nodded. "I saw him being carried into a room. They are bringing him to Fala now."

"Let's go then," she told him, already pushing through the door.

Tristan led her down the dirt hallways to a chamber where the others had gathered; an unconscious man was tied to a chair in the center of the room. The Viper and The Defiant gave Tristan a nod in greeting. Maleya stepped toward the man and uncorked a bottle under his nose, causing the man to jump in alarm.

He looked around, wide eyed for a moment, confused by his surroundings, until his eyes rested on Dahlen. He then smiled, giving a small chuckle.

Dahlen exchanged glances with her comrades. "Do you know who I am?" she asked the bound man.

The man, badly bruised from his beating, shrugged. "Prolly I do," he responded haughtily.

"Why have you come to our woods?" Fala asked, her voice cold and unwelcoming.

The man looked over at her and huffed. "I don't know you though." His voice was gruff and his accent harsh. Dahlen thought he could be from Bornnen or the mountainous regions of Skahrr.

"What weah you and your people looking foh?" Fala pressed.

The man gave her a defiant look, indifferent to her presence.

"You would do well to answah our questions," Fala warned him.

The man spit on the ground. "I would do well tuh do nothin'," he growled.

Fala looked over at a young woman waiting in the dark corner of the room. She nodded at her and the woman emerged from the shadows holding a cup of brown liquid.

"Hold him," Fala ordered.

The Viper and The Defiant stepped forward without hesitation and held the man still while the woman poured the contents of the cup down his throat. The man kicked and sputtered, some of the liquid running from his mouth and down his chin, but it was no use. After the cup had been emptied, the woman bowed to Fala and returned to her place in the corner. The Viper and The Defiant also returned to their places as the man choked and coughed where he sat.

After a few moments, the man's head drooped and hung limply on his chest. Dahlen looked at Fala questioningly, but the older woman would not break her gaze on the man. For a few minutes, the room remained silent as everyone stared at the bound man.

Becoming angry that he could be dead, Dahlen moved to say something when the prisoner threw his head back and screamed. Those who were not expecting it jumped, taken aback by the shrillness of the sound. Fala and Maleya, however, remained motionless.

Dahlen watched in horror as the man's eyes rolled to the back of his head.

"You have poisoned him!" Dahlen exclaimed. "How are we to get any information from him now?"

Fala held up a hand to silence Dahlen without looking her way, her gaze fixed upon the man who had begun to seize. Dahlen gave a panicked look to Tristan who looked on in horror as foam began to form at the corners of the man's mouth. He thrashed and jolted about in his seat making his chair tilt and jump until it fell over, his spasms continuing on the ground. After several intense minutes, all movement stopped. The man's head dropped limply against the earthen floor, drool dribbling from his slack mouth.

Dahlen frowned, her breathing fast and shallow. "What have you done?" she shouted. "What have we gained from this man's death? He had so much information that we needed and you just killed him, rendering the point of bringing him here entirely useless!"

Again, Fala did not look at her. "Sit him back up," she commanded gently.

The Viper and The Defiant shot each other confused looks, but obeyed, pulling the still-bound man up causing his head to roll about on his chest.

"Why ah you heah?" Fala asked in her stern voice.

"Fala, he's dead," Dahlen asked after a few seconds. "You can't ask him questions anymore."

"We've come on thee orders of Vron," the man said softly, his head still hanging.

The Viper nearly fell backward with surprise while The Defiant cursed loudly taking several steps behind her. Dahlen's skin prickled as a chill coursed through her. Tristan only stared in amazement.

"What weah you looking for?" Fala continued.

"Beraxium," the man complied more easily. "We mus' find it an' present it to Vron so 'e can regain 'is full power and defeat 'is enemies."

"And wheah is he?" Fala demanded. "Wheah is the god of watah?"

The man's head slowly raised, a smile on his lips, his eyelids flickering slightly. "'e's everywhere," he replied matter-of-factly. "'is eye reaches the farthest co'nahs of thee realm."

Fala finally looked at Dahelen. "The potion has taken affect," she informed her. "Ask what questions you would like."

Dahlen opened her mouth to say something to her, but nodded instead. She then turned her attention back to the man. "What is your name?" she asked him.

"Me mothah called me Danick," he replied, his head bobbing a bit.

"And where are you from, Danick?"

"The Stronghold Mountain region of Skahrr," he told her.

"Is that where all people from the Order are from?"

His head rolled from side to side. "No," he answered. "We from all ovah thuh place."

"You are not from the Island of Zeln?" Dahlen pressed.

The man gave a small laugh. "Everyone is from thee Island of Zeln," he assured her. "'Tis where thee gods are from. And we are all from thee gods."

"What do you know of the Brotherhood of the Nameless?" Dahlen inquired cautiously.

The man's eyes once again rolled around in his head as he smiled. "I know prolly more than you," he taunted. "'Tis always good tuh 'ave uh well-trained assassin or spy on 'and."

Dahlen exchanged glances with The Viper and The Defiant who looked grave. "Did you know The Thorn?"

"We all did. 'ell of uh drinka! Deadly with 'is daggers."

"Who else from the coven has aligned themselves with you?"

The man smiled eerily. "We've several. We've more than you think. The Thorn was only one o' many."

"Who are they?"

The man gave what could have been a shrug. "Don't know 'em all. Met only uh few."

"What are their titles?"

Danick's brow furrowed as his eyelids continued to flitter. "Can't remember. The Whisper was one maybe."

Dahlen looked up at The Viper and The Defiant who shrugged and shook their heads.

"The Claw anothah."

This time The Viper raked a finger across his throat and made a face indicating the member was dead.

"And what about Ohtt? Why was he giving orders like he was in charge?"

The man's smile widened. "'e *is* in charge."

Dahlen shook her head. "Not anymore," she told him. "I saw him die."

The man began to laugh, softly at first before he threw his head back and let out a terrible cackle. "You know nothin'!" he proclaimed. "You, the prophet, are just uh small part in thee grander scheme o' things! Ignorant tuh what's before ya! Oh, but your mothah knew. She knew everythin'."

Dahlen gaped at him. "What do you know about my mother?"

The man sneered. "Lovely she was," he told her.

Dahlen's blood boiled and her lip quivered in anger.

"She saw it comin' too," Danick continued. "Said Vremir 'ad warned 'er. Told 'er of what was tuh come. Said 'er life was a small sacrifice and 'er gift would not die with 'er."

Gift, Dahlen thought.

"We didn't know 'bout you, o' course, back then," he replied. "Seems you inherited 'er position."

"My mother was the prophet before me?" Dahlen whispered almost to herself.

He nodded lazily. "She's the one 'oo caused uh stir all those years ago with 'er prophesies. Tried to kill 'er then but she was gone."

Dahlen took a deep, calming breath through her nose and let it out slowly. "Where can we find the rest of your companions? Where does the Order hide when they aren't killing innocent women and children?"

"We 'ide where ye least expect. 'idden in plain sight."

"No more riddles! Tell me how to find your brothers in arms," Dahlen commanded trying to remain calm. "Where is the summer castle?"

Danick shook his head. "Never 'eard o' it."

"Is that where you meet?"

"Vron tells us when tuh gather. We wait for 'is word." Danick's head rolled from side to side.

"How? How does he tell you?"

"The wa'er is calm before the storm."

Dahlen frowned. "What?"

"But there are troubled wa'ers ahead."

"I said no more riddles!" Dahlen shouted angrily. "Where do you gather?"

Danick laughed. "Thee end is where thee beginning will start. Where thee sound of wa'er can always be felt crashing over you."

"What are you talking about?" Dahlen asked angrily. "Answer my question!"

"Thee end is where thee beginning will start. Where thee sound of wa'er can always be felt crashing over you," he repeated, rocking as much as his bindings allowed.

"Where do you gather, Danick?"

"Thee end is where thee beginning will start. Where thee sound of wa'er can always be felt crashing over you. Thee end is where thee beginning will start. Where thee sound of wa'er can always be felt crashing over you."

"Stop it," Dahlen ordered.

"Thee end is where thee beginning will start. Where thee sound of wa'er can always be felt crashing over you," Danick repeated again, ignoring her.

"Shut up."

"Thee end is where thee beginning will start. Where thee sound of wa'er can always be felt crashing over you."

"Enough!" she screamed.

"Thee end is where thee beginning will start. Where thee sound of wa'er can always be felt crashing over you."

"This is getting us nowhere!" Dahlen stated heatedly as she stormed out of the room, Danick continuing his chant even as the door slammed behind her.

"You ah upset," Maleya commented as she followed Dahlen out of the room.

"I am angry, yes," Dahlen agreed. "This mode of questioning is getting us nowhere. He isn't answering any of our questions."

"But, he is," Maleya corrected. "He has ansahed all questions asked of him."

Dahlen creased her brow and shook her head. "Nothing he has told me makes any sense."

Maleya gave her a soft smile. "The potion we give might make one sleepy or slow, and sometimes might cause a slight eupho-rria but it always ends in the ta-ruth."

Dahlen blinked at her. "Is that what it was supposed to be then?" she asked. "A truth potion?"

Maleya nodded. "You might not undahstand his ansahs, but they ah the ta-rruth as he knows it."

CHAPTER 27

"WHAT ARE YOU GOING TO DO WITH THE PRISONER?" DAHLEN ASKED as they were led to their horses the next day.

"We will decide his fate soon," Fala replied, walking steadily beside her. "Pahhaps, we will keep him locked up. Or, we shall execute him. Foh now, we hope to gain more knowledge fu-rrom him."

"I want to thank you for helping us," Dahlen told her. "Though it didn't result in what we had hoped, it had the potential to turn out much worse. I will forever look upon the Bame le gochen as my friends and allies."

Fala smiled, bowing slightly as she walked. "Your wohds bu-rring me much joy as we will also look upon you the same way."

The two turned to each other as they pushed through the brush where the horses were waiting. They gave each other a small smile and bowed.

"We will ask Bame to bless you on your path," Fala told her.

"Thank you," Dahlen replied. "You must also thank your daughter for me. I was sorry to miss her on our way out."

"Theah is no need," Fala replied. "You will have plenty of occasions to thank hah latah as she will be joining you."

The Viper, who had been solemn all morning under the impression

205

he would never see Maleya again, immediately brightened up.

"Joining us?" Dahlen repeated.

"Yes," came Maleya's voice from a different part of the path.

Dahlen turned to see her leading her own horse to join theirs.

"Helping the chosen one on hah path is my destiny," Maleya explained. "And now that you ah heah, I can fulfill it."

"The more the merrier, I always say," The Viper exclaimed.

The Defiant sucked her teeth in annoyance. "You have never said that," she grumbled.

"I think I have heard him say something quite opposite to that more than once," Tristan commented.

"My daughtah will sahve you well, Dahlen," Fala told her.

Dahlen didn't reply right away as she watched the other three in the group interact with their newest member.

"You hesitate," Fala observed.

Dahlen looked over at her. "Wise decisions are not made rashly," she replied. "I am just thinking through what has been put before me."

Fala nodded. "I undahstand."

"You are sure you can do without her?" Dahlen questioned. "This journey we are making is uncertain and dangerous."

Fala smiled. "My daughtah has known both all hah life."

Dahlen bowed deeply. "I do not deny she will be useful." She gave a small smile. "We will be glad to have her."

Fala bowed in return.

Dahlen turned and fixed her things on her horse, patting it on the nose. "Is everyone ready?" she asked as she mounted.

Maleya looked over at her smiling mother and approached her.

"Hateye," Fala said opening her arms.

Daughter.

"Maheka," Maleya replied as she fell into her mother's embrace.

"Remember," Fala told her softly in Mehtian, "when your head can no longer understand, follow your heart. Let my love guide you." She planted a kiss on her daughter's forehead and took a step back.

Maleya bowed to her mother and turned to mount her horse.

Dahlen gave her crew a nod before she turned her horse around on the path and galloped away, the others not far behind her. Maleya lingered only long enough to wave her mother good-bye.

Part 3

COMING HOME

CHAPTER 28

THE BOAT MADE PORT IN GARESH, AN EASTERN CITY OF THREN, IN THE early morning hours after more than two weeks at sea. The soft knocking of the boat against the pier and chatter of the crew awakened some of its passengers, causing a subtle excitement to drift onto the deck. One passenger, however, had already been awake. She had already been pacing the deck for hours rolling over a dream she had again and again in her head.

It was another memory. Something so distant that she hadn't thought about it for years, perhaps not since the incident actually happened.

The dream took place maybe five years after her arrival to The Rest. The Master had just visited her after being away, bringing her another gift. This time it was candied almonds from Ganavan. After The Master left, she remembered a story she wanted to tell him and ran after him, but when she rounded the corner she stopped.

The Master seemed to be in a heated conversation with The Gallant who appeared to have been very angry.

"We made a deal!" The Gallant had said. "You said no contact and I have kept my word, but then you rub it in my face!"

The Master didn't reply, but nearly shrugged indifferently.

"You have never cared for any of the other children we have brought back," The Gallant surmised. "Why do you insist on becoming close with *her*. What are your motives?"

The Master huffed. "Maybe I don't have a motive. Perhaps, I just like this one."

Dahlen had watched as The Gallant pushed The Master against a wall and shook him. She had been scared and, yet, could do nothing. She just stood there and watched as the two of them threw punches at each other. Both of them rolling on the ground, struggling against one another until they sat bleeding and gasping on the floor.

"Stay away from her," The Gallant had warned.

The Master chuckled lightly as he picked himself shakily off of the floor. "Or what?" he taunted putting a gold medallion that had fallen from his person back in his chest pocket.

Dahlen had recognized it. She had seen it once before the last time she was at the Rest—except then it was a necklace. It was a large amulet adorned with black stones. Before she had thought they were made into the shape of a wing, but that was not what she saw in this memory.

"You have no authority over me," The Master had told The Gallant. "And if you try anything else like this, I will tell The Leaders who she is."

I will tell The Leaders who she is.

The words had rung through her and continued to do so the rest of the morning. What did he mean? Had The Master known all along that she was the prophet? And if he knew, did that mean he was her father after all? What deal was The Gallant talking about? A deal involving her?

The dream made her uncomfortable. It showed a side of The Master she had never seen before. Part of her wanted to believe they weren't talking about her, but the other part knew that they were.

"So where do you think this summer castle is?" Tristan asked as he joined her at the hull of the ship, breaking her away from her reverie.

She looked over at him. "I'm not sure," she replied. "It could be just a code amongst themselves. Danick didn't appear to know when I asked him either."

He nodded and took a deep breath, letting it out in a 'whoosh.' "I will be glad to get off this boat. If I had to listen to The Viper flirt anymore with Maleya, I would have thrown myself overboard."

Dahlen laughed. "He is rather obvious, isn't he?"

"I think The Defiant has threatened to hang him by his balls already this morning."

Dahlen laughed again. "If only."

There was a brief silence as Tristan slowly placed his hand on top of hers, causing her to shiver slightly. "I never apologized for what happened between us," he said.

Dahlen slowly pulled her hand out from under his. "There is nothing to apologize for," she told him. "We both just got carried away."

He nodded. "I know. I just wanted to apologize for my behavior."

She didn't reply.

"I don't want what happened to make things strange between us," he continued. "I respect you as the most honest friend I have ever had and I would have hated to have ruined that."

Dahlen slowly turned her head to look at him in slight bewilderment.

He chuckled with a nod. "I know. That makes me sound a little more pathetic than before, doesn't it?"

Dahlen cleared her throat. "Perhaps, a little."

He shrugged. "I mean, it's not that I don't find you attractive, I just don't—"

"Tristan, I take no offense," she stopped him. "There is no need for explanation."

"Thank you," he said, relieved. "I mean, I think the real reason, other than the near-death experience is that I haven't bedded a woman since—"

"I said there is no need," Dahlen quickly interrupted him. "And I meant it. Trust that I understand and please, for the love of the eternal four, let us be done with it."

He smirked. "I guess you can say I am your most honest friend as well."

"Too honest," she grumbled. "Let's get off this boat before you start sharing too much."

He laughed as he complied.

"I have nevah been to The-rren," Maleya claimed happily as they mounted their horses. "I have nevah been anywheah except Meht actually."

"Well, there is much to see here on the mainland," The Viper told her, pulling his horse closer to hers. "Soon you will see Dead Man's Rest. That is where The Defiant, Dahlen, who was previously known as The Tigress, and myself were trained. It is there we obtained our fighting and survival skills."

The Defiant rolled her eyes.

"I would love to see it," Maleya said.

"Ooo," The Defiant replied before The Viper could. "Unfortunately, you can't. You must be a member of the coven to get in. Even Dahlen can no longer enter."

Dahlen kept her face forward though the words hurt more than she cared to admit. The Rest had been the only home she had known for most of her life and she was forbidden to ever set foot there again. Since she had been released of her vows, she was no longer considered a sister of The Nameless.

"You alright?" Tristan whispered seeing her expression.

She nodded silently.

"It is true you cannot enter, but you will be able to see it from the bridge," The Viper continued. "A part of it at least. And once I am there, I will visit the garden for you and bring you whatever herbs you need or want."

Maleya smiled at The Viper and thanked him. "You have been

ve-rry kind to me on our voyage. You have made leaving my home less awful."

The Viper's mouth twitched into what could have been a grin. "My pleasure."

The Defiant quickened her horse's pace so she was next to Dahlen. "So, the plan once we get to the Rest is to find The Master and have him meet you at an offsite location?" she asked.

Dahlen gave a nod. "Yes."

"Sounds simple enough," she replied. "And you think he will actually come and meet you?"

"I don't see a reason why he would not. He was always someone I could count on," Dahlen explained.

"Yes, but that was before you relinquished your vows," The Defiant pointed out.

Dahlen smiled. "I know, but something tells me he will still come." Her smile deepened. "Like the fact that he might be my father," she thought to herself.

"And where would you like us to tell him to meet you?" The Defiant queried. "Have you thought of a location yet?"

"I have," she responded with a nod. "There is a shrine not far from the western coast of the Mahk River."

"The one dedicated to the Goddess Behr?"

"Exactly."

"That is a several-hour's ride from the Rest," The Defiant pointed out.

"I know," Dahlen replied. "But our meeting needs to be on neutral ground. And I can guarantee we are alone in the shrine more than I can in the woods bordering the Rest. I cannot risk someone hearing us."

"It's a shame The Viper will not be able to show Maleya any part of the Rest," The Defiant said sarcastically, a smirk smeared on her face. "And where would you like us when you are talking to The Master? We are privy to this information, are we not?"

"Of course, you are," Dahlen responded a little surprised by the accusation. "Though I would ask that you and the others act as lookouts while we talk. I have a feeling he will be more willing to talk if it was just the two of us. But I will share everything he tells me with you."

The Defiant nodded. "But do you think he would know anything?"

Dahlen shrugged. "If he does, he should tell us." She looked over at The Defiant who seemed unsure. "Do you not trust The Master?"

"I don't know how I feel," The Defiant told her. "My intuition is usually pretty good when it comes to people and situations." She shook her head. "And there is something about this that does not sit well with me."

"How did you feel about all of this when I asked you to join us?" Dahlen asked.

The Defiant smiled. "I felt good," she replied. "It's why I came. But this is different."

"Well, there is no way around it," Dahlen affirmed. "I must talk to The Master and I cannot do it at the Rest. He must be informed about the coven members caught up in the Order."

The Defiant nodded in agreement.

A few hours later, they reached a fork in the road with a directional sign. One arrow pointed north toward the shrine, while the other pointed east towards Dead Man's Rest with a warning attached to it.

Those who are not welcome at the Rest will be killed on sight.

Dahlen smiled at it.

"We shall hopefully see you soon then?" The Defiant said.

"Give it a week," Dahlen replied. "I will be at the shrine from sunrise to sundown every day."

The Defiant and The Viper placed a closed fist over their hearts.

"May your travels be prosperous," the three of them said to one another.

"We will be back soon," The Viper added in a softer voice, turning his attention to Maleya. "And I shall bring you those herbs I promised."

"Come on, idiot," The Defiant ordered as she turned her horse.

"Good luck," Dahlen said.

The Defiant winked at her. "You don't need luck if you're good at what you do." She then dug her heels into her horse and was off, The Viper not far behind.

The other three watched them go before turning their own horses north toward the shrine.

In a different part of Thren, a mother beamed proudly at her baby girl as she took her first steps. Almost a year had passed.

CHAPTER 29

Dahlen paced the shrine on the fifth day. Tristan was napping in the corner on the floor while Maleya had been praying for the past hour. Dahlen paused at the eastern-facing window for a few moments before continuing her pacing, her finger tapping nervously on her leg as she walked. When her finger tapping was not enough to pass the time, she took out one of her knives and twirled it around in her hand.

"Those things are dangerous, you know?" Tristan mumbled from the corner.

"I'm just tired of waiting," Dahlen replied.

"Do you think he will come?" he asked.

Dahlen put her knife away and began tapping again. "Yes," she replied after a few moments.

"Then why are you so nervous?"

"I am not nervous," she corrected. "I just hate waiting."

"We must show patience," Maleya added, standing from her kneeling position. "Patience helps keep our mind focused."

Dahlen took a deep breath and moved back to the window where she saw a small speck in the distance. Her heart jumped for a moment, but she remained silent. It could just be another traveler passing through like it was the day before. But as she watched, the speck grew from one to three specs and, as they came closer, she started to recognize them. She smiled.

They had finally arrived.

She turned to the other two. "They're coming," she said triumphantly.

Maleya and Tristan both moved to the window and looked.

"Tristan, I need you to stand on the northern side of the shrine. Maleya, you take the southern side. I will have The Viper and The Defiant guard the western and eastern corners," Dahlen explained.

The other two nodded and moved to take their positions as their three awaited visitors approached; Dahlen waited inside. Soon voices could be heard from outside and the quick step of The Master came through the doors.

Dahlen smiled softly and bowed. "The Master," she said, relieved, "you look well."

The Master smiled stiffly. "As do you," he replied. "I hope your travels have been prosperous."

She smiled as well. "They have."

He nodded curtly.

She stepped to approach him when she noticed the hesitation in his manner. "You are angry with me."

He shook his head and his shoulders relaxed. "No, I am glad to see you again, my child," he told her, opening his arms to her.

Dahlen embraced him. "Thank you for meeting me here," she said stepping away. "It means a lot that you would take the time to talk to me."

He nodded. "I must say, I am at a loss as to why I am here. What is so important that you could not write it to me in a letter?"

Dahlen shook her head. "A letter can be read by anyone," she explained. "This way I know my words are getting only to you."

The Master folded his hands in front of him, a grave expression on his face. "Then what you have to tell me must be serious indeed," he replied. "Tell me what is wrong."

"Do you remember when I stood in front of The Leaders and spoke of the Order of Zeln?" Dahlen asked after taking a deep breath.

The Master's eyes flashed from her face to another corner of the shrine. He rubbed his mouth with his hand. "Yes, I remember," he replied. "But I cannot recall everything that was said."

"They are a secret order much like the Nameless, except they are ruthless murderers. They have no code of honor and will strike down women and children without remorse," Dahlen explained. "They are the ones the temple sent to wipe out my entire family when the coven refused. They murdered my mother and are now bent on murdering me."

The Master nodded almost imperceptibly. "Yes, yes, now I remember," he replied.

"Recently, my travels have crossed paths with the Order," Dahlen continued, "and I made a disturbing discovery. One of our own—" she caught herself. "One of the coven was part of the Order. The Thorn."

"The Thorn," The Master repeated. "You are sure? But he was at the Rest just a few months ago."

Dahlen nodded. "He was dead but we all saw his tattoo and his title was confirmed later by The Viper. He knew him," she explained. "To make matters worse, he was not the only one. The Whisper was also mentioned as well as The Claw. They were both said to be members of the Order."

The Master shook his head. "The Claw I know to be dead, but The Whisper, I believe she is due back at the Rest any week now." He shook his head again. "You are quite sure they were named?"

"Yes, sir."

"I am sorry to hear this," he replied.

"The Leaders must be warned of the treachery going on under their noses. I am also led to believe there are more than those I named."

The Master gave a nod. "I will bring it up the next time The Leaders meet," he told her. "This is a serious but delicate matter. I will have to approach it with caution."

"This is very urgent. When will you next meet?" Dahlen asked.

"In two days. We are discussing which trainees are ready to receive their titles," he explained. "I would like to keep you informed on this issue. Where are you staying?"

Dahlen smirked. "I have not been staying anywhere lately," she replied. "I have been on the constant move for several months."

"Ah, well then, where are you headed?" he pressed. "I could have a note sent ahead."

"We are not sure actually," she replied. "That was something else I was hoping you could tell me. Do you have any idea where—"

"Dahlen," Tristan interrupted as he came back into the shrine. "The Defiant has spotted several more horses on their way here coming from the east."

The Master started when he saw Tristan, but he soon regained himself. The effect on his appearance, however, was not lost on Dahlen.

"The Master, this is Tristan," she said, gauging his reaction. "Tristan, this is The Master."

Tristan gave a small bow while The Master only nodded, turning his face from him.

"I have heard many things about you," Tristan said politely.

"A new friend of yours?" The Master asked Dahlen, ignoring him.

Dahlen shook her head. "No, actually, I met him about two years ago."

The Master cleared his throat. "Well, I should be going. There is much to prepare for this next meeting."

Tristan's eyes grew wide as he listened to The Master and as he turned to leave, Tristan reached out and grabbed his right hand. "It was you," Tristan said breathlessly as he revealed an unmistakable scar on the back of The Master's hand.

The Master pulled his hand away as if repulsed. "What are you talking about?" he asked defensively.

"You're the one that hired me to deliver Dahlen to the Bornnenians," Tristan replied accusingly.

Dahlen felt the blood drain from her face as she looked from one man to the other.

The Master scoffed. "That is absurd. I have never met you before in my life!" he replied backing away.

Tristan shook his head. "I recognized your voice. I couldn't place it at first, but when you said 'There is much to prepare,' it clicked," he continued. "You said the same thing to me when you hired me. I know it was you. You might have been hooded; I might not have properly seen your face and I might have been a little intoxicated, but I remember seeing your scar when you handed me the money."

"Is it true?" Dahlen asked, her voice wavering slightly.

"My child, how could you believe such a story as that?" The Master shot back. "How could you believe an outsider over me?"

Dahlen looked at Tristan intently.

"I swear it, Dahlen," he told her. "This is him."

Dahlen shook her head. "He might be an outsider," she said looking back at The Master, "but he's not lying, is he?"

"My dear girl," The Master began, "I am ashamed you would think so little of me after all I have done for you."

Dahlen shook her head. "Have you really done so much for me?" she asked. "Or did you only remain close to me in order to watch me? To keep tabs on me?"

The Master frowned.

"You are one of them as well, aren't you?" she accused.

The Master chuckled. "It is really quite unfortunate you figured it out," he replied pulling out a dagger he had hidden in his sleeve. "A shame, really as I am not going to be able to let any of you out of here alive."

Tristan moved toward him, wanting to lunge at him when Dahlen stopped him. "Tristan, don't!" she shouted. "That is not the only weapon he is hiding."

"I am sorry for this, you know," The Master continued. "I was hoping your death would be a little more dramatic than this, but I am sure the Order and even Vron would understand."

Dahlen glared at him. "How could you?" she asked breathlessly. "I trusted you. I confided in you. And all along you were one of *them*." She shook her head. "Why didn't you just kill me the day you found me instead of taking me to the Rest? It would have been easier."

"With your father there?" he shot back. "It would have been the end of me."

"So, what?" she shrugged. "You just pretended to care for me all of these years?"

The Master tried to look shocked. "Pretended? My child, I have looked out for you ever since you came to the Rest. I have treated you as if you were my own."

Dahlen's shoulder's slumped. "But I'm not your own."

"No, you are not," came another voice.

The three of them looked to see The Gallant entering the shrine, followed by The Wind, The Viper, The Defiant and three other men of the coven.

"What are you doing here?" The Master asked in surprise, temporarily putting his dagger back into his sleeve.

"The Wind and I followed you," The Gallant replied. "For years, I have not trusted you. For years, I have known there was something off about you, but, now, now I know what it is. Now I know why you kept yourself close to her all of these years. It was not just to torment me or because you even cared for her; it was because you planned on using her as a bargaining tool."

Dahlen looked from The Gallant to The Master. "What is he talking about?" she asked.

The Master scowled. "Nothing," he replied without hesitation. "He has no idea what he is talking about."

"The Master was hoping to sell you to the Order for a guaranteed role in Vron's new realm," The Gallant continued. "A role of power and wealth."

The Master sneered at him. "Lies."

"You can no longer deny it," The Wind added as she entered the shrine. "We have found some of your letters."

The Master turned a furious eye on her. "How dare you? I am one of The Leaders!" he proclaimed. "I am allowed my privacy."

"Not if that privacy goes against the code or the greater good of the coven," The Wind told him. She snapped her fingers and the three men that came with her stepped forward. "Arrest him," she ordered them.

This time, The Master drew a short sword as well as his dagger. "I will not allow it!" he shouted. "I am not some common criminal!"

The other three men drew swords as well.

"The Master, I recommend you go quietly," The Wind suggested. "We will take you alive or dead. And though I remember your skills as a swordsman, you are not the young man you once were."

He laughed haughtily through his nose. "We shall see." He lunged at one of the men ordered to arrest him, blocking his sword swing with his, as he slashed the man's thigh with his dagger.

The man fell with a scream and The Master moved on smoothly to the next, parrying his attack and blocking the third man as he came from behind. Even for a man of his age his movements were smooth and quick. The three men brought to arrest him had fallen with him barely breaking a sweat.

The Gallant stepped forward and unsheathed his own sword and dagger causing The Master to chuckle arrogantly.

"We have finally come to blows then?" The Master said with a sneer. "It will be your death."

"I have beaten you before," The Gallant reminded him.

"When we were children, perhaps."

"The Gallant," The Wind said sternly.

"It is all right," he reassured her. "I know all of this weasel's tricks."

Without another word The Master rushed at The Gallant, causing their swords to clatter as they blocked each other's attacks. They pushed off each other and regained their footing, not taking their eyes off one another.

"You're weak," The Master spat. "You have always been weak. The breaking of your vows is testament to that."

"You dare talk to me of breaking vows?" The Gallant almost shouted. "I might have a weakness for those I care for, but I would never sell them or myself for power. You are a disgrace."

The Master narrowed his eyes and moved again to attack. The Gallant, however, was ready and shifted in time to evade it. Again, their swords clashed against each other while the others watched on in helpless amazement.

"Should we not help?" Tristan suggested with anxiety.

"No," The Wind quickly replied. "This feud has been boiling for over twenty years. Let it finally come to a head."

After another rush attack, The Master spat in The Gallant's eye, causing the distraction he needed to gain the upper hand. The Gallant flinched from the surprise, loosening his grip and allowing The Master to get in a punch. The Gallant stumbled to floor, his sword clattering on the cold stone.

Dahlen and the others felt their hearts stop as The Master raised his sword overhead, ready to bring it down on The Gallant.

"I told you, you could not win," he said.

"No!" Dahlen moved to help when The Gallant kicked The Master's feet out from under him.

The Master fell to the floor, hitting his head. He groaned for a moment as he tried to get up, but The Gallant was already standing over him.

"I knew it would take a cheap shot for you to win," he growled as he forced The Master back on the floor with his foot who grunted.

The Wind looked relieved. She then glanced at The Viper and The

Defiant, gesturing with her head. "Take him away," she ordered.

The two of them bowed and lifted The Master as he struggled against them, hauling him out of the shrine.

Dahlen looked stunned. "But," she shook her head, "I have so many questions." She looked at The Wind. "Why? Why would he treat me as his own, train me, care for me just to deliver me to my enemies?"

The Wind placed a hand on her shoulder and gave a light squeeze. "Sometimes, we never truly get the answers we seek," she replied. "Because sometimes, it is never just as simple as 'why.'"

Dahlen felt a hole in her chest and she rubbed it, though the pain inside could not be reached. "I feel as if my whole life has just shattered. I had trusted him."

"We all did," The Wind replied quietly. "He has fooled us all."

Dahlen did not reply

"How is the boy?" The Wind asked, referring to Dohrrn. She tried to seem indifferent as she looked around.

Dahlen forced a small smile. "Dohrrn is safe," she told her. "He has adapted well to life outside of the Rest."

The Wind smiled. "I am very glad to hear it." The Wind placed her hand on Dahlen's cheek. "Though we might not often meet, know that you still have friends within the Brotherhood of the Nameless. You might no longer be a sister, but we would never turn our backs on you."

Dahlen nodded. "Thank you."

The Wind then looked at The Gallant. "We should be returning soon," she told him. "We must get The Master back to answer questions."

The Gallant nodded. "Please give me a moment."

The Wind bowed and then turned to Tristan. "You, young man, would you escort an old woman out?"

Tristan gave a look to Dahlen who nodded. "It will be my pleasure," he replied as he hooked The Wind's arm under his and led her out of the shrine.

The Gallant looked a little nervous as just the two of them were left. "You have read the books I gave you?" he asked after an awkward moment.

She nodded. "Yes," she replied. "They have been very helpful. Thank you again."

He gave her a small smile. "What shall I call you?"

"I go by Dahlen now."

He nodded. "You did not choose to go by the name given at your birth?"

She shrugged. "It seemed foreign after so many years," she explained. "It was with the name Dahlen that I found who I was."

The Gallant's mouth twitched. He opened his mouth a moment as if he were going to say something, but stopped himself.

"How did you know?" she asked him after a moment. "How did you know about The Master?"

"A friend of yours told me he hired him to kill you," he replied.

Dahlen's skin prickled. The Viper. She had forgotten Marten had told her the same man that hired Tristan had hired The Viper.

"He told me of what you had been up to. He said that you had swayed him into believing what you were fighting for," he explained. "And he thought The Master would try to harm you again. So, after he got The Master to meet you here, The Wind and I came up with a plan of our own."

She shook her head. "But why would you help me?" she pressed. "I no longer have any connection with you or the coven. I have been outcasted."

The Gallant flushed and averted his eyes for a few moments. "Twenty-two years ago," he began, "when you were only four years old, we brought you to Dead Man's Rest. It was against my wishes. I wanted more for you than the life of an assassin, but there was no other choice. Your mother had been killed and, as awful as it might sound, it was the best way to protect you."

Dahlen creased her brow.

"The Master had figured out who you were to me and a deal was struck," he continued. "I had to promise never to approach you, never reveal to you our true relationship and in return he would keep the secret of my betrayal from The Leaders, keeping you and myself safe."

Dahlen's mouth grew slack as the words The Gallant told her sunk in.

"If The Leaders knew I had broken the vow of chastity, that I fathered a child, it could have meant my banishment or even death," The Gallant explained. "And if I was gone, I could not guarantee your survival, I could not protect you. I would have agreed to anything if it meant you were safe."

"You're my father," Dahlen all but whispered remembering her latest dream.

The Gallant nodded. "Yes."

Dahlen felt the air rush out of her lungs and a sudden lightheadedness envelope her. She pressed one hand to her chest and another on a bench to steady her.

"I wanted so many times to tell you, to hold you, but I could not risk letting anyone else know," The Gallant told her.

Dahlen's lip quivered as she stared at the man she had waited so long to meet.

"I know I have failed you in many ways, but there has never been a day where I have not been proud to be your father," The Gallant told her.

"Vorce told me you were still alive," she said quietly. "But he never told me who you were."

He nodded. "Vorce was always a good friend."

"You do not resent him?" she asked.

"You mean for stealing your mother from me?" he asked. He shook his head. "I have long since forgiven them both."

Dahlen looked at him silently.

"I am sorry for everything," he told her sincerely. "I have always wanted more for you. More than what the coven could have given you."

She blinked and turned to face a window. "It was the right thing to do," she replied. "Where else would I have learned how to defend myself?"

The Gallant laughed through his nose and nodded. "You know, you look more like your mother every time I see you," he said.

"Did you know?" she asked turning to him. "Did you know she was the prophet before me?"

He nodded. "She used to tell me how the gods spoke to her. She told me that the night her family was slaughtered, she awoke with the urge to walk the gardens. So, in the middle of the night, she left her room and began to walk along the fountains and rose bushes. That was where I met her. Her dark hair, glowing in the moonlight. She told me later, it was Mahk that had woken her. He, as the wind does, nudges and pulls you to do certain things."

Dahlen smiled, finding the truth in what he said. "She was right," she replied. "That is how I feel about it anyway. Though, sometimes Mahk can be rather pushy."

There was a brief silence between them.

"I," The Gallant began slowly, "I cannot regret having brought you to the Rest. I do believe it has saved your life more than once. I can only regret the time I lost with you. The time I was forced to spend watching you from a distance instead of being a part of your life."

Dahlen let fall the tears she had not realized she was holding back. She stood, silently crying for several seconds when the arms of her father wrapped around her, embracing her for the first time since she was a child. The embrace was warm and slightly foreign, but it was not unwelcomed as she wrapped her own arms around him.

After several minutes, she recomposed herself and, wiping her face, took a few steps back. She looked up at her father who smiled warmly at her.

"This whole time, I thought perhaps The Master was my father," she said, frowning. "He fooled me for years."

The Gallant nodded. "As The Wind said, he has fooled many

people," he told her. "I know I might not always have been there for you when I should have been, but I have done what I could for you from the shadows."

"I cannot blame you for not telling me," she replied. "There was much at stake and even now, if you take The Master back, he will tell the others." She gave him a worried look. "What will they do?"

"Do not fret," he reassured her. "The Wind and I have been working on a new covenant. I will be punished still, perhaps even stripped of my status, but we do not believe death is the right course for what I have done knowing full well I am not the only one to have broken such a vow."

She nodded. "You," she hesitated, "you are a grandfather."

The Gallant's eyes sparkled with joy.

"A little girl." She shook her head. "And like you, for her protection, I had to give her up."

The Gallant nodded knowingly. He hugged her again and kissed her forehead. "I know it was not easy. It was not for me either."

She rubbed her lips together and nodded.

He took a step back and frowned. "Where is your necklace?" he asked her in a worried tone.

"I gave it to Dohrrn, the little boy I took with me for safe keeping," she replied. She laughed softly. "If you can believe it, he is actually Vremir, reborn."

The Gallant gaped at her for a moment. "He has come?"

She nodded.

"Then the necklace is with whom it should be."

She gave him a confused look. "What do you mean?"

"Your necklace is made from beraxium," he told her.

It was Dahlen's turn to gape. "That is why he always wanted to hold it," she said quietly. "It has been giving him strength all this time."

Her father nodded. "I must go," he told her after a few moments. "We must bring The Master back for questioning." He placed a coarse, but gentle hand on her cheek and smiled. "We shall meet again."

Dahlen watched as he walked away and smiled to herself. She slowly made her way to one of the eastern facing windows and watched as The Gallant and The Wind rode off with The Master. She paused for a moment, however, as a familiar figure brought up the rear of the group.

As if he felt her eyes on him, he turned and looked at her, a sad look on his face. Dahlen took in a small gasp as their eyes met. It was Marten. They had already made it several yards away, but Dahlen would know him anywhere.

She turned and ran from the shrine, blowing past her four companions, she jumped on her horse. She dug her heels into its haunches and sped off in the direction of Marten. She waved one arm in the air and shouted his name, trying to get his attention. Finally, when she was only a few yards away, Marten looked back again and saw her.

He turned his horse and dismounted. The others in his group hesitated but he waved them along. By then, Dahlen had caught up to him and jumped off her horse.

"You were not even going to say, 'hello'?" she asked accusingly, breathing heavily.

Marten gave a weak smile. "I didn't think you wanted to see me," he replied.

Dahlen approached him and wrapped her arms around him. Marten seemed surprised at first, but relaxed after a moment as he held her in return.

"I have missed you, T," he said as they pulled away. "And I am glad you are no longer angry with me."

Her lips twitched into a smile. "I was for several months," she explained. "And that anger only grew the more I thought about it." She took in a deep breath and let it out slowly. "But recently, I realized you were right. You and Dohrrn were right."

He smiled softly. "How much did that hurt to say?" he teased gently.

She laughed. "Not too bad."

He chuckled.

"Have you seen her?"

He looked down at her and nodded. "She is well," he replied. "She has just learned how to walk."

Dahlen pressed her lips together to keep them from quivering. She nodded in reply. "The Gallant is my father," she told him, clearing her throat.

Marten nodded. "I know."

She looked up at him sharply.

"He told me on the way here," he explained.

"How is Dohrrn?"

"He grows stronger every day."

She nodded thinking of him wearing her necklace.

"Mohrr was quite angry when he found out you left," he said when she didn't ask about him. "He went missing for months looking for you."

Dahlen felt her heart pang in what could have been regret. "I had to go," she whispered.

"I know."

There was a brief silence between them.

"Why were you never able to read The Master?" she finally asked.

Marten reached into his pocket and pulled out a golden medallion on a long chain. Dahlen reached out and fingered it. It was the same one from her dream. Her mouth went slack as the image of a black hawk in midflight stared back at her. It was Vron's emblem.

"This amulet protected him," he explained. "Much like what Vremir gave to you."

Dahlen wrapped her hand around the red opal hanging from her neck and nodded. "Do you know where the summer castle is?" she asked remembering what she was unable to ask The Master.

Marten frowned, thinking. After a moment he nodded. "Yes," he replied softly. "It is on the most northern shores of Skahrr. Northwest of Skahrr's Stronghold Mountains, just above the Small Mountains and a few miles north from the Hills." He took a deep breath. "It was your family home before the Order murdered them all."

Dahlen blinked at him. "Is that where they gather?" she asked. "Is that where the Order meets?"

Marten shook his head. "I don't know, T."

Dahlen pulled out Ohtt's letter to the mysterious X and handed it to him. "Do you think you can read this?"

Marten gave her a confused look.

"I know you can read," she clarified. "But I want to know if you can *read* this."

Marten nodded. "I can try," he told her, gently taking the letter. He pulled back his long, baggy sleeves and held the letter in both hands. He skimmed through the contents of it before he closed his eyes and focused. After a few moments of silence, Marten began to spasm, his eyes seemed to roll in the back of his head, and he let out a terrible scream as he fell to his knees.

Dahlen knelt beside him. "Marten!" she shouted as he continued to scream in pain.

Finally, Marten collapsed, the letter hanging limply from his hand. Dahlen took it from him, gently shaking him.

"Marten," she said in a heightened voice.

A few moments later, Marten's eyes opened slowly. He pushed himself up carefully from the ground and immediately wretched the contents of his stomach. Dahlen took the canteen from her horse and handed it to him.

"What happened?" she asked. "I have never seen you react like that before."

Marten swished some water around in his mouth and spit it out. "I am not sure," he replied shaking his head gently. "All I could see was pain."

"I am so sorry I made you do that," she said with sincerity.

He reached out and patted her cheek. "I would do anything for you," he told her. "You know that."

She smiled. "Why don't you join us?" she asked him.

He smiled back weakly. "You actually want me to come along?"

She nodded.

"I am honored."

"But?"

His smile deepened. "Perhaps I should have said *almost* anything." He shook his head. "The Gallant wants me to see what I can read from The Master now that he no longer has the protection from the amulet," he explained.

Dahlen nodded. "You're right," she replied. "That is very important." She helped him stand up.

"I will keep you informed," he told her.

"How will you know where to find me?" she asked.

He placed a hand on her shoulder. "I will always know where you are."

"DAHLEN," THE VIPER SAID SHEEPISHLY WHEN SHE RETURNED TO THE shrine. "Can we talk?"

Dahlen dismounted her horse and squeezed The Viper's arm. "There is no need," she told him. "I understand."

"I probably should have told you when we returned, but I just had to make sure— and with everything going on— I thought— but then of course—"

She squeezed his arm again. "It's alright," she reassured him. "You did the right thing in the end."

"What now?" The Defiant asked.

"Now, we are going to pay our soothsayer a little visit," Dahlen replied.

The Defiant's lips curled into a smile. "You found out where we're going."

Dahlen nodded. "I hope you guys are still in it for the long haul."

"Where are we headed?" Tristan asked.

"The northern coast of Skahrr," she told him. "Seems like the both of us are going home, Tristan."

"The Hills?" he asked.

"Just north of them," Dahlen replied.

Tristan frowned. "The summer castle," he said quietly with a nod. "I didn't recognize it by that name, but if it's where I think we are going," he gave an exasperated sigh, "I know where it is."

"Ooo, fun" The Defiant said raising her brows. "Is Harpren on the way?" She winked.

"I like Harpren," Tristan added. "It would be nice to stop there for a rest before we begin this journey."

"Hahpuh-ren is the capitol of The-rren, yes?" Maleya asked.

The Defiant nodded. "Very nice city. With some very nice brothels."

Dahlen shook her head. "Harpren is not in our path," she explained. "We will, however, be stopping to meet an old friend.

CHAPTER 30

"You have returned!" came the booming voice of Vorce as the five of them were led to his small house on the hill.

Dahlen smiled happily as she embraced him, Vorce squeezing her hard enough to make her back crack. "I'm sorry I didn't say goodbye."

Vorce shook his head. "I knew you had your reasons," he replied understandingly. "Plus, I knew you would return when you were ready."

She smiled at him.

"Now, introduce me to your new fellow travelers. I see a couple of familiar faces," he said nodding his head at The Viper and Tristan. "Though I did not expect to see either of them again," he whispered.

Dahlen coughed to suppress a laugh. "As you said, you know The Viper and Tristan," she began. "This is The Defiant, and Maleya."

The four of them bowed.

"This is my stepfather Vorce Brahn," Dahlen told them. "He is the chief of this tribe of outcasts."

Vorce chuckled, giving a small bow in return. "Welcome to our home," he told them, extending his arms in greeting.

"I am glad to see you again," Tristan said, stepping forward.

"As I am glad to see you in once piece," Vorce replied.

Tristan nodded. "Might Hamon be around?"

Vorce gave a single nod. "You can find him at the prayer circle," he told him, pointing.

Tristan bowed again. "Thank you." He moved away from the rest of the group toward the direction Vorce indicated.

Vorce beckoned the others to follow him. "You are hungry," he said more as a statement than as a question. "You must eat."

"I am glad to find you here. I was nervous you might be at the protected settlement," Dahlen told him as they ventured further into the village. "Is Dohrrn here, too?"

He shook his great head. "That is where my lord is," he replied. "He and Mohrr are helping to prepare for the spring planting season. I am proud of him."

"Of Dohrrn?"

"Of the prince," he clarified. "He has truly embraced his new role."

Dahlen gave him a confused look.

"You do not know then?" Vorce asked.

"I have not been back on the mainland long."

"Mohrr confronted his father about his hunt for beraxium. He tried to encourage the king to join forces with us instead against the Bornennians and forget trying to bring Vron back into power," Vorce explained. "His father did not take it well. He was disinherited and banished from stepping foot into Skahrr ever again."

Dahlen gasped in shock. "He is no longer the crown prince?"

Vorce nodded. "I believe he took it well enough," he added. "His brother-in-law took pity upon him and has guaranteed him refuge in Thren."

Dahlen nodded. "That was very nice of Prince Castuhl."

"Yes," Vorce agreed. "I believe he took his disinheritance better than your abandonment."

Dahlen's cheeks reddened with shame. "I could not tell him I was going," she reasoned. "He would have tried to stop me."

Vorce nodded knowingly. "I know." He cleared his throat. "I assume you will not be staying here long."

She gave a small laugh. "No, we are not. To be honest, I came here to ask for a favor."

"How many of my men do you need?" he asked in anticipation.

Dahlen could not help but smile. "Am I that predictable?"

Vorce snorted. "I know what someone on a mission looks like."

Dahlen looked back at her companions. The Defiant held up four fingers, The Viper five. "We need enough to make a difference, but not too many as to cause concern," she replied.

"Four or five, then," he determined. "Might I ask where you are going?"

Dahlen cleared her throat, hesitating. "The summer castle."

Vorce slowed his gait and looked at her, surprise written all over his face. "What do you think you will find there?"

"We think it could be a location where the Order gathers or it is at least where their soothsayer is hiding," she replied. She watched as Vorce's muscles tensed. "A little slap in the face of the Mahrkai family. First, they try to eradicate our bloodline, and then, they use my family home as their own."

"If that is the case, I will join you," he announced.

"Vorce, no," she said softly. "You are needed here and at the new settlement."

"I cannot let you face the men that took everything from me alone," he growled quietly.

"I will not be alone," Dahlen assured him.

Vorce rubbed his mouth, and stroked his beard. He looked uneasy, but after a moment he nodded. "I will give you four of my best men," he told her. "But you must stay here at least two nights. You need rest and so do your horses."

Dahlen opened her mouth in protest but Vorce held up one of his massive hands.

"I believe I am owed at least that much," he told her. "That will give you enough time to tell me about all of the fun you had after you forgot to say good-bye to me all those months ago." He lifted a brow at her.

Dahlen gave him a stern look, but relented. "Agreed," she said finally.

He wrapped a large arm around her shoulder and pulled her closer to him as they walked. "Small blessings," he laughed.

"What's that?" Dahlen asked.

He shrugged. "It is something your mother used to say when she found pleasure in life's simplicities."

"Small blessings." Dahlen smiled.

Vorce gestured for everyone to follow him into a long wooden building. "Come," he told them, opening the door. "We will find you all some food."

Dahlen allowed the others to eclipse her into the building. "I forgot to mention," she said with a grin, "I met with The Gallant recently."

Vorce smiled back. "Now you know."

She nodded. "He is gracious toward you," she told him. "And remembers you as a good friend."

Vorce smiled solemnly. "I am glad to hear it."

For the next two days, Dahlen and the others stayed amongst Vorce and his men, using that time to ready themselves for what might be ahead. The Viper taught Maleya how to use a spear; The Defiant trained with Vorce's men; Tristan had theological conversations with Hamon; Dahlen wandered, like she had over two years before, around the village, sitting next to her mother's statue or talking with Vorce.

It was a peaceful, rest-filled two days, more rest than they had had since they began their journey.

On the second morning, however, Dahlen woke up early, eager to get a jumpstart on the next head of their expedition. She walked out of Vorce's house into the dark morning to see Vorce talking to one of his men in a hushed voice. When they were done, the man bowed and walked hurriedly away.

Vorce smiled at her as she approached. "I am always glad to see you," he told her, "but I am always more saddened to see you go." He placed an arm around her.

"Thank you for your hospitality," she said.

Vorce shook his head. "You are my daughter, by blood or not—where I am, I hope you will always feel at home."

She smiled. "When I get back, promise me you will tell me more stories about my mother."

He placed a rough hand on her cheek. "That is my favorite subject, as you know."

Her smile broadened more before she gave him a stern look. "You must also promise me you will not tell Mohrr where I am going," she begged of him.

"I cannot understand why you refuse to let him in," he sighed.

"Vorce, promise me."

He nodded. "I promise I will not tell him," he told her.

"Thank you," she replied. "Would you also make sure this gets to Dohrrn?" She pulled the small chunk of beraxium out of her satchel and handed it to him. "The mine, unfortunately, collapsed. This was all we could find."

"I shall deliver it to him myself."

She nodded. "Thank you for everything, Vorce."

Vorce pulled her in for a hug. "Keep yourself safe."

"Oh, there was a young maiden with long red hair," The Viper sang as they rode along, "with sparkling green eyes and skin so fair. Her smile did make my heart beat wild, and her laugh was pure as any child's."

"Her touch was gentle and kisses sweet," Tristan joined in, "and warmed me from my head to feet."

The Viper nodded at him.

"I do miss the fair young maid," they sang together,

> *the way she danced when music played.*
> *There ne'er will be a more beautiful soul*
> *nor another woman to make me whole.*
> *Though I dream of thee maiden e'ry night,*
> *I still search for her with morning light.*
> *Come to me maiden! Come to me!*
> *Life without you is misery!*
> *Oh! Come to me maiden! Come to me!*
> *Save me from my life of tragedy!*

"That was beautiful," Maleya said, clapping. "I did not know you could sing so well."

"Don't encourage them," The Defiant grumbled.

Dahlen shrugged as she took in the sweet floral scent of mountain air. "It wasn't too awful," she replied, noticing all of the pretty, little purple and yellow flowers that lined the trail, following it as far as she could see. She had never seen them before and wondered what they were called when she suddenly shivered.

"I thought we were pretty good," Tristan added. He looked behind him to see the four men Vorce had lent them nodding in approval. "See," he jutted his thumb indicating them, "they agree."

"What about you, Malek?" The Viper asked, referring to one of Vorce's men. "Do you and your men know any songs?"

"No!" The Defiant said. "No more singing please!"

"We know some," Malek replied gruffly, ignoring The Defiant.

"Ours not as cute," added one called Viktor.

The Defiant let out a groan as they began and forced her horse to catch up with Dahlen. "I don't think I can endure much more of this," she told her, cringing as Vorce's men's gruff singing voices violated her ears. "How much longer do you think until we get there?"

Dahlen suppressed a smile. "It's been a little over two weeks since we left," she replied. "We still have a few more days at least."

"Gods be blessed," The Defiant cursed begrudgingly, wiping the spider web she rode into off of her face. "What the hell is a spider-web even doing up in the mountains?" she asked to no one in particular. "This is ridiculous! I feel as if we have been traversing this damn mountain for months." She groaned.

Dahlen eyed her skeptically. "Are you well?" she asked. "You are not one prone to temper tantrums."

The Defiant shrugged. "Do we actually even need any of them?" she asked ignoring Dahlen's questions.

"Who?"

"The men!" The Defiant exclaimed.

Dahlen laughed.

"The Viper has gone soft since Maleya has joined us, Tristan's arm is still healing and is basically useless, not that he was all that fantastic beforehand, and then the giant boars Vorce lent us make us look a lot less inconspicuous. I mean did you see the way those mountain people looked at us the other day? Mountain people judged us. That says something."

"Does their singing bother you that much?" Dahlen asked, raising a brow.

The Defiant looked at her with pursed lips. "Yes."

"They are probably just tired of traveling and need something to stimulate their minds," Dahlen replied with a smile. "I think it is a harmless distraction, though it would probably be more helpful if we were a little less noisy."

"Exactly," The Defiant agreed. "How are we supposed to hear an ambush, or a wild animal, or even think with all of this noise?"

"Awe, don't be such a sour-puss," The Viper said catching up to them.

The Defiant glared at him. "Don't make me cut out your tongue," she snarled.

"Ouch!" The Viper commented. "Don't do that. What's a snake without its tongue?" He stuck it out at her.

The Defiant reached over on her horse and hit him in the arm.

"Ow," The Viper frowned, rubbing his arm. "That was uncalled for."

The Defiant rolled her shoulders. "I am just itching for a fight and it has been a long time since I have—" She waved her hand dismissing her thought. "Forget it."

The Viper smirked knowingly. "A long time since you have slayed the dragon?" he teased. "Since you have let your temple be prayed in? Since you have reached the highest peaks of the Stronghold Mountains?"

The Defiant sucked on her teeth, annoyed. "I will throw you from your horse and trample you," she finally said, not looking at him.

The Viper chuckled. "Unfortunately, there probably aren't any brothels on the way from here to where we are going. So, you might just do us all a favor and do *yourself* a favor."

"Are you quite sure we need him?" The Defiant asked Dahlen who coughed to suppress her laugh.

"Yes, I am sure that we all need each other right now," she replied. "None of us are any good alone. Not for this mission."

"Who do you think we will meet at this summer castle?" The Viper asked. "I know their soothsayer is there, but who else?"

Dahlen shook her head. "I am not sure," she confessed. "The soothsayer must have protection. None of the letters I read indicated she was alone and unprotected. My guess is Bornnenian soldiers since it was Ohtt who was the one communicating with her."

Tristan nodded. "It is forbidden, you know."

The Defiant rolled her eyes. "Of course it is! There is always a forbidden place! Wherever you go!"

"What are the legends behind it again?" Dahlen asked.

Tristan shrugged. "They aren't legends so much as ghost stories to keep people from coming too close."

"Anotha Bame le gochen tale?" Maleya asked.

Tristan tilted his head from side to side. "Sort of, yes. But the stories didn't start until maybe ten or fifteen years ago." He cleared his throat. "The summer castle, or the falling castle as it is known in the Hills, is near the ocean, so the sounds emanating from it tend to carry further. It is said, that a monster inhabits it and ten or fifteen years ago, it held a woman captive, forcing her to give birth to their half-breed spawn. It is said that the woman's screams were heard for months until they were replaced by the screams of a child."

"There's nothing scary about that," The Defiant muttered.

"No, but it's said the child is hideous to look at."

"So are half of the people I meet," The Defiant shrugged. "Present company not excluded."

"The child has sharp fangs and long claws, with dry scaly skin," Tristan continued. "And, as legend has it, ate its own mother right after its birth."

The Defiant exchanged glances with The Viper and they both laughed.

"And stories like this actually keep people away?" The Viper asked.

Tristan shook his head. "There have been some that have tried to get a glimpse of the demon spawn, but those that have tried have either never been seen again, or are found in pieces that had washed up on nearby shores."

The Defiant huffed and rolled her eyes again. "Therefore, giving some validity to the stories."

"What do you make of this story, Maleya?" Dahlen asked.

Maleya smiled. "It is much like what the Bame le gochen do," she replied. "We make up tales and tell them to keep people away. And because we want the tales to seem ta-rue we must make good on them. We cannot have someone come into Halana Neya and not eitha be fu-rrightened away or leave alive." She gave a nod. "This is the same," she concluded. "Theah is no monstah, but they have to make it seem like theah is."

"In other words," Dahlen added, "they are hiding something."

"Or, pu-rotecting something," Maleya added.

"Perhaps we should tell my uncle about this," Tristan suggested. Everyone slowly turned their heads to look at him.

"Why would you ever think getting King Breht involved is a good idea?" Dahlen asked. "He is the worst."

"Yes, but shouldn't he at least know that the Bornnenians have been harboring a secret in his country?" he asked. "He might send a few of his soldiers to help us."

"And then what?" Dahlen asked. "You think he will let the soothsayer go? Or let her come with us?"

"In my opinion," The Viper piped in, "he will take the soothsayer for himself and use her for his own agenda."

"Which is the opposite of what we want," Dahlen added, shaking her head.

Tristan held his hands up. "Understood."

"This place has strong magic," one of Vorce's men said from behind them. "We are getting close."

Dahlen stopped her horse and turned to look at him, the others halting as well. "What do you mean, Hanek?" she asked.

The man lifted a hand in the air palm up for a second before rubbing his fingers together. "I can feel it."

"Magic as in spells and witchcraft?" Tristan asked.

The brute of a man nodded.

"I thought the last of the witches was killed off centuries ago," Tristan stated.

"Not where we are from," Hanek told him matter-of-factly. "Where we are from is where those that practiced the art of magic fled when those on the mainland began to hunt them."

"Where are you all from again?" Tristan asked him.

"We come from the lost tribes, an island west of Skahrr," he explained. "We do not fear magic like those of the mainland. We learn from it."

"Though, our witches and wizards are not as powerful as they once were," Malek added. "It is a dying art."

"This that I feel though is stronger than I have felt in a long time," Hanek explained.

"Southern Lost Tribe," Viktor piped in. "They have strongest magic."

"Yes, but Eastern Lost Tribe has darkest magic," the fourth and the quietest of Vorce's men said, making this statement his first complete sentence since they began their journey.

"Do any of you know magic?" The Viper asked.

The four of them laughed as if he said something funny.

Hanek grinned. "We all know some, but Thane here is the reason no one has found our hideout in the woods," he replied. "His magic is only rivaled by that of his grandmother. She was shaman for the Northern Lost Tribe."

"Runs in my blood," Thane replied.

"So, what we are about to walk into," Dahlen started, "is it a dark magic?"

The four men exchanged glances and shrugged.

"It is protection spell," Hanek replied.

"We are far from the epicenter, but its effects are still being felt," Malek added, nodding his head at The Defiant.

"What are you talking about?" The Defiant replied, annoyed.

"The spell repels those that do not belong," Thane explained. "You are already wishing to be far away from here."

"That doesn't mean anything," The Defiant grumbled, shifting uncomfortably in her saddle. "I can't be the only one who doesn't want to be here."

No one responded.

"Magic can have a greater effect on some than others," Viktor told her. "*You* seem to be extra sensitive to it."

The Defiant huffed.

Thane reached into one of his saddle bags and tossed her something. "Willow bark," he told her. "Chew it. It will chase away the feelings of doubt you might have."

The Defiant looked skeptical but did as she was told, scrunching up her face at the bitter taste of the bark.

"It's better as tea," Thane told her.

"Thanks for the warning," she mumbled.

"We should make camp here," Dahlen said, sliding off of her horse. "I would like to know more about this magic."

"It is not something those of the Lost Tribes talk about outside of our island often," Malek explained as they sat around their fire, cooking freshly caught rabbits and vegetables in a pot. "If we do on the mainland, we are immediately outcasted or met with mistrust."

"People think we can control them with our magic," Hanek added. "But that is not the case."

"Magic is nothing more than a manipulation of herbs and perception," Thane said.

"And what would you call the magic you felt earlier?" Dahlen asked.

"Both," Thane replied without hesitation. He pulled a little purple flower from his pocket, the same Dahlen noticed on the side of the road. "This is called witch's lavender. It is used for several things. It can heal burns quite nicely if made into an oil; made into a tea, it can help you sleep—"

"Though you will have terrible nightmares," Viktor interrupted.

"—if burned and inhaled, it will cause hallucinations. And this," he pulled out the yellow flower she had earlier seen mingling with the purple ones, "is sunheart. Alone, it can soothe fevers and if made into paste, can stop wounds from festering, but if paired with witch's lavender, it can cause confusion and irritability."

"Why was The Defiant the only one affected by it?" Dahlen asked.

Thane shook his head. "Soon we all will be if we do not take care," he replied. "The Defiant is only more sensitive. It does not take as much to affect her."

The Defiant scowled from where she sat.

"Different magic affects us all differently," Malek said reassuringly to her. "It might only be this spell you are this sensitive to."

Dahlen nodded. "How much of that willow bark did you bring?" she asked.

Thane smiled broadly. "Enough."

She smirked. "I knew about the protection spells you have put over the settlement and your hideout, but, tell me, can you do more than just that?"

Thane's smile never left his face. "Why do you think Vorce chose us to accompany you?"

CHAPTER 31

A DAY LATER, THEY CROSSED THE GHER RIVER INTO SKAHRR AND pushed northwest past the Hills, the trail of purple and yellow flowers leading the way. All of them now chewed on the willow bark, or brewed it into a tea when they camped to drink the next day as they tried to keep the feelings of anxiety the flowers induced at bay.

"Do you want to make a stop at the Hills?" Dahlen asked Tristan seeing his eyes follow the trail back home.

He took in a deep breath and let it out. "No," he finally said with a shake of his head.

"You don't want to check in on how the business is doing?" Dahlen pressed.

"Are you trying to get rid of me?" he inquired back.

She shook her head. "No," she replied. "It is just you usually have excuses why we shouldn't go to a certain place and I haven't heard you complain once." She shrugged. "I thought you might be waiting until the Hills were in view before you did."

He smiled slightly. "I told you I entrusted my brothers with the decision making. They were schooled to take over. I would only run the operation into the ground."

Dahlen nodded. "So, you are deciding to continue your travels with us instead of going home?"

"Sometimes, home isn't a place," he said with a sigh.

She didn't reply but nodded.

"That down there is your father's land?" The Viper asked, pointing.

Tristan nodded. "Was. Now, it is mostly mine."

The Viper nodded. "Nice."

"Oooo, you're a rich priest," The Defiant commented.

Tristan shrugged.

"Looks like a nice little vacation spot after we're done here," The Viper joked.

"Who is looking after your brothers and sister, Tristan, now that your father and stepmother are gone?" Dahlen asked.

Tristan sighed. "My brothers are being advised by a good friend of my father. My oldest brother is eight years younger than I am at twenty, while the middle one is a couple years younger than him. Esther, however, is only fourteen. She has been moved to King Breht's court by now, no doubt."

"What?" Dahlen gaped at him.

"He is her godfather," Tristan explained. "He thought it only right to bring her to court to continue her education. At least that is what she had told me in her last letter."

"Why are you just now telling me?" Dahlen asked. "It's not safe for her there."

Tristan shook his head. "He won't hurt her," he replied blandly. "Oddly enough, he adores her." He gave a small laugh. "She was supposed to marry Mohrr when she came of age, you know?"

The color drained from Dahlen's face. "They were betrothed?"

"Wait," The Viper interjected, "aren't they cousins?"

He nodded. "But Prince Mohrr thought the match beneath him, so he backed out. Decided he was better than it," Tristan explained bitterly.

"When was this?" Dahlen asked.

Tristan thought for a moment before giving half a shrug. "I guess it's been about two years now. He said he was told by some fortune teller that he was to fall in love with someone else and he didn't want to dishonor my sister or some bullshit excuse like that." He snorted.

"This is why there is so much animosity between the two of you?" Dahlen surmised.

Tristan nodded. "My sister had been crushed by the news. She adored Mohrr. She was being raised to be a queen and he just dropped her like she was nothing."

Dahlen looked away, realizing she was probably the reason Mohrr broke off his engagement to the girl.

"Yeah, but they're cousins, so," The Viper shrugged, "it was probably for the best."

"Cousins? Who cares about that?" The Defiant interjected. "The girl is still a child."

"Yes, except now the king will most likely marry her off to some foreign dignitary for his own political gain," Tristan retorted. "She has barely ever been outside the Hills. At least with Mohrr she would have been close to home. They should have been married this summer."

Dahlen had an uneasy feeling, but remained silent as they continued.

A few hours later they passed through a small village. They stopped, hoping to replenish their replies, but soon found the place completely deserted.

Tristan shivered. "This reminds me a little of Goun," he said.
The Viper nodded.

"It seems the villagers left in a hurry from here," Malek pointed out.

"Voluntarily or by force?" The Defiant questioned.

"I think we should press on," Dahlen stated.

Without complaints, everyone led their horses out of the dead town, moving silently for several miles until they reached the top of a little knoll. They stopped and looked down the other side. Dahlen frowned as she pulled out the map.

"This forest seems a little random," The Viper commented.

"How so?" Tristan asked.

The Viper shrugged. "It's just a feeling."

"Are we going the right way?" The Defiant asked.

Dahlen looked down at her map and nodded. "I believe so, yes," she replied. "Though there isn't a forest on the map."

"Maybe the map is an old one," Maleya added. "A foh-rrest can gu-row in the-ty yeahs."

Dahlen looked into the darkness of the forest before them and shook her head. "Not this thick it can't," she replied.

"Did we miss a turn?" Tristan asked.

Dahlen shook her head as she studied the map. "I don't think so. We can't be more than a few miles away," she stated. "Less than ten if the map is right."

"Let me see it," The Viper asked, reaching his hand out.

Dahlen gave it to him without hesitation.

He nodded after a couple of minutes. "No, you're right," he agreed. "We could reach the castle in less than an hour if we pick up our pace."

The Defiant reached over and took the map from him. She nodded after a minute. "I agree. The end shouldn't be that far, but this forest," she shook her head, "it's out of place."

"What do you think, Thane?" Dahlen asked.

He exchanged glances with the other three tribesmen. "I believe we should proceed with caution," he told her.

Malek nodded. "We know this magic," he added.

"It is the same we use to keep our hideout hidden," Hanek stated.

"But different," Viktor commented shaking his head.

"It's the same or it's different?" Dahlen asked.

"Both," Thane replied.

The nine of them stared into the abyss of the forest in front of them, some of their horses braying uncomfortably.

"Everyone, stay close," Dahlen ordered as she pressed them forward.

THE LIGHT ALL BUT VANISHED AS THEY ENTERED THE FOREST, THE rays from the sun unable to pierce through the thickness of the trees.

"This is even more dense than the Scattered Forest," The Viper said, looking around.

Dahlen pulled out her red opal and held it out in front of her, lighting the way.

"I think I prefer the Scattered Forest to this," Tristan mumbled.

"The path seems straight enough," Dahlen told them as she led the way slowly.

"Here," Viktor said from the back. "Everyone, hold onto this rope. It will help us stay together." He passed a rope up the line to Dahlen, everyone making sure to put one hand on it as they went along.

"It's oddly quiet," The Defiant commented. "I don't even hear birds or the wind."

The Viper sniffed the air. "It smells stale and a little dank in here, too. Not like a regular forest."

"It is not a regular forest," Thane told them.

"I think we should all remain as quiet as possible," Dahlen ordered. "Eyes and ears open for anything. Our journey has been too easy up to this point. We are bound to have something go wrong sooner or later."

Everyone nodded silently as they moved forward, their eyes flitting about them in search of whatever might be waiting for them in the dark.

After what seemed like hours, the soft buzz of noiselessness became almost too much to bear. Becoming antsy and irritable, it was Tristan who broke the silence first.

"Are we sure we're going the right way?" he asked, annoyance apparent in his voice. "We have been going at this steady pace for what seems like forever. If our destination was only ten miles, we must have gone beyond that by now."

"He's right," the Viper agreed. "The terrain has been smooth and straight and, yet, I feel as if we have been going in circles."

Maleya nodded. "I feel the same. I think I have seen this chu-ree," she pointed to a tree with a distinctive knot on it, "at least fohr times."

"So have I," The Defiant chimed in. "I thought it was just a coincidence at first, thinking maybe it was just a tree that looked similar, but now," she shook her head, "I know it's the same one."

"We have neither seen nor heard anything in these woods the entire time we have been traveling them," The Viper pointed out. "No birds, no squirrels, no bugs." He looked around him. "Is that unsettling, or is it just me?"

"No," Tristan replied. "It is unsettling."

Dahlen nodded. "Something is not right."

"Shh," Thane whispered. "We are being watched."

Everyone cautiously looked about them, searching amongst the trees for signs of movement, but it was difficult to see through the darkness. Dahlen moved the red opal from one side of the trail to the other to try and penetrate the overwhelming blackness between the trees, but it only succeeded in casting eerie shadows.

"Keep moving," Dahlen ordered softly.

"You should have stayed away," came an echoing whisper.

The horses brayed uneasily as everyone grabbed tighter on their reins to maintain control of them.

"Dahlen?" Tristan said in a tense voice.

"You should not have ventured this far," the voice echoed again.

"Weapons at the ready," Dahlen told them.

Just then, several objects were thrown in their direction, hitting the ground with a 'thud' followed by a small flash. A hissing could be heard as smoke rose from the ground.

"Do not inhale it!" Thane cried out as he covered his mouth and nose with his cloak.

Dahlen tightened her veil around her face as her horse stomped and shook its head in a nervous manner. "The smoke is affecting the horses!" she yelled as her horse began to rear. She jumped off, grabbing her horse by the reins trying to calm it, but it was no use. Her attempts only agitated it more.

She looked behind her as the other horses began to act in the same way, forcing their riders from their saddles.

"Grab what you can and leave them," Dahlen shouted over the noise of the panicked horses.

The others did what she said, hopping off of their horses and grabbing what they could before the horses bolted off in the other direction.

Dahlen and The Defiant nocked their bows, while the others held up their swords, searching the darkness for whatever it was taunting them.

"Leave! Leave! Leave!" came the echo. "Turn back! Turn back!"

Dahlen turned around to see a figure standing in the middle of the trail in front of them, shrouded by the dark. "There!" she yelled, releasing an arrow. But the figure had vanished.

Suddenly, the sound of hundreds of footsteps enveloped them, coming from every direction. All of them stood back-to-back, their weapons raised, as they looked out for whatever was making that noise.

"Some counter magic would be good right about now!" The Viper yelled over the noise. "You think you could help us out there, Thane? Hanek? Any of you?"

"Cover me," Thane said as he pushed into their circle. He crouched on the ground as he opened his bag, rifling through the herbs.

Dahlen held the red opal up high trying to shed light on what was coming, when a dark figure jumped from the trees, hissing. The figure did not get far before The Defiant sunk an arrow into its chest, causing it to drop to the ground with a thud and a gurgling noise.

It was soon followed by another figure that slashed at Tristan with metallic claws. Tristan let out a yelp as he jumped back, avoiding the attack before thrusting forward with his sword, hitting its mark. He gasped when he looked into the dark eyes of his attacker.

"What the hell are these things?" he yelled as more rushed from the woods at them. He gawked at their grey skin and animalistic behavior as they hissed and growled.

Viktor, the great bulk that he was, caught one of them by the throat, throwing them to the ground before he thrust his sword into it. Hanek easily brought down his axe on another.

"They are the Godless!" Dahlen finally said as she stabbed through one and threw a knife into the throat of another.

"Then the rumors are true!" The Viper yelled over his attack. "They have joined Bornnen!"

Maleya let out a yell as one of the Godless succeeded in striking a blow, its metal talons raking across her arm.

"Maleya!" The Viper screamed as he moved to save her, thrusting his sword through the man. "Are you hurt?" he asked her, his voice dripping with concern.

"I will be fine," she replied, through gritted teeth. "Please, help the others."

"Thane!" Dahlen called out as she fought another one of their attackers off. "Are you any closer to being done with whatever you're doing?"

"You must be patient. Magic cannot be rushed," Thane yelled back calmly.

"Ah!" Malek grunted as he smashed the heads of two Godless together. "There is time for patience later! We need you to be done now!"

"Alright," Thane said, standing. "The Defiant, light an arrow!" he commanded.

The Defiant quickly wrapped a piece of cloth around one of her arrows. Dahlen then took the red opal and touched the tip of the arrow with it, causing it to ignite.

"Ready!" The Defiant called out.

"Cover your ears and do not look at it," Thane told them as he threw a small bundle in the air further up the path. "Fire!"

The Defiant released the flaming arrow as everyone crouched and covered their heads. The arrow found its target causing an explosion of bright, white light. The sounds of screeching could be heard from the woods, the figures of the Godless writhing in pain on the ground. The nine of them slowly stood as the surrounding trees slowly began to fade and the darkness was replaced by the late-afternoon sun.

"What in the greater realms?" Tristan breathed.

"What just happened?" Dahlen asked, confused.

"I have neutralized their illusion," Thane replied.

"At least the horses didn't go far," The Defiant pointed out, seeing the now-calm animals grazing on grass a hundred yards away.

"Ugly bastards, aren't they?" The Viper said walking up to one of the Godless trying to crawl away and stabbing him. He uttered a small, stifled cry before he died.

"Do the Godless do magic as well then?" Dahlen asked.

Malek, who had a small knife sticking out of his thigh, shook his head as he pulled it out with no more than a grunt. "No, this is from the Southern Tribes," he replied.

"That one over there," Hanek pointed out.

There on the ground, several yards from them, a woman struggled to stand. She was breathing heavily, squinting as she pressed her hands to her head.

"I'll get her," The Defiant said starting to move in her direction.

"I will come," Thane called out. "She might still have a trick up her sleeve."

The Defiant hesitated enough for Thane to catch up, the both of them moving cautiously towards the tribal witch.

"Ugh, these creatures are seriously hideous," The Viper commented as he stabbed another one.

"They are not creatures," Dahlen replied. "They are just unfortunate looking men." She moved the corpse of one with her foot and frowned, gazing at their strange grey skin and teeth filed to a point.

"They come from a barren wasteland, don't they?" Tristan asked. "Living underground in caves, or something like that."

"As far as I know," Dahlen replied. "They live beyond Bornnen and the land between that and theirs is a desert vaster and harsher than the Desert of Vremir." She shook her head. "Not many people care to travel through it to find out more about the Godless."

"Yeah," The Viper commented, "and the rumors of cannibalism probably don't make it a desirable place to visit either."

"That is why they file their teeth to a point," Hanek surmised. "So they can rip flesh from your bones."

Tristan shivered. "Pleasant."

"Are you well?" Viktor asked, approaching Maleya. "Does your wound trouble you?"

Maleya, who had been nursing her hurt arm forced a smile. "It's not so deep," she replied just before she fainted.

The Viper turned and ran to her, gathering her in his arms. "Maleya!" He brushed back her hair, noticing the beads of sweat falling from her brow. "She has a fever."

Dahlen came over and looked at her arm. "She's right, the wound is not that deep and it's too early for infection to set in," she told them. "The blades must have been poisoned."

"No, no, no," The Viper whispered shaking his head as he pressed a hand to Maleya's damp cheek.

"We must figure out what poison was used," Hanek told them. "That is only way we can stop its effects."

Dahlen nodded. "Malek, what about you?" she asked. "How are you feeling?" She motioned to his bleeding leg.

Malek, who had started to breathe a little heavier, said, "I think all of their weapons are laced with something," as he fell to his knees.

Hanek caught him before he fell to the ground.

"What the hell is going on here?" The Defiant asked, confused.

Thane placed the unconscious witch on the ground.

"The Godless, their weapons were laced with some kind of poison," Dahlen replied.

Thane frowned and walked over to Maleya, using a thumb to open one of her eyes. He then picked up her arm and inspected her wound.

"Here," Tristan said, handing him a knife he took from one of the corpses.

Thane took it tentatively. He studied the blade, sniffing it before nodding. "White oleander oil," he said, moving toward his pack and pulling out a few herbs.

"Is there an antidote?" The Viper asked nervously. "Can you save her?"

Thane nodded. "Yes, but the healing is slow," he replied. "We must start a fire and mix what I have for them. It will take some time, but they will recover."

The Viper pulled Maleya close and kissed her forehead. "You're going to be okay," he told her.

The Defiant sighed. "Too bad the trees are gone," she replied. "I'll go find something to burn.

"I will help," Viktor added, following The Defiant.

Tristan and Dahlen exchanged glances.

"What can we do?" Dahlen asked.

"For now," Thane replied, "make them comfortable."

THE WITCH WOKE WITH A JOLT, SURPRISED TO FIND HERSELF ALIVE and tied up.

"Took her long enough," The Defiant muttered. "I didn't hit her that hard."

"Tell us what we want to know," Dahlen started, "and your death will be painless. Lie," she narrowed her eyes at the witch, "and it won't."

"Te asssssaaaaa hirrrraaa shekourrrrmaaaaa," the witch hissed, her teeth black with decay.

Dahlen tried not to flinch at her hot breath. "You will only die with honor if you don't scream while doing it," she replied in the same acidic tone. She pulled out one of her throwing knives and pressed it against the woman's throat.

The witch's lip twitched.

"Tell me the layout of the castle," Dahlen demanded. "Who guards it and how many?"

The witch only glared at her.

"Bartenou saer elthen enkroush ehir!" Dahlen yelled in the witch's tribal dialect.

The witch remained silent.

The Defiant rolled her eyes and, taking her own knife, jabbed the edge of it into the witch's knee before popping the joint loose.

The witch howled it pain.

Dahlen shot The Defiant a silent glare.

"Ask her now," The Defiant told her with a shrug.

"Atlan? Atlan klat goshure themalt?" Dahlen asked. *Now? Now will you speak?*

"Jaharet!" she cried. *Never!*

The Defiant backhanded her, but it only resulted in the witch laughing at her efforts.

Dahlen rubbed her mouth with her hand, frustrated. She stood and walked away for a moment. "Thane!" she called.

Thane came over. "Yes."

"How do we get her to talk?" she asked in a hushed voice.

Thane shot a glance in the witch's direction, The Defiant's knife still sticking out of her knee. "I doubt torture will work," he replied.

"Do we not have any of that stuff the ghosts gave that one guy from the order?" Tristan asked, approaching them.

Dahlen thought for a moment. "The only person who would know that is Maleya and she's not exactly lucid right now."

Thane furrowed his brow. "What did they give this man?"

Dahlen shook her head. "Some sort of dark brown liquid that made him tell the truth."

Thane gave a pensive nod. "I have heard of it," he replied. "But I have never made it before. Its ingredients are rare."

"Check Maleya's pack to see if what you need is in there," Dahlen told him.

He nodded, doing as he was told.

Dahlen turned back to the witch just as she finished freeing herself from her bindings. She pulled the knife from her knee with a grunt and held it out in front of her.

Dahlen started and moved to stop her when she held the knife to her own throat.

"No!" Dahlen shouted, holding her hand out.

"Yah abath rendat, fer ander pendash!" she screamed as she raked the knife across her throat and toppled to the ground. *I fear nothing, not even death!*

CHAPTER 32

THE GROUP, NOW DOWN TO SIX WITH MALEYA AND MALEK HURT AND Thane staying to watch over them, made it to the edge of the cliff that overlooked the summer castle. Dahlen paused as she looked down at it, taking in not only the layout but the connection the place had to her past.

She blinked at it, realizing that its layout made it easy prey to any siege, but recognized its beauty. The castle was surrounded by lush grass and fauna, but was also shrouded by the mist that floated from the waves as they crashed onto the neighboring beach. The castle itself was nothing to boast. It was no bigger or grander than any other lord's, but the view was more picturesque than anything she had ever seen. The light of the moon only enhanced its natural beauty.

"And of this, I might have been mistress," she thought to herself. "This all could have been mine had fate thought kinder on my family."

"What is the plan?" The Defiant asked, shaking her from her reverie.

"Well," Dahlen started, searching the grounds, "I think it safer if we take the path down the mountain, though it would cut our time down significantly if we grapple down."

The Defiant nodded, looking out into the valley. She pulled out a looking glass and placed it over her eye.

"Where did you get that?" Dahlen asker her.

The Defiant, without looking away, shrugged. "I swiped it off of one of the ghosts before we left the Scattered Forest," she replied, indifferently.

"You swiped it?" Dahlen repeated. "You mean you stole it?"

"Don't worry," The Defiant said, reaching into her bag and producing another one. "I swiped you one, too."

Dahlen narrowed her eyes at The Defiant slightly, before taking the proffered object and pressing it to her own eye.

"The coast looks pretty clear," The Defiant said as she scanned the area. "It might actually be safe to grapple down."

Dahlen nodded. "Agreed."

"I'm sorry," Tristan started, shaking his head. "Grapple down?"

The other five in the group slowly turned their heads and blinked at him.

"Yes, we can tie our ropes to these trees here and go down two at a time," Dahlen continued. "Sound good?"

Everyone except for Tristan nodded.

"Let's go," Dahlen said moving to prepare their decent.

After the ropes were tied, Dahlen explained to Tristan what to do. She handed him a pair of leather gloves and told him to put them on.

"You don't have to go down fast," she told him. "But, also, time is important so don't take all night."

Tristan gulped. "Yeah, no, sure. It'll be fine. I'll be fine. I obviously do this all of the time."

She smiled at him. "You've made it this far," she replied. "And I am sure you will make it further. I have yet to find a reason as to why Mahk made me bring you along."

Tristan seemed to calm at her words.

"You have yet to serve your purpose," she added moving to the edge of the cliff and pulling on the rope to make sure it was secure.

The Defiant took the other rope and did the same. "See you girls on the bottom," she said as she jumped off the cliff.

Dahlen and The Defiant made it down to the bottom without issue followed by The Viper and Hanek and then Viktor and Tristan. Tristan struggled, inching his way slowly down the rope.

"Gods be blessed," The Defiant mumbled at his slow pace.

"I should have strapped him on my back," Hanek mumbled. "It would have been faster."

"So would pushing him," The Defiant commented.

Dahlen lifted a brow in her direction.

The Viper sighed. "He is taking too long," he said. "What if they have a scout that looks out and sees him still making his way down a half an hour later?" He rolled his shoulders.

"Tristan!" Dahlen half yelled, half whispered. "You need to hurry up!"

Tristan let out a shaky breath. "I am not sure I have ever told you this before, but I am very much afraid of heights."

"Oh," The Defiant uttered, pressing a hand to her forehead, "that's wonderful. Perhaps, you could have told us this before you started climbing down the damn cliff!"

"You're doing great, Tristan," Dahlen encouraged. "But you would do better to hurry. It would be appreciated."

"Or I will shoot you down myself!" The Defiant yelled up.

"Not helping," Dahlen told her.

"Damn priest," The Defiant grumbled, pacing impatiently.

"Keep going, Tristan," Dahlen coaxed, trying not to sound annoyed. "Just a little faster. You're almost there."

"I am doing the best I can," he replied, a little disgruntled.

"Oh, for the love of the Goddesses," The Defiant said pulling out her bow and firing a single arrow, hitting the rope a few feet from Tristan's head and causing it to fray.

Tristan let out a yelp as he clung to the rope.

"The Defiant, what is wrong with you?" Dahlen hissed.

"What?" The Defiant shrugged nonchalantly. "I thought he could use some encouragement."

"You might want to go a little faster, Tristan," The Viper told him. "For your sake more than ours now."

Everyone looked on as Tristan scrambled down the rope at a significantly faster speed, all the while watching as the rope continued to fray.

"The Defiant, you are crazy!" Tristan yelled.

"You're doing great, priest," The Defiant called back. "Keep up the good work."

Before he could reach the bottom, however, the rope snapped, and Tristan gave a small yell as he fell the rest of the way right into Viktor's arms. He opened his eyes to see the brute smiling down at him. Tristan scrambled out of his arms and stood, regaining his bearings.

"See?" The Defiant chuckled. "My plan worked."

Without warning Tristan walked over to The Defiant and punched her square in jaw.

"Tristan!" Dahlen called out.

"That is enough!" The Viper said at the same time.

The Defiant shook her head, dazed for a moment as she rubbed her jaw. She nodded at Tristan. "Point taken, priest," she told him shooting him a grin. "That's a nice right hook you got there."

Tristan straightened his robes and stood a little taller. "Now, we have a soothsayer to find," he said pushing his way through the grass and toward the castle.

The Defiant shrugged. "You heard the man." She pulled another arrow out. "Let's do this."

CHAPTER 33

Viktor, Tristan with Hanek, and The Viper with Dahlen. The plan was
to sweep the castle in search of the soothsayer and to meet back at
the top of the cliff before dawn.

"We will take the path back up," Dahlen started. "If you are not at
the top by dawn, we will assume you are dead. We cannot wait not
knowing the dangers that lie before us. If you are not dead, then we
shall see you back at the settlement."

The others nodded.

"The only thing I know of the soothsayer is that she is a woman
and her name either starts with an 'x' or that is what she is known
by," Dahlen continued. "That is all I have to go on."

The Viper shrugged. "Specific enough."

"The Defiant and Viktor will enter from the north, Tristan and
Hanek will enter from the south, and The Viper and I will enter on
the eastern side. We will make our way to the western part of the
castle which is where I am assuming she is, given the layout. Clear
out what guards there might be and then take her."

Everyone nodded once again, shooting each other final glances
as they parted.

Dahlen and The Viper ran, half hunched to the eastern side of the castle, finding a lattice that led up to a vast balcony. They climbed it, jumping over the stone railing. Dahlen took a moment to take in the scene before her. It was not just a balcony, but a garden with fountains and trees and ivy crawling up the walls.

"Is this where my father found my mother?" she thought.

A noise was heard and the two of them ducked behind one of the fountains just as two men from the Order walked out onto the balcony. They appeared drunk as they laughed and stumbled their way outside. They rested against the railing talking closely to one another before they embraced.

Dahlen and The Viper exchanged glances before shrugging, hesitating only a moment before both of them shot and killed them with their bows.

"I feel a little bad about that one," The Viper told her. "I mean, they were just trying to—"

"Not the time," Dahlen interrupted, moving toward the door.

They continued on, ducking around corners when they saw the light from torches dancing on the walls. They waited until whoever was holding the torch rounded the corner before killing them and continuing.

They made their way further to the western side of the castle when Dahlen stopped. She looked to her right and saw a door, feeling an encouraging breeze as she stepped towards it.

"Where are you going?" The Viper whispered.

"She's in here," Dahlen whispered back.

"You said go to the western part of the castle," The Viper told her.

Dahlen nodded. "I know," she replied. "But she's in *here*."

The Viper nodded and moved toward the door. He pulled on the handle but it was locked. "Perfect," he muttered. "Now we will have to find a key."

Dahlen looked at the door for a moment before she pulled out her red opal.

"Are you crazy?" The Viper asked her, grabbing her wrist. "We want to get out of the castle, not burn alive in it."

"Trust me," Dahlen told him, relieving herself from his grasp. She took a deep breath and let it out slowly as she gently placed the opal on the metal lock of the door.

The Viper took a step back, holding his breath as, to his surprise, only the lock melted away.

"I realized I can control it," Dahlen said triumphantly as she pushed the door open.

"Well, isn't that convenient?" The Viper muttered, following her up a narrow, winding staircase.

"This must be one of the towers," Dahlen whispered as she pulled out two of her throwing knives.

The Viper nodded as he did the same.

Once they reached the top there was another door. They paused at it, listening. They couldn't hear anything, but the glow coming from under the door told them that someone was inside.

Dahlen motioned for him to cover the right while she covered the left. She held up three fingers and counted down before she reached out and pushed the door open. They burst into the room looking around them for any signs of danger and stopped when they noticed the only occupant in the room was a little girl.

The girl, who had been sitting at a desk writing, had jumped up from her seat and faced them. Looking from one to the other, her face wore a terrified expression.

Dahlen's mouth gaped open as hers and the girl's eyes met, a sense of familiarity enveloping her as she continued to stare.

The Viper put his knives away and shook his head. "Well, we obviously went the wrong way," he said.

Just then, the little girl let out a scream and ran at The Viper stabbing him in the arm with her quill.

"Ah! You little brat!" he yelled, backhanding her across the face, causing her to fall to the ground, unconscious.

"The Viper, stop!" Dahlen said, running to the girl and kneeling over her.

"She stabbed me!" The Viper retorted, pointing to the large feather quill sticking out of his arm.

"She's just a little girl."

"Who stabbed me!" The Viper emphasized. "A little girl who stabbed me with her damn quill!" He pulled out the feathered object with a groan and threw it into the dwindling fireplace. "It hurt."

"She thinks we are here to *hurt* her," Dahlen shot back.

"What the hell would we want with her? She's just a child."

"Because it is what she has been told her whole life, no doubt." Dahlen looked up at him. "This is the soothsayer," she told him.

"What?" The Viper retorted. "That little thing is what we have come all this way for?" He shrugged. "At least she will be easier to transport."

"Does she look familiar to you?" Dahlen asked.

The Viper shot the girl another glance and shook his head. "She's not mine if that's what you're asking."

"No, but I bet I know whose she is," Dahlen told him.

The girl stirred, scrambling away from them.

"We didn't come to hurt you," Dahlen said. "I know you know who I am. I do not know what lies they have told you about me, but you can trust me."

The girl shook as she looked from Dahlen to The Viper.

"I promise he will not hurt you either," Dahlen reassured her. "He was just taken aback when you stabbed him."

The girl looked at her, unsure.

Dahlen took a deep breath and let it out slowly. "I know you have been watching me for a long time now. And I want you to think back on every vision of me you have ever had."

The girl swallowed and nodded.

"What kind of person did you see?"

The girl blinked at her for a moment.

"Did you see someone who was cruel? Someone who went back on her word?"

Finally, she shook her head. "No," she squeaked.

"Do you think I would be someone you could trust?"

The girl hesitated another moment before she nodded.

Dahlen smiled. "Then, please believe me when I tell you we are here to rescue you from this prison," Dahlen told her. "We have come to save you."

A tear rolled down the girl's cheek. She nodded wordlessly.

"What is your name?"

The girl swallowed and took a shaky breath. "Xela," she said in a small voice.

Dahlen smiled. "It is nice to meet you, Xela," she replied. "Do you know where your parents are?"

Xela shook her head. "My mother died when I was just a baby. I never met my real father."

"Who raised you?" Dahlen asked.

Xela shrugged. "I have moved around from place to place. Sometimes I stay with priestesses. For a time, I was in King Ahlenwei's court. I knew you were coming. I saw it. I told Vron, and he moved me here. He didn't want me telling anyone else what I had seen."

"You have met Vron?" Dahlen asked.

Xela nodded. "He is the one who owns me."

Dahlen shook her head. "No one can own you, Xela."

"He can," she replied solemnly.

Dahlen nodded. "We are going to take you with you us now," she said softly. "You will be safe and I can take you to your father."

Xela looked at her. "Do you know him?" she asked, a hint of desperation in her voice. "Do you know my father?"

"Yes," Dahlen smiled. "I believe I do. He is one of my greatest friends."

Xela smiled back. "I would like that very much."

Dahlen held out her hand for the girl to take. She hesitated at first, but soon slipped a tiny hand in hers.

The Viper scowled. "Don't go stabbing me again, kid," he grumbled as he followed them out of the room and back down the tower.

"Why can't I read you?" Xela asked as they descended.

"Vremir has been protecting me from your visions," Dahlen explained. She showed her the opal. "He gave me this for protection."

"I am glad it was not because of my own failing," the girl replied. "Vron was becoming impatient with me. I have been fearing his next visit."

"Do you know where Vron is now?" she asked her. "Is he here?"

Xela shook her head. "No, but we should hurry. He will be quite angry with me when he sees I am gone. His anger scares me."

"We are going to take you somewhere he cannot find you," Dahlen told her reassuringly. "You will not have to be scared of him anymore."

"I want very much to believe you, but he is the god of water," Xela replied, an anxious look on her face. "He is everywhere."

"If all else fails, you can just stab him with a quill," The Viper interjected a little bitterly.

Dahlen shot him a look.

"Fine," he mumbled. "You're safe with us, kid," he told the girl in a forced happy tone.

"Come. You are right, Xela. We shouldn't linger."

The little girl nodded.

They made their way down the stairs and through the hallways and back out to the balcony. Her heart raced and she let out a sigh of relief. They moved toward the lattice where they had climbed up just as Prince Mohrr pulled himself over the edge of the balcony.

Dahlen stopped as the two of them stared at each other.

"Dahlen," Mohrr said breathlessly, approaching her.

"What are you doing here?" she asked in surprised confusion.

Mohrr stopped. "Marten came to us and said you would need help."

She shook her head. "You shouldn't have come," she told him.

Mohrr frowned. "You shouldn't have left," he shot back.

"Whoa," The Viper stepped in, "this is not exactly the time to discuss this. I think it would be better if we were to get the hell out of here before you start discussing your issues."

Mohrr pulled out his sword and pointed it at The Viper. "Stay out of this, assassin."

Xela whimpered behind Dahlen who put a reassuring hand on her back.

"Put your sword away," Dahlen ordered. "You are scaring the girl."

Mohrr glanced at the child, noticing her for the first time and sheathed his sword again. He nodded his head at her. "Forgive me."

"Did you come alone or did you bring anyone else with you?" Dahlen asked trying to break the tension, but still visibly angry.

"Vorce and some of his men joined me," Mohrr replied.

"And Dohrrn?"

He nodded. "He is safe. He is observing from the top of the cliff."

Dahlen gave a huff. "You should have stayed away."

"You cannot blame me for what happened!" Mohrr told her. "There was no other way. It had to be done."

"There is always another way!" Dahlen hissed back. "And you didn't even try! You just gave in, no questions asked!"

"She was my daughter too, Dahlen," Mohrr whispered with feeling. "I lost her too."

"Uh, again, maybe you guys can have this discussion at a less pivotal moment," The Viper cut in as shouting was heard coming from the castle. "We kind of need to get out of here."

"The lattice," Dahlen said, taking Xela by the hand and running to the far side of the balcony wall.

"Xela, I need you to hold onto The Viper's back," Dahlen told the girl.

"What?" The Viper said.

"He is going to carry you to safety," Dahlen explained. "I will be right behind him. Okay?"

Xela nodded.

The Viper muttered under his breath as he let the little girl climb on his back. Dahlen and Mohrr closely followed behind them. They ran through the grass where they met back up with Tristan and Hanek.

"What the hell is he doing here?" Tristan yelled when he saw Mohrr.

"This is not the time for our petty squabble, Tristan," Mohrr retorted.

"Where are the others?" Dahlen asked as they continued.

"Keep running!" The Defiant could be heard behind them, answering her question. She paused for a moment to shoot an arrow, hitting its target, before she continued running.

Viktor was not far behind her, slicing his way through men of the Godless and the order alike. He let out a yell when an arrow landed in his back. Everyone paused and looked, wanting to help, but he waived them on.

"Don't stop!" Viktor told them. "I will hold them off!"

"Brother!" Hanek yelled.

"I said, 'Go!'" Viktor yelled as he continued to wield his sword buying the others more time.

"We can't leave him," Tristan said as he took out his sword and ran back to help Viktor.

"Tristan!" Dahlen yelled after him.

The Defiant smirked. "Priest finally grew some balls," she said as she pulled out her two short swords and ran after him.

"Gods be blessed!" Dahlen cursed. She turned to The Viper. "Take Xela up to the horses!" she ordered. "Do not stop!"

"What?" The Viper replied as she turned and ran. "Wait! Don't leave me with her!" He cursed as he watched her run away. "Come on, kid," he grumbled as he took the girl's hand and led her away.

"Dahlen, what are you doing?" Mohrr asked as he ran after her. "We have to go!"

"I can't leave them!" she called back. "They need me." She pulled out her sword and a combat knife.

Mohrr grunted in frustration, but followed her lead.

Dahlen, The Defiant, Tristan, and Mohrr helped deflect attacks from the Order and Godless as Hanek helped Viktor to safety. They succeeded in pushing back a fair amount of them when yelling could be heard coming from the north. They looked and saw several Bornnenian soldiers rushing them.

"There are too many of them!" Dahlen shouted. "I think we should consider leaving!"

Just then, the ground began to rumble as Vorce and his men rode by them on horses. They charged the Bornnenians, breaking through their line.

"On second thought," The Defiant yelled over the noise, "I think the fun has finally begun!" She sheathed her swords and pulled out her bow, running toward the melee.

"I think I might sit this one out," Tristan said, an arrow sticking out of his leg.

Dahlen moved to help him, but he held up a hand.

"I'm fine," he replied. "Go and help."

Dahlen shot a brief glance at Mohrr before she ran to join her stepfather in battle. Mohrr did not hesitate as he rushed after her.

The battle was bloody and loud but was over in a matter of minutes, the last of the Bornnenians and the Order retreating into the castle as the survivors let out a small cry of victory.

Dahlen, catching her breath and smiling, looked up at Vorce. "How many more times are you going to save my life?" she asked him.

He jumped from his horse and wrapped her in a hug. "As long as you continue to find yourself in over your head," he replied.

"I should be angry with you," she told him. "I asked you not to come, but had you not, things would have turned out a little differently."

Vorce nodded. "You are welcome."

"We should leave," Mohrr told them. "We are well within arrow range."

They nodded and began moving quickly toward the path of the cliff, but before they made it too far, Vorce stopped to look back at the castle. He sighed, lingering where he stood, remembering that night all those years ago.

Dahlen turned and smiled at him. "Come, Vorce," she called out. "Let us go home."

He smiled and moved toward the rest of them when, from out of nowhere, Ohtt approached him from behind. Dahlen's eyes grew wide with horror as she watched Ohtt run his sword through Vorce.

"Nooooo!" Dahlen screamed moving to help him when Mohrr grabbed her by the arm.

"You can't!" he told her. "He will kill you too!"

"Let me go!" Dahlen cried as she watched her stepfather fall to his knees. "Vorce, no!" She struggled against Mohrr, who by then, had wrapped his arms around her waist, trying to pull her away.

"Run, my child," Vorce choked out. "Run."

Tears streamed down Dahlen's face as she broke free of Mohrr's grip. She pulled her bow off her back and released an arrow at Ohtt, who laughed as he hit it aside with his sword.

"I saw you die in the Scattered Forest!" she yelled, releasing another arrow that he once again, easily deflected.

Ohtt laughed. "You saw what you wanted to see," he replied.

Dahlen shook her head. "You fell into the collapsed beraxium mine. I saw it!"

Ohtt laughed, a low grumble in his throat. "There are not many ways to kill a god," he started, "and that is not one of them."

Dahlen gaped at him. "No," she replied breathlessly, shaking her head. "No!"

Ohtt laughed as he lifted his hand, palm out, making a pulsing motion. A large ball of water flew from his hand, hitting Dahlen, causing her to fly several feet back.

Drenched, Dahlen coughed and sputtered, as she pushed herself back off of the ground. "Vron," she said with a shaky breath. "You! You're Vron!"

He smiled. "I have been watching you for a long time, prophet," Vron said as he stepped forward deflecting arrows from the rest of Vorce's men.

"Dahlen, we have to go," Mohrr told her. "We cannot take on Vron alone."

"Listen to your prince, girl," Vron sneered. "Lest you end up like him." He motioned his head to Vorce's lifeless body.

Dahlen screamed and moved to charge him when the earth rumbled and several balls of flame rained down on Vron, exploding, sending him flying backward. Vron stood, laughing as he brushed himself off.

"Brother!" he cried, his arms stretched out. "Do you hide from me?"

He was answered with another storm of fire, the earth breaking around him as a rift was created between him and Dahlen and Mohrr.

"You cannot stop me, brother!" Vron yelled. "I buried you once; I can do it again!"

Mohrr was finally able to coax Dahlen onto a horse and ride away back up the mountain pass as the rift between them and Vron grew, the ground beneath him crumbling. Dahlen glanced backwards, wanting to see her stepfather one last time before he was consumed by the flames.

When they got to the top of the cliff, Dahlen jumped off of the horse.

"You should not have come!" she yelled at him, her voice riddled with anger.

"Dahlen, we came to help you," Mohrr replied.

"Yes, and all you succeeded in doing was getting Vorce killed!" she shot back at him.

Mohrr gave her a hurt look. "That is not fair," he replied, controlling his own emotions.

Dahlen.

She whipped around to see Dohrrn approaching her. He was taller than the last time she saw him.

Do not blame him. Had he chosen, Vorce would have willingly given his life for you, over and over again.

Dahlen fell to her knees in front of him and he put a warm hand to her cheek.

"But he did not choose," Dahlen replied, holding back her tears.

Dohrrn nodded. *Yes, he did.*

"Dahlen," The Defiant stepped in, "I think we should be going. We need to get Tristan and Viktor back to Thane so he can look at their wounds."

Dahlen nodded through her pain as she slowly stood. "Come, Dohrrn," she said, holding out her hand as she stood, "you can ride with me."

CHAPTER 34

THANE'S TREATMENT FOR MALEK AND MALEYA HAD WORKED IN SAVING their lives, though the poison greatly weakened them. For the first few days of traveling, they rarely stopped, fearing they might be followed. The two of them, too weak to ride, were forced to share a horse.

The Viper made no complaints as he rode with Maleya's arms wrapped around his waist; The Defiant, though less enthusiastic, rode with Malek. Tristan and Viktor's wounds, luckily, were not deep and were easily treatable though caused them both pain.

The journey back to the new settlement was tension filled. Most of those who came with Vorce parted, headed toward their hide-out, taking with them the sad news of Vorce's demise. Mohrr, however, stayed with Dahlen and her group, bearing the sharp looks he received from Tristan and the silent treatment from her. In contrast, Dohrrn was met with awe by Maleya and a thousand questions from Tristan, all of which had to be interpreted by Dahlen who eventually cut him off as she was getting tired of translating the answers.

"What are we going to do with the girl?" Tristan whispered one night at camp as they were sitting around the fire.

Xela, who had taken a liking to The Viper, was asleep with her head in his lap, and The Viper, having long forgiven her, didn't seem to mind.

Dahlen gave a small laugh at the sight. "We are going to take her to her father," she replied.

"And we know who that is?" Tristan inquired.

"The resemblance is too uncanny," Mohrr broke in, glancing over at the girl.

Dahlen looked at Mohrr for a second and nodded. "I doubt he even knows."

"And then what?" The Defiant pressed. "She is bound to know something of the Order that we don't. Perhaps, she knows where they gather. Maybe she will understand what that one guy said back in Halana Neya."

"The end is where the beginning will start. Where the sound of water can always be felt crashing over you," Tristan recited.

Mohrr furrowed his brow at him. "What did you say?" he asked.

Everyone looked over at him.

Tristan shrugged and shook his head. "It was just something someone we captured from the Order told us about where they meet or whatever."

"Have you heard of it before?" Dahlen asked.

Mohrr rubbed his lips together pensively and nodded. "It sounds very familiar," he replied. "But I cannot remember where I heard it."

"Same." Tristan nodded. "That is exactly what I felt when I heard it. It sounds familiar, but I cannot place where I have heard it before."

"Do you know, Dohrrn?" Dahlen inquired of the boy sitting next to her.

The Order was not formed until after my first coming. I know almost nothing about them.

Dahlen nodded.

The campsite fell into silence for a few minutes.

"I was in Hapren a few months ago," Mohrr said softly, causing the color from Dahlen's face to drain.

She looked up at him.

"My sister and her daughter are doing well."

Dahlen stood abruptly. "I am going to bed," she announced.

"Ehris stayed on with my sister as nursemaid," Mohrr continued as she turned to walk away. "My sister was at a loss for a name, so Ehris suggested Mirabelle."

Dahlen froze for a second.

"Rain loved the name so much, she decided to use it."

Dahlen let out a shaky breath, but refused to say anything.

"Princess Mirabelle has a nice ring to it, don't you think?"

Dahlen stood unmoving as she took a moment to swallow her pain before she walked away.

You should not be angry with him.

Dahlen looked down at Dohrrn riding in front of her. Pretty soon, he would be taller than her. "Angry with whom?"

Dohrrn looked back at her and raised a brow.

Dahlen averted her eyes and cleared her throat.

It feels as if you have long forgiven me and Marten, yet, you still blame Mohrr, though he had the least to do with it all.

Dahlen shifted uncomfortably in her seat. "Maybe he has everything to do with it," she whispered.

Is it because you are scared of what might happen if you let him get close again?

"You may be the god of fire," Dahlen started, "but you are not privy to all of my thoughts and feelings."

Dohrrn shook his head. *I just want you to be happy.*

"I was," she mumbled in response.

"You know, it almost seems as if you are talking to yourself," Tristan said pulling his horse up to theirs.

"Who's to say I am not?" Dahlen shot back.

Tristan shook his head. "I am still amazed by you, my lord," he said turning his attention to Dohrrn. "I feel honored to be riding along-side you."

Dohrrn gave Tristan a small smile and nod.

"How is your leg?" Dahlen asked him.

Tristan nodded. "It is a little tender at times, but I do believe it is healing rather nicely."

"Priest here took that arrow like a champion," The Defiant added. She gave Tristan a nod, not afraid to let her new-found respect for him show.

Tristan sat a little higher on his horse.

"And how about you, Viktor?" Dahlen asked. "How is your back where the arrow hit you?"

Viktor rolled his left shoulder, wincing only a little. "Had I not had my leather armor and fur on," he started, "the arrow certainly would have pierced deeper than it did." He nodded. "I shall heal nicely."

"The Viper," Xela called from her place in front of Thane.

"Yes, child," The Viper called back.

"There is danger ahead," Xela replied.

Everyone pulled on their horses' reins bringing them to a stop.

"What do you mean?" The Viper inquired, calmly, not wanting to frighten her.

"There are Bornnenian soldiers ahead," she explained. "The path we are taking, it leads to a Bornnenian camp that is moving to invade Thren."

Everyone else in the group exchanged glances.

"How many did you see, Xela?" Dahlen asked.

"Over a thousand."

Dahlen and the others frowned. "So little?" she thought out loud. "A thousand soldiers will not last long in Thren."

"But it is far too many for us to take on," Hanek pointed out.

"Perhaps they aren't the main army," The Defiant suggested. "They are just ruffians hired to ransack neighboring villages to send a message."

"At any rate, we would do well to avoid them," The Viper added.

Dahlen looked conflicted. "We should do something," she replied. "A thousand Bornnenian soldiers against unarmed and untrained farmers will do a lot of damage."

"What are we to do?" Tristan asked. "Even if we send word to Harpren, their soldiers would never get here in time to stop them."

Dahlen let out a sigh. "Dohrrn?"

He looked at Prince Mohrr.

"Thren has reinforced its borders since the attack on my sister," he reassured her. "I also suggested to Castuhl that it would be in his best interest to hire mercenaries from the Nameless."

Dahlen blinked at him.

He shrugged. "Marten told us about these raiding parties six months ago," he explained. "There isn't a village along the border that isn't protected. Even some of the village men are being trained to defend their lands."

The Viper lifted his brows and nodded. "Nice," he commented. "It's very convenient to have someone who can foresee the future on your— oh!" He looked at Xela and then over at Dahlen. "Now, I get it."

"Get what?" Tristan asked.

"We're going around the Bornnenians," Dahlen explained.

CHAPTER 35

THE GROUP MADE IT TO THE SETTLEMENT A FEW DAYS LATER WITHOUT incident, tired and silent. They all breathed a sigh of relief as they walked through the gates.

Dahlen turned to them. "The Viper, look after Xela while I seek out Marten," she told him.

The Viper nodded.

"I will summon you when I am ready for you to bring her to him," she added.

"Come on, kid," The Viper said, taking the young girl from Thane's horse. "Let's go see what kind of trouble we can get ourselves into."

Xela gave a small laugh as she took The Viper by the hand and was led away.

"Everyone else, rest, if you would like to," Dahlen said to the others.

"I would like to lay down," Maleya said quietly.

"I can take her somewhere," The Defiant offered helping Maleya from the horse.

Dahlen nodded.

"I should like to tell the others of our loss," Malek replied somberly. "But I can wait if you would like the honor."

Dahlen held back a shiver, a lump caught in her throat. She shook her head after a moment. "No, you should do it," she told him. "They should hear it from one of their own."

He bowed to her and walked off, Thane, Hanek and Viktor following closely behind.

Dahlen's eyes met Mohrr's for a moment before she turned away.

"Dohrrn?" she said looking at the boy beside her.

Go. I will follow.

Dahlen nodded and made her way to Marten's hut.

"Marten is that monk guy, right?" Tristan asked hobbling next to her as she walked. "I met him when we first traveled to Thren together."

Dahlen nodded. "Yes, he is." She glanced over at him. "Thane ordered you to stay off of that leg, did he not?"

Tristan shrugged. "Thane said a lot of things," he replied nonchalantly.

"You forget Tristan only hears what he wants to," Mohrr added in.

Tristan shot him a sharp glance.

"A family trait, to be sure," Dahlen retorted.

Tristan laughed through his nose.

When they got to Marten's little hut, Dahlen called out to him. He appeared at the threshold a moment later. He smiled with relief, hugging her.

"I am glad to see you again," he told her, pulling away.

She nodded and forced a small smile.

"What happened?" he asked. "I had no more visions after everyone left."

Dahlen cleared her throat and blinked back tears. "Vorce is dead," she whispered, unable to say the words any louder.

Marten closed his eyes and rubbed his mouth with his hand, letting out a sigh. After several seconds he nodded. "Come in," he told them softly, motioning with his head for them to follow.

Dahlen entered, and, despite being tired, stood, Tristan and Mohrr following her example. Dohrrn, however, sat cross legged on the floor.

"I am sorry for your loss, T," Marten said softly. "Vorce was a good man."

She nodded silently, rubbing her lips together. "What happened with The Master?" she asked quietly after several seconds. "I did not think you would be leaving the Rest so soon."

Marten nodded. "Nor did I," he replied. "But, once I saw my vision, I left immediately. It couldn't have been three days after I last saw you when I had it. I knew I couldn't waste any time and rode almost nonstop until I came here. Vorce had just arrived himself."

Mohrr sighed. "He had come to tell us about you and where you were headed."

Dahlen scoffed and shook her head. "Then you would have come regardless," she stated.

Mohrr nodded.

"Vorce would have gone knowing he would lose his life if it meant saving yours," Marten added.

Dahlen nodded silently. "Were you able to discern anything from The Master before you left?" she finally asked after a heavy pause.

Marten avoided her gaze. "Only a little," he replied. "He is difficult to read since he had been wearing the medallion for so long. The effects of it have not completely worn off."

"And what were you able to find out?" Dahlen pressed.

Marten took in a long breath through his nose and let it out slowly.

"I am not going to like whatever you are about to tell me, am I?" Dahlen asked.

Marten shook his head. "No," he replied softly. "The Master has long been an agent for the Order."

Mohrr frowned. "Wait, you are speaking of The Master. One of The Leaders of The Nameless," he clarified. "Dahlen's mentor?"

Dahlen looked at the ground. "Yes," she replied emotionlessly. "A man I trusted with my life."

Marten nodded. "The night your family was massacred, Dahlen, he was the one that informed the Order of the coven's rescue mission, forcing them to strike earlier than they intended."

Dahlen balled her fists in anger. "Continue."

Marten rubbed his lips together. "The Order had known for years that your mother was still alive. But it was The Master who found where she was. He had long ago suspected your father at hiding her. Through him, he found out that Vorce was still alive protecting your mother."

Dahlen took a shaky breath calming herself. "It was him, wasn't it?" she asked softly. "He was the one who sent Vorce that letter, pretending to be my father. He lured Vorce away so the Order could finally kill my mother."

Marten nodded. "Yes, but he had no idea you existed until I led them to you."

Dahlen shook her head. "I do not blame you, Marten," she told him softly. "You were meant to find me."

"Is that all?" Tristan asked after a moment. "Were you unable to find out where the Order gathers or hides?"

Marten sized Tristan up for a moment, seeming unsure as to why he was even there.

"It's all right, Marten," Dahlen urged gently. "I have long forgiven him."

Tristan shot a glance at Dahlen; Mohrr blanched; Marten nodded.

"The last thing I was able to see before he began wearing the amulet was a letter, a reply to one of his," Marten began. "It told him to watch over the girl, meaning you, Dahlen. He was ordered to keep close tabs on you, observe you and when the time came, hand you over to Vron and the Order."

"Any idea on who the letter was from?" Mohrr asked.

Marten shook his head. "I imagine it must be Vron, but I cannot tell, and anything else I tried to read from him was foggy and unintelligible."

"What do you mean by read?" Tristan asked, confused.

Dahlen looked over at him. "Marten is a soothsayer, Tristan," she informed him. "He can read the past, present, and future simply with a touch."

Tristan's eyes grew wide as he began to understand. "So Xela is—"

"Speaking of Vron," Dahlen began, interrupting him, "we now know who he is."

"You met him?" Marten asked, his eyes wide.

"I have met him on several occasions," Dahlen told him.

Marten creased his brows.

"General Ohtt of the Bornnenian army," she explained.

Marten gaped at her. "He had whittled himself into a place of power," he said. "Word around the realm is that Ohtt killed Ahlenwei's heir, Prince Alihen. No one has seen or heard from the boy in almost two years."

Dahlen nodded.

"And now Ohtt, or Vron, rules the country," Mohrr commented. "It is only a matter of time before he declares himself king."

"Yes, but we now have his soothsayer," Tristan added.

Dahlen nodded. "Fetch Xela, would you, Tristan?" she asked quietly.

He nodded and soon after left the hut. She shot Mohrr a glance as well and he nodded as he followed Tristan out. Dohrrn remained silent on the floor.

"Xela?" Marten questioned.

"Bornnen's soothsayer," Dahlen told him.

Marten nodded. "How long has she been working for them?"

"Since she was born," Dahlen replied.

Marten furrowed his brow in confusion. "How would they have even known she was a soothsayer when she was born? It takes years for that kind of gift to present itself."

"Perhaps it might be a shot in the dark most of the time, but if the gift is inherent, then you only need to know that one of the parents is one."

He shook his head. "I wouldn't know if that theory was true or not," he replied. "My father was certainly not one, but I never knew my mother, so I cannot confirm or deny whether my gift is inherent or not."

Dahlen smiled at him. "My guess is that it is."

The door to the hut opened and the young girl with pale skin, dark hair and eyes walked in. She stood for a moment in the doorway, unsure, until her eyes met Marten's. She blinked at him for a moment.

Marten started, recognizing her features even in the dimness of the hut. He gaped at the small child, his knees weak until they gave out and he fell, kneeling on the floor. His eyes began to glisten.

Xela looked over at Dahlen who gave her an encouraging nod.

Xela took a few more steps forward. "Good day," she said barely above a whisper. "My name is Xela."

Marten chuckled lightly, pressing a hand to his mouth as a tear fell. "I am very pleased to meet you, Xela," he replied just as softly, his voice riddled with emotion. "I am Marten." He extended his hand to shake hers, but the girl hesitated. "I will not hurt you," he told her reassuringly.

Dahlen made a gesture to Dohrrn to leave, who stood and left the hut, giving the newly reunited father and daughter a moment alone.

"I HAD NO IDEA OF HER EXISTENCE," MARTEN LATER EXPLAINED. "HER mother was a—" he stopped a moment.

"Prostitute," Dahlen finished for him.

Marten smiled weakly. "Yes, from Bornnen. I used to frequent her company for days at a time whenever I traveled through and then one day I came back and she was gone. No one really knew why or where she went." He shook his head. "Skyla was her name."

"Do you think she knew about your abilities?" Mohrr asked. "Perhaps she was—"

Dahlen cleared her throat, interrupting him.

Marten nodded understandingly. "Paid to become pregnant with my child," he sighed. "Perhaps this is another thing The Master is behind. No one else beyond the coven knew about my gift."

"What are we to do with the girl now?" Tristan asked wanting to be a part of the conversation.

"It's obvious we cannot let her fall into anyone else's hands," The Defiant chimed in. "And she obviously cannot go back to Vron."

"She will have to stay here, no doubt," Dahlen concluded. "It is here where she will be undetected and safe."

Everyone nodded.

Xela squealed in delight as The Viper performed a magic trick, pulling a coin from behind her ear.

Marten smiled lovingly in her direction. "How could I have not known?" he whispered a little somberly, more to himself than the others.

Dahlen reached out and squeezed his arm gently. "You couldn't have as long as she remained in Vron's presence," she reassured him. "He would have shielded her from you."

He looked at Dahlen, his eyes glistening. "I understand now," he told her. "What you told me that day in the back of the wagon."

She nodded and shot a small glance at Mohrr.

"She will be sad to see us all go so soon," Maleya commented. "She was stahting to open up the last few days of our tu-rrip."

"What do you mean?" The Defiant asked, confused. "What more are we to do? The beraxium mine is no more, we informed the coven of some of its members' treachery, and we rescued Vron's soothsayer."

"Though it didn't start out as a rescue," Tristan added unnecessarily.

The others slowly turned their heads to glare at him.

"Well, there is still potentially another beraxium mine or store-house in Skahrr," Mohrr replied. "Marten and I have been reading archives on mining."

"Sounds awful," The Defiant mumbled.

"We were hoping it would tell us something useful as to the whereabouts of another possible mine."

"Are we sure there aren't any mines in Bornnen?" Dahlen asked. "They have every other mine. It wouldn't be too farfetched if they had a beraxium one too."

Marten shook his head. "Beraxium mines are always by the sea," he informed her. "And since Bornnen doesn't have any access…"

Dahlen nodded. "At least that narrows down the searching field for a mine, but a storehouse could certainly be anywhere."

"True," Marten agreed.

"Bahxium is important, yes," Maleya began, "but you all ah fohgetting something of much gu-rreater impohtance."

Everyone looked at her.

We have yet to find my brother and sisters.

Dahlen glanced at Dohrrn who had been patiently listening until then. "Maleya is right," she said quietly. "We need to find and release Mahk, Gher, and Behr from their prison."

"Easier said than done, I imagine," Tristan commented. "Much like everything else we have done up to this point."

"If it was easy," The Defiant smirked, "it wouldn't be fun."

"How do we go about finding them?" Tristan asked.

Ask the girl.

Dahlen glanced over at Xela who was being led over to the group by The Viper. She smiled at them knowingly.

"I am ready to answer your questions," she told them in anticipation. "But I wish to ask you, Dahlen, a question first."

Dahlen smiled at the similarities between father, and daughter. "That is only fair," she replied.

Xela blinked up at her. "What happened to your child?"

CHAPTER 36

THE CONFUSION AND ANGER THAT ERUPTED IN THE GROUP FROM THOSE
that were ignorant of what the girl was talking about was almost palpable. Tristan and The Defiant exploded in a torrent of questions and
statements, while Maleya only stood there confused.

"That is why The Viper did not complete his contract," The Defiant
surmised. "He found that you were with child, didn't he?"

"How could you not have told us something like that?" Tristan
asked angrily. "How could you have kept something so important
from us?"

"Theah must be an explanation," Maleya said calmly, trying to pla-
cate the other two. "She would not have hidden such a thing if it was
not impohtant."

"So, when I asked you if there was anything else you were hiding
from us back in the Scattered Forest, you lied to me?" The Defiant
interrogated. "All of the months we have been traveling together, and
everything we have been through mean nothing if all you are going
to do is lie."

"If you cannot trust us," Tristan said gesturing to himself and The
Defiant, "how do you expect us to trust you?"

"Which we have!" The Defiant exclaimed. "We have trusted

you! We went on this self-serving journey almost unquestioningly because we put our trust in you and you couldn't even show us the respect to be forthcoming about everything!"

"So that *is* the real reason Mohrr *bought* you from the coven," Tristan huffed. "Didn't take him long to get you flat on your back, did it?"

Mohrr, no longer able to control his own anger, punched Tristan in the face. Tristan tumbled backward, but didn't fall. He paused for a moment wiping the blood forming on his lip and glared at his cousin before he lunged at him, tackling him to the ground.

Mohrr grunted as he fell on his back, barely blocking Tristan's punch. The prince rolled, throwing Tristan off of him, the both of them struggling to gain control as they swung at each other.

Marten and The Viper jumped in pulling the two of them away as they continued to reach and curse at one another.

"You are the filthiest of scum, Mohrr!" Tristan yelled struggling against The Viper as he pulled him away. "All you have ever done is use your money to get what you want."

"You are only jealous!" Mohrr shot back, yanking his arm out of Marten's grasp and straightening his vest. "You have always been jealous of me. Because you are nothing but a bastard!"

"Enough!" bellowed Dahlen.

They all looked at her.

"Mine and," she cleared her throat, "Mohrr's daughter has nothing to do with any of you." She looked from one to the other. "Her existence does not change what we have to do. It does not change the fact that Vron is growing an army. Has made allies with the Godless and the Southern Lost Tribes." She shook her head. "I will not apologize for not letting you in on *my* personal business as I have rarely asked as much from any of you. I wish you could respect that."

"So that is it?" The Defiant asked. "We are just supposed to let it go?"

"Yes," Dahlen replied matter-of-factly.

The Defiant crossed her arms. "Where is she, then?"

Dahlen narrowed her eyes. "Gone," she told her, rolling her shoulders. "I was forced to give her away. Forced to allow another woman take over the duties I was prepared to do, duties that I never realized I yearned to do. Because of who I am, she would never be safe with me."

Tristan and The Defiant avoided her gaze.

Dahlen huffed through her nose. "Yes, I omitted the truth about her, just as I omitted the truth about Vremir. But I did not do it out of spite, or out of mistrust for any of you," she explained. "I did it because her existence is none of your damn business. And I don't have to justify all of my actions to you." She looked from one to the other. "Now, you can either respect that, or you can leave."

Neither of them responded as she glared at them.

She nodded curtly. "If you'll excuse me, I am going to rest." She turned and moved away from the group, walking the familiar path to the little hut that had been built for her over a year ago before she left. The hut she had thought she would share with her daughter. Mohrr had caught up with her by the time she made it to the door.

"Dahlen," he said softly.

She turned and looked at him.

"Might we talk in private?"

Dahlen was too tired to argue. She simply nodded and allowed him to follow her inside. She opened a window and lit a few candles to let in some light. She gave a brief look around the large one room hut, recognizing that someone had been keeping it clean for her. She smiled gratefully as she sat on her bed and removed her shoes.

"Why?" he asked her almost breathlessly.

She looked up at him.

"Why did you leave? Why did you leave without telling?"

Dahlen avoided his gaze but took out a handkerchief and threw it to him. "You're bleeding above your eyebrow," she told him quietly.

Mohrr opened his mouth to say something, but thought better of it, pressing the cloth to his wound.

After a few moments, Dahlen cleared her throat. "I couldn't stay," she finally replied. "The pain was too fresh, too raw, and everything here reminded me of it."

"I was hurting, too," Mohrr told her.

Dahlen nodded. "I know." She looked up at him as a tear rolled down her cheek. "It was your pain I couldn't stand," she clarified. "I— I wasn't," she took a deep breath and let it out shakily, "I wasn't strong enough to handle my pain and yours." She shook her head. "I couldn't deal with it, so I left."

"We could have helped each other," he replied. "But instead, I lost two of the most important people in my life."

Dahlen turned her head to avoid his gaze.

"I lost my daughter and you," he continued. "Both out of my control. Both absences forced upon me."

Dahlen finally turned to look at him, fearing the anger she might see in his eyes, but was met only with sadness. She took a long time to blink. "I did not leave because I did not care," she started. "I left because I— I was scared of how I felt."

He blinked at her.

"I was scared it would happen again," she confessed. "I thought if I stayed, you and I would continue how we were and I would fall with child again only to be forced to give the baby up once more and I wouldn't be able to handle another heartbreak like that." She closed her eyes and took a deep breath.

Mohrr knelt in front of her and took her hands in his.

She looked down at him, blinking back her tears.

He nodded knowingly and kissed her hands.

"I'm sorry I hurt you," she said quietly.

He shook his head. "You did what you had to."

She placed a hand on his cheek. "And I'm sorry I have been nothing but angry and resentful toward you since—"

He gently shushed her and kissed the palm of her hand.

"I have missed you," she whispered tenderly taking his face in her hands.

Mohrr closed his eyes and placed his hands over hers. "No more than I have missed you," he replied.

Dahlen's heart pounded in her chest. "Show me."

Mohrr obeyed.

"Xela," Dahlen started, sitting across from the little girl, "do you know where the Order meets?"

Xela looked up at Dahlen and creased her brows pensively. She took a deep breath and let it out slowly as she shook her head. "They never spoke about anything important in front of me," she said, ashamed.

Dahlen shook her head. "That's alright," she reassured her. "It's okay if you don't know something. You do not have to be afraid with us."

Xela nodded. "I did, however, have a vision of it before," she replied.

Dahlen exchanged glances with Marten and the others. "That's very good," she told her. "Can you describe it to me?"

The girl closed her eyes. "The end is where the beginning will start. Where the sound of water can always be felt crashing over you," she whispered. "There is a waterfall," she started. "It acts like a door that leads to a cave system or something. It's dark; the only light comes from torches and it is very loud, as if rushing water is not far away. The walls are damp and covered in a green algae. If you follow the sound of water, you're led to another tunnel which leads to some sort of chamber. Inside the chamber is a large table, the walls lined with weapons." The girl's eyebrows creased harder in concentration. "And on another wall is some kind of map." She shook her head. "I can't fully make out what it says, but it looks like an island with a large mountain in the middle of it."

Marten mouthed the words 'Zeln" to Dahlen who gave a nod.

Xela frowned as she concentrated harder. "I could hear them say something. Drahmin mal gorat, I think," she said after a moment. "But I don't know what it means."

Tristan and Mohrr perked up.

"Do you mean 'drahmine mal gorath'?" Tristan asked.

Xela opened her eyes. "I'm not sure," she replied, timidly.

"What does it mean?" Dahlen asked.

Tristan rubbed his face with his hands. "It's ancient Skahrrian for 'power over everything,'" he replied with a sigh. He looked up at Dahlen, his face grim. "I now know why Mahk led you to me."

"Do you know where their hideout is?" Dahlen asked him.

Tristan nodded. "Those are my family words," he told her. "Their hideout is in the Hills."

"The Hills?" The Viper repeated. "Didn't we just come from there?"

Tristan nodded. "Yes, we did, or not far from it."

No one spoke as Tristan took in this new revelation.

"I remember it now," he continued. "The end is where the beginning will start." He shook his head. "My father's youngest brother, Goran, used to say it."

Mohrr nodded. "I remember him, though vaguely."

"Where is he now?" Marten asked.

Tristan and Mohrr looked at each other for a moment. They both shook their heads.

"We don't know," Tristan replied. "My father threw him out of the house one day after an argument. I haven't seen my Uncle Goran since I was probably ten."

"Nor I. After my mother passed away, he was never invited back to the castle," Mohrr added. "My father never really liked him."

"What was their argument about?" The Defiant asked.

Tristan shook his head. "I never knew. My father refused to talk about it. After a while, I stopped asking about him."

Dahlen nodded. "Then I guess we are going back to Skahrr," she concluded.

The others nodded.

"Xela, do you know when they are going to meet again?" The Viper asked her.

She shook her head. "I'm sorry," she replied a little dejectedly.

"Don't worry about it," Marten reassured her. "You did a great job."

Tristan shook his head. "I bet I know when they do," he spoke up. "On the new moon."

"How can you be so sure?" The Defiant asked.

"That's part of the riddle," he explained. "The new moon is the end of an old cycle and the beginning of another."

The Defiant shrugged.

"It's a stretch," Mohrr commented, "but it's more than we have."

"When is the next new moon?" The Viper asked.

"The last one was a few days ago," Marten replied. "If you leave soon, you might make the next one by the time you reach the Hills."

Dahlen nodded. "We are going to need more men," she said.

"Then you can count on us."

They turned to see Malek, Hanek, Viktor, Thane and several more of Vorce's men on bent knee, bowing their heads. After a moment, Malek stood.

"We all discussed it," he started. "Vorce loved you like a daughter. He viewed you as his own, as his heir. Therefore, we will be honored to follow you wherever you lead. We will be honored to fight with you."

Dahlen swallowed the lump rising in her throat. She glanced from Mohrr to The Viper to Tristan to The Defiant to Maleya who all nodded at her.

Still, Dahlen hesitated. "Malek, I appreciate the honor you are bestowing on me, but I am ill equipped to lead so many men and women."

Malek shook his head. "Vorce believed in you, had faith in you. And we believed and had faith in him. Therefore, your orders are our command."

Vorce's, and now her, men stood, pressing a fist over their heart as they bowed.

She felt a warm hand wrap around hers and looked down to see Dohrrn smiling up at her.

It is your destiny.

She took a deep breath and bowed in return to them all. "I will be more than honored to fight by your side."

Part 4

THE END IS WHERE THE
BEGINNING WILL START.

CHAPTER 37

DAHLEN SAT UP IN A PANIC, PANTING. IT TOOK HER A FEW SECONDS to realize where she was, that she was safe in her little house in the settlement. Mohrr stirred softly next to her. She took a deep breath, trying to calm her rapidly beating heart, and wiped her damp forehead with her hand.

Something was wrong; she could feel it.

She got up quietly and crept out of her little house into the darkness of the night, shivering despite the warmth. She listened for a moment before she began walking toward the center of the settlement. It was calm, silent, yet something was wrong. Something was on the verge of happening.

When she made it to the center, where everyone gathered and a fire was usually burning, she found Xela alone, sitting on the ground. Dahlen paused when she noticed her and watched for a moment as the young girl rocked back and forth, whimpering.

"Xela," Dahlen said cautiously.

"It's too late," the girl cried softly. "I found out too late."

"What do you mean?" Dahlen asked, her uneasiness growing. "What did you find out too late?"

"The Order is riding southeast. They are headed beyond the Mahk

River," the girl explained. She looked up at Dahlen, her face appeared to be wet from crying. "The children. They will kill the children."

Dahlen gaped in horror at the little girl as the realization of what she was saying came over her. "Dead Man's Rest," she said breathlessly.

"They are going to try and free The Master."

"When, Xela?" Dahlen asked as calmly as possible, trying not to frighten the girl.

Xela shook her head. "Less than a week," she replied. "You won't be able to make it."

Dahlen turned and ran, yelling as she did. "The Viper! The Defiant! Marten!" She ran between the huts continuing to shout. By the time she made it to their huts, most of the settlement was awake. "The Order is moving on Dead Man's Rest," she told her group as they sleepily emerged from their tents.

"What?" The Viper asked, confused, rubbing his eyes of sleep.

"Xela saw it happening," Dahlen explained. "She thinks it will take place in less than a week."

"I can be ready in ten minutes," The Defiant said disappearing back into the hut she was sharing with Tristan. Tristan nodded and followed in after her.

"What can we do?" Malek asked her.

Dahlen turned to him. "Prepare provisions for us. Gather the men and have them ready," she told him. "We leave as soon as possible." She turned to her own house to gather her things.

Marten fell in line with her. "Xela saw this?" Marten asked her.

Dahlen nodded. "I found her crying at the circle. But before that something had woken me up." She shook her head. "I knew before she even said anything that something bad was about to happen."

Mohrr gently took her arm. "I am coming with you," he told her. "You can't stop me this time."

She smiled and nodded. "We leave now," she replied. "Take only what you need."

Less than half an hour later, the lot of them saddled their horses. Marten, however, looked conflicted.

"Stay here," Dahlen told him. "You only just found out about your daughter and she needs you."

"I cannot let you go in blind," he told her.

Dahlen shook her head. "We will be fine," she replied. "You're not much of a fighter anyway."

Marten smiled at her, placing a gentle hand on her cheek before pulling her into an embrace. "Keep yourself safe," he told her.

An intense heat was felt by them all as Dohrrn, better known as Vremir, the god of fire, knowledge, and truth approached them, seemingly engulfed by flames. He smiled at Dahlen who grinned in return.

Dahlen mounted her horse. "Let's ride!"

CHAPTER 38

DAHLEN AND HER FOLLOWERS RODE HARD FOR DAYS. THEY STOPPED only to eat and take small rests before they pressed on, moving quickly through Behr wood. For almost a week they nearly exhausted their horses as they tore through the terrain. They barely talked or rested; there wasn't any time for it. Dahlen's heart seemed to race the entire way, unsure of what she was going to find when they finally arrived.

They saw the smoke first; even through the dark of the night, they could still see the smoke from the fires rising into the sky. Dahlen brought her horse to a stop as she crossed the Mahk River and looked on in horror.

"No," The Viper whispered as he pulled up alongside her. He shook his head in disbelief. "We're too late."

"We don't know that," The Defiant replied.

Dahlen took an angry breath in through her nose. "Kill anything wearing yellow!" she bellowed as she dug her heels into her horse and raced towards Dead Man's Rest.

The others thundered behind her, pulling out their swords in preparation to cut anything or anyone down.

The sounds of screaming reached them as they approached what should have been the guarded gates. Children called out for help just before they were slaughtered. Dahlen watched on helplessly as a man from the Order stabbed a young boy through.

She let out a scream as she jumped off her horse and tackled him to the ground, pummeling him with her fists before she pulled out a blade and slit his throat. She pulled out her sword as she stood rushing toward another of the Order cutting him down before he had time to defend himself.

The sounds of metal clashing together rang out paired with the yells of those who fell. After a few minutes, the screams were replaced with silence as Dahlen and her men cleared the area. She paused a moment to regain her bearings and realized she was standing in what should have been the market. Its carts were now spilt over and the items for sale were scattered over the blood-stained ground. Bodies were left in piles or hung as a warning. Flies and smoke hung in the air, making it difficult to see or hear while the smell made it difficult to breathe.

"What have they done?" The Defiant asked in a shaky voice, her eyes glancing mistily on the dead children. She pressed a hand to her mouth to suppress the overwhelming feelings of grief and rage.

"They will repay blood with blood and flesh with flesh," Dahlen replied.

"It is not enough," The Viper told her, "but it is a start."

It had been decided on the way to the Rest that they would split into three groups. The Viper would lead a group south toward the docks; The Defiant would lead a group north toward the student housing; Dahlen would lead a group further east where the capital building was. With its thick stone walls and eastern side facing a cliff, it was partially sheltered. If there were survivors, they would be held up in there.

"Strike fair," The Defiant told them as they gathered their groups.

"Strike true," The Viper added.

"And I shall see you on the other side," Dahlen replied with a bow.

She gave a weak smile to Mohrr as she turned and led her group east.

"This is weah you chu-rained?" Maleya whispered.

Dahlen nodded. "This is where I grew up," she explained. "This was my home."

This is the place of my rebirth.

Dahlen looked down at Dohrrn whose hands were alight with fire.

"What monsters treat children as such?" Hanek asked as they passed the forgotten bodies of trainees, those too young and inexperienced to have been titled.

"Vron's monters," Malek replied.

"Maleya," Dahlen began as they pressed on, "I will need you to be ready with your healing skills. We have no idea what we will be up against. I only hope there is someone left to save."

"I have bu-rrought all of my herbs, and have been given some fu-rrom Thane," she replied. "We have shared our skills with each otha. I am moh than rready."

Thane, who had gone with The Defiant's group to look after what children might have survived, had prepared countless remedies for healing. He and Maleya probably slept less than the rest as they worked tirelessly to prepare for what they might run into when they arrived. Dahlen could not have been more pleased or grateful for their work.

After turning down an alley that led toward the houses, Dahlen held up a hand signal to stop. She pointed to her ear indicating for everyone to listen and motioned for them to remain hidden.

"Do you continue to deny us?" came a booming voice.

Dahlen peered through the smoke of the burnt down buildings, barely making out a figure.

"Release The Master and we will leave the rest of you and the children unharmed," the voice called out. "Or, we will continue to kill another child every hour until you do."

They will kill them anyway.

Dahlen nodded.

"You cannot hide in there forever!" the man shouted.

They could hear a child screaming for help through the smoke.

"Can you see?" Dahlen asked Dohrrn.

I can sense them.

"How many are there?"

Dohrrn motioned for Dahlen to kneel.

Close your eyes and ready your bow. It is time for you to speak for the gods.

Dahlen hesitated for a moment, confused, but knelt before Dohrrn and bowed her head as she took her bow from her back and nocked an arrow.

Dohrrn placed a warm palm on her forehead. *May you always see your enemies.*

Dahlen felt a surge of warmth course through her, making her skin tingle. She let out a small gasp as a wave of energy fired within her. She tensed for a brief second with the sensation before she finally relaxed.

She stood slowly, facing the direction of the voice, and, though her eyes were still closed, she saw him. She saw his life force glowing in the thick of the smoke and darkness, a struggling girl held closely against him.

She scanned the area and saw more men, their bodies strange beacons in her mind's darkness. She smiled at her luck. There were only fifteen.

She took a steady breath as she pulled back on her bow and released.

The man with the child fell almost silently. Buying Dahlen time to drop three more before the others knew what was happening. Calmly, she walked forward as she was charged, pausing only a moment to drop her bow and pull out her sword to cut the man down.

"It is an ambush!" came a cry in the dark.

Dahlen remained calm. "Mahk," she began, "I pray to thee. Give us the power of wind."

As if on cue, her men stormed past her with the wind on their heels, dispersing the smoke. The men of the Order were almost no match as Vorce's men, now Dahlen's, clashed against them, metal clanging against metal as battle cries filled the air and blood painted the ground.

Dahlen deflected an attack, pushing the man away to take a swing of her own, but he easily jumped aside.

"It is you, then," the man said. "The prophet has come."

Dahlen gave him a cold look. "Yes, and with me I brought death."

Dohrrn walked slowly past her and with nothing more than a small pulse of his hand, the man ignited into flames and was soon nothing more than ash.

Dahlen, in the silence of the night, stood tall, as the last of the Order fell to the ground. Her men breathed heavily from exertion, some bleeding but still alive. Seeing that the area was clear, she approached the small child who had, until then, been a hostage of the Order.

"Are you alright?" she asked her.

The girl, no more than twelve, nodded.

"Do you know who is in there?"

"Some of The Leaders with some of the younger children," she replied.

"Are they the only survivors?"

The girl shook her head. "No, there are more of us. They are keeping some of the children in the barracks with some of The Teachers." The girl's lip quivered. "They killed my brothers and sisters," she told her. "They have killed so many of us."

Dahlen knelt in front of her and pressed a hand to her cheek. "We will make them pay for what they have done. I promise you this. There will be time for mourning later, but for now, I need you to be strong. For you, me, and your brother."

The girl nodded.

The doors to the capitol slowly opened and The Gallant

stepped out.

"Dahlen," he said in relief.

"Father," she said breathlessly as she stood and ran to him. He winced as he embraced her. "You're hurt."

"It is just a bruised rib. Nothing compared to what others have suffered," he explained. "Bring your men inside."

Dahlen signaled for her men to follow, waiting for everyone to enter before barring the door once more.

"How long have you been held up in here?" Dahlen asked.

"Three days," he replied leading them down the long hallway. "Three days we have had to endure watching them kill one of our members after another." He shook his head. "They came fast and without warning, scattering most of us and with most of our mercenaries in Thren, we were caught off guard to say the least."

"And The Master?"

The Gallant huffed. "He is locked away in the upstairs tower."

Dahlen nodded. "How many of you are in here?"

"There were forty of us, but thirteen have succumbed to their wounds. The Mountain being one of them."

Dahlen gasped. The Mountain was of The Leaders.

"He gave his life for those of us in here. Fended them off just long enough so we could shut the door."

"Then he died well," Dahlen said. "It is a noble death for a man like him."

"And, if I am being honest, I do not think The Fist is far behind him."

Another one of The Leaders.

"What about The Wind?"

He nodded. "She is well."

"I have broken my men up into teams," Dahlen told him. "This is not all of us. We will drive the Order out or kill them all."

"We are grateful," he replied opening the door that led to the assembly room.

Dahlen stepped into the crowded room, taking in the sight of the bruised and broken bodies before her.

"Maleya," Dahlen said, turning to her. "Please, see to the injured. Malek and Hanek, help her."

They bowed and did as they were told.

"The Tigress," came a familiar voice, "you have returned."

Dahlen turned and smiled. "The Rose," she replied, locking arms with her friend. "I am glad to see you unharmed."

The Rose shook her head. "Physically, yes, but I am not sure how one can recover from seeing their brothers and sisters slaughtered."

Dahlen scanned the room for other familiar faces. "Do you know what has happened to The Horn, or The Hawk?"

The Rose shook her head again. "The Horn is no longer with us," she replied. "I saw him fighting until the last. The Hawk, thankfully, has been away on a mission."

Dahlen thought for a moment. "Was there anyone else who was away on a mission, The Gallant?"

He frowned. "There are a few I know of, yes."

"Those names should be written down," Dahlen suggested. "We might need to question their loyalty later."

"You are saying that some of our brothers are with these men who attacked us?" The Rose asked.

"That is exactly what I am saying," Dahlen replied.

"You have returned," The Wind said approaching her, her age showing more than it ever had before. She stopped when she saw Dohrrn, the child she had nursed after his mother passed away. "You have both returned." Her eyes misted.

Dohrrn smiled at The Wind who clasped her hands together to keep from reaching out to him.

Her father placed a hand on Dahlen's back. "I must see to the others," he told her bowing to The Wind, who returned the gesture, before he moved to another side of the room.

"The Wind," Dahlen said. "I am glad to see you are unharmed."

The old woman smiled. "What difference would it have made?" she asked. "I am too old to be of use."

Dahlen shook her head. "Your wisdom is more useful right now than your ability to hold a sword."

The Wind laughed through her nose. "Your kindness is appreciated, but I even fall short on that aspect of usefulness." She wrung her dark hands a little fretfully. "I am afraid that all of my ideas have dried up."

Dahlen exchanged a glance with Dohrrn who reached out and took The Wind's hand.

The Wind looked surprised at first, either by the gesture or by the intense warmth of Dohrrn's hand, but she soon smiled.

"What we are experiencing now," Dahlen began, "we will get through together."

Dohrrn tugged gently at The Wind's hand, urging her to walk him around the room. She gratefully complied.

"Who is that child?" The Rose asked watching the pair of them walk away.

Dahlen studied The Rose's curious demeanor. "He is the child born of the Mehtian pirate woman who washed up on our shores nine or so years ago," she answered cautiously.

The Rose nodded, but not before something flashed in her eyes.

Dahlen regarded her for a moment.

The Rose, realizing she was being stared at, smiled. "That is why I recognize him. You brought him to the gardens with you the last time you came to the Rest."

Dahlen smiled, her shoulders relaxing. "Yes, I did."

"He has grown very tall," The Rose commented.

Dahlen nodded. "Yes."

There was a brief pause between them.

"I am glad to see you again, The Tigress," The Rose finally said.

She smirked. "And I you."

"I am told you now go by another name."

"Dahlen."

"A true name," The Rose replied with a smile. "Is it strange?"

Dahlen thought for a moment before shaking her head. "No. It seems natural. Even after all of those years of being called nothing, it feels like I have always had this name."

The Rose smiled at the floor. "It must seem like such a silly, simple pleasure to those that could never know what it is like not to have a name."

Dahlen studied her friend for a moment before nodding. She recognized the look of longing and regret in her eyes. There was something else behind that look as well, something she could not place.

"Dahlen!" The Gallant called breaking her from her observations.

Dahlen turned to her father's voice. "I must go," she told her friend. "We will talk again soon." She clasped her friend's forearm against her own and walked back to where her father was standing next to The Fist.

Dahlen's heart skipped a beat as she saw The Fist, one of The Leaders, lying propped up on a table, his face bruised and body bandaged. He gave a painful cough, spitting up blood.

"The Tigress," The Fist began, "I thought we agreed you were never to step foot in the Rest again?" Despite his tone, he grinned.

"I believe you did, sir," she replied.

He huffed softly. "I suppose we should all be glad you don't always choose to listen."

"Rules are great for keeping order," Dahlen told him. "But in some circumstances, certain rules are best broken."

He smiled somberly. "I am glad you know the difference." He fell into a coughing fit, falling back exhausted when he was done.

"We have brought a wonderful healer with us," Dahlen told him. "I will bring her over."

"No," The Fist told her. "She has already come to me." He shook his head. "I told her not to waste what she has on me but to focus on the others. I am old," he explained. "I lived a long, exciting life. If I am to die by the blade of a sword, it is a death I have always expected to receive." He shot The Gallant a grin. "I just didn't think it would take this long."

"But, sir—"

He held a hand up. "In the grander scheme of things, I am not that important," he explained. "But these children, the recently titled, the experienced, they are the future of the coven. I am but a piece of its past."

Dahlen felt disappointed. She had hoped to find The Leaders strong, passionate and ready to fight back the invaders that had taken the lives of so many they had sworn to look after, to protect. Instead, she found them dejected, beaten, and tired.

She shook her head. "I refuse to believe that you don't have an ounce of fight left in you," she told him.

"Look at me," The Fist replied. "I can barely keep my head up. I doubt I would be able to lift a sword."

"I am not talking physical fight," she clarified. "I am talking about spirit."

He looked at her.

Dahlen sighed. "Even if you are unable to hold a sword, you can still encourage those around you to not lose hope. Give them the fire that once burned inside of you when you went on a mission. When you were ambushed by a group of unknowing bandits, or silently killed the armed guards of your intended target before setting onto him as well." She looked from him to her father. "Give them the fire so that they might fight."

The Wind approached them, still holding the hand of Dohrrn.

"What has been your plan this entire time?" Dahlen pressed. "To sit and wait it out, hoping the Order would lose interest and leave?"

The Leaders looked ashamed.

"We have been talking about giving them The Master," The Gallant finally replied.

Dahlen gaped at them. "Without a fight?" She shook her head. "I don't understand. This is not what I would have expected from any of you."

"We have prepared our flock for multiple scenarios," The Wind replied. "Taught them what they should do if ambushed in the woods, how to take out multiple men at once, or how to disappear into the shadows or crowd after making a kill, but we never could—" She shook her head. "We have been too arrogant to think we never needed to teach them what to do if ever we came under siege. We have been arrogant thinking no one would dare try."

"And now," The Gallant added, "we are at a loss."

"You are looking at those who have never been defeated and, therefore, never learned how to fail," The Fist concluded.

"I don't understand," Dahlen said. "Is that not what training was for? Did you not learn to fall and pull yourself back up back then?"

"Back then was a long time ago," The Wind explained. "The years have made us forget, have made us comfortable."

"There is still time to fix it," Dahlen urged. "I have two groups of warriors being led by The Viper and The Defiant looking for other survivors, trying to drive the Order out. You are not alone in this. If you just concede or do nothing, then all of those that died trying to protect you died for nothing."

"Perhaps you are right," The Fist replied. "But we can no longer watch the children under our care be murdered."

Dahlen huffed. "If you think that giving them The Master will prevent them from killing anyone else, then you are a fool," she told him.

The Fist raised his brows, not used to being talked to in such a way.

"These men do not fight with honor or rules," Dahlen explained. "They fight to terminate, and they will reach their goal by any destructive means possible. Collateral damage is nothing to them."

Dahlen turned to look at the group of coven members moving about the room. She watched as Maleya applied medicine to those in need, noticing the looks of disillusionment on all of their faces. This siege had broken everything they thought the coven was. Her eyes rested on The Rose for a moment who was staring out the window, fidgeting with a necklace.

She shook her head. "The Order will not stop killing when The Master is in their possession," she informed them. "What you see now is only the beginning."

"She is right," The Gallant said. "We have hidden for too long behind what we thought the Nameless was. It is time to adapt and change into what we should be."

"You propose we fight then?" The Fist began. "I do not disagree, but with what will we fight? Half of us are unarmed."

The Gallant thought for a moment. "Dahlen, could your men provide cover as we take what the fallen Order members have dropped?" he asked.

Dahlen nodded. "Yes."

"Good," The Gallant began. "That at least takes care of that."

We need to talk to him.

Dahlen looked down at Dohrrn and nodded, but not before she noticed the both of them were being watched intensely from across the room. She frowned and took a deep breath. "I think we need to pay The Master a little visit."

CHAPTER 39

"WELL, WELL, WELL, LOOK WHO HAS RETURNED," THE MASTER SAID as The Gallant showed Dahlen and Dohrrn into the tower cell of the capital building.

Dahlen scowled while Dohrrn remained his usual stoic self.

"And, so you have come back to save the place you once could not wait to leave?" he continued. "You are so predictable." He looked down at Dohrrn and shifted uncomfortably where he stood.

"I see you are still afforded a few luxuries," Dahlen replied, looking around to see a small desk with books stacked on it and a comfortable looking bed.

The Master huffed. "Whatever it is you came for, you are wasting your time," he told them. "I will tell you nothing."

"What could you tell us that we would even care to hear?" Dahlen asked him. "What could you say that we would even trust?"

The Master rubbed his lips together and narrowed his eyes. "Then why are you here?"

Dahlen walked over to his desk and pulled the chair out for her to sit in while Dohrrn fingered through his books.

"Those are rare items," The Master protested. "Stop touching them!"

"We are here because we are wondering what it is you have that the Order is so desperate for," Dahlen said, ignoring his plea.

The Master looked at her and blanched for a moment.

She smirked at him. "You have information that the Order wants, don't you?" She stood and took a few steps toward him. "You didn't think I would figure it out, did you?"

The Master laughed haughtily through his nose.

"What was the deal?" she continued. "You do some work for them, spy a little, they give you the power you crave, and then you tell them what you know?"

The Master looked away from her. "I already told you I was not going to tell you anything."

"Because there actually isn't anything to tell, is there?" The Gallant said.

The Master jerked his head in The Gallant's direction, almost surprised to see him still there. "Oh, I have plenty to tell," The Master replied haughtily.

"Perhaps you can tell us why you chose to betray your brethren for a band of dishonorable men set out to help Vron imprison the realm," Dahlen said.

The Master sneered. "What brethren?" he retorted. "Are you referring to the coven and their little puppets?" He laughed. "I have been disillusioned with this place since I was first titled over thirty years ago." He shook his head. "We are trained to the bone, beaten for the smallest infractions and told we are free?"

"You believe you were not?" The Gallant asked.

The Master looked him up and down. "We have *never* been free," he explained. "We are set out into the world in order to make money to pay for whatever the coven needs. Our decisions, though supposedly our own, are restricted. We can't take a shit without the coven's approval."

"Why have you never voiced your opinion before?" The Gallant inquired. "You were one of The Leaders. You had the power to help change everything that you hated about us, yet you chose to sell us out instead."

The Master shook his head again. "It was too late by the time I made it to The Leaders," he explained. "I had already been working for the Order for over twenty years at that point. They are not something you just walk away from."

"Do you know who else has defected?" Dahlen asked.

"I told you to stop touching those!" The Master bellowed at Dohrrn who was beginning to flip through one of the books.

Dohrrn looked up at The Master for a moment before shooting Dahlen a look. She looked away to hide a smile.

"What are you doing bringing a child here anyway?" The Master asked angrily as he snatched the book from Dohrrn's hands.

The Gallant frowned from the doorway. "You specifically asked for these books, didn't you?" he said curiously.

The color drained from The Master's face for a moment. "What does that matter?"

Dahlen looked from The Master to his small stack of books and gently plucked one from the desk. The Master looked like he wanted to react but reluctantly stayed where he was as he watched her flip through some of the pages.

At first, the book appeared to be nothing more than worn-out pages in a leather binding, but somewhere in the middle, Dahlen noticed several words and passages either underlined or circled. Dahlen looked up from the book, wide eyed.

"These books," she started, "they hold the information he has for the Order."

"Let me see," The Gallant said.

Dahlen threw him the book she had been holding. "He has circled specific words and underlined missing letters to spell out his message," she explained. "Turns out we don't need you after all."

The Master scowled at her as she took the book he had grabbed from Dohrrn. She picked up the rest of the books and motioned for

Dohrrn to follow her.

"I am sure everything we want to know is in here," she continued with a triumphant smile.

The three of them moved toward the cell door with The Master glaring at them where he stood. Dahlen was half disappointed he didn't try anything so that Dohrrn could turn him into a pile of ash, but as they stepped out of the cell, a flash of movement caught her eye. The blade of a knife glistened in the torch light, coming down swiftly towards The Gallant, but just before it landed, Dahlen wrestled the would-be assassin to the ground, the knife clattering across the floor.

The two off them struggled against each other in the shadows, grunting and swearing, until The Gallant lifted the assassin up by her hair.

The Rose let out a yell as her small frame almost dangled from The Gallant's hand.

Dahlen smiled as she stood and brushed herself off. "It's no wonder you stopped being an assassin to care for the Rest's gardens," she said as she approached her friend. "You were terrible at it."

The Rose, holding onto The Gallant's wrist, spit at her.

Dahlen wiped her face. "You make yourself too obvious," she continued. She stepped forward and pulled out the necklace The Rose had been fiddling with earlier from under her garbs and frowned when she saw Vron's emblem staring back at her. She ripped the necklace from The Rose's neck causing her to flinch.

"How did you know?" The Rose asked through her gritted teeth.

Dahlen let out a small breath. "Everyone else in the building is covered in dirt and blood, looking defeated. You are the only one who looks as though she walked in here by choice with a plan, albeit, a terrible plan."

The Rose struggled against The Gallant.

"How were you recruited?" The Gallant asked. "Did The Master bring you in?"

"You better just kill me," The Rose replied, screaming as The Gallant shook her by her flame red hair.

"How many more of you are there?" Dahlen asked.

The Rose gave a pathetic laugh. "Forget it," she growled. "There is nothing you can do to me that will make me talk."

Dahlen narrowed her eyes at her. "I am sure we could find something," she told her as she took her red opal from around her neck and took a step forward.

No!

Dahlen stopped and looked down at Dohrrn.

It is not my way.

Dahlen looked from The Rose to Dohrrn. "Then what do you propose we do?" she asked him.

Dohrrn looked at Dahlen who sighed.

"Put her down," Dahlen reluctantly told The Gallant.

The Gallant gave her a curious look, but released The Rose who fell to her knees. Dohrrn stepped forward and gently took The Rose's face in his hands. He brushed back her red curls and bore his sunset eyes into hers. She looked up at the child angrily, but the hatred she felt quickly melted away the longer she stared back into his eyes. A warm air surrounded all of them, seeming to pulse and vibrate as Dohrrn continued to hold The Rose's gaze.

Then, The Rose let out a scream as if in pain before she began to cry. She hung her head to hide her shame and clung to Dohrrn's garbs. "I did not know," she wept as she crumpled to the floor at his feet. "I am sorry! I did not know!"

"Will you help us now?" Dahlen asked her.

The Rose sniffed and nodded. "I was approached by a man a little over two years ago while I was in Karad, a western port city in Skahrr."

"That is not far from the Hills, correct?" Dahlen pressed.

The Rose nodded. "He offered me a life of my own, a life where—" She sighed and shook her head. "It doesn't matter what he offered me. I believed him and I took it." She looked ashamed. "I refused him at first, I did," she justified, "but it was almost as if he knew I would change my mind, because I saw him again two days later, waiting for me." She sniffed again.

"Do you remember his name?" The Gallant asked.

The Rose nodded. "Goran."

Dahlen furrowed her brows. "Goran Stahrrs?"

"Yes," she replied with surprise. "Do you know him?"

Dahlen shook her head. "Only in name."

"Are you in contact with him?" The Gallant asked.

"Yes," The Rose replied meekly. "He is the one I—" she took a shaky breath, "he is the one I have been trading information with."

"And what is it you have told him?"

The Rose wrapped herself in her arms. "I have given him maps, layouts of the Rest. Information on possible weaknesses and the best areas to breach our defenses. It was me who informed him when all of the mercenaries moved out, leaving us vulnerable." The Rose let out another sob. "Gods be blessed! The children! They have killed so many children!" she cried. "This is all my fault!"

"What is the Order planning?" The Gallant asked her.

The Rose took a shaky breath. "They were going to free The Master and burn what was left," she replied softly. "No survivors."

Dahlen glared at the woman she thought was her friend. "Was this ordered by the temple or did the Order move on us freely?"

The Rose shook her head. "You don't understand," she began. "The Order *is* the temple. The temple cannot do anything without the Order's permission."

"Then Vron has more control than we thought," Dahlen stated.

And his influence only grows.

Dahlen nodded. "We are wasting time here," she told The Gallant. "I have to go help my men."

"Go," The Gallant replied, gently taking The Rose under the arm. "May the gods protect you."

Dahlen flashed a small smile to Dohrrn. "They always do." She turned and moved quickly down the hall with the god of fire by her side. "What did you do to her, by the way?" she asked him.

I showed her the pain and devastation she has caused, and, then, I forgave her.

"Is that not something you could have done to The Master to make him talk?"

Dohrrn sadly shook his head. *His heart has been hardened against too much. Even against himself.*

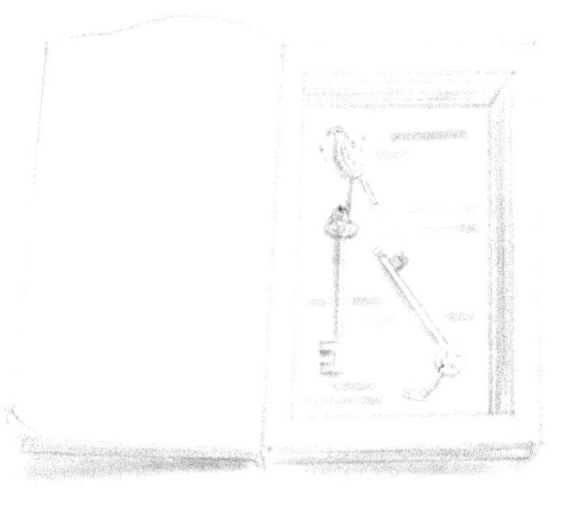

CHAPTER 40

DAHLEN LED HER MEN AND THOSE OF THE COVEN WELL ENOUGH TO fight down the rows of housing and markets to where the dormitories were. They slipped quietly behind those of the Order patrolling the streets, taking them out without a sound and trying not to let their eyes linger on the dead bodies of their fallen brethren.

They moved through the darkness of the night glad for the extra cloud cover. They stopped just around the corner from the trainees' housing to listen. It was quiet. A little quieter than Dahlen had thought it would be.

She held up a hand and took a deep breath as she counted down from three. She then whipped around the corner, her sword at the ready almost letting out a yell of surprise as a drawn bow was aimed not two feet from her face.

"Dahlen."

She let out a sigh of relief. "The Defiant, you were successful?" she asked.

The Defiant nodded and lowered her bow. "To a degree," she replied. "The Order did a lot of damage before we arrived."

"The children?"

"We saved about thirty of them."

"Did we lose anyone?"

The Defiant nodded. "Four men. I sustained a few nicks, but am otherwise unharmed. You?"

Dahlen nodded. "The capitol building is secure. Though The Mountain has passed and The Fist grows weaker by the minute. He refused Maleya's help."

The Defiant shook her head.

"Tristan and Thane? Are they well?"

The Defiant snorted. "Thane is tending to the children. Some were brutalized. Tristan has earned himself another scar, but he should heal. He is helping Thane."

Dahlen nodded. "Where are you headed?"

"I left Viktor in charge of a few men to stay with Thane and the children," she explained. "I was leading the rest to get you and go to The Master's house."

"What for?"

"Rumor has it, the Order is looking for something there."

"How do you know?"

The Defiant sneered and held up a knife. "I asked nicely."

Dahlen suppressed a chuckle. "Do you know what they might be looking for? We might already be in possession of whatever it is."

The Defiant shook her head. "The man I asked said he didn't know."

"And you believed him?"

"A man never lies when you threaten to cut his balls off," The Defiant said matter-of-factly.

A few of the men behind them cleared their throats.

"I guess we are going to The Master's then," Dahlen replied.

THEY APPROACHED THE MASTER'S HOUSE, SURVEYING IT FROM THE lush trees that lined the long path to the front door. It was the only one of The Leaders' houses still standing. The others had already been burned to the ground.

"The Arrow," Dahlen whispered, gesturing to a small, seasoned female.

She approached, bow in hand.

"I need you to lead a few of my archers, making a wide perimeter of the house," Dahlen told her. "You will be our cover if any more of the Order comes."

She nodded. "Gladly."

"Should I go with them?" The Defiant asked.

Dahlen shook her head. "No, I want you to go inside with me," she replied. "I need someone I know I can trust covering my back."

"Let me lead a small team of men around back," came an unfamiliar voice.

Dahlen looked up to see one of the younger assassins who had been taking refuge in the capitol building. "The Bull, is it?" she asked.

The young man bowed.

"What, were you titled yesterday?" The Defiant whispered.

"A year ago."

"Still rather green, aren't you?" Dahlen replied.

"What I lack in experience, I make up for in heart," he told her. He bowed his head slightly. "The Mountain died saving me. I don't want his death to be in vain," he continued when neither of them replied. "Let me help."

Dahlen and The Defiant exchanged glances.

"There is nothing more dangerous than a young man trying to prove himself," Dahlen finally said. "Do not let arrogance guide you, but reason."

The Bull looked up.

"Hanek," Dahlen said, "take three men and go with The Bull. He will guide you safely around the back. Clear the house from that end and we will do the same from the front."

Hanek bowed.

The Bull let out a sigh. "I will not let you down."

Dahlen reached out and took him by the arm. "I trust you will have my men's backs as they will have yours," she told him.

The Bull bowed. "As I would my own brethren."

Dahlen and The Defiant watched them go.

We should hurry. The sun will be rising soon.

Dahlen nodded. "Malek, stay here with Brog, Faut, Lo, and Pralt," she ordered. "Stay to the trees."

Malek bowed.

"The rest will come with us," Dahlen continued. "Let's move."

Dahlen and her allies ran to the broken-down front door, their weapons at the ready as they quietly crept in one by one. She held her hand up for everyone to stop as she listened. Muffled voices could be heard coming from just down the hall.

Dahlen signaled for three of her group to clear the dining area, and for three more to cover the hall by the stairs while she, The Defiant, and Dohrrn moved toward the study where the voices were coming from.

They moved slowly, cautiously, toward the cracked door, staying close to the wall. They stopped for a few moments to listen.

"They have to be in here," came a harsh voice. Dahlen could hear him ruffling through The Master's desk. "There isn't another place he would think to put them."

"We have been looking for days," came another voice, as the sound of books hit the floor. "Perhaps he has entrusted them to someone else, or maybe even had them stored away in a Bank in Ganavan. You would never find a more secure place than a Ganavanese Bank."

"No!" the first voice hissed. "The Master doesn't trust anyone enough to do either of those things. The keys are here!"

Dahlen and The Defiant exchanged glances. "Keys," they both mouthed to one another.

The Defiant held up two fingers. *"Two men?"*

Dahlen nodded in agreement. She indicated one of the men was likely in the corner of the room, while the other was just beyond the door.

"This would have been easier if those damned fools would just release him to us," came the second voice, obviously frustrated. "I want to get the hell out of here."

"Getting nervous?"

"You know Vron does not like to be kept waiting. He expects results."

The first voice sighed. "Yes, and we are running out of time."

Dahlen indicated to The Defiant to take out the man in the corner, rifling through The Master's desk, while she took the man ripping books from the shelves. She held up three fingers and began to count down, but before she got to one, Dohrrn walked past them and threw the doors open.

Both men started and reached for their weapons, but before they could, the man by the bookshelves burst into a pile of ash. The other man stood frozen by the desk.

"Well, that is one way to make an entrance," The Defiant said as she walked in with her bow raised at the last man.

"Warn somebody before you do something like that," Dahlen said, lightly scolding him. "God of fire or not, we're a team."

You were taking too long.

"Then it is true," the man said, looking at Dohrrn with a scowl. "The god of fire has returned. A mere child."

"What are you looking for?" Dahlen asked him, ignoring his comment.

The man huffed. "Death does not scare me. I will tell you nothing."

The Defiant let an arrow go, striking the man in the arm. The man screamed and fell backwards against the wall.

"The Defiant!" Dahlen said in a scolding tone.

The Defiant shrugged. "What?" she replied. "It's just a flesh wound."

Dahlen sighed. "I suggest you tell me what it is you are looking for before my pain-enthusiast friend here turns you into a pincushion."

"Oooo! I like the sound of that," The Defiant said, nocking another arrow.

The man spit on the ground next to him, holding his shoulder. "May Vron drown you both."

"Oh, I see how it's going to be," The Defiant said putting her bow down and taking out a knife. "Pull down his pants."

"What?" the man squeaked. "Why? What are you going to do?"

"Luckily for you, we are not going to do whatever she has in mind," Dahlen reassured him, "*if* you tell me about the keys you're looking for."

The Defiant smirked and stepped forward, brandishing her knife.

Dahlen.

Dahlen held up a hand to Dohrrn while taking out a knife of her own and pressing it to the man's throat. The Defiant untied his pants and let them fall to the ground while the man shook.

"Do you think this blade is sharp enough?" The Defiant asked, letting Dahlen look it over.

Dahlen made a face. "It will make for a messy job, but," she shrugged, "it will get it done nonetheless."

"Right," The Defiant said, holding the knife in one hand while reaching out to take the man's manhood in the other.

"He will kill me if I say anything," the man said.

"I thought you didn't fear death," Dahlen whispered.

The man gulped.

"Now, what keys are you looking for?" Dahlen asked again.

The man held strong, glaring straight ahead.

"Now, Dahlen," The Defiant began, "do you prefer top to bottom or bottom to top?" She moved the knife as she spoke, indicating what she was saying. "Or, I could take both at the same time by cutting from the side."

"It's not my manhood," she replied. "Maybe we should ask him."

"Nah, from the side sounds fun," The Defiant said. "I love a good eunuch." She pressed the blade of the knife against his bare flesh, holding him tightly in her other hand. "Deep breath," she told him.

No sooner had the blade barely dented the skin the man screamed. "I'll talk! I'll talk!" he cried, beads of sweat forming at his brow. "Please stop!"

"We're listening," Dahlen replied.

"One of the keys opens a hidden stash of beraxium, though I don't know where," he replied breathlessly. "The other," he gulped, "the other releases the other gods from their prison."

"Do you know where Vron has imprisoned them?" Dahlen pressed.

The man hesitated and The Defiant once again pressed the knife against him.

"On the Isle of Zeln!" he shouted.

"The Isle of Zeln doesn't exist!" Dahlen replied. "Thousands of men have lost their lives trying to look for it, but no one has ever discovered it."

The isle is real. Only a god can find it.

Dahlen looked at Dohrrn.

"You shouldn't lie to the person with your d—"

"He's telling the truth," Dahlen said, stopping The Defiant. "Let him go."

"Oh," The Defiant said, disappointed and frowning. She put her knife away and took a step back. "Then I guess I have no more use for you."

The man slid down the wall in a sigh of relief.

"You know," Dahlen whispered to The Defiant, "one of these days you're going to have to make good on your threat."

"Who says I haven't?" she replied with a shrug. "Oh, don't look so surprised. You yourself have performed a castration, if I recall."

There was no need for torture, Dahlen.

"There was no torture performed," she replied. "Just the promise of torture."

It is not how I wish my people to act.

"Listen, you cannot be the god of free will and expect people to do everything you want," Dahlen told him with a shrug. "It defeats the purpose of 'free' will."

Dohrrn lifted a disapproving brow at her.

"You know, it's weird when you do that," The Defiant said. "Looks like you're talking to yourself."

Dahlen shrugged. "We should look for those keys," she said, indifferent to The Defiant's comment.

The man was right. They are in this room. One of the keys is made of beraxium. I can feel it.

There was noise coming from the hall and The Bull soon burst into the study.

"The house is secure," he said triumphantly.

"Don't get cocky, kid," The Defiant warned. "But good job."

"Any of the Order around?" Dahlen asked.

He nodded. "There were a few in his garden, they appeared to be digging for something."

Dahlen faced the bookshelves. "They are looking in the wrong place," she replied, distantly.

She walked along the shelves, fingering the spines of the books as she went along. She squinted in the dark as she tried to read, taking out her glowing necklace to help guide her. Most of The Master's books were on politics, war, and history, except for one. In the back, right corner was a book of fairy tales. Dahlen frowned at it. The Master was too practical of a man for such books.

She plucked it from its place and opened it. She smiled as she looked at the hollowed-out pages where two keys hung from little hooks. One was gold, with a black hawk made of gemstones on it. The other was silver in color with the Marhkai family seal, the wing of a dohrrn bird.

She handed the keys to Dohrrn and placed the book back on the shelf, smiling. "Let's go find The Viper and the others."

"What about him?" The Defiant asked, indicating the Order member still clutching his shoulder with the arrow sticking out of it.

Dahlen looked over at him. "I'm sure we have room for him somewhere," she replied. "The Bull, why don't you see him properly secured in a cell in the capitol tower?"

The Bull beamed. "With pleasure!"

CHAPTER 41

THE VIPER, MOHRR AND THE OTHERS HAD ALREADY MADE IT TO THE capitol building before Dahlen and her troops returned. The Gallant approached them as they entered the main hall.

"It appears the Order has been beaten," he told them. "The prince of Skahrr, The Viper, and Vorce's men have forced them back onto their ships." He bowed his head. "Though, I guess I should be calling them your men. They told me what happened to Vorce."

Dahlen reached out and squeezed her father's arm. "I am sorry I did not tell you sooner," she replied somberly. "It wasn't quite the time or place."

He nodded. "I understand," he said with a sad smile. "Go, see to your men."

Dahlen and the rest waded through the crowd of people who thanked them for saving them, each one wanting to shake her hand. She smiled at them as she passed, grateful to see familiar faces among the survivors. When she finally made it to the back of the room, she saw Maleya and Mohrr hovering over The Viper who was lying on his back on a makeshift bed.

Dahlen and The Defiant rushed over to them.

"What happened?" Dahlen asked looking into the pale face of her companion.

The Viper smiled weakly at her. "We won is what happened," he replied.

She looked from Maleya to Mohrr.

"Ah," The Viper continued. "You mean what happened to me." He winced. "It appears the Order does not take kindly to losing."

"Someone shot an arrow from one of their ships as they were leaving," Mohrr explained. "Went straight through his arm."

"I believe the bone is completely shattahed," Maleya added.

"I'm fine," The Viper reassured her drunkenly. "I barely feel it."

"That is because of what I gave you to dull the pain," Maleya clarified.

He winked at her. "You're so pretty."

Dahlen turned to Maleya who looked grave. She pulled her aside. "How bad is it?" she whispered.

Maleya's eyes misted over. "He will live," she replied, "but I cannot set the bones. It is too bu-roken." She bowed her head. "I believe it will need to be taken befoh infection sets in."

The Defiant took in a deep breath, balling her fists in anger.

Dahlen put a hand on her shoulder to calm her. "He is too stubborn to let something like this keep him down," she told Maleya, forcing a smile. "And under your care, I know he has the best chance of recovery."

Maleya nodded. "I will do all that I can."

"See to him," Dahlen told her before turning to Mohrr. "I am glad to see you are safe."

He gave her a small smile. "I am glad as well." He sighed. "The Order seems to be growing bolder by the day," he told her. "They care less about who knows about them"

Dahlen nodded in agreement. "Perhaps, they are growing desperate."

"Perhaps, they now know what is at stake," The Wind said from behind them. She smiled gently. "I have read through this." She handed Dahlen one of The Master's books taken from his cell. "It leads to the location of a warehouse, or more likely a cave where beraxium is stored. I have written it all down for you."

"Thank you," Dahlen replied, taking what The Wind proffered.

The Wind nodded. "I have only gotten through half of another one," she continued. "It appears to describe a way to," she paused, "kill a god."

A chill ran down Dahlen's spine.

"I will have the rest of it to you soon."

Dahlen reached out and squeezed her arm. "You should get some rest," she told her. "It has been a very long night."

The Wind smiled at the two of them. "There will be time enough for rest when I am dead," she replied. "Until that time comes, I plan to be useful." She gave them a half bow and walked off.

Mohrr let out a breath. "She is a tough woman."

Dahlen nodded, staring off into the distance.

"Are you alright?" Mohrr asked.

Dahlen nodded slowly. "I'm just trying to absorb what she said." She looked around the room for Dohrrn who was busy walking around and observing everyone. "I need to talk to The Master again."

"I'll come with you."

She shook her head. "No," she told him. "This is something I need to do on my own." She smiled at him. "I'll be fine. In the meantime, we should send a team out to help bring Thane, Tristan, and the rest of the children back here."

Mohrr nodded. "I'll put one together."

"Be careful."

"You too."

"Back again, I see," The Master said as he looked out of his little barred window. "You have more questions that I will refuse to answer, no doubt."

Dahlen regarded him from the other side of the cell. "The Wind has been working on deciphering your little messages in your books."

The Master huffed.

"Tell me, did Vron know you were going to betray him?"

The Master became rigid. After a moment, he turned to look at her.

"How in fact, do you kill a god?" Dahlen asked. "Is such a thing even possible?"

The Master resumed his staring out of the window. "It is, in theory," he finally replied. "And once you do, you take on all that was theirs. Their strength, their power, their abilities."

Dahlen looked at him in horror. "That has been your intention this entire time," she said breathlessly. "You never intended to help Vron with anything. You intended to become him."

The Master laughed through his nose.

"And that is why you needed to get rid of me," she continued. "Because you knew I could stop you."

"You were a bargaining piece to get me what I wanted," he corrected. "Without you, I never would have made it into Vron's good graces."

Dahlen shook her head. "You are far from your plan now," she told him, turning to leave.

"I wouldn't be so sure of that," he taunted. "The Order will not let me rot here while I have what they need."

"You mean your keys?" Dahlen replied over her shoulder.

The Master didn't reply.

"We are in possession of them now," she informed him. "They are safe in the hands of Vremir."

He swallowed hard.

Dahlen let out a small sigh. "May the gods have mercy on you, though you have done little to deserve it."

Dahlen continued toward the door again when the earth began to shake. She braced herself against the wall as the tremors threw her off balance.

"It is too late for mercy," The Master said. "Vron is already here."

Panic gripped Dahlen as she made it out of the cell, moving as quickly as she could along the walls for support. Screaming could be heard from down below as she descended the tower, stumbling multiple times down the stairs. She finally regained her balance after the tremors stopped and she was able to reach the bottom of the landing.

"Everyone, outside!" she heard The Gallant yelling. "To the gardens!"

"What is happening?" Dahlen asked as she made it to her father.

"Vron has come," The Gallant replied directing people to the front of the building. "We must get everyone to higher ground!"

"Higher ground?" Dahlen repeated, watching as the people ran by her.

He is sending a great wave to destroy us.

Dahlen fell to her knees in front of Dohrrn. "What do we do?" she asked clinging to his cloak. "These people will die! We will die!"

Dohrrn took her face in his warm hands. *Have faith and follow me.*

Dahlen watched as The Gallant continued to move people out of the great hall to the door, urging them calmly to vacate the building. She watched as the scared children, crying, were ushered out. She watched as the injured were helped along, as The Viper was all but carried.

She looked into Dohrrn's sunset eyes and felt a calm rush over her and nodded. She stood and took her father's hand in hers, giving it a squeeze. "Get yourself to safety," she told him.

He looked down at her, confused. "What are you going to do?" he asked.

She gave him a smile before she ran out of the building, slipping by the refugees, following Dohrrn. Her father shouted for her to stop, but it was no use; she was already gone.

The two of them ran the opposite direction of the gardens,

avoiding the fallen debris and bodies that littered the street until they came to an avenue of trees. From the slight incline, Dahlen could see the hundred-foot wave looming in the distance.

She shuddered as she gazed upon it, her mouth open in horror. Dohrrn's warm hand wrapped around hers, a small comfort in the face of their impending doom.

"You cannot have life," Dahlen said, "without sacrifice." She looked down at Dohrrn and gave him a soft smile as her other hand wrapped around the warm, smooth surface of her opal. She pulled it from its strap and took a deep breath.

They watched for a few more seconds as the wave came closer at an alarming speed. Dahlen let out her breath as she and Dohrrn fell to their knees. Dahlen slammed her opal against the hard dirt ground while Dohrrn slammed his fist against it.

The earth shook and split as flames seared the ground, pulling itself apart. Dahlen screamed as the heat singed her flesh, but still she held her ground watching as a canyon grew between them and the wave.

Keep holding!

Dahlen closed her eyes against the hot air throwing particles of sand and rock as she continued to press the opal into the ground, still holding tight to Dohrrn's hand. She could feel the rumble of the earth shift as the wave rushed toward them; she could feel the spray of the salt water, and hear it as it crashed into what was left of dwellings and other structures.

Fear gripped Dahlen as she felt the wave coming closer.

Do not lose faith!

Dahlen opened her eyes and watched as the wave crashed into the rift, losing height, but not force as it toppled over her. The force of the water threw her backward, tearing her hand from Dohrrn's. She rolled and somersaulted as the water controlled her every move until she was forced to the ground and the world went black.

CHAPTER 42

DAHLEN OPENED HER EYES, HER VISION HAZY IN THE MISTY AIR. SHE blinked in the bright light of the sun trying to focus.

"It does not only take someone with great power to do what you did," came a distantly familiar voice, "but great courage."

Dahlen shook her head and rubbed her eyes as they tried to adjust to the light. Finally, she saw a woman standing near her, but looking off into the distance. Dahlen blinked at the image.

The woman turned and smiled at her, her dark curls surrounding her face. "You have come a long way."

Dahlen let out a short breath as tears filled her eyes. "Mother," she whispered.

The woman's smiled broadened as she approached her. "I am proud of you, AnnJella."

Dahlen's lip trembled. "Am I dead?"

Dahlen's mother placed a hand on her cheek. "No, my child," she reassured her. "You are just caught between consciousnesses. You still have so much left to do."

"I have missed you," Dahlen told her, a tear rolling down her cheek.

Her mother wiped the tear away. "There has been no need when I have always been with you."

Dahlen shook her head. "All of this, this prophecy, this role I have to play, it has been too much. How am I to fulfill all that is expected of me?"

Her mother pulled her close to her. "You must rely on others," she whispered. "You do not have to share this burden on your own." She pulled away, holding Dahlen by the arms. "Vron will work to tear you and those you love apart. But you mustn't let him."

"I am scared."

Her mother smiled softly at her. "Fear is natural. You are only human, after all."

"Dahlen!" came a distant voice.

Dahlen looked around her, but there was only the bright light and her mother. "I am sorry I could not do more to save you that day," she told her mother.

"Shh!" her mother softly cooed. "What more could you have done? You were only a child."

"Dahlen!" came the voice again.

Dahlen turned behind her and saw a free-standing door in the middle of the vast light.

"It is time for you to go," her mother told her softly. "You are needed back there."

Dahlen whipped back around and shook her head. "No," she replied in a shaky voice. "I still have so many questions, so many things I want to tell you, so many things I need you to tell *me*."

Her mother reached out and stroked her cheek with her thumb. "The only thing you need to know is that even in death, I have never stopped loving you."

Dahlen's lip trembled again.

"Dahlen!" came the voice.

"Go, my child," her mother told her. "And know that, even if you cannot see me, I will always be with you." She planted a kiss on her daughter's forehead and took a step back.

Dahlen smiled through her tears and walked through the door.

"Dahlen!"

It was Mohrr.

Dahlen coughed and turned to her side as she spewed the rancid sea water while Mohrr patted her on the back. She rolled onto her back again when she was done and winced. She touched the back of her head, not surprised to feel blood.

"What happened?" she asked breathlessly as Mohrr tried to help her up. "Where is Dohrrn?"

Mohrr shook his head. "I had just returned from bringing the children and the others back to the capital building when The Gallant told us what was happening. I rushed here just as the wave dissipated into the canyon with the rest sweeping you and Dohrrn away."

"Did you not go after him?" she asked struggling to stand.

"Dahlen, you shouldn't move!" he told her.

"We have to find him!" She stood with his help and walked unsteadily where a steaming river now ran where the precipice had been. "Dohrrn!" she yelled, flinching as her head throbbed. She paused a moment, grabbing onto Mohrr for balance. "Dohrrn!"

They stopped at the edge of the river, staring into its murky waters filled with floating debris.

Dahlen searched the water, turning to scan the surrounding area. "Where could he have gone?"

Mohrr shook his head.

"Well, we should— we need to—" Dahlen shook her head. "He has to be here somewhere!"

"He's gone, Dahlen," Mohrr said somberly.

Dahlen fell to her knees. "He can't be," she replied breathlessly. She buried her face in her hands. "I can't do this without him."

Just then, the water before them began to bubble and froth as steam rose from it. Dahlen looked up as the water boiled before her and began to glow. The water continued to seethe and foam as a human form rose from the middle of it.

Dahlen and Mohrr stumbled backwards as the tall, dark, glowing figure of a man stepped out of the water and onto the solid ground. The two of them gaped at the naked man as he stepped towards them, his sunset eyes staring back at them.

Our time has come. The prophecy has truly begun.

Afterthought

King Breht sat on his throne stroking his kempt, graying beard as the droning sound of his advisor's voice played on in the background of his mind. He wasn't listening, however. His mind was full of more than the troubles of his kingdom, more than the latest uprisings of peasants in one of his southern cities. Yet, this is what he was dragged out of bed for. Squabbles of ungrateful subjects fighting over wages being too low for the price of bread.

"We should try to appease them, my king," the advisor dragged on. "Come to good terms with them as the harvest will come soon and there will be no one to work the fields if they continue to strike. Giving them a larger wage, making wages higher throughout the land would solve more than just this. Or, if we perhaps slightly dropped the price of grain."

The king gave a small laughing huff, barely listening.

"Mercy, my king, would be the best course," he continued, "as it would be a testament to your legacy. A merciful king with happy subjects is a king who lives without fear."

A shadow in the rafters caught the king's attention and he looked up to see a black hawk perched on a buttress. The king's heartbeat quickened and he sneered.

"Send troops to dispatch the peasants and hang the leaders," King Breht ordered.

"But, my king—"

"I will not tolerate disobedience," the king interrupted. "Make an example of those men, and let it be known that the harshest punishment is reserved for such behavior. It is treason and I will not stand for it."

His advisor stood motionless before him; his mouth slightly open as if in shock.

"You have my orders," the king growled. "Now leave me."

The advisor gave a shaky bow as he walked backward a few steps before turning and exiting the large hall.

"Everyone, leave me!" he bellowed causing the guards to stir from their positions. They only hesitated for a moment before mimicking the advisor and clearing out.

"I am honored," King Breht said once the last of the guards had left.

A figure landed at the foot of the stairs in front of the throne with a subtle thud. After a moment, the figure stood, and smiled at the king.

"I assume you know who I am?" he asked.

King Breht stood and nodded. "I have held many a dignified personnel within the walls of my castle," he began, descending the stairs, "but never a god." He knelt at the bottom of the stairs, bowing. "Lord Vron, I am glad you have come."

"I was assured it would be worth my while," Vron, the god of water, chaos, and deception replied.

King Breht pulled out a small satchel from his jacket and chuckled. He handed it to Vron. "I have no doubt it will be."

Vron took the bag and opened it, an even wider smile growing on his face.

"There is more where that came from," the king told him. "And I know where it is."

"What's in it for you?" Vron asked.

King Breht shook his head. "The kingdom of Bornnen under my control, taken without a fight."

Vron sucked his teeth. "You are quite bold with your request," he answered blandly.

"Yes, but I shall rule in your honor, through your glory," the king told him, standing his ground.

Vron regarded him for a moment. "How much more of this did you say you had?"

King Breht's lips curled and his eyes narrowed. "Enough for two kingdoms, my lord," he replied almost in a whisper.

Vron gave a soft, guttural chuckle. "I agree to your terms," he finally said after a brief pause. "But if it is any less than you have said, your punishment will be long, and unbearable."

"I would not dream of lying to you, my lord."

Vron gave a small nod. "Bornnen is yours then."

King Breht knelt before the god once more, lowering his head. "Thank you, my lord," he said. "I will not fail you."

When he looked up, he was alone. The shadow of a hawk disappearing into the night.

www.ingramcontent.com/pod-product-compliance
Lightning Source LLC
Chambersburg PA
CBHW060621100726
47907CB00006B/1712